Run Wild
SAYE

NOVEL
1

Run Wild
SAYE

NOVEL
1

WRITTEN BY
Wu Zhe

TRANSLATION BY
amixy, Nande M

INTERIOR
ILLUSTRATIONS BY
Ding Yue Rong

Seven Seas

Run Wild: Sa Ye (Novel) Vol. 1
Published originally under the title of 《撒野》 (Sa Ye)
Author© 巫哲 (Wu Zhe)
English edition rights under license granted by 北京晋江原创网络科技有限公司 (Beijing Jinjiang Original Network Technology Co., Ltd.)
English edition copyright © 2025 Seven Seas Entertainment, LLC
Arranged through JS Agency Co., Ltd
All rights reserved

Seven Seas press and purchase enquiries can be sent to Marketing Manager Lauren Hill at press@gomanga.com. Information regarding the distribution and purchase of digital editions is available from Digital Manager CK Russell at digital@gomanga.com.

Seven Seas and the Seven Seas logo are trademarks of Seven Seas Entertainment. All rights reserved.

Follow Seven Seas Entertainment online at sevenseasentertainment.com.

TRANSLATION: amixy, Nande M
ADAPTATION: Monica Sullivan
COVER DESIGN: M. A. Lewife
INTERIOR LAYOUT & DESIGN: Clay Gardner
COPY EDITOR: Pengie
PROOFREADER: Kate Kishi, Hnä
EDITOR: Harry Catlin
PREPRESS TECHNICIAN: Salvador Chan Jr., April Malig, Jules Valera
MANAGING EDITOR: Alyssa Scavetta
EDITOR-IN-CHIEF: Julie Davis
PUBLISHER: Lianne Sentar
VICE PRESIDENT: Adam Arnold
PRESIDENT: Jason DeAngelis

Standard Edition ISBN: 979-8-89160-468-1
Special Edition ISBN: 979-8-89373-559-8
Printed in Canada
First Printing: January 2025
10 9 8 7 6 5 4 3 2 1

CONTENTS

1

WHEN HIS PHONE VIBRATED in his pocket for the fifth time in the span of three minutes, Jiang Cheng opened his eyes.

He'd been on this train for almost three hours. Outside, the sky was as gloomy as it'd been the last time he'd looked out the window. The stranger beside him was still asleep. Her head rested heavily on his right shoulder, which had gone numb.

Jiang Cheng shrugged in irritation, but the girl only shifted in place. With one finger, he nudged the girl's head away from him, but it was back on his shoulder within a few seconds. This was absolutely not the first time he'd done this. He was starting to wonder whether she was really asleep or actually comatose.

Ugh.

He didn't know how much longer it would be until his stop; it wasn't something he'd paid attention to when he got the ticket. He only knew that the destination was a city he'd never even heard of before embarking on this trip.

Life... It was nothing if not absurd.

The sixth time his phone vibrated, Jiang Cheng sighed and pulled it from his pocket.

– What's going on?

– How come you never mentioned leaving?

– Why'd you leave so suddenly?

– Why didn't you say anything?

What what how how why why why blahblahblahblah...

The messages were from Yu Xin, who must not have been able to call him because she was in cram classes over the holiday. He glanced at the screen: It was filled with question marks.

Jiang Cheng was about to put the phone back in his pocket when a seventh message came in.

– If you don't reply, we're over!

Finally: a message without a question mark. He breathed a sigh of relief, turned his phone off, and stuffed it back in his pocket.

Breaking up didn't mean very much to him. All a two-month-long high school romance like theirs meant was talking to each other a little more than everyone else, having someone to bring you breakfast, and having a dedicated cheerleader by the basketball court... They hadn't even gotten to the "doing stuff" stage.

As Jiang Cheng watched the landscape outside the window—shifting, but somehow constant—he finally heard the conductor call his stop over the intercom. Beside him, the girl stirred as if she was about to wake up. He quickly pulled a red marker from his backpack, pulled the lid off, and twirled it between his fingers, moments before the girl woke up and lifted her face.

There was a prominent imprint on her forehead where it had been pressed against his shoulder, as if she was a practitioner of some kind of divine cultivation. When she met his gaze, the girl wiped the corner of her mouth and took out her phone.

"Sorry about that," she said, tapping around the screen with her head down.

What a surprise—Jiang Cheng couldn't make out so much as a hint of actual regret. He chuckled pointedly. There was a pause as the girl's gaze fell on the marker twirling in his hand.

Jiang Cheng popped the lid back on the marker with a loud *snap*.

The girl was still for two seconds. Then she suddenly covered her face with her hands, jumped up, and bolted down the aisle to the bathroom.

Jiang Cheng stood and glanced out the window. It had been over-cast the whole way here, and now it was finally snowing. Retrieving his suitcase from the overhead luggage rack, he put on his jacket and walked to the door, then pulled out his phone and turned it on again.

His notifications were quiet. There were no more messages from Yu Xin, nor were there any missed calls. This was the most pleas-ant Yu Xin had been since they got together, he thought. What a feat. But apart from Yu Xin, nobody else had tried to contact him, either—for instance, there was no sign of the person he'd thought would come pick him up.

As he followed the crowd out of the station, Jiang Cheng zipped his puffer jacket all the way up to his chin and looked out at the city, bleak and gray in the chill of winter. This was his first impression of the city: the decay and disarray around the train station.

But no—it was his second impression. His actual first impression was the stunned confusion when his mom had said, "Go back there, then—that's your real home."

He dragged his suitcase to the southernmost edge of the station square, away from the crowd. Nearby was a side street lined with all sorts of sketchy-looking inns, the kind people probably entered and never came out of, and small restaurants that looked like they'd give you food poisoning. He sat on his suitcase and checked his phone periodically. Still, nobody tried to contact him.

Jiang Cheng had been given a phone number and an address; he was just reluctant to move from this spot. In fact, he didn't feel like moving or talking at all. He pulled a cigarette from his pocket and put it between his lips. Inside him was a deep, inexplicable, confused, and hopeless anger about how he'd come to be in this situation. He stared at the ice on the ground and fumed, fumbling in his pocket for a lighter. When he finally managed to light the cigarette, his back hunched against the bitter wind, he watched the smoke disperse before his eyes and sighed.

If only his old homeroom teacher could see him now.

But that didn't matter anymore. He was here now, a million miles away. He might never again see the people who'd lived under the same roof as him for more than a decade, so what did a mere teacher matter? Whatever run-down school he wound up going to in this run-down city, he doubted anyone there would give a crap if he smoked.

By the time Jiang Cheng was halfway through the cigarette, he couldn't stand the cold anymore. He stood up, planning to hail a cab to go get some food first, but he'd barely taken one step with his suitcase when he felt a surge of pain—something had knocked hard against his ankle.

He turned with a frown. There was a skateboard on the ground behind him. Before he even had a chance to work out where it had come from, someone fell to the ground next to his feet.

"Are you...?"

Out of reflex, he reached out to help, but his hand paused in mid-air.

The person had a mop of untidy hair, as uneven as if it'd been chewed on by a dog. Their clothes were dirty, too... Was this a beggar? A homeless person? A scam artist, or a thief, or something?

It wasn't until the person raised their head that he clearly saw it was a little girl, probably eleven or twelve years old. Her face was streaked with mud, but he could still see that she had a fair complexion and incredibly large eyes.

Before he had a chance to offer a helping hand again, the girl was dragged away roughly by four or five other little girls who came chasing after her. One of them even landed a kick on her back, making her stumble forward and almost fall again.

Jiang Cheng immediately understood what was happening. After a moment's hesitation, he turned to continue on his way. But a peal of laughter behind him made him pause again.

He didn't like to get involved in other people's business when he was in a bad mood—and it just so happened that at this very moment he was in an extremely, extraordinarily, exceptionally terrible mood. But in the end, the lingering image of those large, dark eyes made him turn around.

"Hey!" he called out.

The group of girls stopped. One, who looked like she might be their ringleader, narrowed her eyes at him.

"What?!"

Jiang Cheng walked over slowly, dragging his suitcase behind him, keeping his eyes fixed on the girl who still had Big Eyes' clothes in her grasp. After a couple more seconds of staring, the girl loosened her grip.

He pulled Big Eyes to his side and looked at the other girls. "Nothing," he said. "Go on, then."

"Who the hell are you?" their leader blurted out in obvious displeasure, despite her apprehension.

"I'm a big brother with a knife." Jiang Cheng glanced at her. "I can give you the same haircut she has in just thirty seconds."

The leader clearly wasn't used to this kind of confrontation. She was a little cowed by his words, but she didn't want to give in so easily. "I'm gonna tell my brother to get you!"

"Then tell him to hurry up." Jiang Cheng yanked on his suitcase with one hand and grabbed Big Eyes with the other. "I'm scared to death, so I might run."

As the other girls walked away, Big Eyes shook off his hand.

"Are you all right?" Jiang Cheng asked.

She nodded and walked back to the skateboard. She stepped on it with one foot and looked back at him.

"Yours?" Jiang Cheng asked again.

Big Eyes nodded. She pushed off lightly with one foot and rolled to his side before coming to a steady stop, her eyes still fixed on him.

Jiang Cheng nodded as well. "Then...you should go home."

He pulled out his phone and walked away with the intention of calling a cab. After a few steps, he heard a noise behind him; he turned and saw Big Eyes slowly following him on her skateboard. He looked at her.

"What's wrong?"

Big Eyes didn't say anything.

Jiang Cheng sighed. "Afraid they'll come back?"

Big Eyes shook her head.

Jiang Cheng was starting to feel irritated. "What? Are you mute?"

Big Eyes continued to shake her head.

"Let me tell you something. I"—Jiang Cheng pointed at himself—"am in a very bad mood right now. Very grumpy. I'm not gonna go easy on you just because you're a little girl, understand?"

Big Eyes didn't move.

Jiang Cheng stared at her for a while. It was clear that she had no intention of speaking, though, so he bottled up his annoyance and continued on his way.

Cell reception was bad around here; no matter how he tried, he couldn't get the ride-hailing app to work. He sat down on a stone post by the bus stop and lit another cigarette.

Big Eyes was still standing on her skateboard next to him.

"Is there something else you need?" Jiang Cheng asked impatiently. He was starting to regret interfering and bringing this strange trouble onto himself.

Still silent, Big Eyes pushed lightly on the ground with one foot and rolled up to the nearby bus stop sign. She raised her head and stared at it for a long time. When she rolled back to Jiang Cheng's side, he realized the cause of her confused expression. He sighed again.

"Are you lost? Don't know how to get home?"

Big Eyes nodded.

"Do you live here?" Jiang Cheng asked.

A nod.

Jiang Cheng handed his phone to her. "Call and tell your family to come get you."

She accepted the phone, but hesitated. After a few taps on the screen, she handed it back to him.

"What do you mean?" Jiang Cheng looked at the number displayed there. "You want me to call for you?"

A nod.

"Shit." Furrowing his brow, Jiang Cheng pressed the call button and listened to the dial tone. He asked her, "Which family member does this number belong to?"

Someone picked up on the other end before Big Eyes could answer—although, of course, she probably wouldn't have said anything.

"Hello?" Jiang Cheng said.

There was a male voice on the other end. "Who's this?"

"A passerby." Jiang Cheng was a little unsure of how to explain the situation. "I have a little girl here—"

"Not interested," said the voice. The line was dead before Jiang Cheng had a chance to respond.

"Who the hell was that?" Jiang Cheng spat out his spent cigarette stub and pointed a finger at Big Eyes. "If you're not gonna talk, then get lost. I'm running out of patience."

Big Eyes crouched down beside his legs and picked up a rock to write a crooked "big brother" on the ground. Then she lifted her head to look at him.

Jiang Cheng figured this little girl might really be mute. "Okay. Got it."

He called the number again. On this attempt, it only rang a few times.

"Who's this?"

Jiang Cheng glanced at Big Eyes. "I have your little sister here—"

"Go ahead and get rid of her," was the answer from the other end. The line went dead again.

"Fuck me!" Jiang Cheng had a sudden urge to smash his phone. Pointing at Big Eyes, he demanded, "Your name!"

Big Eyes lowered her head and scribbled out her name with the rock.

Gu Miao.

Jiang Cheng didn't call the number again. Instead, he sent a message, attaching a photo of Big Eyes with the words: *Gu Miao. mute. skateboard.*

Thirty seconds later, the same number called him back.

Jiang Cheng picked up. "Too late, I already got rid of the body."

"Sorry about that," said the voice from before. "Can you please tell me where you are? I want to see if I can still piece her back together."

"...East Station, the really run-down one." Jiang Cheng knitted his brow. "She got lost. Hurry up, I have to go."

"Thank you, thank you so much," the voice answered. "I'll be there right away. You can go ahead and leave if you're in a hurry; just tell her to wait there for me."

Jiang Cheng picked up the cigarette stub he'd tossed earlier and flicked it into a nearby garbage can, then lit a new one. He was going to call a cab and head out, but it occurred to him that nobody cared whether he came or went, or where he was. He supposed he wasn't in any particular rush.

Gu Miao sat for a while on her skateboard, then stepped back onto it and began to zip back and forth along the sidewalk. Jiang Cheng watched her in amazement. He thought the little girl was just fooling around, but he was shocked to see her handle going uphill, downhill, accelerating, braking, and turning with such ease. That head of tumbleweed hair and the dirty face and clothes kept breaking his illusion, though.

After a while, Gu Miao rolled to a stop beside him, kicked the skateboard up with her toes, and caught it in her hands. She raised her hand and pointed behind Jiang Cheng.

"Real cool." Jiang Cheng gave her a thumbs-up and turned around.

A black motorcycle had stopped behind him. The rider wore a helmet that obscured his face, and the legs that rested against the curb were wrapped in form-fitting gray pants and boots. It was all very eye-catching—especially those long, straight legs.

"Your brother?" Jiang Cheng asked Gu Miao.

She nodded.

"What's wrong with your head?" The rider removed his helmet and dismounted. His eyes were glued to Gu Miao's hair as he walked up to them. "And your face and clothes... Did you fall in an outhouse?"

Gu Miao shook her head.

"Bullied by classmates is more like it," Jiang Cheng said.

"Thank you." Only now did this person direct his gaze toward Jiang Cheng. He extended a hand. "Gu Fei—I'm her brother."

Jiang Cheng stood up and shook his hand. "You're welcome."

Gu Fei appeared to be around the same age as him, though it was difficult to tell that he was Gu Miao's brother from his eyes alone—the shape was similar, but Gu Miao's were larger... His face was just as fair, though.

Up until this moment, Jiang Cheng's mood had been nothing but rotten tomatoes all the way down, but he found himself sparing a couple glances through the tomato spiral at Gu Fei's hair, which was every bit as eye-catching as his long legs.

Gu Fei sported a very short buzz cut. When he turned his head, Jiang Cheng saw music staves and notes shaved into the shorter fuzz on each side—a bass clef on one side, and a rest on the other. He couldn't see from here how many dots the rest had.

"Did you just get off the train?" Gu Fei asked, glancing at the suitcase beside him.

"Yeah." Jiang Cheng picked up his phone to open the ride-hailing app again.

"Where are you headed? I can give you a ride," Gu Fei offered.

"That's okay." Jiang Cheng eyed the bike. As large as it was, a motorcycle was still a motorcycle.

"She doesn't take up any space," said Gu Fei.

"It's all right, thanks."

"Say 'thank you' to this big brother," Gu Fei said to Gu Miao, pointing at Jiang Cheng, "you ball of poop."

Jiang Cheng turned to face the "ball of poop," curious to hear her speak. But instead, Gu Miao clutched her skateboard tight and gave him a full 90-degree bow.

Gu Fei straddled the bike and put on his helmet, while Gu Miao climbed deftly onto the back seat and held on to his waist.

"Thanks again," Gu Fei said before turning the bike around and speeding away.

Jiang Cheng sat back down on the stone post. The signal was good enough now, but all the same, he waited for a long time and no one accepted his ride request. None of the passing cabs stopped, either, when he tried to flag them down.

What kind of shitty place is this?

He'd been in a rotten mood for a while now, but he hadn't had a chance to savor it properly. His life had been turned upside down and it left his mind numb with shock and confusion. He had no room to catch his breath. He hadn't even gotten a chance to wonder why he'd accepted this arrangement in the first place before he found himself here already.

Was it rebellion? His mom had said, "There's never been anyone in our family as rebellious as you. You're covered in thorns."

Of course, they had never been a family—hell, over the past few years they'd practically become enemies. When they looked at each other, all they saw was rage.

Jiang Cheng frowned. He hadn't had a chance to ponder any of that. At least, not until now—not until this very moment. It was only in this cold, unfamiliar, snowy city that he'd finally been jolted back to reality.

Pained, hopeless, and resistant to the unknown that lay ahead, his nose twinged. He lowered his head, his tears leaving furious streaks down his face.

✦ ✦ ✦

Jiang Cheng was sitting in a KFC in the middle of nowhere when his phone rang. He glanced at the unknown number and picked up.

"Hello?"

A middle-aged man's voice boomed through the receiver. "Jiang Cheng?"

Jiang Cheng held the phone away from his ears. "Yes."

"I'm your daddy," the man said.

"...Oh." Jiang Cheng answered. This exchange was somehow amusing to him, and he couldn't help but laugh.

The man laughed along with him for a second before continuing, "My name is Li Baoguo. You know that, right?"

"Yeah." Jiang Cheng took a sip of coke.

"Has your train arrived yet?" Li Baoguo asked.

"Yeah." Jiang Cheng glanced down at his watch. *Two hours ago.*

"Do you have the address? I don't have a car to pick you up, just take a cab over and I'll meet you out by the main road," said Li Baoguo.

"Okay."

He had better luck this time; he was able to hail a cab right away. The driver had the heat on full blast, and it was so warm that Jiang Cheng felt a little feverish. The driver was chatty, but Jiang Cheng just leaned against the window and stared outside quietly. After a few false starts, the driver finally gave up and turned on the radio.

Jiang Cheng was trying his best to get a good look at the city, but night had descended and the streetlamps didn't do much in the way of illumination. Besides, watching snowflakes dance in the halo of the lights made him a little dizzy.

He closed his eyes.

And then he quickly opened them again. What was wrong with him? How lame. He was acting like a sissy.

When the taxi finally brought him to his destination, Jiang Cheng got out with his suitcase and stood on the side of the street.

There was nobody there.

Not even a shadow of "your daddy" Li Baoguo, who'd promised to meet him out by the main road. Fighting the irritation in his heart and the pain of his wind-blown face, Jiang Cheng pulled out his phone and called Li Baoguo.

The call rang for a long time before Li Baoguo picked up. "Agh, this hand sucks... Yeah?"

"I'm out here on the main road." Hearing the noise from the other end, though, Jiang Cheng had the sudden urge to hang up and look for a hotel instead.

"Huh?! You're here already?" Li Baoguo exclaimed loudly. "I'm here, I'm already here, I'm coming out right now."

That so-called "right now" was *right about* five minutes. Just as Jiang Cheng was reaching out with one hand to flag a cab, dragging his suitcase along with the other, a man wearing an ushanka hat ran up and pushed his arm down.

"Jiang Cheng, right?" he shouted.

Jiang Cheng was silent. He saw the apartment building Li Baoguo had run out from. It was right next to where he'd been waiting.

Right now?

When he noticed heads poking out from a second-floor window looking in their direction, he almost wanted to keep his mouth shut forever.

"I was over at a friend's place. Let's go." Li Baoguo patted his shoulder. "Come on, let's go home... You look taller than the photos, huh."

Jiang Cheng kept his eyes down, glued to the muddy road, as he followed.

"Hey." Li Baoguo slapped his back a couple of times for good measure. "How many years has it been now? Gotta be more than ten, eh? I finally got to see my son! I should take a good look."

Li Baoguo peered round in front of Jiang Cheng and stared straight into his face.

Jiang Cheng pulled up the face mask he'd left scrunched up on his chin, fixing it over his nose. In that instant, he suddenly felt hollowed out. Even the air around him was charged with a sense of wandering aimlessness.

2

His MOM HAD SAID—

It suddenly occurred to Jiang Cheng that it might be a little absurd to refer to her that way, and this particular notion was so intrusive that it cut off his train of thought. He couldn't remember exactly what she'd said.

In all of his seventeen-odd years, his parents and family were the only ones he'd known. Regardless of their relationship, Mom was always the woman named Shen Yiqing, and Dad was the man named Jiang Wei. And then there was the little brother whom he'd never been close with… But now, out of nowhere, he had an extra set of family members. Li Baoguo, and…some other names he'd already forgotten.

It was hard to accept.

His relationship with his family had always been tense, for sure. Whether it was his parents or his brother, every interaction with them came with a risk of explosion. It had already been about a year since he and his brother last spoke to each other. Even his mom, who was always calm, had lost her temper a handful of times.

But even though this atmosphere had lasted from the beginning of his middle school years all the way until high school, even though he was always thinking that he never wanted to go home again, never wanted to see his parents again, and especially never wanted to see that face that looked like it'd come from the same mold as their parents... When this moment had finally descended upon him like a wish fulfilled, it still completely blindsided him.

Yes, blindsided.

Extremely blindsided.

It all felt like a nonsensical dream which had started the moment his mom said, "There's something I have to tell you," followed by several months of cold silence and paperwork, all the way until now.

Most of the time he wasn't too upset about it, nor was he in a lot of pain.

He only felt blindsided.

"It's cold, eh?" said Li Baoguo as he turned to Jiang Cheng, coughing loudly. "It must be way colder than where you used to live."

"Mhm," Jiang Cheng answered behind his mask.

"It'll be warmer once we're inside," Li Baoguo said, his loud coughs and equally loud voice spraying saliva all over Jiang Cheng's face. "I tidied up a room especially for you."

"Thanks," Jiang Cheng said, pulling his mask higher.

"Well, there's no need for that between father and son." Li Baoguo laughed as he coughed some more, then clapped Jiang Cheng on the back. "No need for 'thank you' between us!"

Jiang Cheng wasn't able to respond; the slaps were quite forceful. Breathing in the chilly air had already left a tickle in his throat; hearing Li Baoguo cough only made the urge for *him* to cough even stronger. Those two slaps made him double over in a hacking fit that almost had him in tears.

"You're not in very good health, huh?" Li Baoguo watched him. "You gotta exercise. When I was your age, I was strong as a bear."

Jiang Cheng didn't say anything, just gave him a thumbs-up, still bent over.

Li Baoguo laughed boisterously. "Exercise! I'm counting on you to take care of me in the future!"

Jiang Cheng straightened and looked at him.

"Come on." Li Baoguo gave him another slap on the back.

Jiang Cheng frowned. "Don't touch me."

"Oooh." Li Baoguo paused and looked at him with wide eyes. "What's wrong?"

Jiang Cheng held his gaze for a few moments, then pulled down his mask and said, "Don't slap my back."

Li Baoguo's home was on an old street lined on either side with various decrepit little shops overflowing with the flavors of life, selling food, clothes, and various sundries. Above these shops sat several stories of low-rise residential apartments.

Jiang Cheng looked up, sweeping his gaze over and past the countless cables that crisscrossed above their heads. It was tough to tell whether the outer walls were truly painted in such ambiguous colors or simply looked that way due to the darkening skies.

He followed Li Baoguo into one of the buildings, his heart a tangle of emotions. They passed through heaps of produce and junk crowding the short hallway on the first floor before stopping in front of a door.

"It certainly won't be able to compare with what you had before," Li Baoguo said as he unlocked the door. "But what's mine is yours!"

Jiang Cheng stayed quiet. He stared back into the hallway at a cobwebbed lightbulb hanging from the ceiling, and imagined the lightbulb must be suffocating.

"What's mine is yours!" Li Baoguo opened the door and turned to give his shoulder a couple of hard thumps. "And what's yours is mine! Now that's real father and son stuff!"

"I said don't touch me," Jiang Cheng snapped.

"Whoa." Li Baoguo entered the room and flipped the lights on. "Spoiled rotten you are, talking to your elders like that. Let me tell you, I never spoiled your older brother or sister. If you grew up here at home, I'd have beat you into submission long ago... Come on, you'll sleep in this room. It used to be your brother's..."

Jiang Cheng dragged his suitcase into the room, not bothering to listen to whatever else Li Baoguo had to say. He wondered how a whole family had managed to fit into this two-bedroom apartment in the past.

Without looking, he could tell by his nose alone that this "tidied" room probably wasn't tidied often...or ever. The smell of dust mingled with a faint odor of mildew in the air. The room held an old wardrobe, a desk, and a bunk bed. The bottom bunk had indeed been cleared out, while the top one was still packed with junk. The sheets and covers were all freshly changed.

"Set your stuff down; you can unpack tomorrow," Li Baoguo said. "Let's have a few drinks first."

"What drinks?" Jiang Cheng was a little taken aback. He glanced at his phone—it was almost 10:00 P.M.

"Alcohol, of course. It's been more than ten years since we last saw each other. We gotta have some drinks to celebrate the occasion!"

"...That's okay." Jiang Cheng could hardly believe his ears. "I don't want to drink."

"Don't want to drink?" Li Baoguo's eyes widened by another degree, and he stared at Jiang Cheng for a couple of seconds before his eyes returned to their original size. He started to laugh. "Have you never had alcohol before? But you're in high school already—"

"I don't feel like drinking," Jiang Cheng interrupted him. "I just want to sleep."

Li Baoguo froze in place. "Sleep…?" After a long pause, he turned and walked away with a wave of his hand, saying gruffly, "Okay, okay. Sleep. Sleep away."

Closing the door behind him, Jiang Cheng stood in the middle of the room for nearly five minutes. Then he opened the doors to the wardrobe. An overwhelming smell of mothballs rushed at him in a wave as he did, catching him off guard. More than half of this double-door wardrobe was stuffed with a variety of comforters, old sweaters, and blankets with edges so frayed they could have been tassels.

It was hard to describe the feeling. Jiang Cheng was certain he hadn't started to miss his old family and home, which were hours away now. What he did miss, sincerely and madly, was his old room.

He pulled out some clothes from his suitcase at random and hung them up, leaving the rest in the suitcase, which he crammed into the bottom of the wardrobe. He pulled out a bottle of fragrance and sprayed it into the wardrobe a dozen times before he finally shut its doors and sat down on the edge of the bed.

His phone rang. The call display showed "Mom." He answered.

"You've arrived?" came his mom's voice from the other end.

"Yeah," Jiang Cheng answered.

"The environment there isn't as good as it is back home," she said. "You might need some time to adjust."

"No need."

There was a pause, then, "Xiao-Cheng, I still hope you don't think that—"

"I don't."

Her voice took on the usual stern note. "We didn't treat you poorly over the years. Your dad and I never once let on that you were adopted, did we? You never knew."

"But somehow, I know now," Jiang Cheng said. "And I got thrown out."

She raised her voice. "Don't forget—it was your fault your dad had that fit and had to be rushed to the hospital on New Year's! He still hasn't been able to come home!"

Jiang Cheng said nothing. He didn't understand what he had to do with his dad's pneumonia-induced hospital stay. As to whatever else his mom had to say after that...amazingly, he didn't catch any of it. It was his superpower: He could block things he didn't want to hear from entering his brain.

Her severe yet hollow accusations and her completely ineffective methods of communicating with him were the catalysts for his own breakdown. He didn't want to listen. The last thing he wanted was to get into a fight while he was in the middle of this unfamiliar environment that made him queasy all over.

By the time the call ended, he couldn't remember the rest of the conversation. What his mom said, what he said—he'd forgotten it all.

Craving a shower, Jiang Cheng rose and opened the door. He peered into the living room—no one was there. He cleared his throat and coughed a few times. No one answered.

"Are...you there?" He walked into the living room, unsure of how exactly to refer to Li Baoguo.

It was a small apartment. Standing in the living room, he could see the doors of all the rooms with one glance: the bedrooms, the kitchen, and the bathroom. Li Baoguo wasn't home. Must have gone off to play mahjong again, Jiang Cheng thought, since the man would steal a few minutes to play a few hands even when he was passing by on his way to pick someone up at the corner.

"*Come now—play a few hands—got plenty of time anyway,*" Jiang Cheng sang as he pushed open the bathroom door. "*Come now— take a shower—got...*"[1]

There was no hot water tank in the bathroom.

"*Got...*" He continued singing as he turned back to look at the kitchen next to the bathroom, but he didn't see a hot water tank there either, only a small electrical heater attached to the top of the kitchen faucet. "*...Got...*"

He couldn't continue. After doing a couple rounds around the apartment to confirm that there was indeed no hot water tank, he felt a stuffiness in his chest. He smacked the faucet.

"Fuck."

He'd spent the whole day traveling; he couldn't possibly fall asleep without a shower.

Finally, he had to reopen his suitcase and pull out a collapsible pail. Stripped down to his underwear, he carried the hot water from the kitchen to the bathroom one pail at a time, and finally managed to take a haphazard "shower."

When he was finished, a cockroach scuttled past his feet as he walked out of the bathroom. He jumped up to get out of its way, and narrowly missed hitting his head on the door frame.

It was only after he'd gotten back to his room and turned off the lights in preparation for some forced shut-eye that he noticed the room didn't have any curtains. The reason he'd never seen the view outside the window, and thus never noticed, was because the windowpane was too dirty.

He pulled the covers over himself, hesitated, then sniffed at them. When he verified that they were clean, he let out a breath of relief;

---

1   *Jiang Cheng is ad-libbing his own lyrics to the song Itch, by Huang Ling.*

he didn't even have the energy to sigh.

After half an hour of lying on the bed with his eyes shut, long enough that his eyes were sore from the effort, sleep still wouldn't come. He was just about to get up for a smoke when his phone chimed with a notification.

It was a message from Pan Zhi.

– Wtf, you left already? What's going on?

Jiang Cheng lit a cigarette and dialed Pan Zhi's number. With the cigarette between his lips, he walked to the window and tried to open it. Dust and rust covered the window and its frame. He struggled for a while, but the window still hadn't budged an inch even by the time Pan Zhi picked up the call.

"Cheng?" Pan Zhi said in a hushed whisper, as if they were in the middle of a heist.

"Ah—fuck." Jiang Cheng grimaced and cursed as he pricked his finger on something sharp. He gave up on trying to open the window.

"What's going on with you?" Pan Zhi was still whispering. "I heard from Yu Xin today that you left already. Didn't you say you'd let me know when you were leaving? I even bought a bunch of things to give to you!"

"Just ship them over."

Jiang Cheng put on a jacket and walked out of the room, cigarette still between his lips. He was about to head outside when he remembered he didn't have a key and had no choice but to retreat into the living room and open a window there. The irritation in him was like a storm; all his bad mood needed was one more spark and it could all go up in flames of rage.

"So you're there already?" Pan Zhi asked.

"Mhm." Jiang Cheng leaned over the windowsill and looked out at the pitch-black street.

"So? How's that biological dad of yours?"

"You got anything important to say?" Jiang Cheng said. "I don't feel like talking right now."

"Fuck, it's not like I sent you over there." Pan Zhi tutted. "What are you lashing out at me for? You didn't hesitate for a second when your mom said they needed the adoptee's consent, but now you're mad?!"

Jiang Cheng blew out a puff of smoke. "Being mad and not hesitating aren't mutually exclusive."

In the empty street outside, a tiny figure suddenly jumped and flitted by on a skateboard with shocking speed. Blinking into the darkness, Jiang Cheng remembered the little girl named Gu Miao from earlier. Who'd have thought there would be so many skateboarders in this shitty town?

"How about I come over?" Pan Zhi said suddenly.

"Huh?" Jiang Cheng's attention was elsewhere.

"I said I'll come visit you," Pan Zhi said. "There's still a few days before school starts, right? I can bring over the stuff I bought for you."

"No," Jiang Cheng declined immediately.

"Don't be stubborn, it's not like you told anyone else about this. At this point, I'm the only one who can offer you some warmth." Pan Zhi sighed. "Let me come cheer you up."

"Cheer me up how?" Jiang Cheng retorted. "Are you gonna blow me?"

"Screw your uncle, Jiang Cheng, can you try having a shred of shame?!"

"What would I need that for? If you're so passionate about coming thousands of miles just to see me, no doubt I'll have to co-operate."

Jiang Cheng circled the apartment a few times holding his

cigarette stub before he found an old Eight Treasure Porridge can covered with cigarette ashes. When he opened the lid, the stench of positively ancient cigarette ends almost made him vomit before he even took a look inside. He tossed the stub in and quickly closed the lid, feeling in that moment that he never wanted to smoke again.

This strange and upsetting environment, this strange and upsetting "family"...

Jiang Cheng thought he'd have insomnia under circumstances like these, but when he lay down, the agonizing sleeplessness he felt earlier was gone. He found himself surprisingly drowsy. Not just drowsy—seriously tired. It was like he'd just pulled weeks of late nights to study for a test.

It came suddenly. He closed his eyes and fell into a deep sleep, as if he'd lost all senses.

It was a dreamless night.

When he woke up the next morning, the first thing he felt was a soreness all over his body. As he rolled out of bed, Jiang Cheng felt that perhaps he was actually a dock worker who hauled loads to and from the pier; some newbie who hadn't even been working for a full week.

He checked the time on his phone: It was still pretty early, just past eight in the morning. When he got dressed and walked out of the room, he could see that everything was the same as it had been the night before—even the empty bed in the other bedroom.

Had Li Baoguo been out all night?

Jiang Cheng frowned. Once he'd washed up, he started to feel a little bad; his attitude yesterday hadn't been all that great. Li Baoguo didn't mean any ill will by dragging him along for drinks, it was only a difference in their habits. But he'd rejected him so bluntly. Was that why Li Baoguo hadn't returned the whole night?

He hesitated for a moment, then pulled out his phone to give Li Baoguo a call. They didn't drink together the night before, but they could still have breakfast together.

Just as he was dialing, the sound of jangling keys came from the other side of the door, followed by the sound of the lock turning. The noise went on for another twenty or so seconds before the door finally opened.

Li Baoguo walked in, bringing the chill outdoor air in with him, with a look of exhaustion on his dull, sallow face.

"You're up already?" Li Baoguo said loudly once he spotted him. "Pretty early riser, huh? How did you sleep?"

"...Not bad." Jiang Cheng noticed the pungent aroma of cigarettes coming off him as he answered, mixed with some other inexplicable stink—it was like the smell you got on the old green and red trains.

"Have you had breakfast yet?" Li Baoguo shrugged off his jacket and gave it a shake. The foul smell only got worse, permeating the tiny living space.

"Not yet," Jiang Cheng said. "Maybe we can—"

"There's breakfast stalls right outside—quite a few of them. Go eat something," Li Baoguo said. "I'm dying to sleep, let me doze for a bit. If I don't get up by noon, you just go ahead and eat on your own."

Jiang Cheng watched him walk into the other bedroom and throw himself onto the bed without removing any of his clothes, just pulling a blanket over himself. A little stunned, he asked, "Where did you...go last night?"

"Mahjong. Been having shitty luck lately, but yesterday wasn't too bad! Must be you bringing me the good fortune!" Li Baoguo yelled happily before closing his eyes.

Jiang Cheng took the keys from the table and headed out. He felt naïve for feeling bad earlier.

The snow had stopped, replaced by a bone-piercing chill that swept through the air.

The morning streets were livelier than they had been at nighttime. There were pedestrians and cars, and even the sounds of firecrackers going off. But now that the sun was out, the neglect and decay that the cover of night had concealed was out in the open along with everything else.

Jiang Cheng walked up and down the street a few times before finally entering a bun shop. After a few meat buns and a bowl of tofu pudding, the soreness in his body still hadn't subsided. Not only that, it seemed to have gotten worse, as if it'd been awakened by the nourishment.

Feeling like he had a cold coming on, he finished his breakfast and went into the pharmacy next door to buy a pack of cold medicine. After that, he stood on the side of the road, feeling a little lost. Should he head back...? The mental image of Li Baoguo falling asleep engulfed in weird smells irritated him to no end. What was there to do if he went back? Sleep, or stare off into space?

After standing outside the pharmacy for a few minutes, he decided to take a stroll around and familiarize himself with the neighborhood. Even if he wasn't sure how long he was going to stay here.

He wandered aimlessly from the side street to the main road, then turned a corner onto another side street parallel to the one he was on before. He wanted to see if there was a way up ahead that would take him back to where he was without having to turn around.

On this little street, he found a tiny musical instrument shop and an ice cream parlor decorated in pastel colors. But other than that, there was no discernable difference between his street and this one.

He stopped at a convenience store masquerading as a supermarket and walked in, wanting to buy a bottle of water to wash down the medicine. But just as the burst of warm, lemon-scented air greeted him, Jiang Cheng froze in the doorway. He had an urge to turn around and leave the way he came.

From where he stood, he could see four people squeezed together in the tight space behind the cash register, each one sitting or leaning on a stool. When he entered, the idle chatter abruptly halted, and all four heads turned simultaneously to stare at him.

Jiang Cheng studied the four people—their appearances and their expressions, their clothing and the way they carried themselves. Each one of their faces seemed to spell out a word:

Fresh. Out. Of. Jail.

As he wavered between turning around and leaving or going in for the water on the shelf, Jiang Cheng caught something else out of the corner of his eye—there were three other people crammed in front of a row of shelves. As he turned, before he was able to make out any faces, he noticed a shiny bald head and tufts of hair scattered all over the floor. And a pair of large eyes.

Run Wild
SAYE

3

T HE SHINY HEAD between the store shelves belonged to
Gu Miao—although now, post-haircut, it was difficult to tell
that it belonged to a little girl. She had on a boy's-style blue-
gray puffer jacket, and if it weren't for her eyes, Jiang Cheng wouldn't
have recognized her.

Behind her stood Gu Fei with a cigarette in his mouth and an
electric shaver in his hand, paused in mid-air. He was surprised to
see Jiang Cheng here, apparently.

He looked different from when Jiang Cheng had seen him
yesterday. Wearing a sweater and joggers, he looked relaxed and
comfortable. His appearance and mannerisms differed dramatically
from his four friends by the door. He was eye-catching, the kind of
person who stood out immediately in a crowd.

Emanating from every pore of his body was the message: *I'm the
top dog.*

Personally, Jiang Cheng never thought of himself as someone who looked like a bad guy, though he scared even himself
sometimes when his temper flared. He assumed he'd just never
gotten over the transitory affliction of adolescent rebellion and
had turned it into a chronic condition. But today, when all he
wanted to do was purchase a bottle of water in peace, he was
pretty sure he looked completely harmless. So when all eyes in the

convenience-store-pretending-to-be-a-supermarket simultaneously converged on him with a silent expression that all but screamed "you're looking for trouble," he was more than a little perplexed.

In the midst of this tension, a bit of ash fell from the tip of Gu Fei's cigarette onto Gu Miao's newly shiny scalp, and she ducked her head and brushed at it roughly with both hands.

Jiang Cheng didn't let the attention get to him. Growing up, he had never shied away from trouble and wasn't intimidated by any "what are you looking at" stares. Especially when he wasn't feeling well, mentally or physically. He walked to the shelf to grab himself a bottle of water. But when he glanced up, he saw Gu Fei standing on the other side of the shelves.

After a brief exchange of eye contact through the gap between two cans of chips, Gu Fei finally said, "Welcome."

"This your family's store?" Jiang Cheng asked.

Gu Fei nodded. "Yeah."

"What a coincidence."

Since Gu Fei said nothing in response, and Jiang Cheng didn't feel much like making more small talk at the moment, he tossed the bottle gently in his hand and headed straight to the checkout.

A young man walked behind the cash register. Propping his hands on the counter, he leaned forward to stare at Jiang Cheng. "Two bucks."

Jiang Cheng swept a glance at him. The "Fresh Out of Jail" quartet were still in their respective spots. This new guy was the one who'd been standing next to Gu Fei when he first came in.

He hadn't noticed earlier in the dim lighting, but under the fluorescent ceiling light that hung over the counter, a cursory glance showed him a rather pretty face, almost feminine featured. Aside from the long, tapered eyes, the rest of his facial features actually made him seem more like Gu Miao's older sister...no, brother. He looked the part more than Gu Fei did, anyway.

Jiang Cheng handed over a ten-yuan bill from his pocket. The young man looked down and punched it into the cash register, then gave him another look.

"You Da-Fei's friend? I haven't seen you around."

"No." Jiang Cheng popped a couple of pills from the pack of cold medicine he'd just bought and washed them down with some water.

"No?" The guy's gaze traveled over his shoulder and landed somewhere behind him. He placed the change on the counter. "Ah."

Jiang Cheng threw the half-finished bottle of water into the trash can by the door, then lifted the heavy curtains to go outside.[2]

"Geez, you should've gotten a smaller size." The cashier's voice sounded from behind. "How wasteful."

"...I didn't think about it," Jiang Cheng said.

The guy was right, of course. Why hadn't he gotten the smaller bottle? He wasn't going to finish it anyway. Must've been the intensifying soreness all over his body short-circuiting his brain.

He stood on the steps outside, having trouble remembering where he was heading before he went into the store... Should he go back? Back where? Li Baoguo's—no, *his* new home?

At the mere thought of the disgusting state of the apartment and Li Baoguo's thunderous snores, he felt a tightness in his chest that crawled all the way up his throat. He suddenly found it difficult to get air into his lungs—it was like he couldn't breathe at all.

Bright stars spread across the black background of his vision.

---

2   In the northeast provinces of China, it's common to cover doorways with heavy-duty curtains to keep out the cold wind.

Having lost control of his body, Jiang Cheng felt himself drop to the ground, spinning like a sack of flour. With his last remaining shred of consciousness, he sighed.

This should be good.

Gu Miao rubbed her smooth head as she walked toward the door, skateboard in hand.

"Your hat." Gu Fei picked up his jacket from a chair, pulling out a green knitted cap decorated with little flowers from where it was bunched up in one of the pockets, and tossed it onto her head.

Gu Miao yanked it roughly over her ears. Eyes on the ground, she went out the door...then immediately came back in, slapping the counter.

"What is it?" Li Yan leaned over the cash register and tugged on her hat, then raised his eyes at Gu Fei. "You really went and knitted her a green hat?"[3]

"She picked the color herself." Gu Fei put the electric shaver away and turned his attention to Gu Miao. "What is it?"

Gu Miao pointed at the door.

"Is there a dog?" Gu Fei kicked his chair to one side and walked over, lifting the curtain.

The baller who'd bought a bottle of water just to throw half of it away was currently ass up on the sidewalk outside the store, hugging the ground with his face.

"Hey." Gu Fei walked out and nudged Jiang Cheng's leg with his toes. He didn't even know the guy's name. "You all right?"

The baller didn't move. Gu Fei bent down to study his face where it was pressed against the ground, noticing that the tip of his nose

---

3   A green hat is considered the symbol of a (usually male) cuckold. As such, they're usually avoided even by people like Gu Miao, to whom the insult wouldn't apply to.

was flattened against the sidewalk. He carefully lifted Jiang Cheng's head and tilted it slightly so he could breathe, then turned and shouted into the store.

"Hey! We got a man down!"

Li Yan was the first one out the door. He froze at the scene before him. "Was he stabbed?"

"What, were you the one who stabbed him?" Gu Fei touched the baller's face and felt its scorching temperature. "He's burning up."

"You can pass out from a fever?" Li Yan was clearly a little stunned. He turned to look at the others who had followed him out. "What do we do? Call an ambulance?"

"I say don't bother." Liu Fan looked around. "If some hypervigilant auntie sees and calls the cops, they'll blame it on us for sure. I only just got out yesterday..."

"Drag him inside," Gu Fei said.

"Drag... You know him, right?" Liu Fan asked.

"Just do as you're told. Even if they don't know each other, Da-Fei touched him just now," Li Yan said. "If some auntie calls the cops, do you think they won't think to ask us about it?"

"He's passed out from a fever is all. Your non-existent screenwriting career must be a real disappointment to your mom and dad." Gu Fei flipped Jiang Cheng over. "Hurry it up."

Together, the bunch of them carried the unconscious body into the store and left him in the spare room Gu Fei usually used for breaks and naps.

"Tch, I didn't even get to sleep properly in this bed," Li Yan said once everyone else was out. "This weakling who popped out of nowhere got to enjoy it first."

"You go out there and eat shit, and I'll tuck you in right away," said Gu Fei.

"You've got no shame," said Li Yan.

"And you've got the most shame, all right?" Gu Fei gave him a shove. "Now get out."

"Hey." Li Yan resisted and stayed where he was. Turning, he lowered his voice. "The guy said you're not friends?"

"Mhm." Gu Fei pushed a little harder and Li Yan stumbled out. Gu Fei followed and closed the door behind them. "He's the one who found Er-Miao yesterday."

"That was *him*?" Li Yan was a little surprised. "Must be destiny."

Gu Fei ignored him. He sat down behind the cash register and started playing a game on his phone.

Li Yan leaned over the counter. "He's pretty handsome," he said in a low voice.

Gu Fei gave him a look, and Li Yan turned away and didn't say anything more. Gu Miao came over then and stuck out her hand in front of Gu Fei with her palm spread open, wiggling her fingers.

"Go ahead and eat. Look how much weight you've gained in these last couple of months; nobody's gonna play with you anymore." Gu Fei took out a ten-yuan bill and pressed it into her hand. "Your face is almost a perfect circle now."

Gu Miao ignored him. She put the money in her pocket, patted it for good measure, then walked out with skateboard in hand.

"With a bald head like that, no kid is gonna play with her no matter what shape her face is," Li Yan sighed.

"Nobody plays with her anyway, even when she's not bald." Gu Fei kept playing his game. "She's never had any friends—who's going to play with a mute?"

"Don't say that," Liu Fan said beside them. "It's not like she really can't talk. She just *won't* talk. What's the big deal?"

"What's gonna happen if she goes on like this?" Li Yan sighed again. "School's just one thing; if she doesn't wanna go, then don't go. But if she's only willing to talk to Da-Fei, then—"

"There's a high probability the world's gonna end if you don't keep worrying about it," Gu Fei interrupted him. "You should really apply for the Nobel Peace Prize."

"Fuck you." Li Yan slapped the counter and pulled up a chair next to Liu Fan.

The store slipped into silence. Liu Fan and the others sitting by the radiator were slowly nodding off to sleep, a glazed look in their eyes. Their facial muscles were starting to droop from relaxation, which made for a rather disturbing scene: three customers in a row had lifted the curtains to come in, only to turn on their heels and leave at the mere sight of them.

"You guys." Gu Fei rapped his knuckles on the counter. "Get going."

"Go where?" Li Yan asked.

"I dunno, go wild," said Gu Fei.

"I don't feel like going outside, though." Liu Fan stretched lazily. "Too damn cold and nowhere to go."

"You've been scaring away customers who've already stepped through the door." Gu Fei put a lit cigarette in his mouth.

"I promise, the next person to come in, we'll hold them here for you." Liu Fan laughed and clapped his hands together. "We won't let a single one escape."

"Hurry up and get out," Gu Fei said. "Annoying little shits."

"Go, go, go, go." Liu Fan tutted and stood up to give the other stools a kick each. "Your Uncle Gu is throwing a fit again—another minute and he'll come at us with a knife."

None of the others wanted to move, but they stood up anyway. They put their jackets on and left reluctantly, cursing under their breath all the while.

Li Yan was the last one out the door, but at the last second, he turned around and said, "There's another one in there. You're not going to get rid of him?"

Gu Fei just looked back at him silently. Li Yan lifted the curtain and walked out without another word.

After finishing a cigarette, Gu Fei glanced at the clock. He estimated that about twenty minutes had passed. According to standard fainting procedure, the guy should've been awake in a fraction of that time.

He pushed open the door to the spare room and peered inside. Mr. Baller was still unconscious, lying there with his eyes closed in the exact same position as before.

"Hey." Gu Fei walked over and gave him a push. "Don't die at my place."

Still, Mr. Baller didn't move.

For a while, Gu Fei just stood there and stared at him.

Jiang Cheng's face was a little dirty, but it didn't take away from the attractiveness of his features. The very slightly downturned eyes gave him a haughty air. According to Gu Fei's standards—which judged pretty much everybody he met as inadequate—the guy was handsome enough. It was just that their first meeting yesterday had left him unimpressed with the prickly air he had about him—only low-key prickly, but Gu Fei felt it just the same.

After a few minutes of staring, he lifted the covers, rummaged around in Mr. Baller's pockets, and found his wallet. His ID was slotted among a number of what looked like membership cards.

Jiang Cheng.

He put the wallet back, leaned down, and shouted into Jiang Cheng's ears, "Hey!"

"Mmm..." Mr. Baller finally stirred and grunted quietly, sounding thoroughly vexed.

Gu Fei gave the edge of the bed a kick and turned to leave.

Jiang Cheng was confused.

When he opened his eyes, it felt like he had amnesia: *Who am I? Where is this?*

The last thing he could remember was the not-very-clean ground rushing toward him, bringing with it some snow that had been trampled into sludge.

He'd passed out? That was a lifetime first for him.

He sat up and lifted the blanket covering him. When he saw the mud all over his clothes, he immediately grabbed the blanket to check and found a few clumps of mud on it as well. He gave it a few pats in a futile attempt to clean it off. Just as he was considering getting some water to see if he could get the dirt out, his brain suddenly decided to work again.

Who am I?

Jiang Cheng.

Where am I?

No idea.

It was a small but well-kept room, much cleaner than the one Li Baoguo had given him. He threw off the covers and went to open the door.

When he saw the three rows of store shelves outside, he finally realized that he was still in Gu Fei's store.

Sitting in a recliner by the cash register, Gu Fei glanced up at him for a second, then turned his attention back to his phone. "You're finally awake."

"Yeah." Jiang Cheng patted the dried mud on his clothes. "Thank you."

"Don't mention it." Gu Fei's eyes were glued to his phone. "It might've been more trouble if I'd left you out there."

"Ah." Jiang Cheng turned and looked back at the small room. "The blanket...got dirty."

"There's a sink out back," Gu Fei said. "You can wash it there."

"What?" Jiang Cheng was stunned, and a little mad, but couldn't find an appropriate way to express his emotions. After all, there was nothing logically wrong with Gu Fei's words.

Gu Fei finally lifted his gaze from the phone screen to scrutinize Jiang Cheng's face. "Why mention it if you don't plan to wash it?"

Jiang Cheng said nothing, so they stared at each other in silence.

At first he'd been grateful to Gu Fei for bringing him inside, but Gu Fei's attitude made it hard for him to express that gratitude. The only reason he didn't lash out was that he hadn't entirely recovered from fainting.

After a few more minutes of the staring contest, Gu Fei directed his eyes and his attention back to his mobile game.

Jiang Cheng turned and walked out.

It was nice and sunny outside. The sun was the only source of warmth against the north wind, though it wasn't much help—it was still freezing cold.

His head was killing him. Jiang Cheng pulled a ski cap out of his pocket and pulled it over his head, along with the hood of his jacket. He checked the time and was glad to see that he'd only been passed out for about half an hour. Not bad—he hadn't wasted too much time in the end.

Not that he had a clue what else there was for him to do.

Standing at the edge of the road and looking out to either side of him, he finally decided to continue wandering forward and circle back once he found the connecting lane between the two streets. He didn't much like the idea of going back to listen to Li Baoguo's snores, but he had to change his clothes.

As he trudged through the muddy snow, he suddenly felt a little lonely.

There had been many days like this in the past, when he'd spent hours wandering around aimlessly outside, sometimes without going home for days at a time. But he'd never felt loneliness the way he did now.

He wondered why.

Perhaps it was the intense sense of loss from being abandoned and exiled. Perhaps it was this strange and decrepit environment. Perhaps it was the lack of friends around him, or perhaps...it was simply because he had a cold.

When his phone made a sound, Jiang Cheng pulled it out to see a message from Yu Xin.

- I changed my mind.

He sighed and texted back.

- A lady always keeps her word.

Yu Xin didn't send another reply—perhaps she was mad that he wasn't giving her any face, or maybe just preserving her anger for another more suitable moment to blow up on him again.

He returned the phone to his pocket and pinched the bridge of his nose. It hurt like hell, he realized—he hadn't noticed before. It must've smashed into the ground earlier when he faceplanted.

Tsk.

He carefully pinched his nose from bridge to tip to make sure that nothing was broken before sticking his hand back in his pocket. After a few more steps, he saw a small side street up ahead, likely the connecting lane he was looking for.

Suddenly, a green-colored head emerged from the side street and rolled over like a gust of strong wind. By the time Jiang Cheng could make out that the green head was Gu Miao with her skateboard, she had already zoomed past him—so fast he could barely get a look at her.

Ah, skater girl.

He turned for another look. What a cool little girl. Too bad all her hair was gone.

He idly wondered if Gu Fei was really her brother. Even if she got a bad haircut, was it really that hard to find a salon and fix it with a shorter style? Did he really have to shave the whole thing off, especially on a chilly day like this...? Wait, was that a green hat?!

By the time Jiang Cheng had turned around again to confirm what he saw, all that was left of Gu Miao was a distant black dot.

Before he turned back to continue on his way, three bicycles came charging out of the side street. The rickety bikes rattled and clattered as they went, but they were nonetheless very quick.

"Shit, she's fast!" shouted one of the riders on the rickety bikes.

Jiang Cheng was amazed. *Does that mean...Gu Miao is being chased by bullies again?*

He didn't have it in him to even feel sympathy this time around, only an inexplicable annoyance.

What kind of fucked up place is this?!

Li Baoguo was still asleep when Jiang Cheng got back to his new "home." Though he had let up somewhat on the snoring, he'd been coughing from the moment Jiang Cheng stepped through the door, hacking and rasping like he was about to cough his lungs out. Jiang Cheng couldn't help but check on him a couple times, but both times, Li Baoguo's eyes were closed and he appeared to be sound asleep.

Certainly, this was a skill Jiang Cheng did not possess; if he coughed while he was sleeping, it'd definitely wake him up. This had to be a Li Baoguo specialty.

After he changed, Jiang Cheng wet a towel he got out of his suitcase and wiped his jacket clean. Then, he sat on the bed and stared off into space. He didn't know what else to do with himself.

Li Baoguo had stopped coughing next door, but his snoring started up again. Jiang Cheng found it hard to pin down his feelings right now. This man was his biological father, his flesh and blood. To think that he was actually born in a home like this was shocking enough. Although he hadn't met the rest of the family yet, Li Baoguo alone was the perfect embodiment of "EXCITEMENT AHEAD" in all-caps bold font.

Recently he had been careful to avoid thinking about it, but sitting here now, looking at the decay within and without, it was no longer possible to avoid the subject.

A long time ago, he had even discussed the concept of adoption with his parents.

It's a pointless exercise. Some things are simply carved into your bones; no amount of nurture can overcome it.

He didn't remember what they had to say on the matter, only what he'd said. His own words were now sharp slaps stinging his own face.

He should've known... His younger brother's personality was just like their parents': He was sensible, a boy of few words, preferred

the quiet, and was an avid reader. Jiang Cheng was the opposite—
though it wasn't like he was a chatterbox, either...

Even their neighbor had said so once, that he didn't seem like
part of the same family.

Right... Almost as if the incompatibility was built into him.

A torrent of coughs suddenly erupted from Li Baoguo's room,
like he had choked on something. It went on for a long time without
pause. Jiang Cheng thought he must be awake this time, then immediately heard the sound of cursing.

Not long after that, the snores started up again.

Jiang Cheng suddenly felt a rush of fear, a horror that carried
with it an intense feeling of suffocation. He stood up and grabbed
the keys from the living room so he could make a copy for himself,
and perhaps look for a hospital while he was out, so he could see a
doctor. He really wasn't feeling good; perhaps he had a fever.

Gu Fei crouched by a flowerbed outside the store, watching
Gu Miao zip proudly past him for the third time, as if showing off.
The cold air had turned her face almost bright red.

When she passed him for the fourth time, Gu Fei waved at her.
Gu Miao made a sharp U-turn and slowly rolled to a stop in front
of him.

"It's time to head home for lunch." Gu Fei stood up. "Go get ready."

Gu Miao walked into the store, skateboard in tow, as Gu Fei
lit a cigarette and pondered what to eat for lunch. A minute later,
he heard Gu Miao screaming from inside the store. Chucking the
cigarette, he immediately shot up and raced inside.

The screaming was coming from the bathroom out back. He bolted out to the courtyard behind the store and pushed open the bathroom door. Gu Miao was standing there, screaming at the sink with her hands covering her eyes.

Gu Fei turned off the tap and carried her out of the bathroom, all the while gently patting her back. "Shh... Quiet now. There's no more water, no water..."

Gu Miao stopped screaming. Leaning against his shoulder with her arms around his neck, she said quietly, "Hungry."

"I'm hungry too." Gu Fei held her in one arm and picked up the skateboard with his free hand. "Let's go eat something good."

GU FEI BROUGHT the motorcycle around outside the store, and Gu Miao deftly climbed onto the backseat with her skateboard in tow. She grabbed onto Gu Fei's sides and pressed her face against his back.

Gu Fei turned around. "Let me see your face." Gu Miao tilted her face up at him. "There's still tears. Give it a wipe."

Gu Miao rubbed her eyes with the back of her hand, then rubbed her nose with her sleeve.

"Ay..." Gu Fei sighed. "Even if you were a boy, you'd be the most rough-and-tumble kind."

Gu Miao smiled and pressed her face against his back again.

Rolling out on the motorcycle, they headed straight for downtown. For Gu Miao, "something good" could only mean the all-you-can-eat barbecue joint in the shopping mall. The little girl had a remarkable stubbornness when it came to certain things, one of which was that she refused to eat at any other restaurant whenever they went out.

One of the benefits of a small city was that there was only one downtown; no matter which neighborhood he set out from, it didn't take very long for Gu Fei to get there. By the time they arrived, it was the height of the lunch rush and there were hardly any free tables left in the restaurant.

"Do you have any specials today?" Gu Fei asked the server as he pulled out his phone to check for digital coupons. He flicked Gu Miao's head with his finger. "Hey you, go find a table."

Gu Miao set the skateboard on the floor and put her foot on it, but Gu Fei quickly stopped her with his own foot. "Walk."

"Do you need to keep the skateboard at the front counter?" the server asked with a smile.

Gu Miao shook her head, then swiftly bent down, grabbed her board, and held it tightly in her arms.

"She'll hold onto it herself," Gu Fei said as Gu Miao ran inside with the skateboard.

◆ ◆ ◆

"Geez, you're making me hungry." Pan Zhi gulped on the other end of the phone. "I'm serious. I'll go visit you in a couple days and you can take me out to eat. There's no way we can get that much food here for that price!"

"Did your family donate all their money to charity during the New Year or something?" said Jiang Cheng, holding the phone between his head and his shoulder. He had a plate in one hand, a pair of tongs in the other, and was methodically filling his plate: pork belly, sliced beef, pork belly, sliced beef... Honestly, no matter how varied the food selection was, he'd always get the same things. These were his favorites.

"It wouldn't be the same," Pan Zhi said wistfully. "Last semester we agreed to eat barbecue together at New Year's. But now there's no meat to eat and no you to eat with."

"You can stay at a hotel when you get here." Jiang Cheng put the tongs down, stacked another empty plate on top of the one he'd already loaded with meat, and piled more meat onto the new plate. "And book it yourself; I don't feel like doing anything these days."

"But I can just stay with you," said Pan Zhi.

"No." Jiang Cheng frowned. Where he was living now... He didn't want to stay there any more than he had to himself. "Just book a standard room. I'll go to you."

Pan Zhi thought about it for a second. "...You don't have a great relationship with your biological dad, huh?"

"There's no relationship to speak of just yet." Carrying the two plates of meat, Jiang Cheng went to grab a bottle of beer. "So there's no telling if it'll be good or bad..."

As he made his way back to his own table, he stopped in his tracks.

The table was a four-top, and one of the seats was currently occupied by a skateboard. A little bald kid dressed in blue sat in another. And on the table was...a green knit cap adorned with pink flowers.

Jiang Cheng looked at her in shock. "Gu Miao?"

Gu Miao nodded, though she didn't seem at all surprised. She stowed her skateboard under the table.

"You..." As he set his plates down on the table, he noticed that Gu Miao was already eyeing the grill in eager anticipation. He waved a hand in front of Gu Miao's eyes. "Who are you here with?"

Gu Miao stood up and pointed toward the door, then waved her hands. Turning in the direction she pointed, Jiang Cheng spotted an equally surprised Gu Fei.

"We'll find another table," Gu Fei said as he walked over. "Gege is already sitting here."

Gu Miao took one look around, swallowed, and didn't budge from her seat.

"The server just told me there's still a few tables over on that side." Gu Fei pointed to the back of the restaurant. "We'll go sit over there."

Still, Gu Miao stayed put. She tilted her face up and held Gu Fei's gaze, expressionless. It was anyone's guess what she was trying to say. Gu Fei remained in a stalemate with her for a few seconds, then turned to Jiang Cheng.

"Hm?" Jiang Cheng looked back at him inquisitively.

"You here by yourself?" Gu Fei asked.

"Yeah," Jiang Cheng answered, sitting down.

The server came by and turned on the gas, then laid down some parchment paper. Jiang Cheng picked up a few slices of meat and placed them on the grill, preparing to brush on the marinade.

"Then how about we..." Gu Fei hesitated for a long time before he finished his thought. "Sit together?"

Jiang Cheng lifted his eyes to peer at him. To be honest, he was inclined to say, "In your dreams! Why don't you go and wash that blanket first?" But Gu Miao was still sitting across the table with her shiny head and her huge eyes staring right at him; he couldn't let those words come out. He brushed some more marinade onto the meat slices, then nodded.

"Thanks," Gu Fei said, then pointed at Gu Miao. "Sit here and wait for me. I'm going to get food."

Gu Miao nodded. After Gu Fei walked away, Jiang Cheng placed another two slices of sliced beef onto the grill. "Which one do you like?" he asked Gu Miao. "There's pork belly and sliced beef."

Gu Miao pointed at the beef.

"Pork belly is good, too—wait 'til it's sizzling hot and the grease seeps out... I can eat five or six plates." Jiang Cheng flipped the meat over and brushed it with oil. "Can you handle spice?"

Gu Miao shook her head.

Jiang Cheng put a slice of cooked beef on the plate in front of her.

"Eat up." But Gu Miao was a little hesitant. She turned and looked in the direction Gu Fei had gone.

"It's fine..." Jiang Cheng trailed off as he noticed a prominent scar stretching across the back of Gu Miao's head. It had to be two inches long at least. He was shocked.

It seemed like Gu Miao couldn't spot Gu Fei, so she turned back around and stuffed the meat into her mouth, smiling at Jiang Cheng.

"Wanna try a piece of pork belly?" Jiang Cheng asked her. Gu Miao nodded, and so he picked up a slice of pork belly and put it on her plate. As he moved the green hat from the table onto the chair beside her, he couldn't help but click his tongue. "Who bought this for you?"

Gu Miao kept her head down and chewed in silence. Well, it *was* bad manners to talk with your mouth full. This little girl was probably the only person he'd ever met who followed that policy to perfection.

Gu Fei quickly came back with their food, though he was clearly not as skilled as Jiang Cheng in the art of all-you-can-eat barbecue—he only managed to bring back three plates. If Jiang Cheng hadn't been talking to Pan Zhi on the phone, he could easily have filled six plates to satisfy his belly and had enough room to throw in some fruit at the end.

Their table was next to the wall. Jiang Cheng had taken a seat by the wall, while Gu Miao was happily chowing down in the seat diagonally across from him. Gu Fei hesitated for a moment, then sat down next to Jiang Cheng.

A somewhat reluctant Jiang Cheng was about to grill some food for him when Gu Fei reached across and gently poked Gu Miao's head. "Go get the drinks yourself."

After Gu Miao left for the drink counter, Gu Fei quickly got up and moved across the table. Jiang Cheng glanced up at him, then continued to grill his pork belly and beef slices.

"Still running a fever and you're eating such greasy food?" Gu Fei asked.

"Hmm?" Jiang Cheng's hand paused in mid-air as he watched the rice cakes cooking on Gu Fei's side. "And you know this how?"

"You were burning hot when I dragged you inside. How could I not notice?"

"Dragged?" An image popped into Jiang Cheng's mind of Gu Fei dragging him by the hair like an old sack.

"What, was I supposed to carry you bridal style?"

Gu Fei picked up two pieces of bacon and placed them on the grill. They each took up one half of the grill—the picture of harmony. Not quite sure how to continue the conversation, Jiang Cheng ate a piece of pork belly instead.

Gu Miao came back from her quest for drinks with a few bottles in her arms. She set all four open bottles of beer one by one onto the table, plus a glass of orange juice.

"You're quite impressive." Jiang Cheng looked at her in surprise. "Didn't spill it all over the floor?"

Gu Miao shook her head and sat down at the table, then pushed a bottle of beer and the glass of orange juice in front of him.

"I don't—" Jiang Cheng was just about to tell Gu Miao to drink the orange juice herself, but as he opened his mouth, Gu Miao had already grabbed a bottle of beer and poured it into her own glass. "You...?"

Gu Miao picked up the glass and took a big gulp, let out a satisfied sigh, and wiped her mouth with the back of her hand. Jiang Cheng glanced at Gu Fei, only to see him wrapping a lettuce leaf around a piece of pork belly without so much as a glance in Gu Miao's direction.

He had to ask. "She drinks?"

"Mm-hmm. Only when we eat barbecue, though." Gu Fei held the rolled-up lettuce in front of Jiang Cheng. "She doesn't drink apart from that."

Jiang Cheng stared at the lettuce wrap. Gu Fei didn't say anything, just continued holding it out.

"...Thanks." Jiang Cheng had no choice but to accept the offering and take a bite.

"Doesn't it feel greasy to eat the pork belly all by itself?" Gu Fei asked.

"It's all right. I really like it," Jiang Cheng said.

Gu Fei assembled two more wraps for Gu Miao. "You're not from around here, are you? Judging by your accent."

"No," Jiang Cheng answered. He suddenly felt kind of irritated. The annoyance that he'd managed to suppress with pork belly and sliced beef made a valiant effort to rear its head once more.

Gu Fei kept probing. "What's your relation to Li Baoguo?"

Jiang Cheng paused—how did Gu Fei know about Li Baoguo? But the question was quickly eclipsed by exasperation. He flung two more pieces of meat onto the grill. "What's it to you?"

Gu Fei lifted his eyes to peer at him, then smiled wordlessly. He raised up his bottle of beer and clanked it gently against the bottle in front of Jiang Cheng, took a sip, then kept grilling.

It was the first time Jiang Cheng had eaten at a table face-to-face with a stranger. He hadn't felt like talking anyway, but now he really had nothing to say. Across the table, Gu Fei didn't seem to be in a chatty mood either—and his little sister seemed to be legitimately mute. She was quite happy alternating between bites of meat and swigs of beer.

Jiang Cheng finished four plates of meat in silence. He felt like his head was about to burst. It seemed like Gu Miao ate about as much as he did; Gu Fei went to top up the plates several times. Jiang Cheng had finished eating by the time she put down her chopsticks. She leaned back in the chair and rubbed her belly.

"You full?" Gu Fei asked.

She nodded.

"You eat way more than your brother," Jiang Cheng put in, unable to keep from doling out this judgment.

"How did you get here?" Gu Fei set down his chopsticks as well. "We can take you back, it's on the way."

"Motorcycle?" Jiang Cheng asked.

Gu Fei nodded. "Mm."

"Drunk driving *and* over capacity?"

Instead of answering, Gu Fei gave Jiang Cheng a long stare, with what might've been scorn or something equally stupid in his eyes, then patted Gu Miao's shoulder. "Let's go."

After Gu Fei left with Gu Miao, Jiang Cheng got up and filled another half a plate with meat and grabbed a small basket of lettuce leaves. The pork belly lettuce wrap Gu Fei made him earlier was pretty good: crisp, refreshing, and not greasy. Once he finished this half plate of meat, he figured he might have to go back on foot in order to walk it all off.

However, it was way too cold outside. Shivering behind the thick curtain at the door of the shopping mall, he pulled out his phone to hail a rideshare, but five minutes went by and nobody accepted his request.

It was then that Pan Zhi called again. "There are two stations on this line, with different arrival times. Which station should I buy the ticket for?"

"East," Jiang Cheng answered. "I only know the East Station."

"All right. Come pick me up tomorrow afternoon at four. Send me your address later. I'll look for hotels nearby."

"There probably aren't any." Jiang Cheng recalled the general vibe of the neighborhood, and it didn't seem like a place that would have hotels. "Just go ahead and book anywhere—it's not that big of a city."

After he hung up, a driver finally picked up his request. Jiang Cheng sat down inside the car, feeling thoroughly unwell. This must be what people meant when they said it took time to acclimatize to a new environment. He was the kind of guy who rarely ever caught colds, but a simple change of scenery had made him a delicate flower. He'd spent all morning fumbling around, and even eating his favorite foods didn't seem to have helped. He was practically wilting.

Jiang Cheng closed his eyes and sighed.

All the people who'd stayed inside over the New Year had begun to emerge; the roads were jammed with cars. The driver was trigger-happy with the gas pedal, alternating frequently between accelerating and braking hard. Not even ten minutes into the ride, Jiang Cheng felt his stomach churn.

It wasn't a long journey—perhaps half an hour in total—but as soon as he saw the turn for Gu Fei's store, he simply couldn't take it anymore. Unable to even open his mouth, it was all he could manage to slap the inside of the car door a few times in desperation.

"Here?" the driver asked.

He nodded, then banged the door a couple more times. The moment the driver stopped the car, he bounded out the door. As though propelled by the power of farts, he rushed to a garbage can by the side of the road and puked.

It was such a devastating scene that he couldn't even bear to watch himself.

After this heaving bout of nausea, his insides finally calmed down, leaving behind an explosive headache. Bracing himself against the wall with one hand, he fished for a pack of tissues in his pocket, but after several minutes of rummaging, he came up empty.

Just as his temper was about to shoot all the way up from the soles of his feet, a small arm reached over from one side, holding out a few tissues. He grabbed them and wiped his mouth a few times before glancing to the side.

There really was no lack of coincidences in this universe. It was Gu Miao standing beside him in her green hat, with Gu Fei three steps behind her, looking thoroughly entertained.

"Thank you." Jiang Cheng nodded at Gu Miao. It was kind of depressing to feel embarrassed and stuck in a spot where he couldn't just turn and walk away, or say something like, "The fuck are you looking at?"

Gu Miao reached for his hand and tugged on it, as though wanting to walk with him.

"No thanks." Jiang Cheng pulled his hand away.

Gu Miao grabbed his hand again, still trying to help.

"No, really," Jiang Cheng insisted. "I'm fine."

When he tried to take his hand away again, Gu Miao held on tight and didn't let go.

"Er-Miao…" Gu Fei walked up to them. Still, Gu Miao didn't let go.

Jiang Cheng had no idea how to communicate with her. All of his errant irritations converged to one point, and he shook off Gu Miao's hand in annoyance. "I said I don't need your help!"

Gu Miao didn't move, her hand still raised in the air, frozen in place. Before Jiang Cheng's guilt had time to spread and fester, he felt pressure on his throat as Gu Fei yanked on his collar from behind, forcing him to stumble.

"Fuck…"

He turned, jabbing his elbow behind himself at the same time. Gu Fei caught his elbow with one hand and tightened his grip on Jiang Cheng's collar. Jiang Cheng had no choice but to back up and get cozy with Gu Fei. The chokehold he had on his throat was making him nauseous again.

"She likes you a lot." Gu Fei spoke low in Jiang Cheng's ear. "But she has trouble reading other people's emotions sometimes. I politely ask that you try to be understanding."

Jiang Cheng wanted to blurt out that in all seventeen fucking years he'd been alive, he'd never seen anyone "politely ask" for anything like this, but that was more words than he was capable of getting out right now.

Instead, he managed to squeeze out three words from between his teeth: "I'm gonna puke."

Gu Fei let him go. Jiang Cheng braced himself against the wall and dry heaved a couple of times.

After accepting a bottle of water from Gu Fei and gulping down two large mouthfuls, he finally caught his breath. Then he turned to Gu Miao and said, "I'm fine. I can walk on my own."

Gu Miao nodded and retreated to Gu Fei's side.

"I'm going, then." Jiang Cheng threw the half-finished bottle of water into the garbage, then turned and headed down the block.

Fuck!

When Jiang Cheng got back to Li Baoguo's place, the smell of home cooking was the first thing to hit his nose. Li Baoguo was standing in the living room, calling someone on this phone.

Jiang Cheng was just about to say something when his phone rang in his pocket. He pulled it out and saw Li Baoguo's name on the caller ID. "You—"

Hearing the ringtone, Li Baoguo turned around. "Hey!" he yelled in his usual loud voice. "When did you get back? I was just calling you!"

"Just now." Jiang Cheng closed the door. "You...didn't hear me?"

"My hearing isn't the best." Li Baoguo pointed to his ears. "Gotta turn my head toward the sound to hear clearly."

"Oh."

"Where were you?" Li Baoguo brought out a crock of soup from the kitchen. "I've been here waiting for you to eat lunch for a while."

"I..." Jiang Cheng hesitated. He didn't mention that he'd already indulged in all-you-can-eat barbecue. "Went to the hospital."

"The hospital?" Li Baoguo immediately started hollering again, reaching over and feeling around Jiang Cheng's cheeks. "Are you sick? Where does it hurt? Got a fever? Is it because of the new environment?"

"I already took some medicine. It's not a big deal." Considering the meal in front of him, Jiang Cheng tried his best not to reflexively slap away the dirty yellow hand that stank of old cigarettes.

"Listen, if you're not feeling well, there's no need to go to the hospital," Li Baoguo said.[4] "There's a community clinic on the next street over, and it's pretty good. It's just that the front of the

---

4   In China, it's common to go to a hospital for things like cold and flu. Smaller health clinics are relatively uncommon and generally not seen as very trustworthy.

building is kind of far back, so it's hard to notice. It's next to the little supermarket."

"Oh." Jiang Cheng pondered for a moment. "The little supermarket? You mean Gu Fei's—"

"How do you know Gu Fei?" Li Baoguo whipped around in shock. "You just got here, and you're already hanging out with him?"

"Nah." Jiang Cheng couldn't be bothered to go into detail. "I just bought some stuff there this morning."

"Listen." Li Baoguo's voice got even louder. His voice was always loud, but now it was especially emphatic. "Don't get mixed up with him—that guy is bad news!"

"...Oh." Jiang Cheng took off his jacket and tossed it into his room.

Li Baoguo watched him, probably waiting for him to ask why. After a while, when Jiang Cheng didn't say anything, Li Baoguo leaned in again, looking eager to gossip. "Do you know why he's bad news?"

Jiang Cheng played along despite having zero interest in any of this. "Why?"

"Because he killed his own dad!" Li Baoguo boomed.

He was leaning a little too close, and his excited spit sprayed over half of Jiang Cheng's face. Jiang Cheng jumped up from the chair to get out of the way, roughly rubbing at his face. Just as his temper was about to erupt, he suddenly realized what he'd heard.

"What? Killed who?"

"His dad!" Li Baoguo said, half yelling. "Drowned his own father."

Jiang Cheng stared back at him in silence. From the gleeful expression on Li Baoguo's face, he knew that they could spend a whole afternoon on gossip like this if he wanted to. Too bad Jiang Cheng didn't believe it.

He sat back down by the table and pinched the throbbing area between his brows. "If he killed his father, wouldn't he have to go to jail?"

"It was years and years ago—what jail?" Li Baoguo also sat down. "Plus, there were no witnesses."

Jiang Cheng smirked. "Ah, so nobody saw it..."

"We all know what happened. When the police arrived, his dad was in the lake, and he was standing on the shore, making that face..." Li Baoguo clicked his tongue several times in a row for effect. "He obviously did it... Hurry and eat up, see if the food is to your liking."

Without a word, Jiang Cheng picked up a piece of short rib.

"He did it for that Er-Miao of theirs," Li Baoguo added, seeing that Jiang Cheng didn't seem to believe him. "His dad threw her so hard there was blood all over her head, and after that, she didn't even know how to talk anymore."

Jiang Cheng chewed on the rib, remembering the shocking scar on the back of Gu Miao's head. "Ah."

5

WHEN PAN ZHI'S CALL came in, Jiang Cheng was deeply asleep, practically in hibernation. His cell phone rang for a long time before he finally picked it up, groggy.

"Hmm?"

"Fuck, I knew it," Pan Zhi said. "Open your dog eyes and see what time it is."

"Is it four o'clock?" Having regained consciousness, Jiang Cheng held the phone in front of his face to look at the time. His eyes hadn't woken up yet, though, and everything was blurry.

"It's already three-thirty!" Pan Zhi said. "I knew you'd be like this, so I'm calling you early."

"There's still time." Jiang Cheng sat up. "I'll be waiting for you outside the exit gates."

"Which exit gate?" Pan Zhi asked.

"There's only one exit." The window was so dirty it might as well have been frosted glass, but he could see the weather was pretty good today; everything was draped in a layer of glittering gold. "Talk later."

He rolled out of bed and got dressed, feeling much better than he did yesterday. Other than not getting quite enough sleep, the all-over unpleasant feeling from yesterday was gone, and so was the accompanying crankiness that made him want to beat up anyone he laid eyes on.

Checking the time, he realized that he'd been sleeping since yesterday afternoon—an entire day had passed. He felt a little unsteady on his feet.

Li Baoguo wasn't home; who knew where he'd gone off to. Jiang Cheng found this "home" a little perplexing. When his mom started the process of reversing his adoption, Li Baoguo had keenly made several trips to their city, tail wagging, even though Jiang Cheng hadn't wanted to see him. But now that he was here, there was no sign of the eagerness to take his son back that Li Baoguo had shown before. And as for the rumored older brother and sister—he'd been here for two days and they were still nowhere to be seen.

Jiang Cheng was not at all interested in this new home, nor did he have any expectations. All the same, it didn't feel particularly great to wake up every day and find yourself alone in a completely lifeless apartment, no matter what time of day it was. If he hadn't been in a low-rise building, he would've thought it was some ancient hut. The whole place was suffused with a sense of decay.

That was also the reason he didn't want Pan Zhi to stay here. His old room had been clean and immaculate—he'd even had a piano. The contrast would have Pan Zhi sobbing his eyes out for the length of his visit.

Frankly, though, even without seeing this place, the state of the East Station alone would be enough to make Pan Zhi weep.

"Fuck." Dragging a large suitcase and carrying a large backpack, Pan Zhi exclaimed at the first sight of Jiang Cheng. "Ahh—this place is kind of unbearable!"

"You should head back, then." Jiang Cheng pointed at the ticket booth. "Hurry up, go get your ticket."

"What happened to our brotherly bond?!" Pan Zhi lamented. "I came all this way, dragging all this luggage just to see you! Shouldn't you be touched?!"

"Wow. I'm so touched," Jiang Cheng said.

Pan Zhi glared at him for a long time, then finally opened his arms. "I really was starting to miss you."

Jiang Cheng went over and gave him a hug. "I haven't had a chance to."

"Do you know why I'm your only friend?" Pan Zhi said as he let go.

"Yes." Jiang Cheng nodded. "Because you're a dork."

He'd had quite a few friends back in his old city, but they were the non-essential kind. They would hang out and idly trudge around town with him, swarming like bees around small conflicts, but would disperse like startled birds if they ran into real trouble.

Pan Zhi was different. They met for the first time in ninth grade and were put in the same class when they started high school the year after. It hadn't even been three years, but their friendship was as solid as steel. Ever since he'd come to this shitty little city, the only person Jiang Cheng missed was Pan Zhi.

"Hey boss, you know where this address is, right?" Pan Zhi asked the driver when they got into the cab.

"How could I not?" The driver chuckled in response. "It's the best hotel we got here."

Jiang Cheng threw Pan Zhi a glance. "You sure know how to pick them."

"What's there to pick? They have the most expensive rooms." Pan Zhi rummaged in his pocket for a while, then finally produced a lighter and placed it in Jiang Cheng's hand. "Here, do you like it?"

Jiang Cheng looked at the lighter. It was the kind of style he liked: minimalist and sleek. Two letters were engraved at the very bottom. He leaned in close and squinted. "What's this you carved here? 'J.C.'... Like Jesus?"

"J.C., your initials," Pan Zhi said. "Neat, huh?"

"...Real neat." Jiang Cheng tucked the lighter away in his pocket. "How long are you staying for?"

"Two days," Pan Zhi said with a sigh. "School's starting soon."

"What's the big sigh for?"

"It's just annoying—classes, tests, homework, worksheets." Pan Zhi frowned. "If I was like you and absorbed everything without even trying, and I ranked in the top ten without even going to class, I wouldn't be sighing either."

"Who said I don't try?" Jiang Cheng gave him a side-eye. "It's not like you don't remember any of the times I stayed up all night studying."

"But the point is, it doesn't make a difference even if I stay up *ten* nights in a row," Pan Zhi whined. He sighed again. "Oh, fuck, I know why I missed you so much. Now that you're gone, I have no one to show me the answers during tests!"

"Time to drop out," Jiang Cheng said.

Pan Zhi glared at him. "Where's your humanity?"

Jiang Cheng grinned and didn't answer.

Pan Zhi might not have been happy with this little city, but he was satisfied with the hotel. When they arrived at his room, he carefully inspected the bed, the shower, and the toilet before announcing his verdict: "Not bad."

"Let's go get something to eat." Jiang Cheng checked the time. "Barbecue?"

"Mhm." Pan Zhi opened his suitcase. "I have another present for you."

"Hm?" Jiang Cheng sat down on the edge of the bed.

"Why don't you take a guess?" Pan Zhi reached inside his luggage and rummaged around.

Jiang Cheng swept his gaze over the suitcase. It was stuffed to the brim with small and large packages of various snacks and food; it didn't look like there was room for anything else. "A tin whistle," he said.

"Shit." Pan Zhi laughed as he pulled out a long black leather pouch from the very bottom. "Was that too easy, or are we just too in sync?"

"It was way too easy." Jiang Cheng accepted the pouch and pulled out a black tin whistle, turning it over in his hands. "It's nice."

"A Susato, in D," Pan Zhi said. "I bought the right one, right? Isn't it exactly the same as your old one?"

"Yes." Jiang Cheng gave it a try. "Thanks."

"Don't smash it again—this one's a gift from me."

"Yeah." Jiang Cheng put the tin whistle back in its pouch.

He wasn't in the habit of smashing things out of anger. After all, he had been trained in the virtue of restraint for nearly two decades. He might get into fights and beat people up, but it was only rarely that he'd take his temper out on inanimate objects. The only reason he'd broken his tin whistle was because there was no other outlet for his rage; it wasn't like he could go have it out with his old man.

Since he wasn't going home tonight, he hesitated for a moment over whether to text Li Baoguo or give him a call. He eventually settled on calling, and Li Baoguo took a long time to pick up.

"HELLO!"

He could tell from the noise in the background that Li Baoguo was playing mahjong again. Jiang Cheng didn't know what to think. He wondered if his mom knew about this particular habit. But then again, considering the family dynamic had been ruined by his very existence, perhaps it wasn't a big deal to her at all.

"My friend is here to visit me, so I'm not going back tonight," he said. "I'll be staying at the hotel."

"Ah, a friend visiting?" Li Baoguo coughed a few times. "Go play with your friend, then. What are you calling me for? I thought something happened to you."

"...Bye then."

Li Baoguo simply hung up without another word.

"This dad of yours..." Pan Zhi looked at him. "What kind of person is he?"

"Dunno. He smokes, coughs, snores, and gambles."

"But you smoke too—and coughing? Everyone coughs sometimes..." Pan Zhi attempted to analyze the man. "Snor—"

"Are you done?" Jiang Cheng cut him off.

Pan Zhi waved his hand. "Barbecue!"

The barbecue wasn't anything special, but Pan Zhi enjoyed it immensely. Jiang Cheng didn't eat as much as he had the day before—after all, he was a delicate flower freshly recovered from illness—but even so, coming out of the restaurant, he still felt bloated from eating too much.

"You really are in a bad mood," Pan Zhi said. "That pork belly was pretty good, but you only ate a little..."

"Good eye." Jiang Cheng nodded. His mood wasn't so low that he had no appetite, but he didn't want Pan Zhi to know he threw up the day before on top of running a fever.

"Let's walk for a bit." Pan Zhi patted his stomach. "Is there anything fun to do around here?"

"No," Jiang Cheng said. After a pause, he added, "I don't know."

"Hey, where's your new school at?" Pan Zhi said suddenly. "Shall we go check it out?"

"Now?" Jiang Cheng tugged at his collar. "Nope."

"Tomorrow, then. It's winter break anyway, it's not like there's gonna be anyone there. Let's go see what the campus looks like." Pan Zhi slung an arm around his shoulder. "Didn't you go take a look when you filed the paperwork or anything?"

"It's not like you don't know whether I've been or not." Jiang Cheng was growing a little irritated.

Pan Zhi chuckled. "Oh, right, you just got here."

His new life and environment exasperated and unsettled Jiang Cheng, but the presence of Pan Zhi brought him a little solace. In this strange and unknown territory, there was finally a familiar person by his side.

Jiang Cheng stayed up most of the night talking with Pan Zhi, though he could hardly remember what either of them said. It was just like the days they spent chatting on the edge of the school field, talking about nothing and everything. It didn't really matter what they talked about—the important thing was having someone he could confide in.

They finally dozed off for a while just before dawn, only to be rudely awoken a little past eight by the blaring horn of a semi-truck passing outside.

"What the... Aren't we in the city?" Pan Zhi held on tightly to the duvet. "Since when can trucks drive straight up to the entrance of a hotel?"

"Dunno." Jiang Cheng kept his eyes shut.

"They have breakfast. Should I get them to send it up now?" Pan Zhi asked him.

"Sure," Jiang Cheng said. "Did you sleep?"

"I might have," Pan Zhi said, laughing. "What's the plan for today?"

"Let's go check out the school together," Jiang Cheng said. "Then we can see if there's anything fun to do around here, but I doubt we'll find anything in the dead of winter."

"It's all right. I'm the kind of guy who's very focused on mental fulfillment," Pan Zhi said. "I came here to see you, so I'm good."

"How about I take a nap later, and you can pull up a stool and keep watching me?" Jiang Cheng said.

"Hey." Pan Zhi leaned in and stared at him for a while. "Have you not been talking very much the last couple of days?"

"Why?" Jiang Cheng yawned.

"You're talking more than you used to. Have you been bottling stuff up?" Pan Zhi asked.

Jiang Cheng considered it. "...Maybe."

Maybe Pan Zhi was right. Before he got here, Jiang Cheng had had nothing to say, and no one to say it to.

They located the new school on the map; it wasn't very far from Li Baoguo's place. As for what kind of school it was, Jiang Cheng hadn't looked it up, and wasn't particularly eager to find out.

There was a lot of bureaucratic nonsense involved in the process of transferring high schools. From the minute his parents began the administrative process without a hint of reluctance, he had lost interest in practically everything in his life. He couldn't even get his spirits up for a fight. It was as though something had been wrenched out of his body. He was a pile of mud looking for an appropriate hole in the ground to fill.

After looking up the route, Pan Zhi dragged him to the bus stop.

"Did you know that the view from a bus window shows you the most authentic side of a city?" Pan Zhi said.

Jiang Cheng gave him a look. "Mm-hm."

"Don't you think that's very profound?" Pan Zhi was rather proud of himself.

"Mm-hm." Jiang Cheng continued looking at him.

Pan Zhi held his gaze for a while. "Oh," he said at last. "You were the one who said that."

Jiang Cheng shook his hand.

There weren't that many people on the bus. The daily commute in a small city was much more relaxed; people weren't pressed up against each other like sardines and nobody's hair got plastered all over another passenger's face. The bus never got so packed that it couldn't fit another person, and no one ran the risk of getting physically squeezed out of a crowded bus.

"This is much more comfortable than back home." Pan Zhi expressed his approval upon getting off the bus. He checked the map on his phone. "Fourth High... Go straight for five hundred yards, then make a turn."

"They probably won't let people go inside." Jiang Cheng tugged on his collar.

"Then we'll just look around the outside and take a walk around the neighborhood. This is going to be your main haunt for the foreseeable future." Pan Zhi held his phone up to Jiang Cheng's face and tapped on the screen.

Jiang Cheng glanced at Pan Zhi. "What are you doing?"

"Just taking a photo," Pan Zhi said. "When Yu Xin heard I was coming here she cried on her knees for me to take a photo of you for her. Thing is, it's really hard for me to turn a girl down..."

"She bribed you, didn't she?"

"Yes." Pan Zhi nodded solemnly.

Jiang Cheng failed to hold in his laugh. "You're shameless."

Pan Zhi snapped another couple of photos of him with his phone. "Are the two of you really through? I thought she was all right."

"There wasn't much point to it."

"Is it because she's a girl?"

Pan Zhi was still holding his phone up, keeping him in frame, like he was filming an interview. Jiang Cheng gave him a look and didn't answer.

"I think...it'd be better for you to get with a girl if possible. It's too difficult to find a guy, and society right now isn't exactly the most accepting." Pan Zhi put away his phone. "Don't be fooled by the flocks of fujoshis on the internet—they hardly count for anything when you toss them into the real world."

"You must've been bottling up your words for a while too, huh?"

"Ever since winter break started and you disappeared, I haven't really talked to anyone." Pan Zhi clutched his chest. "I've been so emotionally repressed that my man-boobs grew from an A to a B."

"I'll buy you a lingerie set before you go home," Jiang Cheng said.

"We're here." Pan Zhi pointed in front of them. "Fourth High... The outside looks pretty big—bigger than our school, at least."

The front gates were open. The guard glanced at the two of them when they walked through, but didn't say anything.

"He doesn't care?" Pan Zhi said.

"You want him to care?" Jiang Cheng side-eyed him. "Are you a masochist or what?"

"Come on, let's take a walk." Pan Zhi lifted his arms and stretched.

"It's..." Jiang Cheng glanced around the grounds. "Pretty big."

"Has to be. Our school is smack-dab in the middle of the city, where every inch of space is worth its weight in gold. They couldn't expand even if they wanted to," Pan Zhi said. "Look how great you have it here—you probably have a big sports field, too... Should we check out the gym?"

"Mm-hm," Jiang Cheng hummed his agreement.

The thing Jiang Cheng and Pan Zhi cared about the most was the basketball court. Jiang Cheng's old school only had a couple of indoor basketball courts; even the soccer field had been plowed over to make space for new lecture buildings. Neither of them played soccer, but they still resented the decision.

The fields at Fourth High were much more comfortable in comparison. There was a soccer field where a bunch of people were playing a match, even though it was freezing outside. Next to the field were two outdoor basketball courts, and even one for volleyball.

Pan Zhi nudged Jiang Cheng with his arm. "There are indoor courts, too; wanna go check them out?"

The wretched mood that Jiang Cheng had been stewing in over the past few days was noticeably soothed by the Fourth High campus. Compared to Li Baoguo's home and the street where it sat, these wide-open spaces put him at ease, like he could finally catch his breath again.

He closed his eyes and inhaled deeply, then exhaled, patting Pan Zhi's shoulder. "Let's go."

The indoor courts weren't that big, but there were spaces for volleyball, badminton, and basketball, even if the markings on the floor occasionally overlapped with each other. Both basketball courts were occupied, and everyone looked over when they noticed them walk in.

Pan Zhi stopped walking, but Jiang Cheng ignored the stares they were getting. He stuffed his hands in his pockets and leisurely sauntered over to the few chairs placed courtside to take a seat.

It had been a long time since he'd last played, so he wanted to scratch his itch by watching others. The guys on the court eyed them for a while, then went back to playing.

"Is this the school team holding practice?" Pan Zhi asked as he sat down beside him.

"Can't be," Jiang Cheng said. "They're total amateurs."

"Wanna go shoot some hoops?" Pan Zhi said with a smile. "We can team up."

Jiang Cheng stuck his foot in front of Pan Zhi and wiggled it. He wasn't wearing basketball shoes today.

"Ay," Pan Zhi sighed as he leaned back with his arms behind his head. "Who knows when we'll be able to play together again?"

"Don't go changing your vibe. Acting emo doesn't suit you," Jiang Cheng said. Somebody on the court landed a smooth three-pointer, and he called out, not very loudly, "Nice shot!"

The person glanced at him, smiling, and clapped a hand over his fist in a salute.

Even though he wasn't playing, just sitting courtside with Pan Zhi and watching people play brought him a little respite. It cut away all the threads of irritation from his mind... As long as he didn't stop to think about the bleak life he'd go back to once Pan Zhi left tomorrow.

He was so engrossed in the game that he didn't even notice when more people entered the gym—at least, not until the guys on the court all stopped and looked at the door with complicated expressions.

"Why do I feel like there's going to be some action?" Pan Zhi whispered next to him, excited.

"What..." Jiang Cheng turned to the door and froze. "Action?"

One, two, three, four, five, six—a total of six people had walked in.

Jiang Cheng thought he might dislocate his jaw from the shock. It was the Fresh Out of Jail quartet, followed by the guy who'd been manning the cash register when he bought water the other day. Bringing up the rear, wearing a baseball cap that covered up the snazzy music symbols on his head, was Gu Fei.

Jiang Cheng was a little impressed with his own ability to remember these guys' faces—especially considering he'd been practically delirious with fever the last time he saw most of them. It was truly a miracle to simultaneously run into the same six strangers in this strange city at a strange school.

He must've been infected by Pan Zhi's enthusiasm, he thought, because he found himself watching the guys approach with the anticipation of someone waiting for the curtains to open at a show. It looked like they'd come here to play: Gu Fei wore track pants and basketball shoes, while one of the other guys had a ball in his hand.

Someone spoke up on the court. "Da-Fei?"

"Uh huh," Gu Fei answered.

"What are you doing here?" the guy asked.

"I'm here to play, of course," Gu Fei said. His voice was level and calm, without even a hint of hostility.

"Are...all of you joining us?" the guy asked, after hesitating for a beat.

"The sick, weak, injured, and elderly are staying on the sidelines," Gu Fei said, then took off his jacket.

As he turned, about to toss it onto the bench, he spotted Jiang Cheng sitting there and promptly choked on his own spit. He broke into a coughing fit, staring at Jiang Cheng the whole time.

Jiang Cheng contained his disappointed expression. He'd wanted to see some action, but the action had ended before it even had the chance to start.

"What a coincidence," he said.

"Good morning," said Gu Fei.

"Are you together?" someone on the court asked.

"No," Jiang Cheng replied.

Out of the six people in Gu Fei's group, three of them decided to play, while the remaining three came to sit beside them. The one from the cash register sat down next to Jiang Cheng and extended a hand.

"I'm Li Yan."

"Jiang Cheng." Jiang Cheng slapped his palm lightly, then pointed to Pan Zhi. "My bro, Pan Zhi."

"You both Fourth High students?" Li Yan looked the two of them over. "Haven't seen you guys around before."

"I will be." Jiang Cheng didn't want to go into too much detail. "Are you all from Fourth High?"

The two guys behind them started laughing. Perhaps it wasn't intentional, but their voices were tinged with a familiar mockery. Li Yan turned and glanced back at them.

"Do we look like students?"

"Who knows." Jiang Cheng was a little annoyed. "I don't make a habit of staring at every person I come across."

Li Yan's face suddenly dropped. He directed his attention back to the people on the court, no longer paying any attention to Jiang Cheng.

The guys behind them must not have perceived the tense atmosphere, as one of them piped up, "Da-Fei is in second year."

"Oh," was Jiang Cheng's reply.

What a coincidence indeed.

6

JIANG CHENG SAT with his arms crossed and legs stretched out in front of him, a little irritated.

The guys who'd been playing before were mediocre at best; if he were wearing the proper shoes today, he could easily partner up with Pan Zhi and take them on two against five. It was still kind of fun to watch them play, though. He enjoyed the feeling of superiority, as though he was looking down from the highest peak.

But once Gu Fei and his friends joined, the whole atmosphere changed. Gu Fei was…very good. If this had been his old school, Gu Fei would be on the receiving end of deafening cheers from all the girls during inter-high tournaments. Beside him, from the Fresh Out of Jail group, Fresh and Jail also played pretty well. Their teamwork on the court was surprisingly smooth, in stark contrast to the way they'd slouched and slumped like hooligans all over the chairs in the convenience store. It made the remaining two players on their team seem almost redundant.

Watching a game like this didn't make Jiang Cheng feel good about himself at all.

He didn't necessarily dislike Gu Fei, but he definitely didn't like him, either. He was torn between thinking, *Heeey, that fucker's pretty good at this,* and forcibly correcting himself with, *Pretty good, my ass! More like a pretty big show-off...*

"That guy's pretty good, huh?" Pan Zhi said, clearly not on the same wavelength as his best friend. "How do you know him?"

"He's just about average compared to our team," Jiang Cheng said.

Before Pan Zhi could answer, Li Yan spoke up beside them, his voice taunting. "Ooh, you're on the basketball team? Maybe you can swap in for someone on the other side."

Jiang Cheng turned and gave him a look. "No."

"No?" Li Yan blinked. He'd clearly assumed Jiang Cheng would rise to the challenge; he didn't expect him to flat-out refuse. "Why not?"

"Guess." Jiang Cheng stood up and walked toward the exit.

Pan Zhi raised his arms in a stretch before following him out, leaving the others sitting on the bench in confusion.

"This mood of yours certainly came out of nowhere." Pan Zhi turtled his neck in the cold as they stepped outside. "You got beef with that guy?"

"This is only my third day here," Jiang Cheng said.

"True—you haven't been here long enough to make any enemies." Pan Zhi sighed. "You just get pissed at anyone who crosses your path, that's all."

Jiang Cheng glanced at Pan Zhi. "You're all right."

Pan Zhi laughed. "But hey, for real, how do you know that guy? Is it because he's a junior too?"

"...He's a neighbor."

"Same building?"

"The next street over," Jiang Cheng answered simply.

"Ah."

Jiang Cheng thought that Pan Zhi might not be able to immediately grasp the concept. They both grew up in typical gated residential compounds, where there were only two types of neighbors: ones who lived in the same building, and ones who lived in the same compound. The first type you'd nod to in passing, and the second type you'd spare only a glance.

And as for the next street over... They'd never even meet those neighbors.

Jiang Cheng sighed softly. He felt almost as if he was here to film a reality show about city-to-country identity swaps.

Pan Zhi clapped his hands together. "You got mountains here? Let's go look at the snowy view."

"Hiking on a day this cold? Aren't you afraid your brain will freeze over? Not that it works that well normally," Jiang Cheng said. "Haven't you seen snow before?"

"But there's more snow here than back home." Pan Zhi slung his arm around Jiang Cheng's shoulder. "Cheng-er, my dude, let me take you out to get some fresh air. You've had a change of setting, so what's the big deal? You've had a change of parents, so what's the... Okay, that one's kind of a big deal. Give me a second to rephrase this..."

Pan Zhi made Jiang Cheng laugh. "All right, let's go hiking." He flung his arm up. "Hell, what's the big fucking deal."

After a basketball game, Gu Fei felt like his whole body had been warmed up. The lethargic feeling that had been plaguing him for the last couple of days was finally gone. He put on his jacket and looked back at the guys on the court, whose eyes were shining with joyous relief that he'd finally decided to leave.

"Thanks," he said.

"Leaving already?" one of them asked, probably out of habit.

"Did you wanna go again?" Gu Fei said.

They all went quiet at that, awkwardness spreading across their faces.

Gu Fei laughed and zipped up his jacket. "Let's go."

Outside the gym, Liu Fan leaped up and hopped for a few steps. "That was no fun. I told you we should've rented a court in the sports center, but you just *had* to come to your school."

"How much more fun were you looking for, exactly?" Gu Fei asked.

"What's the point of playing with high schoolers?" Liu Fan said.

Li Yan eyed him sideways. "You're only two years out of high school yourself."

Gu Fei gave Liu Fan the middle finger. "If you can beat me one-on-one, you can keep saying that all you want."

They all laughed.

"Shit." Liu Fan slapped his hand away. "Let's go eat something, I'm hungry."

"Count me out." Gu Fei glanced at his phone. "I'm heading home."

"Back to the store?" Li Yan asked. "Isn't your mom there today?"

"I have to take Er-Miao to the hospital. They asked for a follow-up last time, and the appointment is today," Gu Fei said. "I have to coax her out every time she goes to the hospital. It's time-consuming."

"We'll come over tonight and hang out," Liu Fan said.

"We'll see." Gu Fei pulled out his keys. "Bye for now."

"Don't you usually just shut up and leave?" Li Yan said. "What's with all this mushy stuff today? I'm not used to it."

"You looking for a fight or what?" Gu Fei turned and walked away.

Time passed slowly when the days were meaningless and bleak. But as soon as they were imbued with even the slightest meaning, the days thundered by like a crashing waterfall—utterly unstoppable. The happiness and ease Pan Zhi brought with him quickly came to an end.

Jiang Cheng stood in the departure hall of the train station, watching departure and arrival times scroll by on the giant screen. "You're really not gonna take that pile of snacks back with you?"

"If I say yes, will you go back to the hotel right now and grab them for me?" Pan Zhi said.

Jiang Cheng glanced at him. "Don't take it seriously. I was just making conversation."

"I brought the snacks for you, anyway. I was worried you wouldn't be able to find anywhere to buy that stuff yet." Pan Zhi sighed. "So, will you be coming back for the week of the May 1st holiday, or should I come over again?"

"I'm not going back," Jiang Cheng said. "I already said I'm never going back there again."

"I don't know what the hell you're being so stubborn for," said Pan Zhi. "I'll come here then, and bring those fuckers from our class, too—how about that?"

"We'll see when the time comes." Jiang Cheng leaned against the wall. "It's not like we were all that close to begin with. A few months from now, who knows if anyone'll be bothered to travel all the way here. It's not like this is a tourist destination or anything."

Pan Zhi nodded. "Okay, we'll talk about it later."

The two of them were quiet for a moment. Then, Pan Zhi, who had been sitting the entire time, abruptly stood and came face-to-face with Jiang Cheng.

"What are you doing?!" Jiang Cheng pointed at him, startled. "Keep your mouth to yourself! Or I'll smack you."

"Give me a hug." Pan Zhi spread his arms.

"Shit." Jiang Cheng didn't know what to say, but he opened his arms and hugged Pan Zhi.

"Don't forget about me," Pan Zhi said. "I'm serious."

Jiang Cheng let out a quiet sigh. "Come visit me in May, and I won't."

Pan Zhi laughed. "All right."

◆ ◆ ◆

In the days leading up to the start of the new semester, Li Baoguo had cooked a total of one meal. He was away from home for all other mealtimes.

Jiang Cheng thought he'd try to make some noodles on his own, but his motivation died as soon as he walked into the kitchen and saw the mess of pots and pans piled all over the place and all the seasoning bottles covered in a thick coat of grease. Over the next few days he tried all the interesting-looking places within a mile radius on the food delivery apps, and managed to survive the rest of winter break.

The day before school started, to Jiang Cheng's surprise, his new homeroom teacher called.

"Your dad hasn't been answering his phone," the teacher said.

Now *that* wasn't a surprise; Li Baoguo didn't have the greatest hearing, and he was always preoccupied with mahjong, anyway. Jiang Cheng sometimes passed by the building where Li Baoguo played, and he could always hear the clamor all the way from the street.

The homeroom teacher's surname was Xu. He sounded middle-aged, and very warm and welcoming. It alleviated some of the unease Jiang Cheng was feeling about facing a brand-new environment.

On the first day of school, snow began to fall first thing in the morning. It was just as Pan Zhi said—he'd never seen snowfall as heavy as this before. The sight of it was somehow satisfying.

As he walked through the gates, Jiang Cheng took note of the students around him. They didn't look all that different from the students at his old school, but although a crowd of high school students whose faces he didn't recognize was hardly a new sight, there was still an irrefutable sense of foreignness to them. He took special care to seek out Gu Fei's face among them, but he had no luck.

"Jiang Cheng, not a bad name." The middle-aged-sounding Mr. Xu, the homeroom teacher, was indeed middle-aged, and apparently the type of uncle who'd already had something to drink this morning. "My surname is Xu, full name Xu Qicai. I'll be your homeroom teacher—I teach your Chinese class. My students all call me Lao-Xu, or Xu-zong."[5]

"Lao-Xu...zong." Jiang Cheng gave a polite little bow as he acknowledged his teacher, but he couldn't help feeling weird about this style of address.

"Let's chat for a bit. The first class after the morning self-study period is Chinese class. I'll walk you over." Lao-Xu gestured to a chair nearby. "Have a seat."

Jiang Cheng sat down.

"It's pretty rare to see transfer students in second year." Lao-Xu smiled. "Especially to a place like this... I looked at your old report cards; you get pretty good grades."

"Not bad, I guess," Jiang Cheng said.

"Not just 'not bad,' they're very good! No need to be humble." Lao-Xu laughed, then sighed. "It's a pity you came here," he added in a quiet voice.

---

5   Lao- is a prefix attached to a name, used to refer casually to someone older and suggesting a closeness with the other person; it literally means "old." -Zong is a suffix attached to a name when referring to the other person as boss or CEO. When used between students and their teacher, it also suggests a casual closeness.

Jiang Cheng didn't respond, just watched Lao-Xu in silence. His old homeroom teacher had said the same thing: It was a pity that he was moving to a city like this one, where the quality of the teachers, the students, and the education were all lacking... Jiang Cheng was a little surprised to hear Lao-Xu say the same thing.

"I noticed that your STEM subjects are stronger than your humanities," Lao-Xu said. "Why did you choose to go into the humanities stream?"

It wasn't an easy question to answer. "Because my parents wanted me to pick STEM" was so embarrassingly immature and contrarian that he couldn't bear to say it aloud; even though he'd already done it, admitting to it would make him feel like the biggest clown in the circus.

After a great deal of hesitation, he finally said, "I liked our home-room teacher, and the homeroom he led was in the humanities stream."

"Ah, is that so?" A little surprised, Lao-Xu paused for a moment. "Hopefully you'll like me, too. It'll be hard to transfer to the STEM stream now."

"Oh."

Jiang Cheng stared at him. Lao-Xu stared back for a while, then started laughing, and Jiang Cheng laughed along with him. This homeroom teacher was an interesting guy, at least.

After the early bell for the first class sounded, Lao-Xu stuck a briefcase under his arm and a USB key into his pocket, then said to Jiang Cheng, "Come on, I'll take you to our classroom."

"Okay." Jiang Cheng slung his backpack onto his shoulder and followed Lao-Xu out.

Lao-Xu might not have thought much of Fourth High as a school, but it had a big campus with creatively arranged buildings. All other classes were grouped by grade level, except for second- and third-year classes in the Humanities stream, which were singled out in an old three-story building. The stairs in the center served as a divide, with the second-years to the left and third-years to the right.

Jiang Cheng was quickly becoming a believer in destiny. Even when transferring schools, he had the luck to end up in a run-down building. It even had wooden floors—the floorboards were so old and worn that the original color was no longer discernible, and it made him worry that a couple of hard stomps would be all it took to fall straight from the third floor to ground level.

"This is an old building," Lao-Xu explained, "but don't let its age fool you! It's very well designed. In these classrooms, the teachers don't have to use a mic or raise our voices to be heard even by the back row."

"Oh." Jiang Cheng nodded.

"Our classroom is on the third floor. Despite the height, there's not much of a view, but at least we can look out onto the field."

"Mhm." Jiang Cheng kept nodding.

"So, our school…" Lao-Xu kept talking as they walked, but after a turn in the stairwell, he harshly whispered, "Gu Fei! You're late again!"

Jiang Cheng raised his brow reflexively and lifted his gaze. A guy who'd been slowly walking up the stairs ahead of them turned around, a small bag of milk dangling from his mouth. He had his back to the light, but Jiang Cheng could still see that it was indeed Gu Fei, not just someone with the same name.

"Morning, Xu-zong." Gu Fei mumbled around the milk pouch as he swept his eyes over Jiang Cheng's face. At this point, he was probably just as unsurprised as Jiang Cheng at their impromptu meetings.

"Why are you still loafing around when you're already late?! Might as well crawl up the stairs while you're at it!" Lao-Xu pointed at him. "School only just started, and you're already slacking off!"

Gu Fei didn't speak, just turned and ran up the stairs in a few large strides before disappearing down the third-floor walkway.

Fourth High really couldn't compare to Jiang Cheng's old school. The second bell had already rung and the teachers were already inside the classrooms, and yet the walkway was still filled with students leaning against the railing and chatting. They didn't seem to have any intention of going to class.

Everyone seemed to slack off on the second years' side of the building, and the third years' side was filled with much of the same idleness. He looked a little harder, but there was no sign of the newly-arrived Gu Fei among them.

Lao-Xu entered the classroom right by the stairs. As Jiang Cheng followed behind him, he checked out the nameplate on the doorframe. It read: "Year Two (8)."

Eight—not bad. Finally, a good omen, even though he had no idea how this lucky eight was going to make him a fortune.

There were quite a few people loitering outside Class Eight as well. They didn't stir when they saw Lao-Xu walk into the room, but when Jiang Cheng walked in behind him, curiosity seemed to finally spur them to go inside.

Lao-Xu stood at the lectern looking out at the dozens of loudly talking students, apparently waiting patiently for everyone to settle down. The whole time, Jiang Cheng stood there beside him, on the receiving end of all sorts of stares and hushed discussions.

It was uncomfortable. Normally Jiang Cheng would stare back at whoever was staring at him—the typical rebuke of "what are you lookin' at?!" never did have any effect on him. But right now, under the weight of dozens of pairs of eyes, he was somewhat at a loss. There were too many people, and therefore there was no one to focus on; all the faces blurred together.

Irritation writhed inside of him. He held back his temper as he glanced toward Lao-Xu, who still stood there, calmly watching the uncalmable students. Jiang Cheng suddenly realized his judgment of his homeroom teacher might have been a little off. He wasn't the affable uncle type—he was the kind of easygoing pushover who held no sway over his students at all.

The noise in the room showed no sign of stopping. Struggling desperately to pull himself back from the edge of an outburst, Jiang Cheng finally couldn't help asking, "Are we supposed to wait until all of them are quiet?"

Lao-Xu turned to look at him. At the same time, the persistent buzz in the room, almost like demonic chanting, suddenly died down.

It was a little difficult for Jiang Cheng to control his temper once it flared. He usually tried to suppress it before he got really worked up, but if that didn't work, it sucked to be on the receiving end of it. And right now, being left standing like a fool for upward of three minutes as all these people stared and blatantly discussed him... It was no different from setting off a pack of dynamite right between his legs. Like his balls had been blown off and there was no trace of him left.

Lao-Xu smiled and clapped his hands. "All right, let me introduce—"

"Jiang Cheng. Transfer," Jiang Cheng interrupted him in a dark voice. "Can I sit down now?"

Lao-Xu blinked.

Someone in the room whistled, suddenly setting off another round of commotion, with a few louder voices breaking through the din. "Cocky, isn't he!"

"Have a seat, then. You can sit..." Lao-Xu shifted his gaze toward the last row. "Right there. Gu Fei, raise your hand for me."

Starting from the first row and moving back, the heads swiveled around one by one like the passing of a baton. Jiang Cheng's eyes followed theirs all the way to the back. Finally, his gaze landed on a desk at the end of the classroom, where Gu Fei had his foot propped against his desk drawer, with half a piece of fried dough still between his teeth.

Jiang Cheng suddenly felt like there was a powerful force screaming inside him, compelling him to write a novel, the title of which would be "King of Tropes: The Proud Owner of Every Coincidence on This Planet."

Gu Fei raised his hand halfheartedly in response.

Jiang Cheng used to sit in the last row at his old school. Every week, the seats in the class would rotate to ensure everyone had a chance to sit at the front, but he'd always managed to switch back to the last row. He liked it there. It was quiet, with no one to disturb him. It was also easy to take a nap or sneak out the back door.

But sitting in the last row here wasn't anywhere near as comfortable. None of the desks and chairs were lined up properly, and as a result, there was very little space to move; his back was practically pressed up against the wall. On top of that, not a single person was quiet. People chatted and played on their phones; not to mention the guy sitting beside him was leisurely munching on a fritter.

Jiang Cheng didn't know what to make of it. Back in his old school, the only thing his teachers found acceptable about him was his grades. However, at the end of the day, he was still in a school that went head-to-head with other top high schools when it came to graduation rates and elite university acceptance. He had truly never

experienced an environment where going to class felt like attending a tea and chat session.

He took out his textbook. As he flipped it open to follow Lao-Xu's lecture, he could feel himself being judged as a freak by the people around him.

Gu Fei wasn't chatting with anyone, nor was he asleep. He only took out a pair of earbuds, stuffed them into his ears, and started listening to music.

A guy in the row in front of them started leaning back and pushing their shared desk. Every time he bumped it, he would turn and call out, "Da-Fei."

The desk lurched.

"Da-Fei."

The desk swayed.

"Hey, Da-Fei."

The desk swayed again.

"Da-Fei?"

Jiang Cheng stared at the words on the page, pondering the answer to the multiple-choice question of whether to smack this guy's head with his hand or his book. He eventually reached over and yanked out Gu Fei's earbuds.

When Gu Fei glanced at him, he stared back without a word.

The guy started pushing their desk again. "Da-Fei! Hey, Da-Fei."

"Yeah?" Gu Fei answered, still looking at Jiang Cheng. Jiang Cheng held his gaze, unperturbed.

"Let me borrow your camera, okay?" the guy asked. "I'll give it back to you tomorrow."

"No," Gu Fei said, and turned away.

"Shit, don't be stingy! I just need to take a couple of photos."

"Fuck off," Gu Fei said simply, then put his earbuds back in and went back to his music.

"Just for one night." The guy bumped the desk again. "I'll give it back first thing tomorrow."

The desk wobbled.

"Damn it, Da-Fei. Da-Fei—!"

He kept on bumping the desk. Jiang Cheng didn't understand why he had to talk about this during class, or why he had to bump his desk while he did it, for that matter. And why was he so persistent, even after being told no? He also couldn't figure out why Gu Fei refused to lend out his camera, why he was being so stuck-up, or how he was able to tolerate their desk having a seizure.

Jiang Cheng lifted a leg and kicked it hard against the chair in front of him. The impact sent the guy careening forward to slam abruptly into his own desk.

He whipped his head around. "The fuck?"

All the eyes in the room were suddenly focused on them.

"Please don't bump against my desk," Jiang Cheng said calmly, looking him in the eye. "Thank you."

The guy seemed a little shaken; he opened his mouth, but no words came out.

Run Wild
SAYE

7

GU FEI LIFTED AN EYEBROW, took out his earbuds, and turned to look at Jiang Cheng.

This guy really was prickly. He was practically covered in thorns—and it seemed that sharp exterior didn't get any less sharp in an unfamiliar environment like this.

Gu Fei looked at Zhou Jing in front of him with great interest. He was still gaping in shock. If Gu Fei hadn't already finished eating his eggs, he'd have loved to stuff one into Zhou Jing's mouth right now.

Jiang Cheng had certainly picked a good target—Zhou Jing was a total pushover, an annoying kid with no temper. *If it was someone else instead...* Gu Fei snuck a glance to his right. *A fight would've broken out by now.*

"What's the matter? What's going on?" Lao-Xu slapped the lectern. "We're in the middle of class here! Gu Fei, what are you doing?"

Gu Fei froze, then pointed his finger at himself and mouthed silently, "Me?"

"Who else?!" Lao-Xu said. "You must be bored now that you've finished your breakfast, huh?"

There was laughter from the desks around him. Gu Fei couldn't help but laugh as well, and he turned to look at Jiang Cheng.

"What are you looking at him for?" Lao-Xu pointed at him. "The guy's grades are eight hundred and seventy-four entire street blocks ahead of yours!"

A round of shouts rang out in the class.

"Yo—!"

"Ooooh, an overachiever!"

"Lao-Xu finally found someone to focus his energy on, huh?"

Gu Fei sighed. Lao-Xu acted like a naïve, purehearted teaching trainee. It was like he'd never taught a badly-behaved class before. With just one statement, Lao-Xu had raised a three-foot-tall barrier around Jiang Cheng that would keep him from integrating with his peers.

Looking at Lao-Xu, Jiang Cheng seriously considered whether this man was an undercover agent sent by his mom to torture him. He wasn't afraid of any sort of provocation, nor had he made any effort to calm his temper since he walked in, but he'd still rather not be praised for his grades by the homeroom teacher of a class this rowdy. The title of "overachiever" was practically an insult.

"All right." Lao-Xu cleared his throat. "Let's continue... We were just talking about..."

Jiang Cheng hadn't been listening to what Lao-Xu was saying up there, and now he gave even less of a damn. He slumped over the desk and pulled out his phone.

In his old school, he had to sneak around like a thief every time he wanted to use his phone in class: ringer off, volume on mute. Then, after he plugged in his headphones, the cable had to be snaked through his sleeve and held to his ear with his hand covering it. The homeroom teacher's drawer was like a sidewalk stall selling used goods, filled with heaps of confiscated cell phones.

Clearly, Fourth High was different. Jiang Cheng shot a glance at Gu Fei, who already had his phone out—it was even propped up on a stand. He was very obviously wearing headphones, leaning back in his chair with his arms crossed, watching a video.

Jiang Cheng flopped on his desk. Up at the lectern, Lao-Xu droned on like a monk chanting scriptures. Even the low-frequency chatter around him sounded like chanting. Amidst the noise, Jiang Cheng drifted in and out of consciousness for over half the class. When he couldn't suffer through the boredom any longer, he took out his phone to send Pan Zhi a message.

– grandson.

Pan Zhi quickly messaged back.

– Gramps. What class are you in right now? You busy?

– Chinese, you?

– English. The old donkey gave us a pop quiz, I'm dead

– Not like it's a formal exam, what's the big deal

– I don't know the answer to a single question. Plus the old donkey said he wanted to get a feel for our foundation, I feel like he's plotting something!

Pan Zhi had sent a photo along with the message. Jiang Cheng looked at it and sighed. It was a page of multiple-choice questions, shot from a very sly angle. He could tell right away that Pan Zhi had risked not seeing his phone again until the summer break in order to take this photo.

Jiang Cheng glanced at the time and zoomed in on the picture, then grabbed a pencil and started quickly writing the answers on a notebook as he read through the questions. Not even two questions in, Pan Zhi sent three more photos in a row. Jiang Cheng peered at his phone, a little speechless. The bastard must've sent him every single question on the quiz.

– Wait.

He sent a reply back to Pan Zhi, then continued to go through the questions. Frankly, they weren't very difficult at all; he could pretty much guess all the answers. He wondered why Pan Zhi was struggling so much.

The classroom was still very noisy. Jiang Cheng had to admire Lao-Xu's patience. Perhaps teachers who were used to teaching these classes eventually built up a strong tolerance for bad behavior. He remembered the chemistry teacher from his first year of high school; her lectures were pretty boring, so people liked to chat in her class. The volume was nothing compared to the noise in his current classroom, but it still made the teacher so angry that she cried. If she were transferred here, she'd sob until she shattered like a glass flower. Lao-Xu was seriously powerful in comparison.

Jiang Cheng continued scribbling down the answers for Pan Zhi, occasionally lifting his eyes to look at the teacher. Students everywhere were sleeping or chatting, but as long as nobody got up to dance, Lao-Xu didn't even blink.

Tsk, tsk.

Pan Zhi had only sent him multiple-choice questions, and Jiang Cheng made short work of them. He glanced at the clock as he typed the answers into his phone. There were still a few minutes before class ended—enough time for Pan Zhi to copy everything down.

As for the other questions... Pan Zhi never bothered with the open-ended ones. Sometimes he was too lazy to even copy answers.

After he sent the message, Jiang Cheng was still bored, so he tapped open his WeChat Moments and started slowly scrolling. He saw that Jiang Yijun—his dear little brother—had posted a selfie yesterday. His mom and dad were in the background—it looked like the whole family was out eating together. A happy family of three.

Jiang Cheng felt a tightness in his chest which swiftly turned into a bizarre wave of nausea. He put the phone back in his pocket, but not before muting the three of them.

Just as he was about to look up, something fell on his head. Before he could figure out what was going on, he felt even more things land on him. It felt like someone was pelting him with a handful of pebbles. Next, he saw a pile of white dust, and caught a whiff of plaster.

He looked up in surprise. "The fuck?"

A large slab of grayish-white plaster lay on his desk, with more fragments of various sizes scattered across the surface. Jiang Cheng's knee-jerk reaction was to dust off his head. Then, he glanced toward Gu Fei next to him.

Gu Fei's cell phone still sat on the desk. Whatever was playing on the screen was no longer visible, concealed behind a layer of dust—as were Gu Fei's hair and face. Gu Fei's arms were still crossed. He hadn't moved at all; the only difference was that he looked kinda pissed off.

Their heads and desks were covered in bits of plaster. Jiang Cheng looked up at the ceiling and located the missing section. With the plaster gone, strips of wooden beams were exposed.

This sure is an ancient building, huh?

When Jiang Cheng looked back down, he noticed a small black rock at the corner of the desk that couldn't have been part of the ceiling.

The bell rang right on time, and Lao-Xu closed his book. "All right, class dismissed... Ah, did the ceiling fall again? Who's on janitorial duty today? Sweep that up, please."

The moment Lao-Xu left the room, the class erupted into chaos; everyone turned to stare at the last row. Jiang Cheng quickly sized up the situation right then and there. Judging from the little rock on his desk, Gu Fei's darkened expression, and everyone who'd stood up to watch as soon as the bell rang, all clearly eager to watch the show... the ceiling might rain plaster on its own from time to time, but that definitely wasn't what had happened today. This was intentional.

He remained in his seat, pulled some tissues out of his pocket, and slowly swept the dust from his desk to the floor. In a situation like this, where he had no clear adversary, it was much easier for him to keep his anger under control.

Gu Fei stood up, his movement shifting the desk forward. He took off his jacket and shook it a few times before lifting his eyes to look at Wang Xu.

"Apologies, Da-Fei." Already on his feet, Wang Xu walked over and slung an arm around Gu Fei's shoulders, then dusted off his jacket. "C'mon, we'll go to the snack stand. I'll buy you a drink."

Gu Fei flung Wang Xu's arm away, put his jacket on, and walked out through the back door. Wang Xu quickly followed, side-by-side with him as he walked down the stairs.

"Hey, Da-Fei, that was friendly fire, I swear!"

"Mm-hm," Gu Fei answered. He'd rather not waste time talking to Wang Xu. The dust in his hair was irking him; some of it had even gotten into his eyes.

"I just wanted to give that kid a warning," Wang Xu went on. "A transfer student acting so fucking arrogant on the first day of class... If nobody teaches him a lesson, he won't know that we do things different here!"

Without a word, Gu Fei reached the ground floor and turned left.

"Hey, what about the snack stand?" Wang Xu said. "Where are you going?"

"To pee," Gu Fei replied.

"You use the bathroom on the teachers' side? It's so far."

"There are less people there."

"All that trouble just to take a piss... I'll bring a bottle of milk tea for you, then," Wang Xu said. "Is Assam okay?"

Gu Fei turned back slightly. "Drink it yourself."

"Assam it is!"

Gu Fei sighed.

The restroom on this side of the field was close to the teachers' offices, so most students preferred not to use it. In fact, not many teachers came here either, since there were bathrooms in their office building. It was a rare spot where he could have some peace.

Gu Fei pulled a cigarette out of his pocket and lit it as he walked inside. He only managed to take one drag when the door to the stall beside him opened and Lao-Xu walked out.

"Xu-zong," Gu Fei greeted him, mumbling around his cigarette.

"What's your problem? You just had to come have a smoke in the teachers' washroom?!" Lao-Xu said, careful to keep his voice low as he pointed at him. "Are you flaunting your power or something? Who exactly are you trying to impress?"

"What's powerful about smoking a cigarette?" Gu Fei laughed and stepped in front of a urinal. "If I'm flaunting, does that mean you're scared of me?"

"I don't even know what to say to you." Lao-Xu walked over, pointing at the cigarette. "Put it out!"

Gu Fei sighed and flicked the cigarette backward into the squat toilet behind him, then looked at Lao-Xu as he held onto his pants zipper. "I'm going to pee now."

Lao-Xu sighed and turned to leave.

Gu Fei unzipped his fly and was just about to pee when Lao-Xu suddenly stopped in his tracks. "And that Jiang Cheng—"

Because he was a little further away now, Lao-Xu spoke loudly, his voice echoing magnificently through the washroom.

"Holy shit!" Gu Fei braced a hand against the wall. Lao-Xu's sudden voice had startled him so much that he'd almost pissed on his shoes. "Xu-zong, sir, can you give me a moment?!"

Lao-Xu walked out, and Gu Fei zipped up his fly and lit another cigarette. Then he walked into a random stall and closed the door so he could smoke. Besides the peace and quiet, the more important reason he liked to come here was that it didn't stink as much.

Lao-Xu was an earnest teacher at heart, but unfortunately he wasn't the greatest lecturer. Nobody listened to him in his classes, and as a homeroom teacher, his people skills were nothing to write home about, either. As a result, no matter how hard he tried with his students, nobody took him seriously. Gu Fei sometimes felt exhausted on his behalf.

When he walked out of the bathroom, Lao-Xu was waiting for him outside in the snow.

"How about you find him a different seat?" Gu Fei said, tugging on his collar.

"Don't want to share a desk with him? Or don't want to share a desk, period?" Lao-Xu looked at him. "Oh, Gu Fei, you need to stop being so antisocial."

"Don't psychoanalyze me," Gu Fei said. "You've been doing it for two years and you haven't been right once."

"Give it some time, it's only his first day of school." Lao-Xu smiled. "That Jiang Cheng... His grades really are quite good. He'll be a positive influence on you as a deskmate."

Good grades? *Positive influence*? Jiang Cheng had just spent an entire class slumped over his desk scrolling on his phone—Gu Fei found the idea of his "good grades" a little hard to accept.

"It's time for class," he said.

"Go on then," said Lao-Xu. "Give it some time."

On his way back to class, Gu Fei ran into Wang Xu on the third-floor landing, and Wang Xu handed him a bottle of milk tea.

"Thanks." Gu Fei accepted the offering and went inside.

Second period was English class. Their English teacher had a short temper and a loud voice; like Lao-Xu, he didn't have much authority over the students, but he did have an affinity for insults. He had such a large arsenal of them that he could go on for half an hour without repeating himself. He had even gotten into physical fights with students before; he refused to back down and would always face troublemakers head-on. Therefore, most people avoided provoking him unless it was a matter of life and death. They all entered the classroom immediately after the warning bell.

The dusty desk had already been cleaned up, but probably not by Jiang Cheng alone. When Gu Fei arrived, he saw Yi Jing walk away with a rag in her hand.

"Thanks," Gu Fei said.

"Oh, it's nothing." Yi Jing brushed her hair aside and smiled. "I'm on janitorial duty today."

Sitting down in his chair, Gu Fei glanced at Jiang Cheng. He sat there calmly with his eyes on the blackboard, leaning back in his seat.

Gu Fei took his phone out to continue watching the movie he didn't get to finish earlier. He had only just pulled up the video when Jiang Cheng suddenly stood up beside him. With a swipe of his hand, Jiang Cheng picked up his chair. In his other hand was a long broom.

Surprised, Gu Fei glanced over at Wang Xu, who had just sat down and was talking cheerfully to his desk-mate. Gu Fei frowned a little. *Is this guy about to start a fight?*

Jiang Cheng had learned who Wang Xu was. After Gu Fei, this was the second name in the class to enter Jiang Cheng's memory. There was very little space in the room between all the desks and chairs, and there was a desk separating his seat from Wang Xu's. To get to Wang Xu while holding a metal chair, Jiang Cheng had to make a detour around the front of the room, which was a hassle.

Jiang Cheng put down his chair and said to the two students sitting beside them, "Excuse me."

They looked at him incredulously, but still stood up and let him squeeze through from behind. After passing through, he dragged one of their chairs out into the aisle.

"Hey! What are you doing?!" the chair's owner shouted.

Jiang Cheng turned to stare at him. He stared back for two seconds, then didn't speak again.

The whole class was looking at them. Wang Xu had realized by now that he was the target, and stood up proudly.

"Oooh! You're here to bust my head open or something? Come on, then, let's see the overachiever prove himself..."

Wordlessly, Jiang Cheng set the chair down next to Wang Xu's seat with a *clunk*, then slowly backed away a few steps. He lifted the broom and threw the handle at the ceiling like a javelin, hitting the spot above Wang Xu's seat with pinpoint accuracy.

Wang Xu had figured it out as soon as Jiang Cheng raised his hand, but when he turned to get away, he was blocked by the chair Jiang Cheng had placed by his legs. He was about to try kicking the chair away when the broomstick came crashing down, bringing a huge sheet of plaster with it. A thick cloud of white dust instantly covered Wang Xu's head and desk.

After a brief silence, the class erupted into tumultuous laughter and shouting, with some students even stomping their feet and thumping their desks. It was total chaos.

"Motherfucker!" Wang Xu yelled, kicking away his chair and charging at Jiang Cheng.

Jiang Cheng didn't move away; he stood still and waited. Wang Xu came straight at him, leaving everything wide open, so he didn't even need to aim his fist to give the guy a nosebleed.

"WHAT'S GOING ON?!"

A roar thundered from the doorway. It was probably the most powerful bellow Jiang Cheng had ever heard in his life; a booming sound that soared straight to the sky and into the clouds. He was so startled that he almost launched himself at Wang Xu.

"What's going on, huh?!" A middle-aged male teacher charged over with a pointer stick and pointed it at Jiang Cheng. "What class are you from? What are you doing here?!"

Before Jiang Cheng could answer, the teacher jabbed the pointer in Wang Xu's face. "And you! Are your ears growing from your armpits? Didn't you hear the bells ring?! Are you deaf or something? Can you hear the sound of my voice now? Can you hear me?! Can you?!"

He didn't wait for Wang Xu to speak. Turning the pointer at everyone else around him, he continued, "Standing around to watch the show, are we? Well, I'll give you a performance all right! A round of applause, please! Clap, clap, clap! Come on!"

After this tirade, the class quieted down. Wang Xu glared, but it didn't look like he would charge at him again. Jiang Cheng looked up worriedly at the ceiling, afraid that the whole ceiling would cave in on them if the teacher yelled any more.

"Back to your seats! Scram!" the teacher yelled again. "What, are you waiting to be carried or something?! Someone take the door off its hinges so I can carry you all!"

The classroom was filled with the sounds of low laughter and complaints as Jiang Cheng turned around to go back to his seat.

"You!" the teacher called out to him. "Which class are you from?"

"He's the newly transferred overachiever," someone piped up.

Staring in astonishment, the teacher looked him up and down at length. "Go sit down! Are you waiting for someone to carry you over?"

The teacher's yelling barely left Jiang Cheng space to breathe. He could only glance at the teacher again before returning to his seat.

"Commencing class!" The teacher smacked the pointer stick on the lectern. "*Good-ah mowning-ah, ey-werey-one!*"

Jiang Cheng stiffened. The heavily accented English almost made him burst out laughing.

After the lecture started, the boy who was pushing his and Gu Fei's desk earlier started to push again, but this time, it wasn't directed at Gu Fei. He turned around and called out to Jiang Cheng, "Hey, overachiever. Pretty damn impressive, casually provoking Wang Xu like that."

Jiang Cheng didn't reply.

"Fuck off," Gu Fei said from beside him.

"What the hell?" the guy said quietly. "I wasn't even talking to you. Is that your automatic response to me?"

"Mm." Gu Fei propped up his phone.

"You're asking for trouble." The guy looked back at the teacher, then turned to Jiang Cheng with a serious face. "Wang Xu definitely isn't done with you. Did you know that our school has a back gate—"

"What's your name?" Jiang Cheng interrupted him.

"Zhou Jing."

"Thank you," Jiang Cheng said, and pointed at his chair. "Don't. Bump. My desk. Again."

"...Oh." Zhou Jing blinked at him, then nodded.

Jiang Cheng flipped open his textbook and stared down at it. Zhou Jing stayed frozen there for a while, still craning his neck back to look at him, before finally turning around.

It was indeed an eventful beginning to the new semester; it was a shame Jiang Cheng didn't have the habit of keeping a diary.

It didn't matter to Jiang Cheng whether this Wang Xu would bother him again or not. At the moment, he only felt despondent. That picture in his WeChat Moments—the family selfie, full of warm affection simply because of his absence—it made him feel suddenly unmoored, weightless.

Of course, it only made sense that people he didn't care about didn't care about him, either. But it depressed him all the same.

Jiang Cheng stared at his textbook. He detected a faintly sweet, milky smell amidst the scent of paper and ink, and suddenly felt a little hungry. He remembered that he hadn't had breakfast yet. Turning, he saw that Gu Fei was unwrapping a milk candy next to him as he watched his video.

Gu Fei exchanged a look with him, paused, then reached his hand into his pocket and rummaged around. He pulled out a piece of candy and placed it on Jiang Cheng's book before turning his attention back to his phone screen.

Jiang Cheng looked at the candy lying on the page, a little bewildered. And yet the aroma of milk candy wafting over from Gu Fei's side was practically making his stomach scream.

After two minutes of hesitation, he picked up the candy and peeled open the wrapper.

...It wasn't milk candy!

He'd given him a *fruit* candy!

He couldn't help himself from turning to glance at Gu Fei again.

Gu Fei swept his eyes over the fruit candy in Jiang Cheng's hand, reached his hand into his pocket again, and put a handful of candies directly on the desk. There were all kinds of packaging and flavors— at least a dozen of them.

"Take your pick," said Gu Fei.

8

JIANG CHENG had never picked candies like this, even when he was little. His family never really allowed sweets, junk food, or soda; he'd always felt as if he was living like an ascetic. As a result, he didn't really crave junk food or sweets. Usually whenever Pan Zhi found something good, he'd shove a bunch of it in Jiang Cheng's direction.

It was a novel feeling to see Gu Fei place a handful of candy on his desk for him to pick from.

There was coffee candy, milk candy, mint candy, fruit candy...and all of these were divided further still into soft and hard varieties. He stared for a while and finally picked out a milk candy. He had only just opened the wrapper when Gu Fei reached out and took away the rest of the pile.

"The hell?" Jiang Cheng was stunned—then he remembered that Gu Fei had said "take your pick," not "take it all." He immediately conceded that the logic was irrefutable, but he couldn't help but ask, "Do you think your stinginess is going to save you enough cash to have Wang Jianlin prostrating himself at your feet tomorrow?"[6]

Without a word, Gu Fei looked down at the sweets in his hand, picked out the other two milk candies, and placed them in front of Jiang Cheng. He then put the rest back in his pocket.

---

6   Known for having been the richest man in China.

...What a weirdo.

Jiang Cheng unwrapped all three pieces of milk candy and stuffed them into his mouth, unable to find anything else to say.

The English teacher's name was Mr. Lu. Because he liked to yell, he was better than Lao-Xu at keeping the students' attention and maintaining a quiet class. He saw overall better results than Lao-Xu did.

Although none of the teachers Jiang Cheng had met today could compare to his old teachers, the entire period taught by Mr. Lu was uniquely invigorating. If someone so much as scratched an itch, he would jab the pointer stick at the student and ask if they needed help with that. Jiang Cheng hadn't been so focused on a lecture in ages. The second his attention strayed even slightly, he'd find himself shocked back to reality by Mr. Lu's roars.

The classroom became rowdy again the instant the bell rang, like a pressure valve being released. Some people even let loose a few howls as they stretched their backs.

"You!" Mr. Lu suddenly jabbed the pointer stick toward the back of the classroom. "Come with me."

The gesture and the "you" covered a fairly wide range of students. There was another wave as everyone once again whipped their heads around one by one. Even when he felt a bunch of eyes on him, Jiang Cheng didn't pay it any heed. He was a new transfer, after all; he doubted the teacher would even remember his name...

"Gu Fei!" Mr. Lu yelled again.

Gu Fei sighed. He'd been looking down at his phone, and at the sound of the teacher's thunderous voice, he dropped it to the ground. He glanced up at Mr. Lu, then gestured with his head at Jiang Cheng.

"He's calling you."

"Hm?" Jiang Cheng froze. "Me?"

"Yes, you! Gu Fei's deskmate!" Mr. Lu pointed at him again with his stick. Several students scrambled to move their heads out of its radius.

Jiang Cheng had no choice but to stand up. He wondered what the English teacher wanted from him. He glanced back at Wang Xu as he walked to the door; he'd stood up too. If the teacher hadn't called Jiang Cheng away, they would have been battling it out by now.

"The name is Jiang Cheng, right?" Mr. Lu turned and started heading downstairs.

"Yes sir," Jiang Cheng answered as he followed. "What did you want to see me about?"

"Your Xu-zong has been bragging to me for days, saying that a capital-R Real overachiever has arrived..."

Jiang Cheng was confused. "A capital what?"

"A capital-R, Real, overachiever," Mr. Lu explained as he gave him a look. "You've never heard the expression before?"

A Real overachiever.

"...Oh. I get it now." It was the first time Jiang Cheng had heard someone specify capitalization out loud.

"Our school started out as a general high school before it got turned into a vocational school, and then it was changed back to a general high school again," Mr. Lu said. "It can't compare to your old school, but I hope it won't affect you. Just continue studying the way you did before."

"Oh." Jiang Cheng thought about how he'd studied in the past and figured the teacher didn't know him very well.

"Students like Wang Xu and Gu Fei... Try not to mess with them. They're all just here to kill time," Mr. Lu went on. "If I hadn't called you out, he'd be looking to pick a fight with you right about now, and he wouldn't give up until he emerged with another demerit point on his shoulder. He has a penalty on his record already."

"...Oh." Jiang Cheng nodded. It seemed that Mr. Lu actually cared about his students.

Mr. Lu shot him a displeased look. "Aren't you going to thank me?"

"Thank you."

"Your English grades were pretty top-notch—why don't you be student rep for my English class?" Mr. Lu suggested. "Yi Jing is the current student rep. She's also the class president, and the student rep for Chinese class..."

"Hm?" Jiang Cheng blinked, then immediately shook his head. "Nope."

"Why not?" Mr. Lu was a little surprised. "I heard Lao-Xu say you used to be class president. You don't think being a student rep for one class is too much work, do you?"

"I was only the class president for one semester."

"How come?" Mr. Lu asked.

Jiang Cheng shot him a glance. "Because I got into fights and skipped class."

Mr. Lu's eyes widened. He stared and opened his mouth, but nothing came out.

"I'll be heading back to class now, then?"

"Hey... Hold on." Mr. Lu mulled over it for a moment. "How about you come work on some course materials for me some day when you have the time?"

Jiang Cheng sighed inwardly. He wanted to say he didn't have a computer at the moment, but since Mr. Lu seemed to be a good person, it was hard to reject him a second time. He nodded.

"Good, good." Mr. Lu grinned. "Go back to class, then."

✦ ✦ ✦

"Fuck, what's taking him so long?" Wang Xu said from his perch on Jiang Cheng's desk. "Is he avoiding me? Does he think he can hide forever?!"

"Lao-Lu wants him for something, probably," Zhou Jing said.

"What the hell could he possibly want?" said Wang Xu. "When have you ever seen Lao-Lu ask a student for something?! He probably just wanted to ask some questions to get to know the new transfer. And the new guy didn't dare come back to class once he was done! Asshole!"

Gu Fei, who had been quietly playing a game on his phone this whole time, finally cut in. "You're planning to settle the score right here?"

"No shit!" Wang Xu bowed his head and ran his fingers through his hair in irritation. "Fuck!"

Gu Fei put his phone down and peered up at him.

"...Or, where else should I do it?" Wang Xu was a little hesitant.

"Not my problem," Gu Fei said. "Just don't bring your mess around me. It's fucking annoying."

"Maybe you can just forget it," Zhou Jing said. "You both got each other once—you're even."

Wang Xu turned and glared at Zhou Jing. "Your great fucking uncle it's even!"

"Go down to the field or do it outside of school," said Gu Fei, still playing his game. "Just not next to me. It's irritating as hell."

"He's back," Zhou Jing said.

Gu Fei looked up, sweeping his gaze across the front of the room. Sure enough, Jiang Cheng was slowly ambling toward them with both hands in his pockets and his eyes on Wang Xu.

"Hiding from me, are ya?" Wang Xu sneered. "You've got guts, coming back before the bell."

"Three things," Jiang Cheng said.

Wang Xu looked at him, not quite comprehending what he just said.

"One: get down," Jiang Cheng said as he stuck out an index finger. He then proceeded to put up another finger. "Two: the one who started it is always the jackass."

Wang Xu finally reanimated. He glared at Jiang Cheng and was about to say something when Jiang Cheng cut him off and held up a third finger.

"Three: just tell me how you want to resolve this. If all you're going to do is keep blabbing on, then I concede."

As he said this, a silence fell over the class, who had all been waiting to see the show unfold. They watched with bated breath for Wang Xu's reaction.

Gu Fei tilted his head back and, leaning against the wall, let out a low whistle. Based on Gu Fei's many years of experience as a popcorn-eating bystander, Jiang Cheng's words and the way he carried himself as he said them immediately put Wang Xu's future career as boss of the class in jeopardy.

The expression on Wang Xu's face went through several quick changes. Jiang Cheng couldn't tell what he was thinking, but he didn't miss the quick glance Wang Xu shot Gu Fei the first chance he got. He saw very clearly that Wang Xu was afraid of Gu Fei—or maybe he subconsciously viewed Gu Fei as someone to lean on.

Ever since Jiang Cheng saw the Fresh Out of Jail quartet at Gu Fei's store that day, he knew that the somewhat polite and mellow "it's none of my business" façade that Gu Fei put up was just that: a façade.

Tsk. What the hell is with him? He's acting like he's some lofty immortal wandering on the fringes of society.

"I'll be waiting for you at lunchtime," Wang Xu announced, hopping off the desk. As he walked back to his own seat, he turned and pointed a finger at Jiang Cheng. "And don't even think about running away."

"Mm-hm," Jiang Cheng answered as he sat down. After some thought, he turned and asked Gu Fei, "Is that guy a big deal in your class?"

He noticed now that the rest note shaved onto the left side of Gu Fei's head had three dots: It was a thirty-second rest.

"Something like that," said Gu Fei.

"What do you mean, *something like that*?"

"It means he'll fight whoever dares to say he isn't."

Gu Fei's eyes were still glued to his phone, his fingers busy swiping around on the screen. Jiang Cheng saw that the game he was playing was *Aixiaochu*, the kind of mindless matching game he'd only played in middle school when he needed to kill some time but had nothing else better to do. He was surprised to see Gu Fei spend his time either watching videos or playing that garbage game—and he seemed pretty into it, too. *How juvenile.*

Jiang Cheng couldn't help himself. "You like to play that game?"

"Mm, it doesn't take a lot of brain power," Gu Fei said. "It's not like I'm an overachiever like you."

Jiang Cheng was already irritated by everything that had happened that morning. At those words, he almost landed a punch directly into Gu Fei's thirty-second rest. He clenched his jaw and stopped himself, though—for one thing, Gu Fei had helped him when he passed out the other day. And he ate three of Gu Fei's milk candies just now, too... *If that even counts?*

"It's courageous of you to face your smooth brain head-on," Jiang Cheng said. "Good for you."

Gu Fei turned, took one long look at him without any expression, and said in an obnoxiously high-pitched voice, "Good luck at lunch time!"

Damn you and your great uncle's big yellow dog! Ugh.

Jiang Cheng didn't listen much in class for the rest of the morning. His chest felt tight. Even after he blacklisted the family of three, he couldn't help going back and tapping on their Moments.

He didn't have a good relationship with them—things had been more tense than anything else—but that was the only home he'd known for more than a decade. It was the "family" he had seen every single day; they were carved into his memory. He couldn't simply throw those sentiments away.

Seeing the calm on the other side made him feel even more miserable than being pushed out of the place he'd called home for more than ten years. It seemed that no one was affected by his absence—his permanent departure, rather... Or perhaps they simply weren't showing it?

He slumped over his desk, stuffed a hat under his head, and closed his eyes. *Forget it,* he thought as he decided to take a quick nap. He wasn't someone who needed to be in his own bed to fall asleep, but he hadn't slept well ever since he got here. Li Baoguo's place was way too old and run-down, and on top of that, the guy lived like a total slob. The house was full of cockroaches and spiders—and rodents, too. Listening to the sounds of mice scurrying around the apartment all night made Jiang Cheng feel like he lived inside a dumpster.

The teachers at Fourth High were much more understanding than his old teachers when it came to slacking off during class. He slept all the way through the period, even dozing through the break in between classes without lifting his head once, and not a single teacher came up to disturb him.

It wasn't until the final bell for the last period of the morning sounded, and Wang Xu slammed a palm onto his desk, that Jiang Cheng straightened up with a yawn. His back felt a little stiff.

Wang Xu glared at him sideways. "Let's go."

Jiang Cheng didn't say a word as he stuffed all his books and notebooks into the desk drawer, then stood up with his backpack.

Wang Xu turned with a flourish and walked toward the back door of the classroom. If it wasn't for the down jacket he was wearing and the fact that there was no breeze, it would almost set the kind of tone that said, "Watch out, the big boss is coming."

A handful of people followed by his side. Judging by their excitement, they were probably his little assistants. The popcorn-eaters hadn't had the chance to catch up yet.

"Hey," Jiang Cheng called from behind them.

"Are you chickening out?" Wang Xu replied immediately.

"Are you bringing these people as your teammates, or as your cheerleaders?" Jiang Cheng asked.

Wang Xu glanced at the guys beside him, then glared back at Jiang Cheng. "What, you scared?"

"Cheerleaders are fine by me," Jiang Cheng said, sizing them up as he approached. "But if they're going to fight, then you better get the order straight among yourselves first."

Wang Xu waved his hand and said to the others, "Don't follow us."

"Are you going to watch?" Zhou Jing nudged the desk.

Still playing *Aixiaochu*—a game only people without overachiever brains liked to play—Gu Fei finished the round and finally stood up. "Nope."

"Maybe you should go take a look. Aren't you worried something will go wrong?"

"And why would that be my problem?" Gu Fei stuffed his phone in his pocket and walked away.

When he got downstairs, those friends of Wang Xu's were still craning their heads in the direction of the back gate. There was no sign of Jiang Cheng and Wang Xu anywhere.

One of them spotted Gu Fei and immediately walked up. "Da-Fei…"

"Shhh." Gu Fei put a finger to his lips. "Don't bother me."

Elementary students hadn't started class for the semester yet, so Gu Miao must have been waiting at the gate for him for an hour already. He didn't have the time to watch Wang Xu get beat up. That was right—he was *that* certain that when Wang Xu went up against Jiang Cheng, the only possible outcome was Wang Xu getting his ass kicked.

That indifference in Jiang Cheng's eyes was something Wang Xu didn't have. Not to mention the displeasure written plainly all over him like countless tightly packed "NO"s—it was enough to scare off someone with trypophobia. Either something had happened recently that left him in a funk, or something was chronically wrong with the guy's head. How could Wang Xu, a kid who harbored the naïve dream of ruling the streets, possibly contend with a legit psycho in a bad mood?

A green head flew past Gu Fei like a gust of wind as soon as he walked out of the school gate, and a chorus of impressed *wow*s rang out around him.

Gu Fei fetched his bicycle from the bike shed. As soon as he climbed on, Gu Miao once again flew past like the wind, pausing beside him for only two seconds—long enough to pilfer a handful of candies from his pocket. By the time he got his bike out to the main road, Gu Miao was standing at the side of the road, peeling open a wrapper. She had picked out all the fruit candies.

"Want a ride back?" Gu Fei asked. "Or do you want to follow behind?"

Gu Miao picked up her skateboard. Just as she was about to hop onto the back seat, he reached out a hand to stop her, taking her chin in one hand and peering at a small scratch by the corner of her eye.

"Did you scrape yourself, or is this from a fight?"

"Scrape," Gu Miao said.

Gu Fei didn't press the issue. "Get on."

Gu Miao got onto the back seat with her skateboard in one arm and held onto his waist with the other.

It might have been just a scrape, or it might have been from a fight. Either way, the little girl was stubborn as hell, so it was useless to even ask. He couldn't nag her about it too much, either. She preferred to take care of her own business, even if it meant getting roughed up occasionally.

"What do you say we go buy a pair of gloves for you," Gu Fei said as he pushed down on the pedal. "Those little leather ones you wanted last time?"

Gu Miao quickly took off the dirty down-filled gloves she was wearing and gave him a thumbs-up.

The streets outside the back gate of Fourth High were busier than the ones out front. It was a strange phenomenon. The back gate opened onto a smaller street which had a more laid-back street management committee than the one by the front gate. Because of this, all kinds of stalls and makeshift stands lined the street's sides, one after another. Most of them sold food, and business was booming.

As Jiang Cheng followed Wang Xu through the various aromas, he fought the urge to say, *How about I treat you to some food first?* However, seeing the indignant anger and determination on Wang Xu's face, Jiang Cheng held his tongue. He didn't want to make the guy cry.

He'd treat this like a tour, then, he decided, and then come back later to eat. There were quite a lot of stalls that appealed to him, selling all kinds of grilled meats: fatty veal, pork belly, lamb kidneys, lamb tendons… Jiang Cheng swallowed.

After they passed the street, the delicious smells disappeared with it. He wondered where Wang Xu was taking him.

"Are we going on a hike or something?" he asked. His hunger was making him cranky.

Wang Xu ignored him, but after a few steps, he suddenly stopped, looking ahead with a frown. Jiang Cheng followed his gaze.

A few yards away from them, three people stood on the side of the road, all facing their direction with their hands in their pockets. After he and Wang Xu both looked at them, they slowly started walking over. Wang Xu reached a hand into his own pocket.

"What?" A tall string bean of a guy who looked like he'd been starving for years grinned. "Are you going to call Gu Fei? He just left with his little sister. He probably won't have time for your problems."

"What do you want?" Wang Xu said gruffly, clearly impatient.

"Oho." The skinny guy put on an exaggerated expression of surprise. "Somebody's got a spine today, huh? Not gonna run?" He shot a glance at Jiang Cheng. "This your new buddy? He must be damn impressive if you don't even need to run away now."

"It was a whole bunch of you last time, and you all ran 'til you wheezed," someone laughed from behind the skinny guy.

The skinny guy looked at the two of them mockingly. "How about I count to three, and you can—"

Jiang Cheng's fist connected directly with the guy's nose. His words were smashed clean away, and everyone on both sides turned to stone.

Jiang Cheng didn't stop there. It was important to be decisive and quick in these matters. After the first punch, he grabbed the guy's hat-covered head and yanked it down to meet his knee.

He didn't use a lot of strength with either strike. In Jiang Cheng's experience, it wasn't enough to break his nose, but there'd definitely be blood pouring out, making it look like the guy had ketchup smeared all over his mouth. Just as he thought, when he released his grip and shoved the skinny guy back, blood came gushing out of his nose. Out of reflex, the guy lifted a hand and wiped it.

Jiang Cheng glanced at Wang Xu, then stepped forward and knocked his shoulder into the arm of another guy, who was about to pull a knife—and for good measure, he headbutted the guy in the face. The guy yelped and covered his nose with his hands.

"Run, dumbass!" Jiang Cheng shouted at Wang Xu before launching into a sprint.

Wang Xu paused for a moment, then hurried to catch up with him. When they reached the intersection, Wang Xu pointed to the left. "This way."

Jiang Cheng followed him, making several twists and turns until they were deep in another alley. They turned a couple more times before stopping in a clear area surrounded by the back walls of other people's backyards.

"What is this place?" Jiang Cheng asked, looking around.

They were at a dead end, blocked on three sides by courtyard walls. The alley looked decrepit. Piles of snow and fallen branches were clumped on the ground along with all sorts of trash.

"This is..." Wang Xu panted, taking a minute to catch his breath, "where I go to fight people."

"You've got unique taste," Jiang Cheng said.

"Um..." Wang Xu looked at him and hesitated for a while, then finally said, "Thanks...for what you did just now."

"Why thank me?" Jiang Cheng pulled a cigarette from his pocket, lit it, and put it between his lips. "It's not like I did it to help you."

Wang Xu stared at him. "Fuck. Are you *really* a top student?"

"Let's get this over with." Jiang Cheng checked the time. "I'm hungry. Hurry up so I can go eat."

"It's already over with." Wang Xu sat on a three-legged stool nearby that looked so rickety it could have been a prop in a haunted house. "There's no beef between us anymore."

Jiang Cheng tutted audibly. "I'm leaving, then."

"Just wait a little longer," Wang Xu called out to stop him. "Monkey's probably still around, and they got the numbers on us. If you go out now, you'll run into them."

Jiang Cheng went quiet.

"That was only three of them you saw just now. You left Monkey with blood on his face, so when you go back out, it's definitely not just gonna be the three of them anymore. I...I'm going to call someone for help." Wang Xu pulled out his phone.

Remembering what the skinny guy said earlier, Jiang Cheng knitted his brow and asked, "Who are you calling?"

"Da-Fei."

"The fuck? Gu Fei?"

Jiang Cheng felt his face shatter into a million pieces and scatter all over the ground.

9

JIANG CHENG TOSSED the cigarette and turned to walk toward the mouth of the alley.

"Hey! Don't go out there!" Wang Xu shouted. "You think I'm just scared? You can't afford to mess with Monkey and his gang! Last semester, they beat up someone from Seventh High so bad that he was in the hospital for months!"

"I can't afford to mess with them?" Jiang Cheng turned to look at him. "If they're so badass, why is it okay to ask Gu Fei to mess with them?"

"Da-Fei's different," Wang Xu said. "He's been roughing it around here since he was a kid. And... Anyway, just listen to me. You helped me out, so I'm not sending you out there to die."

And... And what? And he killed his own father? Suddenly, remembering what Li Baoguo had told him, Jiang Cheng found himself laughing. There were urban legends every few streets in the old districts of small cities like this one; it was kind of amusing.

That just made Wang Xu angry. "The fuck are you laughing at?!"

Jiang Cheng ignored him. He was about to continue walking, but as he put one leg forward, Wang Xu wrapped his arms around him from behind and dragged him back.

"Hey, hey!" Jiang Cheng exclaimed in alarm. "Let go! What's wrong with you?!"

"What's wrong with *me*?" Wang Xu froze, then abruptly loosened his grip. "Nothing! I didn't mean anything by it! Don't get me wrong! I didn't mean it!"

Jiang Cheng gave him a look. "Did I *say* you meant something else by it?"

Wang Xu didn't speak. He pulled out his phone again and dialed a number.

Jiang Cheng sighed. Once again, he lit a cigarette and put it in his mouth. Crouching at the foot of the wall to get out of the wind, he picked up a twig and scrawled aimlessly in the snow.

"Da-Fei, Da-Fei," Wang Xu called out in a hushed voice as he held his phone, as if Monkey's gang was standing guard in the yard next door, "Monkey found us... Yes, we got away. No—we can't leave right now... He's running around with a bloody face, of course he's not going to let us go! Who else? Me and Jiang Cheng."

Wang Xu peeked at Jiang Cheng as he spoke. Jiang Cheng didn't meet his eyes. Wang Xu wasn't that tough, but he wasn't a coward either. If those people scared him this badly, they probably *were* the type you shouldn't mess with. Honestly, even back when he himself had hung around a rough crowd, he was reluctant to offend people outside of school. It was too much trouble.

When he remembered it was Gu Fei on the other end of that phone call, Jiang Cheng almost preferred the idea of going back out there to face a beating. But the rational part of him won out: Going out there could cost him more than just a simple beating or two.

"Da-Fei's coming over soon." Wang Xu hung up and dragged his foot back and forth through the garbage heap. "He took his sister out for noodles. They're still eating."

Jiang Cheng was utterly speechless.

Wang Xu found a stick in the garbage, about three feet long. He chucked it at Jiang Cheng's foot. When rummaging earned him nothing else, he began to take apart the raggedy, three-legged chair.

Jiang Cheng stared at him. "What are you doing?"

"Getting us some weapons," Wang Xu said. "Monkey's gang knows this place pretty well, too. What if they find us before Da-Fei gets here?"

Jiang Cheng sighed. He rifled through his school bag and found a knife, which he threw at Wang Xu's foot. "Use this."

"Fuck me!" Wang Xu leaped in shock the instant he saw the knife. He whipped around to glare at Jiang Cheng. "Are you really a top student? What kind of top student carries a knife in his bag?!"

"I've never used it," Jiang Cheng said. "It hasn't even been sharpened. It's just for scaring people."

Wang Xu picked up the knife and studied it intently for a while, then walked over and crouched before him. "Jiang Cheng, I'm no match for you."

Jiang Cheng looked at him in silence.

"This is the end of our disagreement," Wang Xu continued. "After this, we'll stay in our own lanes. How's that?"

"Sure, you can keep that in mind," Jiang Cheng said. "Overachievers like me are too busy studying to waste time screwing around with guys like you."

Neither of them spoke after that. They crouched, facing each other in silence.

They had been crouching for some time before Wang Xu spoke again: "A word to the wise."

"Uh huh." Jiang Cheng gazed at the lit cigarette between his fingers. The smoke that rose from it twisted madly in the air for an instant, then vanished without a trace.

"If Monkey gets here first, just surrender," Wang Xu said. "Sure, we can get rough, but we're only students. We can't tough it out against real-world thugs."

Jiang Cheng looked at him, somewhat taken aback. So there *were* some surviving dregs of sense in this silly little dude's head.

"That's what Da-Fei said," Wang Xu added.

Ah. Jiang Cheng felt a bit like stubbing his cigarette out on Wang Xu's face.

Gu Fei wasn't that late, really; he showed up about ten minutes later on his bike. What perplexed Jiang Cheng was that he brought Gu Miao along. The little girl was on her skateboard, hanging onto one end of a cord that attached to the back of the bike. A whole family of lunatics!

The moment Gu Fei's leg braced against the ground, Gu Miao leaped off her skateboard. She kicked the tip of her foot against the board and caught it in one hand as it flipped into the air. Hugging the skateboard, she walked over to Jiang Cheng and smiled at him, then ran back to Gu Fei's side, leaning against his leg as she stood.

"Who made the first move earlier?" Gu Fei asked.

"Me." Jiang Cheng stood. "What's up?"

"You ran into Monkey?" Wang Xu asked Gu Fei.

"Outside the alleys." Gu Fei glanced behind him. "Probably coming in now."

"Fuck." Wang Xu frowned. "Will we be able to get out?"

"Depends how you want to do it," Gu Fei said, then looked at Jiang Cheng. "Two possible solutions..."

Jiang Cheng knew he was probably in real trouble this time. He sighed and stuck his hands in his pockets as he leaned against the wall. "Go on."

"Let him get you back," said Gu Fei. "Once you're even, it's settled. If you don't want that, I'll escort you both out now, but where and when they get you after that is just luck of the draw."

Wang Xu quickly looked to Jiang Cheng.

"Getting even is fine. But let's be clear," Jiang Cheng said. "One hit more than even, and I'll fight back."

When Monkey showed up, his nose was stuffed with cotton. Jiang Cheng thought he must have a low platelet count to bleed for so long without it clotting. Like Wang Xu had said, Monkey brought a lot of people with him this time. At a glance, there were seven or eight of them. The air was thick with small-town gangsterism.

"Er-Miao, wait for me on the street outside," Gu Fei said.

Gu Miao gave Jiang Cheng a look. She put the skateboard down, got on it, and kicked a few times, shooting out of the crowd like a rocket.

"You go, too," Jiang Cheng said.

Leaning his weight on the handlebars, Gu Fei stared at him for a moment. "Wang Xu, come out with me."

"I..." Wang Xu hesitated, looking at Jiang Cheng.

"Go," Jiang Cheng said. He didn't want an audience watching him get hit.

Gu Fei grabbed the handlebars and swung his bike around. Wang Xu followed.

Monkey walked over to Jiang Cheng, his face dark. When Gu Fei brushed past him, he suddenly seized Monkey's right wrist and yanked it out of his pocket.

Monkey glared at him. "What?"

Gu Fei didn't speak. He roughly ran his fingers down Monkey's wrist and took something from his hand before chucking it at the foot of the wall. The sound of metal clanging against brick was crisp and clear.

Jiang Cheng glanced in the direction of the noise. It was a black brass knuckle.

Motherfucker.

"Rules still apply," Gu Fei said without raising his voice. With a kick of his foot, he rode his bike out of the network of alleys and toward the main road.

"He won't be in trouble, will he?" Wang Xu stood by a bald tree at the mouth of the alley. He tucked his neck in from the cold as he watched Gu Miao spin nimble circles on her skateboard around a heap of snow underneath the tree.

"If you're scared of trouble, don't go looking for it," Gu Fei said.

"I didn't! I always run when I see Monkey," Wang Xu said. "Fuck's sake, how was I supposed to know we'd run into him today? Jiang Cheng didn't know about him, so he went straight for the punch!"

"Are you two settled?" Gu Fei glanced at his face. "Did you kneel down and beg him not to hit you in the face?"

"...It's settled." Wang Xu sighed and turned to peer into the alley. "Today I learned they make all kinds of nerdy overachievers. I can't afford to piss him off."

Gu Fei laughed.

Barely a few minutes later, Monkey and his gang emerged onto the road.

Monkey didn't seem all that pleased, but he looked normal overall. The one behind him didn't look so pretty, though—there was a large bump adorning his forehead.

Wang Xu started in shock the instant he saw it. "He fought back?"

Monkey met Gu Fei's eyes and said nothing more. He led his men away.

"Fuck. Where is that moron?" Wang Xu watched the mouth of the alley.

Gu Fei frowned. By the looks of it, Jiang Cheng had indeed fought back, and it probably wasn't of his own volition; someone had given that one hit more. Monkey wouldn't break the rules again under these circumstances.

So where was Jiang Cheng?

Even if he took several turns around the place, he shouldn't take this long to come out... Gu Fei's phone rang in his pocket. He was surprised to find that Jiang Cheng was calling him.

"Where are you?" he asked as he picked up.

"I...got lost," Jiang Cheng said.

"What?" Gu Fei was flabbergasted. "Lost?"

"Yeah, lost! We went around in circles when we came in, so I don't know where I've circled round to. Did you people build alleyways or a fucking labyrinth?" Jiang Cheng grumbled, pissed off.

"You... Hang on." Gu Fei glanced at Gu Miao. "Er-Miao, go in and lead Jiang Cheng-gege out."

Her foot on the skateboard, Gu Miao turned and sped into the alley.

When Jiang Cheng heard the sound of skateboard wheels, he called out, "Gu Miao?"

Gu Miao's figure emerged from a turn ahead. She waved at him, and Jiang Cheng went over. In fact, that was where he'd just come from; when he followed Gu Miao down another turn, he saw the little street from before.

Damn it. If he'd known how close he already was, he wouldn't have embarrassed himself by calling Gu Fei. He'd made an ass of himself so many times today, you could pin a tail on him.

"You all right?" Wang Xu asked the moment he saw him, looking at his face.

"I'm fine." Jiang Cheng touched his abdomen.

Wang Xu glanced at his hand. "They didn't hit you in the face?"

"No." Jiang Cheng gave him a look. "Why, do *you* want to?"

"Just asking. They hit your stomach? Does it hurt?"

"I'm hungry," Jiang Cheng said.

"Did you fight back?" Wang Xu continued to badger him. "I saw what's-his-name come out with a huge bump on his head—what happened there?"

"I said I'd hit back if they hit more than they were meant to," Jiang Cheng replied, rather impatiently. "So I bumped his head on the wall. What, you wanna try it too?"

"I'm going home," Wang Xu said. "I'm leaving. Hey, uh, Da-Fei, I'll buy you lunch tomorrow."

After Wang Xu left, Jiang Cheng stood there in silence with Gu Fei, watching Gu Miao on her skateboard.

"Thanks," he said, finally.

Though he'd ended up taking a couple of hits—Monkey punched him twice in the gut, and he still felt queasy—if it hadn't been for Gu Fei, that solution wouldn't even have been on the table. If he'd just left, Monkey would probably spend his days prowling the streets looking for him, and he'd never have a moment's peace again.

"Are you really okay?" Gu Fei gave him a look.

"Yeah." Jiang Cheng had absolutely no desire to discuss it further. He thought for a moment. "Did you eat?"

"No."

"Wang Xu said you were eating noodles earlier. He said you'd come over once you were done," Jiang Cheng said.

"You two would've been chopped liver by then," said Gu Fei. "I was eating on the pedestrian street. If I really finished my noodles first, it would've taken me half an hour to get here."

"Come on, then, let's go get some food." Jiang Cheng looked at Gu Miao. "What do you want to eat?"

Of course, Gu Miao didn't answer him. She simply turned to Gu Fei.

He patted her on the head. "Lead the way."

Gu Miao instantly shot off on her skateboard—one look told them she was headed for the roadside barbecue place they'd passed before.

"Come on up," Gu Fei said to Jiang Cheng, gesturing at his bike.

"I'll walk."

Gu Fei didn't waste any more words; he just rode away. Jiang Cheng sighed and pressed his stomach. He felt a bit nauseated, but he wasn't sure whether it was from hunger or from Monkey's punches.

Gu Miao chose the farthest barbecue stall. By the time Jiang Cheng walked over, she'd already picked out a heap of things to eat. When Jiang Cheng smelled the aroma of the barbecue skewers, the discomfort in his gut finally began to subside, leaving only an intense hunger. He went over and pointed at the meat.

"Ten skewers of each, and two pounds of mala crawfish."

They didn't have mala crawfish, so he ran half a street away to buy some from another stall. When he piled the large platters of meat onto the table, Gu Fei had to ask. "Do you always eat this much?"

Jiang Cheng grabbed a skewer of lamb and took a bite. "There's a reason Xiao-Ming's grandfather lived to a hundred and three."[7]

---

7   "Do you know how Xiao-Ming's grandfather lived to be a hundred and three?" "Because he minded his own business." This is a style of silly joke that's used to tell someone not to be nosy.

Gu Fei chuckled and asked the shopkeeper for a bottle of Red Star erguotou.[8] Jiang Cheng felt the urge to ask if Gu Fei needed booze with every meal, but he was stopped by the memory of Xiao-Ming's hundred-and-three-year-old grandfather.

Gu Miao didn't speak, as usual, and the two boys had nothing to say either. Like the last time they ate barbecue together, they finished their meal in silence. It was pretty nice—Jiang Cheng managed to eat until he was full. Whenever he ate with Pan Zhi, he found himself still hungry by the end of the meal because they ended up talking so much. He typically had to eat another meal after.

The only issue was that the other tables at the barbecue stall were so lively that theirs stood out like a beautiful and quiet sore thumb—even the owner shot them a glance every time he walked past. Maybe people thought that they were here to discuss the terms of a duel, and they might stand up with knives drawn at any moment.

When Gu Miao was done eating and took off her hat to scratch her head, Jiang Cheng finally broke the silence.

"Why'd you buy her a green hat?" he asked Gu Fei. It had been bothering him since he saw Gu Miao at the store the other day.

"She likes the color green," Gu Fei said.

"Oh." Jiang Cheng looked at Gu Miao's green hat. What infallible logic—Gu Fei's answers were always impossible to refute. "It's a miracle you managed to buy a hat in that color."

Gu Miao shook her head.

"Hm?" Jiang Cheng looked at her.

"It wasn't bought," said Gu Fei.

"Hand-knitted?" Jiang Cheng touched the hat. He couldn't tell; it was pretty well made. "Who knitted it for you? Your mom?"

---

8   A colorless liquor made from sorghum. Its twice-distilled process sets it apart from other sorghum-based spirits such as fenjiu. Red Star is one of the most popular brands of erguotou.

Grinning, Gu Miao pointed at Gu Fei.

Jiang Cheng turned sharply to look at him. "The fuck?"

"Language," Gu Fei chided him calmly.

"Oh, right." Jiang Cheng gave Gu Miao a slightly abashed smile, before turning back to Gu Fei. "*You* knitted it? You know how to *knit*?"

"Mm," Gu Fei replied.

The edges of Jiang Cheng's mental image of Gu Fei suddenly went fuzzy: a guy who carried sweets in his pocket, knew how to knit woolen hats, and committed murder—patricide, no less...

After they finished their skewers, Gu Fei hopped onto his bike. Gu Miao unwound the rope tethered to the back of the bike and held it in her hand as she stepped on her skateboard.

"Be...careful." Jiang Cheng really didn't know what else to say.

"See you tomorrow." With that, Gu Fei sped off on his bike, disappearing into the bustling crowd of the narrow street with Gu Miao in tow.

It wasn't until Jiang Cheng had finished paying that he thought: *Tomorrow*? Was today over already?

Obviously not. There were three more periods in the afternoon, and two of those were dedicated to Political Science class. The moment Jiang Cheng saw the schedule, he'd felt a wave of drowsiness.

Gu Fei didn't make an appearance all afternoon. Jiang Cheng really wouldn't see him until tomorrow.

Jiang Cheng lay on his desk and slept the afternoon away. The advantage of Gu Fei's absence was that Zhou Jing didn't keep turning back to speak. It was perfectly quiet.

The Political Science teacher had even less presence than Lao-Xu. This was the most invisible teacher he'd seen today; they had to speak louder and louder as the lesson went on to be heard above the uncontrolled droning murmurs of the class.

During the final period, Pan Zhi texted him.

– No teacher wanted to take self-study period. Niiice

Jiang Cheng glanced at the teacher at the lectern and replied to Pan Zhi.

– It's always niiice here, going to class is like going to the marketplace

– Even when it's quiet, all you do is sleep. I bet the noise is just interfering with your naps

– You don't get it

Jiang Cheng sighed. Pan Zhi really didn't understand. Sure, he often slept in class, but he wasn't always asleep; there were times when he would listen to the lecture with his eyes shut, and during exams season, he never slept through or skipped class. In an environment like Fourth High, he really was a bit worried that his top-student status would lose its value.

When the final bell rang, his class erupted with noise. Almost everyone packed their things instantly. Some left, some chit-chatted; everyone was cheerful.

Jiang Cheng packed his bag and left the classroom. When he reached the walkway outside, he sensed a number of people were watching him. He snuck a glance out of the corner of his eye. Students were leaning against the railing and staring at him; he couldn't tell if they were juniors or seniors, but their eyes were curious and probing.

Tsk.

He turned to look for Wang Xu. That miscreant must've said something—probably bragged about the earlier incident like it was something impressive.

When he got downstairs, his phone rang. He thought it would be Pan Zhi, but when he took it out, he saw that it was an unknown number.

"Hello?" he answered the call.

"Is this Jiang Cheng? You have a package. Please come and collect it."

Jiang Cheng blanked for a moment before reacting. After a couple of clarifying questions, he learned that the call wasn't from a delivery service, but a logistics center—he had to go collect it himself. He asked for their address and where the parcel had come from before hanging up.

His mom had sent it. It was probably the mess of stuff from his room. She had set up a bank account for him before he left, and now she'd mailed his things over. How considerate. She'd gone to all this trouble, yet she hadn't even gotten in touch with him.

Jiang Cheng didn't know whether to thank her or hate her for it.

He didn't feel that bad, though. Over the past few days, he'd started to grow numb to it all. His heart still lurched in his chest whenever he thought about it, but the feeling always passed quickly.

Slowly, he walked back home. At this hour, Li Baoguo would still be out; Jiang Cheng might be alone for dinner again. He pondered over it as he walked and finally decided to just have dumplings—he'd eaten a lot at lunch, so he wasn't that hungry yet.

Near Li Baoguo's place there was a small square surrounded by various eateries. Jiang Cheng had passed by on a walk before—it was quite busy, and there was a dumpling place that looked very clean.

There was an overpass on his way to the square. As he neared the bridge, he glanced up ahead, then paused. The snow had stopped falling around midday; all afternoon, the sun had shone brightly. Now, even though the sun was setting, half the sky was still colored with golden light, spreading like ink in water. Even the little bridge was dyed in warm hues.

For an instant, Jiang Cheng felt his heart at peace. All the misery this chaotic day had brought him dissipated.

He quickened his steps toward the overpass. If he'd been earlier by half an hour, he thought, it would have been even more beautiful. In all the days he'd spent in this crappy little city, this was probably the most beautiful thing he'd seen.

There weren't many pedestrians here. When he approached the middle of the bridge, he saw someone holding a camera, likely to take photos of the bridge and the sky. Just from his profile—no, just from his legs—Jiang Cheng could tell who it was.

Gu Fei.

It wasn't surprising in the least that he could recognize Gu Fei by now. What *was* surprising, however, was that Gu Fei was here after skipping lessons all afternoon, holding a camera bag and what looked like a professional-grade camera. No wonder he didn't want to lend it to Zhou Jing.

Jiang Cheng hesitated, trying to decide whether he should walk over, or cross to the other side and pretend he hadn't seen him. They had nothing to say to each other, anyway.

Before he could take a step, Gu Fei turned in his direction and started walking—he must have finished taking his pictures. Pretending not to see him was now out of the question. Jiang Cheng sighed and walked toward him.

Just as he was about to greet him and force some small talk, Gu Fei caught sight of him, paused, and lifted the camera in his hands. In his surprise, Jiang Cheng didn't have time to block his face with his hand before he heard the shutter go *click*.

Son of a cockeyed calico cat!

Run Wild
SAYE

10

"THE FUCK?! What do you think you're doing?!" Jiang Cheng swore at him—little Gu Miao wasn't here right now, so he didn't give a damn about minding his language.

Gu Fei didn't answer, merely pointing the camera at him and letting the shutter click a few more times. Jiang Cheng figured he'd captured every ugly contortion of his face.

He walked over to Gu Fei, reaching out to grab the camera. "I'm talking to you!"

Gu Fei swiftly pulled it back. "Two hundred and sixty-seven years."

"Huh?" Jiang Cheng blinked. "Two hundred and sixty...what?"

"Two hundred and sixty-seven," Gu Fei repeated.

"What's two hundred and sixty-seven?"

"Xiao-Ming's grandfather."

Jiang Cheng stared at him for a full thirty seconds, partly because he was speechless, partly because he was trying not to laugh.

Finally, he pointed at Gu Fei's camera. "Give me that. Or delete them."

"Why don't you look at them first?"

Gu Fei handed the camera over. Jiang Cheng was nervous as he took it. It was a hefty device—he kept feeling like he might accidentally drop it. He looked at the bevy of buttons, perplexed. Forget deleting the pictures—he didn't even know what button he was supposed to press to *look* at them.

"Here."

Gu Fei reached out and pressed something, and a photo appeared on the screen. There were four in total. Jiang Cheng flipped through each one in silence. He'd never been very interested in photography, whether they were his own photos of scenery or other people's photos of him; he'd rather see the world with the naked eye. And although he usually thought himself rather handsome, he'd always get jump-scared by the front-facing camera on his phone, so he didn't expect his appearance on Gu Fei's camera to be so... *Hmm*.

So much like himself. That was it.

His face wasn't twisted in a scowl like he was worried it would be. He only looked a bit impatient. He actually really liked the first photo. The bleak, chaotic background was a blur, giving it a slightly melancholic feel. It inexplicably brought a phrase to mind: *a home elsewhere*. As for his own figure—pictured walking toward the dying rays of light—there was hardly a need for words. He was spectacularly handsome.

Jiang Cheng flipped through the handful of photos of himself twice. He didn't know what to do.

"The delete button is on the bottom right," Gu Fei said.

"I know," Jiang Cheng replied awkwardly.

He was the one who'd wanted to delete them, but now that he'd looked at them, he didn't want to delete them anymore. After all, he'd never had photos of himself that showed so much character.

Last New Year, his whole family had gone to a studio to take a family photo. He thought it would look good, but when he saw the picture Jiang Cheng almost ripped it up. He'd even fought with his parents and stayed out for two nights over it...

His thoughts were wandering too far. He collected himself and looked at Gu Fei.

"You're pretty photogenic," Gu Fei said. "If you don't mind, I'd like to keep them. I've taken lots of photos of my classmates—I keep all of them."

Gu Fei had given him a very well-timed out. Jiang Cheng hesitated for two seconds. "Why do you take so many photos of people?"

"For fun."

"...Ah." Jiang Cheng nodded. He respected Gu Fei's ability to kill a conversation dead every time. "An amateur photographer."

"Here, let me add you as a contact," Gu Fei said, taking his phone out, "so I can send you a copy when I'm done editing them."

Jiang Cheng wanted to turn him down and say he didn't care. But when he opened his mouth, he found himself nodding and saying, "Sure."

He was still holding the camera, not knowing what else to do. Gu Fei didn't say anything, either, apparently extremely comfortable with the awkward silence.

"Can I look at the other photos?" Jiang Cheng asked. He still couldn't believe that someone like Gu Fei would have such an impressive, professional camera.

"Go ahead," said Gu Fei.

Several of the photos were of the bridge and the sunset. From the way the light hit, it was clear that Gu Fei had been here almost all afternoon. There were a lot of photos—some of scenery, others of people walking along the bridge.

Jiang Cheng didn't really understand photography, but he could tell when a photo looked good. Gu Fei's photos were totally professional. The composition and color balance suffused them with warmth. If he hadn't been standing in the bitter northern wind right now, looking at the photos would have made him feel as if he were sitting next to a radiator, comfortably basking in sunlight.

As he continued flipping through the pictures, he came across photos that must have been taken before today. Many of them were street scenes. There were trees and old buildings, snow piles and stray dogs, fallen leaves and the feet of passersby... The ordinary things you saw every day, yet looked right past.

Just as he began to get a handle on Gu Fei's photography style, he came across a backlit image of Gu Miao in bright sunlight, bending and grabbing her skateboard as she soared through the air. It made Jiang Cheng let out an involuntary "*Oh.*"

Gu Fei was leaning over the bridge rails and smoking; he turned at the sound. "Hm?"

"This photo is really striking. Gu Miao looks so cool." Jiang Cheng turned the photo toward Gu Fei. "Like she's flying through the air."

Gu Fei grinned. "It was a candid shot. She flew like a dozen times, and this was the only shot I caught."

Jiang Cheng gave him another look. Gu Fei was a difficult person to label. He usually seemed as indifferent as a heavenly immortal, an ender of conversations before they began—but when he was with Gu Miao, or whenever anyone mentioned her, he came across very gentle. Like a kind elder.

Jiang Cheng thought of Gu Miao's woolen hat. *The thread in the hand of the kindly brother...*[9]

The mental picture even came with its own background music.

"*Wake up and make love with me, wake up and make love...*"

The music was a bit inappropriate, though.

"Your phone's ringing," Gu Fei said.

---

9   A play on a Tang dynasty poem on maternal love by Meng Jiao, variously translated as "A Traveler's Song," "Wanderer's Song," or "The Song of a Wandering Son." The original verse begins, "The thread in the hand of the kindly mother, the clothes on the back of the traveling son."

"Oh." Jiang Cheng returned the camera to him, digging out his phone with slight embarrassment.

"*Wake up and make love with me...*"

"Oh, Chengcheng?" Li Baoguo's voice exploded in his ear.

"What...did you just call me?" Wave after wave of goosebumps spread over Jiang Cheng's entire body.

Gu Fei must have heard. Though he quickly turned away, Jiang Cheng still caught the shape of laughter on his face.

Damn it.

"You're almost home, right?" Li Baoguo said. "Hurry back. Your brother and sister are home—we're waiting for you to eat dinner!"

"Oh." Jiang Cheng abruptly became despondent. His dumpling plan had fallen through, and he was dragged back to reality once again. Forced to confront people who had almost no chance of crossing his path before—people who were now his *family*—he found his legs suddenly unwilling to move. "Got it," he said.

"You're going home?" Gu Fei asked, putting his camera away.

"Yeah," Jiang Cheng responded.

"Let's go together. I'm heading home, too," Gu Fei said.

"On your bike?" Jiang Cheng asked.

Gu Fei gave him a look. "...I walked."

"Oh." Jiang Cheng turned and started walking.

The temperature dropped dramatically the instant the sun disappeared behind the mountains. They strolled back against the biting northern wind.

Once he'd walked enough to thaw out his body a little, Jiang Cheng turned to glance at Gu Fei. "Do you know Li Baoguo?"

"Everyone knows everyone on those streets, more or less," Gu Fei said. "Grandpas and grandmas, uncles and aunts, brothers and sisters... We're all old neighbors."

"Oh, okay. So...what's he like?" Jiang Cheng asked.

Gu Fei tugged his hat down and turned to him. "Who is he to you?"

Unsure of how exactly to answer, Jiang Cheng pulled the mask from his chin over his mouth and nose. With most of his face covered, he could finally relax a little. "My...birth father," he said.

"Huh? Your birth father?" Gu Fei raised his eyebrows in genuine surprise. "Li Baoguo has two sons? Now that you mention it, though...you do look a little bit like Li Hui."

"I dunno." Jiang Cheng bristled. "That's what they told me, anyway... I asked you what he's like. Could you just answer the question?"

"Seasoned gambler," Gu Fei answered, blunt. "Professional alcoholic."

Jiang Cheng's steps paused.

"Want to hear more?" Gu Fei asked.

"What else is there?" Jiang Cheng sighed softly.

"Abuser. Beat his wife 'til she ran away." Gu Fei looked contemplative for a moment. "That's all the important stuff, I think."

"It's enough on its own." Jiang Cheng furrowed his brow, but after a moment's hesitation, he turned to stare at Gu Fei again. "Is that all true?"

Gu Fei laughed. "You don't believe me?"

"All these neighborhood rumors are kinda..." Jiang Cheng didn't finish his sentence. *The neighborhood also says you killed your own father*. But he couldn't say that out loud. Whether he killed him or not, Gu Fei's father was dead.

"Those aren't rumors," Gu Fei said. "You go home every day. You have to notice he plays mahjong."

"Right."

Suddenly, Jiang Cheng didn't want to talk anymore.

They walked in silence all the way to the corner of the street. Gu Fei headed down the road that took him home. Jiang Cheng didn't even have it in him to say goodbye—but Gu Fei didn't say anything, either.

Jiang Cheng tugged at his mask and walked in the direction of Li Baoguo's house. Still a distance away, he could already hear people arguing. It sounded like a vicious fight, and a co-ed group battle at that.

As he got a little closer, he could make out that it was coming from the building next to Li Baoguo's. A man and a woman stood downstairs, and another man and woman were looking out the window from the second floor. He couldn't tell the reason for the argument, but members of both teams were cussing each other out with great dedication, every word perfectly enunciated. Various reproductive organs and indescribable scenarios were spat out, with some of the vocabulary recycled from time to time. Just listening to it made Jiang Cheng embarrassed for them.

When he reached the entrance to the building, the man on the second floor suddenly appeared at the window with a basin. Jiang Cheng took one look and immediately leaped to the side as the basinful of water—complete with vegetable leaves—came pouring down.

Although it didn't land directly on his head, Jiang Cheng still got drenched. Disgust surged so violently through him that it almost busted the mask right off of his face.

"Are you crazy?! Bunch of morons!" he bellowed. "Go outside to fight, you cowards! Or did you max out your stats on being fucking Karens?!"

Jiang Cheng didn't look around after he shouted at them, he simply turned and walked into the building. He didn't know if they were stunned by his outburst or simply didn't understand what he shouted at them. All he knew was that both parties exchanged some more curses at a lower volume, and then the fight abruptly ended.

Jiang Cheng tried to shake the water from his clothes, along with a few leaves the size of his fingernail. *Fuck!*

Just when he'd fished his keys out, Li Baoguo's front door opened. He stuck his head out, his expression full of mirth. "Was that you just then?"

"What?" Jiang Cheng growled, irate.

"Well said," Li Baoguo said with a laugh. "You sure are my son!"

Jiang Cheng walked inside without responding to that remark. The house was just as wretched as always, but it was a bit livelier today. The table was covered with various dishes, and the two men, two women, and three children sitting around the tiny living room filled it to its limit.

"Here, Chengcheng." Li Baoguo shut the door and came over, throwing an affectionate arm over his shoulder. "Let me introduce you."

Jiang Cheng loathed being hugged or patted by people he didn't know well. He had to grit his teeth to resist shoving him away.

"This is your brother, Li Hui. He's the eldest." Li Baoguo pointed at a man who looked twenty-six or twenty-seven, and then at the young woman sitting next to him. "That's your sister-in-law, and those two are your nephews... Come here and say hello to your uncle!"

The two boys watching TV nearby looked round in unison to give them a glance, and then immediately turned back. It was as if they hadn't heard him at all.

"Hey, you brats! I told you to say hello!" Li Baoguo roared. But this time, the two children didn't even turn round. "You..."

Li Baoguo jabbed a finger in their direction. He clearly had more words to say, but he seemed uncertain what exactly those words were.

"It's fine. They don't know me." Jiang Cheng patted Li Baoguo's arm. All he wanted was to escape Li Baoguo's barking shouts and flying spit as soon as possible—not to mention the arm on his shoulders turning his entire body rigid.

"You boys will get it from me later!" Li Baoguo shouted. He then pointed to another woman. "This is your sister, Li Qian, and your brother-in-law... Here's your niece. Greet your uncle!"

"Uncle." A little girl of about four or five called out to him in a tiny voice, sounding frightened.

Jiang Cheng forced a smile. "Hi."

Li Baoguo finally let go of him. Citing a need to get changed, Jiang Cheng rushed into his room and closed the door. He leaned against it, shutting his eyes.

From the moment he entered the apartment, not a single person in that room had shown a smile except Li Baoguo. When Li Baoguo dragged him through the introductions, everyone only nodded; no one said a word. Their indifference didn't feel personal, and it didn't seem to come from any particular displeasure, either. Instead, it was what seemed to be an inborn numbness, with a trace of blank confusion.

It was more terrifying, more suffocating, than simple hostility. Just a minute or two of it was enough to choke Jiang Cheng; it felt like he couldn't breathe. He took his coat off and braced himself against the wall, taking sharp, deep breaths in. He exhaled slowly, then inhaled, then exhaled slowly again. Finally, he let out a small sigh.

He couldn't even count how many times he'd sighed over the past few days. He'd probably sighed enough air to fill one of those big party balloons.

After a few minutes alone in his room, Jiang Cheng heard Li Baoguo holler for him outside. He had no choice but to scrub his face with his hand, open the door, and walk out.

Everyone was already seated around the table, including the two TV-watching brats. In fact, they'd begun to eat, reaching their hands directly into the plates to grab ribs and chew on them.

"Come eat," Li Qian said, stretching out her hand to pick up the bowl in front of Jiang Cheng.

"Thanks, I'll do it myself." Jiang Cheng quickly took the bowl. "You keep eating."

"Let her fill your bowl," Li Baoguo said from his corner. "That's a woman's job."

Jiang Cheng was taken aback. Li Qian took the bowl out of his hand and went over to the pot of rice to fill it.

"Come on, we should drink the good stuff tonight." Li Baoguo picked up two bottles of liquor from the floor—probably brought by Li Qian or Li Hui—but before Jiang Cheng could see what they were, he opened the cabinet next to them and put the bottles in, then retrieved a different bottle from it. "Rosehip wine. I fermented it myself!"

Li Hui wasn't keen on it. "Let's just drink the two bottles Li Qian brought," he said. "You keep offering that crappy wine like it's some kind of ambrosia. It just tastes like dishwater."

"Ha!" Li Baoguo placed the bottle on the table. "Don't think your old man's wine is good enough? Why didn't you bring any drinks yourself, then? You came home empty-handed, and you have the gall to be picky?"

"Dad, what are you saying?" Li Hui's wife said in a deeply dissatisfied tone. "Your son comes home to visit, and all you think about is whether he brought you anything?"

"Shut up!" Li Baoguo glared at her. "Since when do women have a say in this household?!"

"So what if I'm a woman?!" Li Hui's wife raised her voice. "Without *this* woman, do you think you'd have two grandsons to carry on your family name? Where would you get them from, your *daughter*? She can't even pop out a single grandson for her husband's family!"

Jiang Cheng was appalled—appalled that this family could start a fight in two sentences, shocked that they would fight at a family dinner meant to foster some semblance of harmony, and absolutely stunned that Li Qian and her husband stayed silent the whole time.

"I have grandsons because I have a son!" Li Baoguo's yelling was so loud that it threatened to shatter the decrepit lamp above his head. "Now I have another son! If I want more grandsons, I'll have them! Li Hui, are you a man or not? This is how your wife acts, and you can't even say a word?!"

"What's the big deal?!" Li Hui slammed his chopsticks down and stood up; it wasn't clear whether he was talking to his wife or Li Baoguo.

"You're asking me? Don't you know what we're fighting about?!" his wife shrieked.

As soon as she screamed, the two brats—who had been grabbing food with their hands and raising it to their faces in unison—wailed at the same time, their voices as shrill as a police siren. It was a total headache.

Jiang Cheng stood, turned, and went back to his room, shutting the door.

The fight continued outside. Male bellows and female shouts and the cries of children—the lousy door couldn't block out the awful noises at all.

Behind that thin wooden plank of a door was his *real* family. They stressed him out, and they probably would have still stressed him out if they were just characters on a TV show. They were the kind of people he had always disdained—not even disdain; they were the kind of people he would never have noticed to begin with.

If he'd grown up here for the past seventeen years, would he have ended up just like them? His temper, so quick that it could flare from a single touch, and his drawn-out rebellious phase—were they hereditary? Was it all written in his genes?

Maybe his rebellious phase wasn't a phase. Maybe it was a terrifying part of his very nature.

Someone rapped gently on the door behind him. Outside, the voices continued to argue; he even heard someone kick a chair over. If he hadn't been leaning against the door, he wouldn't have heard the soft knock at all.

From outside came Li Qian's voice, just as softly: "Jiang Cheng?"

After a few seconds of hesitation, he turned and cracked the door ajar to look at Li Qian, who was standing there rather anxiously.

"Are you okay?" she asked.

"I'm fine," Jiang Cheng replied. He should've been asking Li Qian if *she* was okay.

"Um..." Li Qian took a glance back at the turmoil unfolding behind her. "Do you want me to bring you some food so you can eat in your room?"

"No, thanks," Jiang Cheng said. "I'm...not hungry."

Li Qian didn't say anything more. Jiang Cheng closed the door again and locked it.

After standing aimlessly in his room for a while, he walked to the window, grabbed the handle, and twisted it. The window didn't budge.

From the day he'd arrived, he wanted to open this window, but he never succeeded. It was sealed tight, practically welded in place. He couldn't even open it by a sliver. He grabbed the handle and twisted violently again, then began to push. He started to sweat from exertion, but he still couldn't manage to get it open.

Glowering at the window and listening to the chaos out in the living room, he felt something about to explode within himself. He reached behind him, picked up a chair, and flung it hard at the glass.

It hit the window pane with a deafening bang.

The sound gave Jiang Cheng a great sense of satisfaction. Every hair on his body stood on end. He picked the chair back up and threw it again, shattering the glass and sending it scattering all over the floor.

As he steadily smashed the window, the shouting match in the living room turned into banging on his door. He couldn't be bothered to listen to it.

Once the pane was completely destroyed, he aimed a foot at the now-empty window frame and kicked it hard.

The window opened.

There was the sound of a key in the door behind him. Bracing one hand against the windowsill, he jumped out.

Fuck you, and fuck this "birth family."

Run Wild
SAYE

11

T HE INSTANT HE LEAPED OUT the window, the winter
wind filled his lungs and rushed into his pores, permeating
his entire body.

It was *satisfying.*

As the shattered glass crunched beneath his feet, Jiang Cheng felt
that suffocating feeling finally disappear.

The sky outside was completely dark now. There were no
streetlamps, and who knew where the moon had gone. The only
illumination came from the weak light filtering out of the windows
of various homes. He could vaguely make out that he was at the
butt-end of these buildings, and in front of him was a large blanket
of snow that hadn't been cleared away.

Jiang Cheng took his phone out of his pants pocket and turned
the screen on. With the faint glow lighting the way, he trudged
through the snow with uneven footsteps, walking around the back
of the buildings until he reached the end of the street.

Ahead was a small factory building. The road ended here. He
stopped, standing in the darkness. After his fit of rage, he'd managed
to slowly calm down in the cold wind. Now, he was at a bit of a loss.

Where should he go?

What should he do?

He had no destination, no goal.

He looked down at the clock on his phone, mulling over what to do next. It was too fucking cold; he forgot to put on his jacket before he jumped out.

There was a smudge on his phone screen. He wiped it with a finger, but instead of removing the smudge, it added another. He couldn't see what it was through the darkness. He could only feel slight moisture on his fingers.

He reacted quickly, shining his phone screen at his finger.

Blood.

"Oh, shit," he whispered.

It was a little terrifying to see his hand covered in blood. It was so cold that his hand had gone numb; he didn't feel any pain. He had to search for a while before he found the source: a cut on his palm. It was deep, and the blood was still gushing out.

Jiang Cheng rummaged through both of his pants pockets, but he couldn't find anything to stem the flow, not even a tissue. He had no choice but to pull up a corner of his sweater and press it hard against his palm. It was cold, but not cold enough to freeze his wound over.

...Oh yeah, it was fucking freezing. And he didn't even have a jacket.

Fucking hell!

For the first time since he'd jumped out of the window, Jiang Cheng felt the icy chill permeate him to the bone—it was a rude awakening. He had no jacket, no money, and a wound that wouldn't stop bleeding.

Roughly guessing at a direction, he ran down a path to the next street. Li Baoguo had mentioned that the community clinic was that way; he could get someone to bandage it for him while he warmed up. He ran a few steps, then, unable to stand the cold any longer, switched from a run to a skipping gait—he could barely feel the warmth of his own breath anymore. It was just too fucking cold!

Li Baoguo had said the clinic wasn't obvious from the outside. He wasn't wrong. "Not obvious" was putting it mildly; Jiang Cheng had already run past when he noticed it. It wasn't even lit.

...Not even lit? He froze. The lights...were off!

He had to go right up to the door to see the sign hanging on it. He was so cold that even his eyes were shivering, and only with great effort could he make out, barely, that the doctor had gone home for dinner.

"...No way!"

He knocked on the door. There was no response.

A phone number was included on the sign, but he didn't call it. He figured that by the time the doctor answered the call and returned, he would have frozen to death on the spot.

Frowning, he turned to look around. Gu Fei's store was about fifteen feet from here, brightly lit.

He hated the idea of Gu Fei seeing him in such a pathetic state again, but...it was just too damn cold!

Jiang Cheng hopped over and pulled the door open, pushing the heavy leather curtain aside with one hand. Warmth rushed at him head-on, banishing the cramping stiffness from his body with a surge of instant relaxation. But the next moment, he stilled again, slightly embarrassed. He didn't know why, but every time he entered Gu Fei's store, he ended up feeling awkward.

The space where Fresh Out of Jail had been loitering last time he was here was now occupied by a small table. On it was a crackling electric stove, with a steaming pot of...mutton soup, from the smell of it. Gu Fei was filling a bowl for Gu Miao. A woman who looked to be in her twenties stood nearby, directly facing the door.

Aside from the age difference, they looked like a family of three. Jiang Cheng felt like his arrival was extremely ill-timed.

"What—" Gu Fei startled when he turned and saw Jiang Cheng. "What happened to you?"

"Can you not ask?" Jiang Cheng said. "I was just...passing by."

"A friend of yours?" the woman asked Gu Fei.

"Yeah." Gu Fei stood and walked over to Jiang Cheng, his gaze landing on his wounded hand.

The woman stood as well. "What—"

"First aid kit," Gu Fei said, turning to her.

"Right." She strode quickly into the smaller room.

Gu Miao was still sitting at the table, unmoving. She gripped her spoon, her eyes very wide as she watched them nervously. Jiang Cheng noticed Gu Fei move slightly to one side, blocking Gu Miao's line of sight. Hurriedly, he hid his hand behind his body.

"Go inside," Gu Fei told him.

Jiang Cheng marched into the smaller room, where the woman had taken out a first aid kit. Seeing him come in, she asked quietly, "Your hand?"

"Yeah," Jiang Cheng answered. "The clinic next door..."

"The doctor's having dinner right now," the woman said. "Is it serious? I'll help you clean it up a little—I can disinfect it."

"It's not serious." Jiang Cheng glanced at the first aid kit. It was quite well-stocked. "I can do it myself."

"Won't be an easy task with one hand," the woman said with a smile. "It'll be faster if I help you."

"Knife wound?" Gu Fei asked as he walked in.

"No." Jiang Cheng hesitated, then loosened his tight hold on his sweater. Even he was shocked when he released his hand: There was a massive bloodstain on its hem.

"You..." Gu Fei frowned at his hand and looked at the sweater. "Maybe I should do it," he said to the woman.

"It's fine. A small cut like this can't scare me." The woman laughed and pushed him. "Go keep Er-Miao company. She looked pretty nervous just now."

"...Okay." Gu Fei hesitated, then turned to walk out. But after two steps, he paused again and turned back to introduce the two of them. "My classmate, Jiang Cheng. This is Ding Zhuxin, my big sister."

"Just call me Xin-jie,"[10] Ding Zhuxin chuckled. She pulled Jiang Cheng's hand closer. "Let me see. The cut looks pretty deep..."

"Does it?"

Zhuxin..."bamboo heart"? It wasn't much of a name, considering bamboo was hollow.

Jiang Cheng was baffled by the literary romanticism of his own musings today.

"I'll rinse it with saline first," said Ding Zhuxin. "Then I'll put iodine on it."

Jiang Cheng nodded. "Okay. Thank you."

Ding Zhuxin smiled. "Don't mention it."

It was very warm in the room, so Jiang Cheng warmed up quickly. However, as his body thawed, the wound seemed to wake up with it, the pain boring into his hand. As Ding Zhuxin cleaned his hand of blood, he realized his wound really wasn't just a small cut.

"Got cut with glass, huh," she said. "That was careless of you."

Jiang Cheng didn't reply.

Gu Fei's sister...with the surname Ding? Did she take their mother's surname? Furthermore, although Ding Zhuxin was very pretty—her complexion was so fair it was almost translucent, and

---

10   Term of address for an older sister, or a woman close enough to be referred to as a sister.

from this angle, her long, thick lashes obscured her eyes almost completely—she looked nothing like Gu Fei or Gu Miao.

"You're Gu Fei's sister?" he asked.

"Not his biological sister." Ding Zhuxin laughed. "He just calls me jiejie. I used to live upstairs from him."

Jiang Cheng smiled. "Oh."

"I watched him grow up. He always used to follow me around as a kid." Ding Zhuxin applied the iodine for him, then wrapped the wound with gauze from the first aid kit. "That's all I can do for now—wrap it up. You can have the doctor take a look at it later."

"Thank you." Jiang Cheng stood.

"What's with all the thank-yous?" Ding Zhuxin packed the first aid kit away. "Da-Fei never thanks me when I clean his wounds."

How rude of him, Jiang Cheng thought, but after a moment's consideration, he figured she and Gu Fei were probably just too close for that. Though Ding Zhuxin and Gu Fei had barely spoken to each other since he came in, he could sense they had a very close relationship. What was more, when Ding Zhuxin turned, Jiang Cheng saw the little musical note adorning her earlobe...

Sister? Tsk, tsk.

Who would have thought Gu Fei was into that sort of thing? This woman was at least four or five years older than him!

"You're Da-Fei's classmate, huh?" Ding Zhuxin said. "I don't think I've seen you around before... Although he doesn't hang around his classmates that much anyway."

"I just transferred here," Jiang Cheng said.

Ding Zhuxin studied him. "I see."

"You done?" Gu Fei pushed the door open.

"Done," Ding Zhuxin said. "He can go have it looked at when Dr. Zhang comes back."

"Is the cut deep?" Gu Fei asked.

"It's just a graze—how deep could it be?" Jiang Cheng said.

Gu Fei glanced outside. "Er-Miao wants me to ask if Cheng-ge's eaten."

"...Not yet," Jiang Cheng answered rather morosely.

"Just in time for you to eat together, then," Ding Zhuxin said. As she walked out, her hand rested very naturally on Gu Fei's shoulder. "I was just saying I bought too much lamb for the two of them to finish tonight."

Jiang Cheng hesitated for a moment before whispering, "Won't I be in the way?"

"In the way of what?" Gu Fei didn't understand, but he subconsciously lowered his voice as well.

"Um..." Jiang Cheng's eyes flitted swiftly over Ding Zhuxin's back. "Your *sister*."

For a moment, Gu Fei looked stunned. Then he leaned against the door frame, with a smile dancing at the corners of his lips. "Oh."

Jiang Cheng looked at him. "Oh?"

"You won't be in the way. Er-Miao's here too, isn't she?" Gu Fei entered the room and took a sweater from the closet. He chucked it on the bed. "Get changed. She gets scared."

After Gu Fei left, Jiang Cheng picked up the sweater. It looked like it was about his size, so he changed into it. He looked down and examined the sweater for a moment. This wasn't knitted by Gu Fei himself, was it...?

"Need a hand?" Gu Fei called from outside.

"No!" he answered in a hurry, folding the sweater he'd taken off and leaving it on a nearby chair.

The moment he walked out of the room, he breathed in the heavy aroma of mutton soup that filled the store. All at once, Jiang

Cheng was so hungry that he could feel his heart pounding in his chest.

"Smells good, doesn't it?" Ding Zhuxin filled another bowl.

"Yeah." Jiang Cheng walked over and sat by the small table.

"It's the first time I've seen Er-Miao ask anyone to stay for dinner. I was only away for two months, and she's made so much progress." Ding Zhuxin picked up two pieces of lamb and added them to Gu Miao's bowl. "You must've moved here a while ago, right, Jiang Cheng? Was it last semester?"

"This semester," Jiang Cheng said.

"Oh." Ding Zhuxin studied him for a few more seconds before smiling and putting a bowl of soup in front of him. "That's surprising."

Meanwhile, Gu Miao kept sneaking peeks at Jiang Cheng's bandaged hand as she ate.

"It's fine now." Gu Fei grabbed Jiang Cheng's hand and put it in front of her. "See?"

Jiang Cheng's wound was on his right hand. His grip on his chopsticks was already shaky to begin with; when Gu Fei suddenly grabbed him, the chopsticks flew out of his grasp and clattered to the floor.

Lightly and very carefully, Gu Miao touched the bandage around his palm.

"Let go." Ding Zhuxin swatted Gu Fei's hand and picked the chopsticks up. "He's injured. Why'd you have to grab him so hard?"

Gu Fei reached out for the chopsticks. "I'll wash them."

Jiang Cheng made to get up. "I'll—"

"Sit, both of you. I'm not eating, anyway." Ding Zhuxin rose and walked out the back door.

"She's not?" Jiang Cheng was taken aback. Noticing the three sets of bowls and chopsticks at the table, he was instantly abashed.

What if three sets were all they had, and there weren't enough to go round because of him?

"She doesn't eat at night—hasn't for years now." Gu Fei handed him his own chopsticks. "I haven't used these yet."

"No rush," Jiang Cheng said.

"No?" Gu Fei turned to look at him. "I thought you were so hungry your eyes were going square."

"Oh, fuck off."

Jiang Cheng accepted his chopsticks and picked up a piece of lamb, putting it in his mouth. He really must have been famished. This lamb was easily one of the top three most delicious things he'd eaten in the past two years.

When Ding Zhuxin returned and saw the chopsticks in Jiang Cheng's hand, she froze for a moment before putting the washed pair in front of Gu Fei. Softly, she said, "I'm heading off."

"Okay." Gu Fei stood and fetched her jacket from behind the counter.

Jiang Cheng stood up as well and forced himself to find something to say. "Won't you eat a little? It's...really good." He felt even more awkward.

"You guys go ahead. Eat up." Ding Zhuxin chuckled and put on her jacket. "I'm on a diet."

"Oh." Jiang Cheng hesitated, then sat back down. Gu Miao pointed at the lamb in the pot, and he nodded. "I'll get some for you."

Gu Miao pointed at his empty bowl.

"I'm...not in a hurry." Jiang Cheng was a little embarrassed. He was so hungry that even the little girl could tell. To show her he really wasn't in any rush, he forced himself to look around at Gu Fei and Ding Zhuxin.

"Keys." Ding Zhuxin stretched her hand out at Gu Fei.

"Isn't it cold?" Gu Fei dug the motorcycle keys out of his pocket.

"I was racing when you were finishing elementary school, kid." Ding Zhuxin took the keys and turned around to walk out through the curtains. Gu Fei followed her to the door and looked out, then came back to sit.

An inexplicable sense of relief washed over Jiang Cheng after Ding Zhuxin left. It was the first time he'd ever felt such intense awkwardness around a girl. Ding Zhuxin was very pretty, the sort of beauty that was neither ostentatious nor aggressive—normally, he'd look twice if he saw someone like that on the street.

He took another piece of lamb. His hand still hurt; when he picked the meat up, he didn't dare use much force. He held himself like he was disarming a bomb, afraid a single tremble of his hand would fling a piece of lamb onto the table.

Gu Fei brought over a slotted spoon and reached straight to the bottom of the pot with it, retrieving a large portion of meat. He held it out to Jiang Cheng. "I'm tired of watching you."

"Thanks." Jiang Cheng shoveled half the meat into his own bowl, then grabbed Gu Miao's and pushed the rest into hers.

"How did you hurt your hand?" Gu Fei asked.

Jiang Cheng didn't reply. He really didn't know how to tell the story. Gu Fei probably knew what Li Baoguo's family was like; if Jiang Cheng told him, it would only be more gossip fodder—even if Gu Fei didn't look like the kind of guy who gossiped.

He fell silent for a moment. "I bit myself."

Gu Miao stared at him. After a moment, she grinned.

Gu Fei nodded. "Nice teeth you got there," he said. "You should value yourself more—go easy on the bite next time."

Jiang Cheng smiled at Gu Miao and lowered his head to slurp up the soup.

"Are you heading back later?" Gu Fei asked.

This time, Jiang Cheng's answer was quick and decisive. "No."

"You got somewhere to stay?" Gu Fei reached into the little basket of vegetables next to them and put two stalks of leafy greens into the pot to blanch.

"Yeah." After that, Jiang Cheng paused. After almost two whole minutes of silence, he opened his lips again with great difficulty. "Do you have cash? Can you lend me some?"

"How much?" Gu Fei put his chopsticks down.

Jiang Cheng thought for a moment. "Five hundred yuan. I can transfer the amount to you on my phone right now."

"No worries." Gu Fei took out his wallet and fished out the bills.

"Thank you." Once he took the cash, Jiang Cheng felt much more secure. As he got his phone out, he said, "Add me on WeChat. I'll pay you back."

"Actually, if you turn right at the corner and walk about two hundred yards, there's a small side street that ends at a HomeInn budget hotel." Gu Fei tapped on his phone a few times. "It won't cost five hundred."

Jiang Cheng watched him wordlessly, then picked his bowl up to drink a mouthful of soup. Although Gu Fei hadn't guessed wrong—there was no way he could have, since Jiang Cheng had no other option but to stay at a hotel—it was humiliating to hear it said out loud.

His phone dinged. He glanced down at the screen to see Gu Fei's friend request: *Good Little Bunny*.[11] The display name almost made him spray a mouthful of broth onto the phone.

He turned the phone toward Gu Fei. "This you?"

---

11   Reference to a nursery rhyme where the Big Bad Wolf sings, "Good Little Bunny, open the door, hurry and open up, I want to come in," and the Good Little Bunny answers, "No, no, no, I won't open the door. Mommy hasn't come home. I won't open for anyone."

"Yeah. Cute, huh?" said Gu Fei, unfazed.

"...Very." Jiang Cheng was at a loss for words. He approved the friend request and glanced at Gu Fei's profile picture. It fit his display name well: a green rabbit. Judging from the color and technique, the artist was probably Gu Miao. "Did Gu Miao draw this?"

Next to them, Gu Miao nodded.

"It's...really good," Jiang Cheng expressed his extremely insincere praise. Gu Miao's artistic talent fell behind her skateboarding skills by at least seven hundred and twenty-four of Xiao-Ming's grandfather's lifespans.

As he was about to transfer the money to Gu Fei, there was a sound from the front door. Someone had opened it, then pushed the curtains apart by a crack. Finding it a bit odd, Jiang Cheng glanced over. It was completely normal to buy things at this hour, so why did they peel the curtains back like they were sneaking a peek...?

Before he could figure it out, Gu Fei had tossed his phone onto the table and jumped to his feet.

"Huh?" Jiang Cheng said blankly, still holding his phone up as he watched Gu Fei rush out to...catch a thief?

Normally, he didn't shove his nose where it didn't belong—he'd probably have no trouble living to a hundred and three—but he was at Gu Fei's place right now. Since Gu Fei had run out, he couldn't possibly stay seated. He rose to follow.

He thought of telling Gu Miao to stay put, but when he looked down, she was eating with her head bowed as if nothing was going on.

"I'm going to have a look," he told her, then turned and sprinted out.

The moment he set foot outside the store, he saw Gu Fei grasping the collar of a man who was frantically trying to break free.

The glow from the shabby streetlamp obfuscated more than it illuminated. All he could tell was that the man was roughly thirty years old, dressed in a trashy leather jacket, with pants stuck so tightly to his slender legs that they looked like a pair of toothpicks—it was an off-putting sight.

"What are you doing?! Let go!" The man was desperately grappling with Gu Fei's hand, but he was clearly no match for him, neither in height nor strength. Though he flailed for quite some time, Gu Fei didn't even budge. All the man could do was yell again, "Let me go!"

"Didn't I tell you not to let me see your face again?" Gu Fei asked, his voice low.

"Who do you think you are? What do I care what you say? So what if you did?" The man stuck his face provokingly close to Gu Fei's. "I'm here right now. You see me, don't you? Well, now what? You—"

But before he could tack another question onto his existing stream of questions, Gu Fei grabbed him by the scruff of his neck and flung him against a tree. The man slammed against the tree trunk face-first, as if he weighed no more than a rag doll.

BANG!

Jiang Cheng felt his eyes widen like saucers at the sound. He never knew the impact of a human body striking wood could make such a loud noise.

After the bang, the world fell silent.

The man stayed upright against the tree for two seconds, then slipped slowly down to his knees before tipping to the side, falling flat and motionless.

"Holy fuck!" Jiang Cheng took two steps in his direction. Was he dead? He stared for a while, but the man didn't move. Jiang Cheng turned to look at Gu Fei, dumbstruck for a long moment.

The man was thin and not very tall, but he was still a grown man. And Gu Fei threw him against a tree with just one swing of his arm—even a slow-motion replay of it would last two or three seconds at the most...

Jiang Cheng felt a sudden chill run down his spine. With moves like that, it was entirely plausible that Gu Fei could have killed someone before.

"Get inside." Gu Fei glanced at him, then started walking back to the store. "Aren't you cold?"

"Who was *that*?" Jiang Cheng exclaimed, having recovered his wits. "You're just going to leave him there? What if he freezes to death?"

"Then I'll just kill you." Gu Fei laughed. "No witnesses that way."

Run Wild
SAYE

12

J IANG CHENG THOUGHT of himself as kind of a delinquent. He'd always been the guy who skipped classes, got into fights, and generally caused trouble. Still, he'd never knocked someone out and left them unconscious in the snow while he went back inside to eat.

"Hey." He followed Gu Fei into the store and stared as Gu Fei plopped back down on his chair. It was hard to speak openly in front of Gu Miao, so he could only hint at it. "Are you really just going to leave...*that*?"

"Don't worry, it's fine. He'll get up and leave on his own soon enough. The most he'll need is a nose job..." Gu Fei gave him a look. "I didn't realize you were so compassionate. I didn't see you worrying like this when you ran into Monkey and his crew."

"Did I..." Jiang Cheng pointed at the door and searched for ages for the right words, "put them to sleep, though?"

Gu Fei looked at him without saying a word, obviously struggling to keep a straight face.

"Fine." Jiang Cheng sat down. "It's not my problem, anyway."

Gu Fei put his head down and continued eating. Jiang Cheng didn't say anything else either, though he really wasn't sure the guy outside could "get up," much less "leave on his own."

Maybe it was the difference in environment. Where he grew up, no matter how much he misbehaved, there was a line he knew not to cross. But for Gu Fei, in this shitty old city surrounded by shitty people, maybe nobody cared about this sort of thing at all. Now that he thought about it, he was grateful to Gu Fei for not letting him freeze to death when he "went to sleep" in the snow outside the other day.

He was getting used to eating in silence with this pair of siblings. It was the same as both times before: Gu Miao didn't speak, he himself had nothing to say, and Gu Fei seemed like he didn't want to talk at all.

Eating like this saved a lot of time. They were done in ten minutes.

When he put his chopsticks down, about to say *thank you*, a stream of bitter curses rolled in from outside. It sounded like Sleeping Ugly had woken up. Jiang Cheng sighed in relief at the noise.

It sounded like swearing took a great effort for the man, probably because his nose was broken, and maybe some other bones too. He spoke in the same style as Li Baoguo's neighbors had earlier—perhaps it was part of the neighborhood's cultural heritage.

However, one especially loud and jarring line in his rant made Jiang Cheng immediately turn his eyes toward Gu Fei.

The man's words were a bit slurred, but still audible: "So I fucked your mother, so what?!"

Gu Fei met Jiang Cheng's eyes, then drank a spoonful of soup before saying, "My mother's boyfriend—"

"What?" Jiang Cheng's jaw dropped enough to fit two pounds of lamb inside—he didn't even wait for Gu Fei to finish. That man *did* look revolting, but he was only about thirty. Even if Gu Fei's mother had had him at the age of twenty, she'd be nearing forty now.

"*One of* her boyfriends," Gu Fei amended.

"Huh?" Jiang Cheng was stunned.

"Done eating?" Gu Fei asked. "There's more meat. If you're still hungry, I'll add it to the pot."

"Oh yes, I'm done," Jiang Cheng said with a hurried nod.

Gu Fei put his chopsticks down. "Er-Miao, clean up."

Gu Miao stood at once. She stacked the rice bowls with a practiced hand and grabbed all the chopsticks in one go, then carried them out the back door. Jiang Cheng felt a wave of displeasure at the sight. He thought of Li Baoguo saying *that's a woman's job,* and reached out to help with the clean-up.

"Sit." Gu Fei stopped him. "She can clean up."

"Because it's a woman's job, huh?" Jiang Cheng glared at him out of the corner of his eye.

A little surprised, Gu Fei laughed. "Did I say that?"

"Not everything needs to be said out loud." Remembering the chaos in Li Baoguo's household, Jiang Cheng's ire began to threaten his hard-won calm.

"I," Gu Fei said, pointing to himself, "cook."

Jiang Cheng looked at him.

"Gu Er-Miao," Gu Fei said, pointing at Gu Miao as she returned through the back door, "washes the dishes."

Jiang Cheng continued to look at him.

"Anything wrong with that?" Gu Fei asked.

"Oh." Jiang Cheng stared, the flames of his ire morphing into embarrassment.

"Oh?" Gu Fei stared right back.

"...Oh." Jiang Cheng really didn't know what else to say.

Gu Fei didn't pay him any more attention. He rose to his feet and walked away, parking himself behind the cash register and lighting a cigarette. Jiang Cheng wanted to leave, but his good manners prevented him from leaving right after a meal at someone else's house; all he could do was sit at the table and watch as Gu Miao cleared everything away in two or three trips.

Just as he was about to ask Gu Fei for a cigarette, Gu Fei stood up, still smoking, and followed Gu Miao out the back door.

...Which left him alone in the store, spacing out at the empty table.

Fuck.

He took his phone out and texted Pan Zhi.

- Grandson.

- Gramps! Up for a chat?

- busy

Pan Zhi sent him a voice message. "Don't you have anything better to do than fuck with me? I just got an earful from my mom—she won't even let me eat dinner!"

Jiang Cheng burst out laughing. He sent a voice message in reply: a full twenty seconds of laughter. After that, he rose to his feet, deciding to go out back and see what the two siblings were up to. If there was nothing else to do, he would take his leave.

Outside the back door was a small courtyard. It seemed to be a common space shared by the shops beside them—it had a bathroom and a small kitchen. The wind slapped Jiang Cheng in the face the moment he set foot outside. He hurried over to the kitchen.

Gu Fei had his back to the door. Gu Miao stood at the sink, washing the bowls with hot water. The little girl was quite adept at washing dishes; her face was full of focus.

Jiang Cheng watched for a while. He didn't really understand why Gu Fei was just standing there. Gu Miao wasn't a young child anymore; if she was asked to clear the table and wash the dishes, then she could do it on her own. Why stand and watch?

"Um..." Jiang Cheng cleared his throat.

Gu Miao was probably too engrossed in washing. She continued as if she didn't hear him at all.

Gu Fei turned. "Hm?"

"I'm gonna go," Jiang Cheng said. "Do you have any jackets you don't wear? One I can borrow?"

"Nope," Gu Fei said.

"The hell?" Jiang Cheng stared at him. "What do you mean?"

"I only have the ones I wear," Gu Fei said. "The closet in the inner room. Help yourself."

"...Oh. Thanks." Jiang Cheng turned to go inside.

Gu Fei stopped him. "Cheng-ge."

Jiang Cheng paused. It made him feel weird to hear Gu Fei call him "Cheng-ge" the way Gu Miao would, but there was something oddly satisfying about it too—he was tempted to reply, "What's up, kid?"

"Will you stay until she's done washing dishes—so you can say goodbye?" Gu Fei asked.

"All right." Jiang Cheng nodded. "Could you, uh...give me a cigarette?"

Gu Fei dug a pack of cigarettes and a lighter from his pocket and handed them to Jiang Cheng, then went back to watching Gu Miao at the sink. Jiang Cheng retreated to the doorway to light his cigarette as he also watched Gu Miao.

He wasn't too sure, and it didn't seem polite to ask, but maybe Gu Miao wasn't like other children. Maybe Gu Fei had to watch her all the time—even when she did the dishes. Then again, if he was so worried about his little sister, why let her go flying about town on her skateboard all by herself? Why didn't he seem worried even when she was bullied?

A mystery. The people here were all very mysterious.

Sometimes it felt like a hallucination. These streets, these scenes, these people he saw, and the things he came across—it all felt a little surreal. It was only when he was in contact with Pan Zhi that he came back to reality.

Had he traveled to another world? Another time? Another dimension? A pocket universe?

He frightened himself into a shiver.

Gu Fei happened to be looking at him. "You should've just stayed inside."

Jiang Cheng ignored him.

Gu Miao finished washing the bowls and put them away, then turned to leave the kitchen, walking by Jiang Cheng as if she didn't see him at all. Jiang Cheng followed her into the store. Now she began to look for him, and she finally turned and spotted him.

"You're very efficient," Jiang Cheng said, giving her a thumbs-up.

Gu Miao rubbed her nose bashfully.

"Hey." Jiang Cheng bent down to speak to her. "I'm leaving now."

Gu Miao shot a look at Gu Fei, then nodded.

"Goodbye?" Jiang Cheng lifted a hand and waved to her.

Gu Miao waved back, and Jiang Cheng chuckled. He thought he'd get to hear her say goodbye, but the silent movie only continued.

Gu Fei went to the room and brought out a long down parka for him.

"Thanks." Jiang Cheng took the jacket and glanced over it.

"Hat? Gloves? Scarf? Mask?" Gu Fei asked.

"...That's okay," Jiang Cheng said. It was only a few hundred yards away. "How about a charger... Do you have an extra?"

Gu Fei went back to the room and grabbed him a phone charger.

"Thanks." Jiang Cheng put it in his pocket.

"...If someone punched you, would you still say thanks out of habit?" Gu Fei said.

"Why don't you try me?" Jiang Cheng replied. He put the jacket on, pushed the curtain aside, and left.

Gu Fei stretched. He picked up his phone and glanced at the time, then gently patted Gu Miao's head. "C'mon, let's go home."

Gu Miao swiftly shut the windows and doors, then went outside to wait for him, hugging her skateboard. Gu Fei collected the money in the cash register and switched the lights off.

"We're walking home today. Xin-jie took our bike." Gu Fei locked the storefront. "Once we get home, go to your room and do your homework. Don't come out until you're done."

Gu Miao nodded. She put her skateboard on the ground and rushed off with a single kick. A dozen or so yards along, she tripped over something and crashed. Gu Fei laughed and whistled, but Gu Miao ignored him. Climbing to her feet, she got back on the skateboard and dashed off again.

By the time they reached home, it was just past eight. In the living room, both the lights and the TV were on. Their mom's bedroom door was shut, but there was light coming from the crack underneath it.

After Gu Miao retreated to her room to do her homework, Gu Fei went over and knocked on the bedroom door. There was no response.

"I'll give you one minute, then I'm going in," Gu Fei said.

He went to the kitchen and boiled some water. After making himself a cup of tea, he returned to his mother's door and knocked twice, then opened the door. The door wasn't locked from the inside. In fact, she couldn't lock it—he'd broken the lock the last time she'd said she was going to kill herself, and they hadn't fixed it since.

"Get out." His mom sat on a small couch by the window, a phone in her hand. Her eyes flared as she glowered at him. "Get out! Who let you in here?!"

"Are you on the phone with that guy?" Gu Fei raised his voice. "Tell him if he doesn't hang up now, I'll go looking for him tomorrow. When I'm done with him, there'll be nothing left of him or the store he works at."

"You—" Gu Fei's mother rolled her eyes at him and brought the phone to her ear. "Honestly... Hello? Hello? Hey! Son of a bitch!" She slammed the phone viciously down on the couch. "The hell is wrong with you?! Sticking your nose in other people's business—can't you let your mother have a love life? It's not like we have some grand inheritance! You two won't have to fight anyone for it!"

"Out of all your little boyfriends, pick one you can be serious with. Just one." Gu Fei took a sip of tea. "Then ask me if I care."

"Which of them isn't serious?!" His mother frowned. "You're such a pain."

"Which of them *is*?" Gu Fei faced her head-on. "Why don't you stop spending money on them and see if any of them care about you then!"

"Why wouldn't they?!" His mom slapped the couch. "Am I ugly? If I were ugly, would people be calling you handsome all your life?"

"Yeah." Gu Fei took a small mirror from the bedside table and looked at himself. "I *am* handsome."

"You—"

Just as his mother spoke, he cut her off. "Everyone tells me, *your mother was so pretty when she was young*." Gu Fei put down the mirror. "When she *was young*, you know? Now girls who are prettier and younger and dumber than you are a dime a dozen. If you didn't have any money, what guy in his twenties or thirties would want to date a forty-something-year-old—"

"Get out! Out, out!" His mother leapt off the couch and pushed him out the door. "I have nothing to say to you! Get out!"

Gu Fei seized her wrist. "Stop taking money from the cash register. It's not like there's a lot in there; I didn't even need to count to know you took it."

His mom didn't reply. She merely went back into the room and slammed the door.

Gu Fei flopped onto the living room couch. He took two sips of tea, then grabbed the remote control and channel-surfed. There was nothing on at this hour but family soaps, with moms and daughters and brothers-in-law all tearing each other up—either that, or saintly clichéd heroines forgiving their asshole romantic interests and reforming them through the power of love.

He switched off the TV after a few moments and went to his room, where he turned on his computer.

Between doing his homework and editing the photos he'd taken today, he chose the latter without a hint of hesitation. When it came to homework, well... He couldn't write anything decent if he tried, the same way he always failed his exams whether he sat for them or not.

Gu Fei uploaded the photos from his camera onto the computer. First, he deleted the bad ones, then selected the ones worth editing from the remainder.

The ones he'd taken of Gu Miao were all decent. That kid never smiled in photos. Her face was so serious she looked like she was planning to blow up a school—but she looked pretty cool regardless.

The street photos weren't any good—they were too messy, with too much in the background—but the snaps he took of the sunset were all right. The colors of the one with someone in a red coat crossing the bridge were particularly striking... And these photos of Jiang Cheng, Jiang Cheng, Jiang Cheng...

He frowned, comparing them. He saved the first one and deleted the rest.

Putting on his headphones, he listened to music as he began to edit. Photo editing was a finicky business, but he found it interesting—much more interesting than going to class.

His music streaming algorithm had been a bit too aggressive lately—each song on his personal channel was more explosive than the last. As a result, every click of his mouse felt like a mini electric shock, disrupting his flow. He changed the music to his own local playlist. It eased substantially. After shuffling through two songs at random, he heard a familiar guitar chord, followed by the piano notes, and then a female vocal:

Stepping into thin air, about to take flight
I look up and I'm lost, I look down to see your face
And you tell me this world is an empty place...

Gu Fei moved the cursor and clicked on the next song. It'd been a long time, he thought. He hadn't thought so when he wrote it back then, but now it sounded childish. The vocalist was Ding Zhuxin, who understood it perfectly, imbuing her languid, husky voice with notes of doubt and struggle.

When he was finished with Jiang Cheng's photo, he glanced at the time. It was almost eleven. That was time for you—never there when you needed it, but impossible to get rid of when you didn't.

He stretched as he looked at Jiang Cheng's face filling the screen. The light was just right, as was the hue. The young man's expression of disdain was perfect, and the way his eyes didn't quite meet the camera... Compared to the model he'd practiced photographing before—the one Ding Zhuxin spent real money on hiring for her crappy online store—Jiang Cheng had a much better feel for the camera.

He compressed the photo slightly, checked for any outstanding issues, then saved it. After that, he opened Meitu.[12]

Reduce saturation, darken, filter. Bokeh, sparkles...

Lastly, he added text to the photo: *With sad music playing, spinning freely, the night feels even lonelier.*

After some typesetting, he sent it to Jiang Cheng.

"Last Of the Wilds"— Jiang Cheng's username seemed to demonstrate his identity as an overachiever. But though these English words meant as much to Gu Fei as any other random combination of the English alphabet, he *had* heard this song before, and liked it, too—bagpipes with a metal vibe.

He looked at Jiang Cheng's display picture. It was a side profile of his face, with his back turned. Though it was blurry, he could tell from the nose that it was Jiang Cheng... It was a pretty good photo.

Not two minutes later, Jiang Cheng replied.

– What's wrong with you?

Gu Fei laughed.

– What?

– Are you a sticker maker or something?! Why don't you make me into one of those stickers old people like? "a toast to our friendship tonight" or something like that

– You want one? I can make you one

– Fuck off

---

12   A popular image-editing mobile app best known for its beautifying filters and plethora of effects.

Gu Fei leaned back in his chair to laugh for a while before he replied.

– What, you don't like it?

– Where's your compassion?!

Gu Fei snickered as he sent over the original photo.

Jiang Cheng went quiet in the chat. It took him a few minutes to send a reply.

– Just one? Any more?

– Nope. The others weren't good, I deleted them

– ...you certainly have high standards for yourself. Couldn't you send them to me so I can delete them myself?

– Weren't you the one who wanted to delete them this afternoon?

Jiang Cheng didn't reply. Gu Fei put his phone down and got up. He flexed his slightly stiff arms and legs and walked out of his room. The lights were already off in Gu Miao's room. He walked over and gently pushed the door open to peek inside. Having done her homework and finished washing up, the munchkin was now bundled up in her blanket, sound asleep.

Nobody was allowed to interrupt Gu Fei when he was doing his thing. Gu Miao knew this, and even his usually unreliable mother remembered it. He didn't know when she had gone out, but she'd done it so soundlessly that it hadn't disturbed him at all.

Gu Fei furrowed his brows. He took the jacket he'd hung by the door and checked his wallet. All the big notes were gone.

"Fuck," he said quietly.

Returning to his room, he took his phone out and called Liu Fan.

"Da-Fei? You coming out tonight? We're out here drinking," came Liu Fan's cheerful voice on the other end of the line. "Li Yan and the gang are all here."

"No, I'm tired. I'm going to bed," Gu Fei said. "Come out with me tomorrow."

"Where to?" Liu Fan asked immediately.

"The CD store we talked about last time."

"The snobby one where everyone from the owner to the staff thinks they're a masterful music connoisseur?"

"The owner is the real deal," said Gu Fei. "I'm looking for the skinny-legged grasshopper guy."

"Got it. You don't have to come." Liu Fan tsked. "It's not right for you to go. I'll bring some people. What kind of result are you looking for?"

"I want him to turn and run when he sees my mother."

"Done."

After he hung up, his phone pinged. It was a message from Jiang Cheng.

– Thanks

Gu Fei cast an eye over his display picture: Jiang Cheng had changed it to the photo he sent him.

– Changed your display pic?

– Yeah, it's got style

Gu Fei chuckled. He put down his phone to get ready to wash up, but as he reached the door, his phone pinged again. He reversed course and picked it up for a look.

– I might have to keep your clothes for one more day. I won't
  have time to buy new clothes 'til after school

– You're not gonna wash them before you give them back?

– ...are you a germaphobe?

– Nope. Why don't you pick one to wash, the blanket or the
  clothes

– I'll give your clothes back after I wash them.

Gu Fei yawned. Maybe it was because he ate too much meat to-night, but he was unusually sleepy. After he washed up, he dropped onto the bed and fell asleep instantly. It was only when it got too cold in the middle of the night that he woke up and tucked himself in.

When he woke in the morning, the house was empty. His mother had stayed out all night, and Gu Miao had gone to school by herself. He checked the time. Forget morning self-study—he'd already missed a good half of the first class.

"Ughh," he let out a long grunt as he stretched, then slowly tidied up and left the apartment.

Just as he reached the ground floor, his phone rang with a call from Lao-Xu. "Back to your old habits this semester? Do you *want* to be expelled?!"

"I overslept," said Gu Fei.

"I don't care what excuse you have today. You and I are going to have a talk at lunchtime! I have to take responsibility for you!"

"...What did you do to me that you need to take responsibility for?" Gu Fei asked.

"Don't be smart with me!" Lao-Xu said. "Before, I didn't know what happened with you. That was an oversight on my part! Now that I know, I need to be responsible!"

Gu Fei's steps paused. "What happened with me?"

"With your dad," Lao-Xu said earnestly. "As your homeroom teacher, I'm hoping you'll open up to me and—"

"I don't need you in my business," Gu Fei said. "I don't care who you are. If you mess with me, you can 'open up' to my knuckles."

13

JIANG CHENG WOKE UP a little late that morning. By the time he opened his eyes, school was about to start.

The longest he'd ever skipped school was for two days—he also didn't go home for three nights—but he was very rarely late. He wasn't sure why, but whenever he decided to go to school, he was reluctant to be late.

The term was just starting, and he wasn't planning on skipping just yet. The second he saw what time it was, he shot out of bed and ran to the bathroom, grabbing the single-use toothbrush and toothpaste.

He didn't usually use these things when he stayed at hotels. The toothbrushes were jumbo-sized and stiff as hell, and there were never any good toothpaste flavors... When he rinsed, Jiang Cheng discovered that his gums were bleeding, either from shakily brushing with his left hand or from the poor quality of the brush.

Looking into the mirror, he saw that his face was pallid from poor sleep and his eyes had faint dark circles under them. That, along with the toothpaste at the corners of his lips...

"Ack—!"

He covered his chest with a gauze-wrapped hand and pointed ahead with the other as he wheezed painfully, "I've...been...poisoned! Agh!"

Jiang Cheng laughed to himself for a good long while until he remembered that he was running out of time. He quickly splashed some water on his face and gave it a quick wash.

When he checked out and left the building, he thought he could see the HomeInn across the road grinning at him. He *had* followed Gu Fei's clear instructions yesterday and found the HomeInn. Even then, with nothing on him but five hundred yuan, a phone, and clothes that weren't entirely his, he wasn't able to make it inside. He had no ID on him and asked the staff if there was any way around it—they threatened to call the police. He was screwed. A shitty old neighborhood in a shitty little city, and it was *this* hard to get a room in a hotel?!

He was already wearing Gu Fei's sweater, Gu Fei's down jacket, and using Gu Fei's charger after eating Gu Fei's food and smoking his cigarette. He really couldn't bring himself to go back and say to Gu Fei, "Hey, let me borrow your ID, too."

Just as he was planning to spend the night at an internet cafe, he caught sight of a little inn across the street. He was saved.

Now he looked behind at the inn once again. Zhou Inn. He noted it down so he could revisit it one day when he was writing his memoirs.

He bought breakfast at a little shop downstairs from the inn, though he had no time to eat it. Jiang Cheng stuffed all the food in his pocket and sprinted like mad to Fourth High. The school wasn't that far from here—only two stops away on the bus, and short ones at that; a distance you could cover on foot in the same amount of time it took for you to wait and get there on the crammed bus. Granted, it wasn't that close, either—running like this still took a lot out of him—but there were no taxis so early in the morning.

When he reached the school gate, Jiang Cheng heard the warning bell ring. The students slowly converging toward the main entrance didn't react to it at all. Those who were eating continued to eat; those who were chatting kept on chatting. With the accompaniment of the warning bell in the background, they ambled into school at a leisurely pace.

Jiang Cheng slowed down, not wanting to be the only speed-walking nerd in the crowd. If he'd trudged in late like this at his old school, the teacher on duty would have come over to admonish him. Instead, the teacher standing at Fourth High's front gate—perhaps too even-tempered, or just out of habit—called out in a kindly manner, "Hurry up! Speed those steps up! Anyone climbing the gate after we close it is getting demerits!"

Climb the gate?

Jiang Cheng turned back and glanced at the school gate. Despite everything, the gate of Fourth High was quite majestic. It was double-layered: The first was a waist-high electric gate, and the second one within was large, metal, and double-doored, with spikes on top.

He suddenly remembered that Gu Fei had been late the day before. Did he climb in?

Tsk. At the thought of that row of spikes, he felt a phantom breeze blow past his crotch.

When he was going up the stairs, someone yelled out from behind, "Jiang Cheng!"

Turning, he saw Wang Xu with an enormous jianbing,[13] taking bites as he ran over.

---

13   *A crepe-like breakfast wrap featuring a layer of eggs, a crispy dough fritter, and meat.*

"Damn, it really is you." Wang Xu looked him up and down. "I thought it was Da-Fei for a second, but the hat was wrong... Why are you wearing his clothes? Those are his clothes, right?"

"Mm-hm." Jiang Cheng continued to climb the stairs.

"Did something happen?" Wang Xu glanced at his hand. "Oh fuck, what happened to your hand? Was it Monkey? Were you hiding out at Da-Fei's place?"

"No, and no," Jiang Cheng replied.

"You don't have to keep it from me." Wang Xu patted his shoulder in a loyal, brotherly way. "This whole mess is my fault. If anything happens, I'll take responsibility. Be honest—"

"*Don't*," Jiang Cheng said, turning to face him, "pat my shoulder."

Wang Xu's hand hovered in the air.

"Or my back," Jiang Cheng said.

"Fuck." Wang Xu stuck his hand back in his pocket, a bit peeved as he leaped a few steps ahead of Jiang Cheng. "What a princess."

Gu Fei didn't show up for the morning self-study period. Jiang Cheng didn't know whether he was going to be late again today or skip school entirely.

Jiang Cheng kept low at his desk, staying out of sight behind Zhou Jing as he slowly ate his breakfast. Half a dozen people around him were eating, too. He sighed as he ate. He was only on his second day here—had he already assimilated, just like that?

His breakfast was pretty simple: pan-fried dumplings and soy milk. He'd carefully selected the dumplings for their napa cabbage filling—he didn't want them to smell too strongly when he ate them in class. Then he looked at the people around him, who were feasting on pungent garlic chive-stuffed buns and garlic chive-stuffed pancakes... And the smell wasn't the end of it: Someone was outright slurping up a bowl of beef noodles!

The first period was English. Lao-Lu came in bellowing as usual, and even confiscated half a bun that the slowest eater hadn't managed to finish over self-study period and break.

"Hey," Zhou Jing said, cocking his head. "Jiang Cheng, Jiang Cheng."

Jiang Cheng glanced at him soundlessly.

"Jiang Cheng?" Zhou Jing called out again. "Jiang Cheng."

"Just say whatever you have to say." Jiang Cheng suddenly understood why Gu Fei couldn't be bothered to respond to Zhou Jing. Every time this guy wanted to say something, he insisted on calling your name until you replied.

"Are you wearing Da-Fei's clothes today?" Zhou Jing asked.

Jiang Cheng frowned. He looked at the puffer draped over the back of his chair. It must have been the one Gu Fei wore most often. Wang Xu had recognized it at a single glance, and Zhou Jing could just fucking tell it was Gu Fei's... Half the class probably knew he was wearing Gu Fei's jacket to class. He looked down at the sweater he had on and prayed it wasn't one Gu Fei wore often.

"The sweater is Gu Fei's too, right?" Zhou Jing asked. "You stayed at Gu Fei's place yesterday?"

Fuck!

Jiang Cheng ignored him and lay on his desk, trying to sleep.

"Hey, Jiang Cheng." At least Zhou Jing had stopped bumping the desk now. "Why isn't Da-Fei here today?"

"If you don't shut up, I'll smack you," Jiang Cheng said with his eyes closed. Zhou Jing sighed and didn't bother him anymore.

The classroom was warm and well-heated, but it wouldn't be appropriate for him to take the sweater off. After all, he wasn't wearing anything else under it, and he could hardly go topless in class.

Gu Fei seemed low-key. He never said more than a few words at school and didn't appear to be close to anyone. He even made a point to go to a separate bathroom...but everyone seemed to remember the clothes he wore.

Fucking bizarre.

Second period was Chinese. After class, Lao-Xu walked over to his seat, looked him up and down, and said, "Hey, step outside with me for a second, Jiang Cheng."

Jiang Cheng rose. He hesitated for a moment before reluctantly pulling on Gu Fei's puffer jacket and following Lao-Xu out of the classroom onto the walkway outside.

"What's up, Xu-zong?"

"Why isn't Gu Fei in class today?" Lao-Xu asked.

"How should I know?" Jiang Cheng didn't know what to say.

"You don't?" Lao-Xu eyed him suspiciously; he clearly didn't believe him for a second. "You really don't know? Or do you not want to tell me?"

"I barely know him, why would I cover for him?" Jiang Cheng said, rather impatiently.

"Oh. I see." Lao-Xu sighed. "I noticed you're wearing his clothes. I figured you were with him yesterday and you'd know why he isn't at school today."

"...Oh." That was all Jiang Cheng could say. Another word and he thought blood would spray out of his mouth from the internal injury he'd sustained.

"Say, Jiang Cheng." Lao-Xu studied his face. "You've known Gu Fei for two days. What do you think of him?"

Jiang Cheng stared at Lao-Xu. If he didn't know that he was in school, that the man standing before him was his homeroom teacher, and that Gu Fei was merely his deskmate, he really would have thought he was talking to a matchmaker.

"*One* day," Jiang Cheng corrected. "Or half a day, to be more precise."

"Right, he didn't come back yesterday afternoon." Lao-Xu furrowed his brows. "So, what do you think—"

Jiang Cheng cut him off. "I don't think anything. Xu-zong, I have no opinion of the guy."

"Gu Fei, well... He's quite intelligent, not like the rest of these underperforming students." Lao-Xu stubbornly pushed forward. "If we can shift his mentality, he should be able to raise his grades."

"Me?" Jiang Cheng pointed at himself. He almost added, *Are you still asleep, sir?*

"No, no, me." Lao-Xu laughed as he gestured at himself. "That's for the homeroom teacher to do, of course."

Jiang Cheng said nothing. He could tell that Lao-Xu was a good man, but his job seemed like a tough one considering how little authority he had over the students. Even someone like Zhou Jing probably wouldn't buy into his spiel, never mind Gu Fei.

"I was just thinking, since you have excellent grades... Could you pair up with him as a study buddy?"

"What?" Jiang Cheng stared at Lao-Xu in astonishment.

A *study buddy*?

He'd only seen that sort of thing in middle school. It always ended up amounting to nothing, or developing into some kind of forbidden puppy-love. He didn't expect to run into this sort of thing in high school. Right now, Lao-Xu's mawkish optimism was almost meme-worthy—the kind of meme an old man might unironically use.

"Not exactly a buddy," Lao-Xu explained, "just someone to help him out sometimes. Get him to listen in class, explain problems he can't solve..."

Jiang Cheng stared at him. He didn't know what gave Lao-Xu the illusion that Gu Fei would be willing to accept anyone's supervision.

"I once asked Yi Jing to tutor him when she had the time," Lao-Xu went on. "Yi Jing's the class president and she's very responsible, but she's a girl. So in some ways, it's not the best arrangement. That's why I'm hoping you'll...look out for your classmate, as long as it doesn't affect your grades."

Lao-Xu's expression was sincere, and his tone diplomatic. It made Jiang Cheng unsure how he should respond. Ever since he was a kid, he'd taken to persuasion better than coercion, sincerity over pretension. But still, he couldn't bring himself to agree to this naïve request.

"Xu-zong, sir," he said, equally sincere, "I think you need to understand who I am before you consider whether *I* should be the one doing this. Grades don't define a person. I didn't even bring my books to class today—didn't you notice?"

The bell rang, and that was the end of the conversation.

Gu Fei didn't come to school all morning. None of the teachers asked after him in any of the classes. It was like they didn't care who did or didn't attend.

The moment morning classes ended, Jiang Cheng was the first out the classroom. He had nothing to pack, so he threw on Gu Fei's jacket and dashed out of school at the speed of light, faster than anyone sprinting to the cafeteria for food.

He was pretty lucky today. The moment he stepped out the school gate, he spotted a taxi dropping off passengers. Jiang Cheng didn't even wait for the car to empty out entirely before climbing into the front seat.

"Apart from the shopping mall in the center of town," Jiang Cheng asked the driver, "where else can you go to buy clothes?"

The driver thought for a moment. "The shopping mall."

"Where?" Jiang Cheng asked.

"The center of town," the driver answered.

"...I see." Jiang Cheng leaned back and shut his eyes. "Let's go there, then."

It was a pretty backwater mall. Jiang Cheng had come here to window-shop with Pan Zhi the day they had barbecue, and nothing caught their eyes. But he didn't have the time to be picky right now—he just needed clothes.

He chose a store that claimed to have cutthroat, fly-off-the-shelves-and-jump-out-the-building discounts, with prices so low that not buying something would be like letting the owner die for nothing. Jiang Cheng tried on a sweater and puffer jacket, thought they were fine, and asked the staff to cut the tags when he paid.

As he walked out of the shopping mall carrying Gu Fei's clothes, he breathed a sigh of relief. The new clothes were average-looking, but their strength was in their decent quality, warmth, and reasonable price. It definitely wasn't a price you'd cut your throat over, though—worth jumping out a first-floor window at the most.

Jiang Cheng made do with some random food in the mall, but he didn't know where to go next. Maybe he could go straight back to school and find a dry cleaner nearby to clean Gu Fei's clothes.

He didn't bother with a taxi this time. His mom had left him a tidy sum in his account, but looking at Li Baoguo's situation, he was going to need to make that money last all the way until college...

He looked around and saw a bus stop up front. Just as he was walking over, his phone rang: It was Li Baoguo.

Rather grudgingly, he picked up. "Hello?"

"Chengcheng!" Li Baoguo's ear-splitting voice called down the line. "You're done with class, aren't you?!"

"Mm-hm." Jiang Cheng carried on walking to the bus stop.

"Where'd you sleep last night?" Li Baoguo asked. "You pitched such a fit that the neighbors must've thought I did something to you!"

Jiang Cheng didn't answer. He stood at the bus route sign, checking if any of the buses stopped at his school.

"Calmed down yet?" Li Baoguo asked. "Come home and eat! I wrapped some dumplings, they're waiting for you to come back!"

"I..." Jiang Cheng didn't want to go back, but he couldn't bring himself to say that now. It was a long time before he replied. "I'm at the shopping mall."

"That's not too far. Just take Route 19 home," Li Baoguo said immediately. "The bus stop is right outside the mall's east entrance!"

When Jiang Cheng got back to Li Baoguo's street, clothes in hand, he noticed there was a dry cleaner not too far away. It didn't look very trustworthy, but there were a lot of clothes in the window. After a moment's pause, he brought Gu Fei's clothes in for a wash, and paid extra to pick them up the same night.

He reached the ground floor of Li Baoguo's apartment and paused. In front of the stairs was a cycle rickshaw dragging a cart full of glass panels. Li Baoguo was standing next to it, unloading several sheets of glass from the cart and carrying them back with some effort.

That was probably to replace the window he broke yesterday. Jiang Cheng sighed and ran over. "Here, I'll take them."

"Oh, you're back!" Li Baoguo boomed. "Leave them, I'll do it. You don't wanna break them, they're expensive!"

Jiang Cheng glanced over them. It really wouldn't be easy to hand them over. Instead, he took Li Baoguo's key from his hand and opened the apartment door.

"Read my mind!" Li Baoguo lifted his head and spoke in a half-yell to nobody in particular, "See, now, this is my son! We're on the same wavelength!"

"Why didn't you get a handyman to install them for you?" Jiang Cheng looked into his room. There was still broken glass on the floor; he grabbed a broom from the kitchen. "It—"

"A handyman?" Li Baoguo glowered. "How much would that cost?! I already had to buy these glass panes on credit, you know!"

"On credit?" Jiang Cheng stiffened, broom in hand.

"From that glass store on the backstreet. The owner plays mahjong with me all the time, so I asked him for them," Li Baoguo said. "I'll pay in a few days when my luck's better."

Jiang Cheng's lips parted but nothing came out. Li Baoguo didn't even have enough money to buy a few panes of glass? He had to gamble for the payment?

"The backstreet?" Jiang Cheng bent and swept up the glass on the floor. "I'll go over later and pay them."

"What a good son!" Li Baoguo put the glass panes on the table and dusted his hands off. "You care about your old man! Your old family must've given you a nice bit of money, huh?"

Jiang Cheng turned and glanced at him without a word. When Li Baoguo went to the kitchen to get the dumplings, Jiang Cheng grabbed his jacket from where he'd tossed it on the bed last night and took the wallet from its pocket. When he opened it for a look, he was dumbstruck.

The cash was probably untouched, but the card was in a different place. He checked the number to make sure it was the original card before putting the wallet back in his pocket. He sat on the edge of the bed, feeling drained.

Gu Fei had just pulled out his pack of cigarettes to take one when he realized he'd finished the entire pack. Frowning, he crumpled the box and tossed it to the ground to join the cigarette butts that surrounded his foot.

It was quiet today. Lao-Xu had called a few times that morning. So had his mom and Li Yan, but he didn't pick up a single call. Eventually, he turned his phone off.

The world was quiet now. Alone, he could fully appreciate the terror rising from the deepest pit of his heart.

The sky had already begun to darken, and the northern wind was blowing harder and harder. It permeated his hat, his earmuffs, and his mask, scraping at his face relentlessly as Gu Fei turned and walked down the path between the two rows of gravestones. Bringing a small broom over, he swept up the cigarette butts, then stared at the photo on the gravestone. He'd spent the whole day here, but this was the first time he'd looked at it. In the dim light, the man in the photo looked even more like a stranger. And yet, he still retained a trace of the aura that had so frightened him.

"I'm leaving now," he said.

As he turned to leave, he felt like someone was behind him. When he turned to look, all he saw was a silent gravestone.

Gu Fei walked on, his footsteps a little heavy. He sucked in a breath and sped up.

The moment he put down the broom, his ears were filled with the sound of roaring water.

He stopped breathing as his surroundings abruptly darkened. It wasn't the sound of flowing water, or normal movement through it. This...was the sound of someone struggling for his life beneath the surface—an immense, desperate, agonizing noise. Waves rose, crested, and splashed; then broke into ripples one by one. Through the chaotic splashing, a pair of eyes fixed on his.

"Why didn't you save me?! Are you asking for a beating?!"

In his terror, Gu Fei gave a vicious kick to the nearby trash can. The sound of it clattering to the ground dragged him back to reality. He tugged his collar up and lowered his head, striding quickly along the empty road toward the main entrance of the cemetery.

Those weren't the last words he'd heard his father say, but on the day he died, they became the words that echoed over and over in the nightmares he couldn't wake from.

His dad hadn't managed to say anything before he died. He couldn't. All he could do was struggle for his life.

Gu Fei didn't know why he dreamt of those words. He never imagined they would follow him through the years, growing into a fear he couldn't bring himself to face. It always felt so real—the feeling of standing by the lake, his whole body drenched—so real that he was compelled to reach out and grab his own clothes every time, to reassure himself repeatedly that he was dry.

The area near the cemetery was actually somewhat lively; the road just beyond the entrance was a thoroughfare. Gu Fei entered a nearby supermarket almost at a jog.

After surrounding himself with artificial light, he finally began to feel some warmth, and the stiffness of his body gradually subsided. He bought two packs of cigarettes, a bottle of water, and a bowl of oden; he only went back outside once he'd finished it in the sitting area.

Standing at a corner sheltered from the wind, Gu Fei lit a cigarette. But he only took one puff before putting it out—he was too nauseous. The top of his throat felt coated in sand.

On the bus, he downed an entire bottle of water and finally felt a little better. Only then did he turn his phone on. There was a whole heap of missed calls, mainly from Lao-Xu. Everyone else had nothing important to say and stopped calling when they realized his phone was switched off. The only one persistent enough to keep calling was Lao-Xu—he was like an earnest, stubborn suitor.

Done with checking the missed calls, he looked at his texts. There was only one, from Jiang Cheng.

- Bringing your clothes over at 8

At the sight of Jiang Cheng's display picture, he thought of the meme he'd made for Jiang Cheng the night before. He leaned against the bus window. Without warning, he burst into a long fit of laughter.

Run Wild
SAYE

14

THE BUS ROUTE back home from the cemetery was long, winding halfway around the city. Gu Fei leaned against the window, swaying along with the bus. He barely sat through two stops before he fell asleep.

When he opened his eyes, he was still one stop from home, but it was already past eight. He pulled out his phone to check: no messages from Jiang Cheng, so he probably hadn't arrived yet.

There was also a message from Gu Miao, consisting of only two words:

– I ate.

Their downstairs neighbor had a small catering business. Sometimes, when he returned too late to make dinner, Gu Miao would go to their neighbor's house to eat, and Gu Fei would pay the neighbor off at the end of the month. Sometimes, when she felt like it, their mother would also cook up a meal or two. Their mother's cooking was delicious—he and Gu Miao both liked it—but they rarely had the chance to enjoy it.

– Did you eat downstairs?

– yeah

Gu Fei put his phone back in his pocket and walked to the door, ready to disembark. The kiddo was getting colder and colder these days. She even skimped on words when she was typing.

In the old city during winter, eight-something was already quite late; for these streets in particular, which were older than old, it was as good as midnight. Stores were mostly closed by now, and nobody went outside except to play cards or mahjong.

As Gu Fei ambled toward his own store, still a long way off, he saw someone standing at the door. In the dim light, he could see the guy jumping back and forth on the sidewalk, like he was dancing.

Jiang Cheng?

He hastened his steps. Now he could make out that the person with his neck tucked into his jacket, his hands in his pockets, and his feet leaping up and down the steps outside the store was indeed Jiang Cheng.

Before he could announce himself, Jiang Cheng turned and saw him.

"Holy shit!" Jiang Cheng exclaimed. Gu Fei couldn't tell if it was from the cold or if Jiang Cheng was trying to sound threatening, but his voice was a low growl. "Get here tomorrow, why don't you?!"

Gu Fei realized it must be from the cold. Jiang Cheng's voice was shaking, and he could even hear the chatter of his teeth knocking together.

"Sorry," Gu Fei said as he dug out the keys. "I was on the bus. It was slow."

"Okay, but," Jiang Cheng pointed at the locked door to the store, "you run a pretty casual business here, huh?"

"Huh?" Gu Fei glanced back at him.

"Before he left just now, the doctor next door said you've been closed all afternoon."

"Really." Gu Fei opened the door and the warm air inside rushed out. "Today was my mom's turn to watch the store. She...must've had something else to do in the afternoon."

"Move-move-move-move—" Jiang Cheng followed him, then pushed him aside and ran into the store. He hopped in place for a while before slamming his butt down on a chair. "Shit, I was freezing to death."

"When did you get here?" Gu Fei brought a space heater over to him and turned it on.

Jiang Cheng tossed the bag of clothes onto the cash register. "Seven-fifty."

Gu Fei was taken aback. "That's early."

"*I*," Jiang Cheng said, pointing to himself, "was raised to be *punctual*."

Gu Fei stared at him. "Why didn't you tell me you were here?" he asked at last.

"Would you have been able to get here if I did?" Jiang Cheng said. "Besides, my phone was so cold it wouldn't turn on."

"Then why didn't you go home first?" Gu Fei brought a glass over and put a slice of lemon in it, then filled it with hot water before handing it to Jiang Cheng. "I could've gone over to pick it up."

"What's with all the useless questions?" Jiang Cheng took the glass and sipped, glaring at the heater.

Gu Fei didn't push the issue. "I'll give your clothes to you tomorrow morning. I brought them home to wash."

"Huh?" Jiang Cheng looked up at him. "They're not easy to wash, though, what with the blood and all."

"It was fine. I've washed it off now anyway."

"Thanks."

"You're welcome." Gu Fei sat down behind the cash register, resting his legs on the counter. He added, "It was mostly because they were too gross *not* to wash. And it's not like you took them with you."

"...Fuck," Jiang Cheng said. "I forgot to."

After that, neither of them spoke.

Gu Fei half-reclined very comfortably behind the counter as he played with his phone. Jiang Cheng had no phone to play with, so he just sat in his chair, zoning out. He knew that all the businesses around here were closing around this time, aside from the gambling dens. Gu Fei was probably waiting for him to leave so he could lock up, but Jiang Cheng didn't want to go.

Li Baoguo's house was a circus today. For whatever reason, he'd suddenly gone crazy and invited a whole bunch of people over to play mahjong. Li Baoguo had adroitly fixed the windowpanes he broke this afternoon, and Jiang Cheng was quite impressed. He had to hand it to the older generation when it came to being handy around the house. But before he had time to collect himself—before he'd even had ten of the dumplings Li Baoguo claimed to have made for him—half a dozen men and women filled the apartment and descended upon him. They surrounded him completely, examining him, asking him all kinds of questions and discussing them in front of him.

What a neat deal, getting someone else to raise your son to this age!
Look at that, kids raised in the big city just aren't the same, are they?
Your adoptive parents must be pretty rich!
They have to be. Look at the way he dresses, the way he carries himself... Tsk, tsk, tsk...

At last, a middle-aged woman with mannerisms so exaggerated she could have been a meme said, *One look will tell anyone he's your son, just look, look! See how much he looks like Li Baoguo! Exactly the same!*

Jiang Cheng had been clenching his jaw the entire time, suppressing so much anger that he was turning into a red bell pepper. When he heard this, he lost it.

Looks like him? Looks like my foot! Exactly the same, my ass!

He pushed the crowd aside and stormed back to his room, slamming the door behind him. Only then did they give up. Li Baoguo's guests then proceeded to eat all the remaining dumplings in the pot, even the three left in Jiang Cheng's bowl that he didn't have time to finish.

Every day, Jiang Cheng found himself living through all sorts of bizarre situations—wherever he looked, something ridiculous was happening. He could barely catch his breath.

When he walked up to the entrance of Li Baoguo's building after school, he could tell they were still in there just from the noise. It didn't seem like they were going to leave anytime tonight, either. He didn't bother going in; he simply turned around and left.

Jiang Cheng went to the dumpling place he'd planned to go to the day before for dinner. After texting Gu Fei, he finished his homework there in the restaurant. He didn't get up and leave until he was the only customer left in the whole place.

He felt a loneliness he couldn't put into words.

He couldn't go back to his old life, nor could he fit into his current one. He was drifting on the outskirts of everything unfamiliar, without family, without friends, and without a place he could stay and feel secure. It was as if his entire being was suspended in mid-air.

Jiang Cheng spent nearly half an hour spacing out in Gu Fei's store. He turned to look at Gu Fei, who was still in the same position, his head buried in his phone screen.

"Are you waiting to lock up?" he asked.

Gu Fei stared at the screen, ignoring him.

"If you're in a hurry to lock up, I'll leave," Jiang Cheng said. "Otherwise, I'll stay a bit longer."

Gu Fei still didn't speak or move. What was he playing that had him so engrossed? Jiang Cheng hesitated, then stood up and leaned over the counter to glance at his phone.

It was that stupid mobile matching game, *Aixiaochu*!

"Damn," he muttered. How could anyone be so absorbed in this game that he didn't hear someone talking to him?

Jiang Cheng looked at the screen. It was a difficult level—there were only three moves left, but you could win as long as you made every move count. Gu Fei was probably trying to figure it out.

Bending over the counter, Jiang Cheng counted the steps and quickly figured out the next move. However, out of basic manners— the way you wouldn't butt into a chess game you were spectating— he waited in silence.

Gu Fei remained still.

Jiang Cheng watched for almost five minutes, and he was still motionless. Including the time before he came over, Gu Fei had been mulling over these three moves for half an hour now...

Jiang Cheng thought back to what Lao-Xu said that morning: *Gu Fei, well, he's quite intelligent...* So *this* was intelligence?

At long last, he couldn't help himself. He reached a finger out to show Gu Fei the way. "Haven't you worked it out?"

The moment his fingertip passed the corner of Gu Fei's eye, before it even reached the screen, Gu Fei suddenly lifted his head and seized his finger, bending it backward.

"Ow!" Jiang Cheng yelled. Gu Fei hadn't used a lot of force, but it gave him a shock. Thirty-foot-high flames of rage shot up inside him. He sent his fist into Gu Fei's chest. "What the fuck's wrong with you?!"

Gu Fei let go.

"What's wrong with you?!" Jiang Cheng shook his hand out.

Good thing he'd used his left; his wound would have reopened if it'd been his right hand.

Gu Fei stood up. Jiang Cheng watched his movements sharply, wondering if some bizarre temper had come over Gu Fei and he wanted to pick a fight.

"I..." Gu Fei tossed his phone aside and grabbed a cup, filling it halfway with water and taking a drink. "I dozed off."

Jiang Cheng was dumbstruck. "What?"

"Sorry." Gu Fei looked at his hand. "Are you hurt?"

"You sleep with your eyes open?" Jiang Cheng asked.

"I must have been daydreaming, then. I didn't hear you speak." Gu Fei sat again and fetched his phone for a look. "Were you telling me which move to make?"

"Yeah." Jiang Cheng looked at him.

"So which move?" Gu Fei asked.

"Meditate on that yourself," Jiang Cheng said.

Gu Fei looked down at his phone for a while, then swiped at his screen. This was followed by a frowning, "Ah."

Jiang Cheng glanced at him. "Dead?"

"Yup," Gu Fei replied.

"Are you—" Jiang Cheng bit back the rest of his sentence.

"Stupid?" Gu Fei finished helpfully. "I'm playing a stupid game, aren't I?"

"Come on, you didn't see the vertical row of bombs you could trigger at the top right corner?" Jiang Cheng said. "Once you got the bombs, there would have been a color match, too. Then you'd only need one more move to get that one below—"

Before Jiang Cheng could finish speaking, Gu Fei nodded and said, "Okay."

Then he swiped twice on the screen. Jiang Cheng glared at him.

"I won." Gu Fei sighed in relief and turned to look at him. "Thanks."

Jiang Cheng was appalled. "Fuck off."

Gu Fei threw his phone onto the countertop and stretched. "Any homework today?"

"Yeah, no shit," Jiang Cheng said. "Are there days you *don't* get homework?"

"Have you done it?"

Jiang Cheng looked at him in silence.

"Let me copy it," Gu Fei said.

Jiang Cheng continued to stare at him. Gu Fei was asking his deskmate of two days—whom he barely knew and hadn't seen at all for one and a half of those days—to let him copy his homework, and there wasn't even a shred of supplication in his tone.

"Please, lend me your homework." Gu Fei sighed. "So I can copy it. Thank you."

Jiang Cheng sighed too, but he also felt like laughing.

"There's quite a lot of homework today, so you might be copying for a while." He pulled out a few workbooks and a worksheet from his bag, dumping them on the counter. "Give them back to me tomorrow morning."

"Never mind the worksheet, I don't have a copy." Gu Fei took a book and flipped through it. "This looks nothing like a top student's handwriting."

"Take it or leave it," Jiang Cheng said. He wasn't offended by that statement. His handwriting *was* ugly, each row wobbling across the page like a drunken boxer. "Beggars can't be choosers."

Gu Fei stood and walked two rounds around the store before he managed to find his school bag in some corner. Just as he put his books on the table, his cell phone pinged. He tapped on the screen. It was a voice message, playing on speaker mode—sitting nearby, Jiang Cheng heard it loud and clear.

"Dage! Ge—oh, fuck! I'm sorry! Dage, I'm sorry... I'll keep my dis—tance—agh! Stop hitting me! Stop hitting me, fuck! Stop, I'm gonna die!"

The message was full of pained cries and pleading. Jiang Cheng was stunned.

"That's enough," Gu Fei said into the phone.

Jiang Cheng stared at him for a good while. "Was that the guy you plastered onto the tree yesterday?"

"Mm-hm." Gu Fei dug through his bag almost twenty times before he managed to find a pen; when he tried scribbling with it, he discovered it was out of ink. He looked at Jiang Cheng. "Got a pen?"

Jiang Cheng pulled out a pen and handed it to him.

There were different tiers of underachieving students. Pan Zhi was an underachiever, but compared to Gu Fei, he was practically a goody two-shoes. At least Pan Zhi had pens, and more than one of them.

Gu Fei lowered his head and began copying the homework. He looked so focused right now that a passerby could have been forgiven for thinking he was a hardworking student.

Jiang Cheng sat for a while until he finally felt he couldn't stay any longer. He could hardly sit here and wait for Gu Fei to finish copying his homework. Getting up, Jiang Cheng said, "I'm leaving."

"I thought you had nowhere to go," Gu Fei said as he copied.

Ding, ding, ding! Congratulations! Your answer is correct!

Jiang Cheng said nothing, filled with a humiliating, helpless bitterness.

"If you have nowhere to go, just stay here," said Gu Fei. "Li Yan and Liu Fan and the rest of them come here and laze around when they have nothing to do, too."

"I'm going."

The thought that he was now equal to the Fresh Out of Jail squad in the eyes of others was a harrowing one. It almost made him lash out. He roughly pushed the curtain aside, only to slam into someone charging into the store.

"Son of a bitch!" It was a woman, and she began swearing before they even broke apart. "Son of a *bitch*!"

Jiang Cheng was too stunned to be angry. He stared at her, wide-eyed.

"Out of my way!" She shoved him forcefully. "Gu Fei, you asshole!"

Jiang Cheng staggered several steps back. When he made out the woman's features, he froze. There was no need for introductions or guesswork; he could tell this was Gu Fei's mother. They had the exact same eyes and nose.

"What are you screaming about?" Gu Fei threw down the pen and stood up, his brow furrowed.

The woman pounced on Gu Fei, aiming a slap at his face. "What did you do?!"

Gu Fei grabbed her hand and glanced at Jiang Cheng.

"Uh..." Jiang Cheng was so uncomfortable that he didn't know where to look. "I'm off. Bye, Auntie."

"Off where?!" The woman turned around and grasped his arm. "You're one of this asshole's friends, aren't you?! Don't you dare leave!"

Jiang Cheng was completely baffled. "Wh–what?"

"What did you all do?!" The woman slapped his arm.

Jiang Cheng didn't dare to grab her hand the way Gu Fei did—she was Gu Fei's mother, after all. He could only stand there and let her hit him. To be honest, she was beautiful. He just didn't understand why she was acting like a lunatic.

"You don't mind making a fool of yourself, huh?" Gu Fei seized her arm and threw her onto a nearby chair. He pointed at her face. "Go ahead then, try that again!"

At last, the woman stopped. Instead of lunging at them again, she suddenly burst into tears. "Am I your mother or not? What's so wrong with me dating someone?! Did you really have to beat him up so badly he won't see me anymore...? Do you want me to stay a widow forever?!"

The look on Gu Fei's face was terrible. Even his hands were shaking. Jiang Cheng had the feeling that if he hadn't been here, Gu Fei might have slapped his mother. But even if leaving meant this woman would get slapped, Jiang Cheng had to leave. He thought he could understand how Gu Fei felt—he felt the same way about people observing his relationship with Li Baoguo.

He retreated to the doorway, and when Gu Fei glanced over, he pointed at the door. Gu Fei nodded wearily and Jiang Cheng swiftly lifted the curtain and bolted outside.

The abrasive winter wind finally scoured away the discomfort and secondhand embarrassment coursing through him. Fucking hell, what kind of wretched mother was that?!

Jiang Cheng scowled. Was there a single normal person in this goddamn city?

He heard the rattle of wheels on the ground from behind him. It was a familiar sound. He swiveled round, and sure enough, Gu Miao was zooming toward him on her skateboard.

She must have heard the noise inside as she passed the entrance of the store—she paused but didn't stop. Instead, she kicked the ground and flew over to him like the wind. She even waved as she reached him. Jiang Cheng was just about to warn her to be careful, but she'd already pushed off on her skateboard and soared through the air, streaking past him before landing solidly ahead. With a graceful turn, she stopped.

"Why aren't you at home?" Jiang Cheng looked at her, though he knew she wouldn't answer.

As expected, Gu Miao didn't speak. She stepped off her skateboard and kicked it gently, and it rolled over to Jiang Cheng's foot.

"You want me to skateboard?" Jiang Cheng asked.

Gu Miao nodded. She tugged at the hat on her head.

"I do know how." Jiang Cheng rubbed his hands. "But I haven't done it in a long time."

Gu Miao simply stared at him in silence.

Jiang Cheng could detect a smidge of defiance in her gaze. He couldn't hold back his laugh. "Are you challenging me?"

Gu Miao leaned against a lamppost nearby, watching him with folded arms.

"Oho." Jiang Cheng threw his school bag onto the heap of snow next to them and put one foot on the skateboard. "The little girl's got attitude."

Gu Miao lifted her chin at him, silently telling him to hurry up.

Jiang Cheng had enjoyed things like skating and skateboarding since elementary school. But in order to prepare for the high school entrance exam in the last year of middle school, his mother had wiped anything "irrelevant to studying" from his life.

He took a deep breath. With a kick of his foot, he rolled out.

Jiang Cheng didn't go very fast; he didn't know the terrain too well. Luckily for him, Gu Miao's skateboard was a double kick—the kind he was most familiar with. Once he got used to it, it was pretty easy.

After skateboarding for a short distance, he heard footsteps behind him. He turned to see Gu Miao running after him. When she saw him turn his head, she immediately began to clap, but he didn't know whether she was applauding him or urging him to speed up. At any rate, a little girl catching up to him on foot while he was on a skateboard...it was pretty funny.

Gu Miao hopped as she ran, mimicking an ollie. Jiang Cheng couldn't embarrass himself in front of her. He steadied himself, then pushed off against the board and leaped over a little mound of snow in front of him, pointing at Gu Miao as he did.

Gu Miao's eyes brightened. She jumped excitedly and snapped her fingers as she waved. The finger snap was so crisp and loud that Jiang Cheng was almost jealous he couldn't replicate it.

Once he landed, he kept on gliding ahead to the corner of the street. This time, he was faster; Gu Miao didn't follow. She stood in place and watched him.

As he turned around and rolled his way back, he risked a humiliating faceplant and jumped onto the step with the board, then back down again. Luck was on his side: He swayed slightly, but didn't fall.

Skateboards were great stress-relievers. When you stepped onto a skateboard and rushed past the people around you like a breeze, you could leave all your boredom and frustrations behind. Doing it against the wind on a brisk winter's day was kind of bracing, but it was also satisfying.

The road back was at a slight downward angle. Jiang Cheng accelerated, gradually getting into the groove of it. He glanced at Gu Miao. She was gazing at him with a face full of anticipation. He kept his eyes on the ground, planning to jump over that big pile of snow when he passed her.

He was at just the right speed now, the wind coursing as he went. Jiang Cheng charged ahead; the pile of snow was approaching fast. In the split second he prepared for the jump, he noticed a small piece of brick on the ground in front of him.

Fuck!

The brick was in his way, and with his rusty skills, dodging it seemed impossible. All he could do was jump early, though it meant he might land on the snow heap itself. It would all come down to the height of the jump.

He pushed off on the board and propelled himself into the air.

This time, he wasn't so lucky.

Maybe it was too cold; maybe he was too nervous. Either way, all he knew was that there wasn't enough power in his jump, and that he hadn't pulled his legs in enough... He could already tell where he was going to land.

The head of the skateboard would lodge itself into the peak of the pile, he figured. As for Jiang Cheng himself, he'd probably crash onto the sidewalk up ahead.

Come on then, kid! Fly!

After a brief moment airborne, the skateboard got stuck in the snow heap, as he'd predicted. But as he began to fall, he suddenly spotted someone in front of him.

Oh, no.

15

I T WAS A LAW OF THE UNIVERSE that if you ran into a red light, you'd get red lights the entire way. It didn't matter whether you sped up or slowed down—they'd still be red.

They should've added a second part: If you embarrass yourself in front of someone, you'll always embarrass yourself whenever you see him. No matter how impossible you'd think it would be, or how carefully you tried to avoid it, your dignity just didn't belong to you.

Take now, for instance: Five minutes ago, Gu Fei had been pointing at his mother, on the verge of violence. But now, he was standing on the sidewalk, almost as if the gods had put him there right in time to watch Jiang Cheng disgrace himself.

Jiang Cheng's flight was exceedingly short, but the human brain was capable of running through multiple clear thoughts in one brief moment. For example, he observed that Gu Fei was in a dreadful mood. His expression alone said his chest was filled with twenty-five pounds of explosives, ready to blow at any second. Another example: He determined that falling from this angle meant knocking straight into an extremely pissed-off Gu Fei.

Example three: He understood that his momentum would make for a forceful impact, and he was probably going to knock Gu Fei over.

And fourth: He knew he had to put his hand to one side imme-diately, or else, when they made contact, the freshly scabbed wound on his palm would split open instantly from the pressure.

In any case, when he opened his arms and flew toward Gu Fei like he was charging toward the sun, the look on Gu Fei's face was incomprehensible.

Jiang Cheng finally bowled solidly into Gu Fei with a *thwack*. The other day, he'd learned how loud the sound of a body slamming against a tree could be; today, he discovered that a body slam-ming into another body could ring out just as loudly.

First his forehead smashed into Gu Fei's clavicle, then his mouth smashed against something else—he felt his teeth close around a zipper or something. After that, he couldn't tell what was happening or in what order. Various parts of his body struck Gu Fei at various speeds.

Gu Fei didn't even stagger. He simply tipped over and tumbled backward to the ground, followed swiftly by Jiang Cheng. He couldn't tell whether anything hurt when he crashed into Gu Fei, but falling to the ground didn't really hurt at all. Gu Fei wasn't fat, but he still made a good cushion.

When they landed on the ground, Jiang Cheng could almost see a cloud of snow puff up around them. He realized several seconds later that it was his imagination: There was no snow under Gu Fei, just the stone of the sidewalk.

Both of them were dazed. When Jiang Cheng heard Gu Fei mut-ter, "Holy fuck," he finally collected himself.

He braced himself with his uninjured left hand, trying to get up as quickly as he could. "Sorr—"

But his hand also had a bad sense of direction and braced against Gu Fei's ribcage instead.

"Fuck!" Gu Fei swore in pain. "Are you a fucking idiot?!"

To tell the truth, Jiang Cheng was in a terrible mood himself. The glimpse of joy that skateboarding with Gu Miao had brought him was a salve, not a cure. The simple fact that he had to occupy himself by skateboarding with a schoolkid late at night was a miserable thought in and of itself.

Now, with Gu Fei cursing at him, he was a little disgruntled. But at the end of the day, he was the one who crashed into Gu Fei. It wasn't a light knock, either; he could see that Gu Fei's jacket had lost a zipper slider.

"Get the fuck off me!" Gu Fei raised his arm and swung at him.

"Fuck your uncle, I didn't fucking mean to!" Jiang Cheng felt his teeth ache as he spoke. There was something in his mouth. He turned and spat: Half a zipper slider came out.

Clink.

Crisp and clear.

Hearing this, he suddenly felt pain burst in his mouth. Jiang Cheng couldn't bring himself to imagine how he'd managed to gnaw off a zipper slider; he couldn't even bring himself to lick his front teeth and check if they were still there.

"It's not easy being a show-off, so stop bringing a whole fucking stage with you everywhere you go!" Gu Fei's face was full of rage; his fall must not have been light. He shoved Jiang Cheng violently. "*Overachiever*!"

Jiang Cheng was thrown back on his ass and instantly felt his temper ignite. "Fuck you! Just try and hit me again!"

Gu Fei didn't even look at him as he launched a kick straight to his stomach. In that moment, Jiang Cheng felt everything else in the world disappear; the only thing left was this fucker Gu Fei in front of him. He bounced back to his feet and kicked Gu Fei in return.

Gu Fei quickly dodged, so he missed, but he chased after him without missing a beat and landed a foot on Gu Fei's back.

"Fuck!" Gu Fei grabbed Jiang Cheng's calf and yanked.

Jiang Cheng fell back down, but he didn't forget to throw his other foot at Gu Fei's face. Gu Fei blocked it with his arm, then flipped over and straddled Jiang Cheng, aiming a fist at his face.

Motherfucker! This guy wasn't pulling his punches!

Son of a bitch!

Jiang Cheng saw a stream of golden sparks flicker in front of his left eye like a little train. He had no time for anything else; he lifted his hand and pushed Gu Fei's chin up, hard. Gu Fei leaned backward.

Seizing his chance, he tried to elbow Gu Fei in the ribs...and failed, because Gu Fei reacted instantly and caught his wrist.

His next move took Jiang Cheng completely by surprise: The bastard pressed his finger straight into the wound on Jiang Cheng's palm.

"Aaaagh!" Jiang Cheng hollered.

It was like a switch had flipped in him—Jiang Cheng abruptly drew his leg up and slammed a knee into Gu Fei's back. Gu Fei fell forward, his hands bracing either side of Jiang Cheng's head.

Dirty tricks? Toddler tricks? Fine! Jiang Cheng turned and bit Gu Fei's wrist.

"Aarghh!" Gu Fei yelped in pain.

Jiang Cheng kept biting and wouldn't let go. Gu Fei hurriedly pinched his cheek. The fucking bastard had a strong grip; Jiang Cheng's cheek hurt so badly that he thought it must be pierced through. But at least now he could tell his front teeth were still there—and they were still pretty sturdy, too.

As the fight continued to escalate in an increasingly ludicrous fashion, the both of them inseparably entwined on the ground, a voice came from close by.

"Gu Fei?"

The two of them were too absorbed in their squabble; they both heard the voice, but neither of them diverted an iota of their concentration away from pummeling each other with earnest devotion.

"Gu Fei!" the person yelled, then paused before shouting, "Jiang Cheng? Why are you... Get up! Both of you, get up!"

Jiang Cheng had known from the first shout that it was Lao-Xu, but he had no time to be surprised or wonder why their teacher had suddenly appeared.

"Stop, both of you!" Lao-Xu walked up and gave them each a kick. "What are you doing?! Have you really got that much time on your hands?!"

At last, they both stopped.

But they only stopped moving. It was like pressing pause: Both of them still held their combat positions. One of Gu Fei's hands gripped Jiang Cheng's collar, while his other hand was in Jiang Cheng's grasp. They stayed exactly where they were, half-kneeling, half-bracing against the ground, neither one daring to let go so easily. Since their fight had devolved into pressing palms and biting wrists, neither of them trusted that his opponent didn't have more kindergartener tricks up his sleeve.

"Let go!" Lao-Xu came over and yanked on their arms. With great effort, he finally pulled them apart.

"What's all this?!" Lao-Xu glared at Gu Fei. "How could you beat up your own deskmate?!"

"Was it just me beating him up?" Gu Fei raised a hand and wiped at the corner of his mouth. "Are you blind?"

Lao-Xu wasn't bothered by Gu Fei's fiery words. He turned to look at Jiang Cheng. "And what's wrong with you?! What's a good kid like you doing; getting into a fight as soon as you get here?"

"I told you." Jiang Cheng shook his wrist out. His palm didn't hurt—it was already numb. "Don't judge someone by their grades. No teacher has ever called me a good kid."

Lao-Xu heaved a big sigh. He pointed across the road and said to Gu Fei, "Isn't that your sister? Look how you've scared the little girl!"

It was only then that Jiang Cheng remembered Gu Miao still standing to one side. Suddenly disquieted, he turned to look and was taken aback. Gu Miao sat alone on a stone bench across the street, one hand cupping her cheek as she watched them calmly. Or perhaps it wasn't calm, but apathy—total disinterest.

"She's not scared of fights," said Gu Fei.

Jiang Cheng stayed quiet. Gu Miao was a bit odd, that was certain... When he hurt his hand, Gu Fei had carefully hidden it from Gu Miao's view, so she was probably afraid of blood. But now, he and Gu Fei had blasted this whole area clean in their skirmish and her face was blank. Jiang Cheng thought of the time Gu Fei threw the man against the tree. She didn't even lift her head, then; she'd just kept eating.

What's wrong with this little girl?

"Clean up." Realizing he wasn't getting any answers from either of them, Lao-Xu simply pointed at the school bag on the ground. "I'm here to pay a home visit, so first, let's talk about your fight."

A home visit? Jiang Cheng was taken aback. A homeroom teacher making a home visit in the biting northern wind, at nine o'clock in the evening... He really didn't know what to say to that.

"Whose home?" Gu Fei straightened his clothes. When he looked down to pull his zipper up, he found the zipper slider missing. He turned and glanced at Jiang Cheng.

Jiang Cheng met his eyes with a dirty look. *Yeah, I fucking ate it! So what?!*

"I walked all the way here. Whose home do you think?" Lao-Xu sighed. "Yours, of course."

Gu Fei fell silent for a moment, then turned to walk back. "Let's go, then."

"Wait." Lao-Xu probably didn't expect him to act so decisively. "I still have to find out why you were fighting."

"We were bored." Gu Fei looked back at him. "You coming or not?"

Lao-Xu didn't quite know what to do first; whether he should visit Gu Fei's family or settle the matter of their fight. He took one step forward, then stopped, then stepped backward, then paused and stepped forward again. Jiang Cheng was tempted to clap in time with him.

"I'm heading back," Jiang Cheng said. "Thanks, Xu-zong."

Before Lao-Xu could speak, Jiang Cheng spun around and walked down the block. Behind him, Gu Fei whistled. Jiang Cheng didn't look back—he figured he was summoning Gu Miao. Sure enough, he immediately heard the sound of Gu Miao's skateboard rolling.

He sighed quietly. Tonight had been so...*satisfying*.

Li Baoguo's mahjong crew was still there, but since they'd spent so much of their lives stewing at the mahjong table, all that existed to them was that square yard before their eyes. No curiosity or desire for gossip could win against those tiles shooting back and forth. After the brief cross-examination at lunchtime, Jiang Cheng disappeared from their field of vision. Even when he walked in and out of the living room, nobody gave him a second look except Li Baoguo.

"Home already?" he said. "We had takeout. Do you want anything to eat?"

"Don't worry about me."

Jiang Cheng went to his room and took his jacket off. It was covered in dust and torn in two different places. *Shit.* He frowned. *I just bought this today!*

He doubted his face looked much better. Walking around the room, he discovered that there wasn't even a mirror in here. He had to take his phone out and try to turn it on. Warmed up from its owner's exercise in the snow, the phone finally lit up.

Jiang Cheng pointed the camera at his face. There was a lump on his forehead, but it wasn't serious. His lower lip was slightly torn—maybe from Gu Fei's zipper. Everywhere else was fine, apart from some grazes.

He sighed, unsure how he felt now. The fight was a bit...messy. He didn't normally fight like that—like a pig in the mud. It was more venting anger than actual fighting.

Jiang Cheng didn't know what he wanted out of a fight with Gu Fei—he just wanted to lash out, to tear into someone, to pitch himself forward and break free from the chains on his body that he couldn't see, touch, or understand.

As for Gu Fei, maybe he'd been influenced by Jiang Cheng. Why else would someone who could throw a grown man with one hand resort to rolling artlessly on the ground, even pinching his palm like that? Fuck! Why hadn't his lackeys been there to see that?!

Hey, did you know your boss is a worm?!

Jiang Cheng looked down at his hand, where blood was already seeping out of the gauze. He rifled through his backpack for the supplies he'd gotten from the community clinic today. Thankfully, they weren't damaged.

He opened the bandage and, with some difficulty, washed and disinfected his right hand with his left. His left hand was clumsy, so he ended up poking himself in his wound a couple of times;

it hurt so much that tears almost ran down his face. He wanted to cry, actually. He'd always thought crying was pointless, but ever since he got here in winter break, he occasionally felt so bottled up that he wanted to cry it all out.

Someday, he thought, he'd have to find a deserted corner just to let loose and give himself a good, violent cry.

When he got up the next morning, the mahjong game was finally over. There were two men sleeping on the living room couch, and Li Baoguo snored thunderously in his bed. After washing up, Jiang Cheng took his backpack and dashed right out the door, unwilling to stay for a second longer.

Before he even reached school, he got another call from the logistics company. "It's been three days. Last day is tomorrow, or we'll start charging for storage!"

"Do you deliver?" Jiang Cheng sighed.

"Sure, two hundred to your building," came the answer. "Extra charge to go upstairs."

Jiang Cheng was quiet for a moment, wincing at the cost. He was rather appreciative of his newfound financial awareness.

"I think you'd better pick it up yourself." The caller was quite considerate. "There are a lot of trishaws around here. Hiring one to your place only costs about a hundred."

"Got it, thanks," Jiang Cheng said.

It was Saturday tomorrow, thank goodness. Still, it worried him a little. His bedroom could barely hold a bed and a closet—even his desk was a tight fit. He didn't know how he was going to put his stuff in there when he brought it back... But maybe his mom didn't pack everything, so it wouldn't be too much?

He walked into the classroom with a mask over his face. The swelling on his forehead was slightly better, and his hair hid half of it, anyway. He wasn't wearing Gu Fei's clothes today, so nobody noticed anything off about him the whole way to his seat.

He didn't know what Lao-Xu said to Gu Fei during that home visit yesterday, but miraculously, Gu Fei came in before the bell for morning self-study. Jiang Cheng lifted his eyes to peek at him, then froze. Aside from a scratch to the side of his chin, Gu Fei's face was unblemished. But what really shocked him was that the bastard had *glasses* on.

The fuck?! Acting like a good student?! Jiang Cheng scowled at him.

The funny thing was that nobody seemed surprised to see Gu Fei like that. Did this mean that...he wore glasses often? He thought of Pan Zhi. Pan Zhi was a bit near-sighted, but firmly refused to wear glasses.

"How could someone with my grades have the nerve to wear them?!" Pan Zhi had said. "I'd rather be blind!"

Pan Zhi is honorable, Jiang Cheng thought. And Pan Zhi even owned more than one pen...

Gu Fei walked over and tossed a plastic bag on the desk in front of him, then sat down. Jiang Cheng opened it to find both his sweater and his homework inside.

Shit! His homework! He'd forgotten to take his homework back after the fight yesterday. He'd let Gu Fei copy his homework after brawling with him! How fucked up was that?

"The swelling hasn't gone down yet?" Gu Fei asked.

Jiang Cheng turned and eyed Gu Fei, trying and failing to tell if his tone was apologetic or gleeful. Gu Fei said it without any affectation, as if he was merely stating the day of the week.

So Jiang Cheng didn't respond.

"Da-Fei." Zhou Jing leaned back against their desk. "Da-Fei!"

Gu Fei pushed his glasses up and looked at him.

"Da-Fei?" Zhou Jing turned. "Hey, Da-Fei..."

Gu Fei slapped the back of his head.

"Why didn't you come yesterday? Were you off traveling some-where?" Zhou Jing asked, rubbing his head.

"No," Gu Fei said.

"I thought you skipped class to go on vacation, like last semester."

Gu Fei sighed and looked at him. "Would *you* skip one day of class for a vacation?"

"...True, one day isn't enough. Hey, are you—"

"Fuck off," Gu Fei curtly ended the conversation.

Today's lessons were no different from the previous days; the teachers talked to themselves, the students played by themselves, and all was harmonious. Gu Fei was the same as usual, too. He first played his stupid *Aixiaochu*, then, probably having run out of lives, put on his headphones and began watching videos.

Jiang Cheng couldn't resist sneaking a few looks at his face. As long as you didn't look in his eyes, Gu Fei gave off a serene air. His clothes were very comfortable, both in style and color, and with glasses on, he really did look like a capital-R Real overachiever.

Jiang Cheng was somewhat shaken by the peculiar mix of charac-teristics in this one person.

After multiple glances, he finally returned his attention to the teacher. No matter how bad their lectures were, no matter whether he was half asleep at his desk, he had to listen when they mentioned the important points.

Jiang Cheng never claimed to be the kind of student who aced tests without studying. He was aware of how much time he needed to spend on his studies. In fact, his current learning environment and the indifferent atmosphere his peers provided made him rather anxious. At his old school he'd never cared much about his grades, but he absolutely refused to let them be dragged down as a result of transferring to Fourth High.

The final period was English. Lao-Lu lectured passionately—maybe because it was almost the weekend and he wanted to shout the whole classroom of sleepyheads awake. Jiang Cheng slumped over his desk and took notes earnestly.

"Let's talk about the homework you handed in today!" Right before ending his lesson, Lao-Lu slapped his desk. "You could run an exhibition with your homework! Call it 'One Hundred Ways to Mess Up a Simple Assignment!'"

"Our class doesn't have a hundred people," Wang Xu replied.

The class burst into laughter.

"You! Wang Jiuri!"[14] Lao-Lu pointed his pointing stick at him. "You're about as useful as cardboard candy! If all of humanity's organ functions started deteriorating, you'd still be left with your mouth!"

Wang Xu pushed his desk in displeasure.

"Don't like that? Come to my office after class!" Lao-Lu bellowed. Before Wang Xu could respond, Lao-Lu's pointer turned in Jiang Cheng's direction, jabbing as he did so. "Gu Fei!"

Gu Fei looked up. "Here."

"What the hell is wrong with you, huh?! You copied your homework, didn't you? Didn't you?!" Lao-Lu said in one breath. "Did you copy it? Tell me if you copied it! Did you or didn't you?"

Gu Fei waited in vain for a moment to answer.

"If you're copying, could you at least use your brain?! Huh?!" Lao-Lu hit the lectern. "Not a single question wrong! Not a *single* one! Let's hear it! Who did you copy from?!"

---

14   Xu [旭] is made up of the characters jiu [九], nine and ri [日], sun. It's like referring to Frank Pentangeli as "Frankie Five-Angels."

This time, he gave Gu Fei room to reply. Gu Fei was silent for a moment, then lifted a finger and pointed at Zhou Jing. "Him."

"Zhou Jing!" Lao-Lu roared immediately, pointing at him. "How very noble of you! I'll mention how helpful you are in your report card comments this semester, how about that?!"

Zhou Jing jumped in fright and turned to see Gu Fei pointing at him. He opened his mouth but didn't say a word.

Lao-Lu picked up their homework and continued to berate them until class ended. He waved his pointer, stuck it under his arm, and walked out of the classroom.

"Damn." Zhou Jing turned. "Whose did you copy?"

Gu Fei looked at him without a word.

Zhou Jing paused for a moment before rising. "Fine, whatever."

After Zhou Jing left, Jiang Cheng looked at Gu Fei, unsure what to say.

"Er-Miao will be waiting at the school gate soon," Gu Fei said as he packed his bag. "Why don't you walk with her?"

"Huh?" Jiang Cheng was perplexed. "I just fought with her big brother. I don't want to walk with her."

"I dare you not to," said Gu Fei.

"Fine, fuck." Jiang Cheng felt his temper flare. "I *won't.*"

Gu Fei was quiet. After a few moments, he took a deep breath. "Do me a favor. Please."

Jiang Cheng suddenly felt gratified. "Wow, was that so hard?"

"Sure was," Gu Fei said.

16

WHEN JIANG CHENG followed Gu Fei out of the school gate, he was strongly tempted to say, *I'm doing this for Gu Miao's sake, not yours.*

But Gu Fei never turned around, so he never had the chance to say it.

When they were finally side by side, he'd missed his moment. Gu Miao was sitting on the railing along the sidewalk with her skateboard in her arms, swinging her legs. Seeing them come out, she jumped straight down and chucked the board in front of herself, then did a running leap onto the skateboard and rolled up to them. She stuck her hand into Gu Fei's pocket and pulled out a handful of candy. Jiang Cheng watched, astounded, as Gu Miao picked all the fruit-flavored ones out of the bunch.

So the candies Gu Fei carried around every day were for little Gu Miao?

Gu Miao unwrapped one and put it in her mouth, then turned and rolled away on her skateboard. She skirted the edge of the sidewalk, probably wary of running into people.

Jiang Cheng had to keep an eye out from behind—though Gu Miao was agile and skilled, she *was* just a little kid... Meanwhile, her brother simply left to get his bike, not even giving her a second glance.

Gu Miao scooted ahead a bit and stopped, turning to look at Jiang Cheng.

"What's up?" Jiang Cheng asked, hurrying over to her side.

Gu Miao jumped off the skateboard and stood aside.

Jiang Cheng wanted to say "I'm sore all over from the fight with your brother yesterday, so I don't feel like skating," but with Gu Miao's round eyes on him, the words wouldn't come out.

"Fine."

He sighed and stepped onto the skateboard, slowly rolling onward.

Fortunately, once they turned the corner, they were on a quieter road with fewer people. Gu Miao ran behind him and suddenly clapped. When he turned around, she sped up and raced over to him, gesturing as she ran: She wanted him to get down.

"You sure know how to play..."

Understanding Gu Miao, he hopped off the skateboard. Gu Miao reached him and bounced onto the board, shooting forward on momentum; she kicked off a few times before looking back at Jiang Cheng.

"Ah..." Jiang Cheng really did feel tired, but he ran toward her anyway. "Why don't you get your brother to do stuff like this with you...?"

Gu Miao jumped off. He rushed to mount the still-rolling skateboard and continued forward. They kept rolling ahead like that, taking turns on the board.

It was pretty fun, to be honest. Gu Miao didn't say anything, nor did she need him to say anything. He just had to coordinate with her. And most importantly, she was a good skater, so Jiang Cheng didn't have to worry about her falling.

Gu Fei kept a dozen or so yards behind them the whole time on his bike, one foot on the ground pushing himself forward. He would speed up and slow down at random, his head bowed as he looked at his phone instead of the road or his sister. Jiang Cheng kept waiting for him to slip into some uncovered manhole so he could applaud. But as run-down as this shitty city was, the roads were well-kept; even the bricks in the sidewalk were all whole. Gu Fei made it safely to their street without an issue.

"All right," Jiang Cheng said as he jumped off the skateboard, his body sweaty from running. "I'm heading that way now."

With one foot on the skateboard, Gu Miao waved goodbye. Jiang Cheng waved back. Gu Miao put her fingers to her mouth and whistled. Gu Fei looked up at her, then stepped on the pedals—all at once, the bike rushed ahead. When it passed her, she reached out and grabbed the back seat, letting Gu Fei drag her along like a water-skier.

Jiang Cheng watched, stunned. "...Fly away, then."

Gu Fei didn't have a father, and his mother probably wasn't very helpful. Gu Miao had likely been raised by Gu Fei like a wolf pup. Where Jiang Cheng came from, if his mother saw an older brother raising his sister that way, she'd rant about it for months.

...Some thoughts just surfaced uncontrollably, compulsive.

Jiang Cheng lifted his head to suck in a deep, ice-cold breath, and felt his heartache ease a little.

Back at Li Baoguo's place, the mahjong players were all gone. The living room was a mess; the unkempt tiles and the filled cans of cigarette ash strewn over the table were a revolting sight.

Jiang Cheng went into the kitchen. He couldn't keep ordering takeout; he had no allowance now, only expenses, so he had to save. Forget getting pocket money from Li Baoguo—it was a mercy if he didn't ask Jiang Cheng for money instead.

He felt like smashing things the moment he walked into the kitchen. After making dumplings yesterday, Li Baoguo had simply left everything there, unwashed and untidied. The pot was still half-filled with old noodle water. Jiang Cheng wanted to wash it, but just as he lifted it, he froze solidly in place: A cockroach had drowned in the pot.

He was too shocked to throw up. He simply held the pot and stood there in the kitchen, feeling as if creepy-crawlies were writhing all over his skin, itchy and uncomfortable and utterly disgusting.

He stood for at least two minutes before clenching his jaw and emptying the pot into the toilet. He placed the pot on the floor of the bathroom, blasted it with the hose for a long while, then scrubbed it frantically with dish detergent. Finally, he filled it with water and boiled it over the stove.

Even when the pot boiled, Jiang Cheng didn't kill the flame. He stared at the bubbling surface. It wasn't until he was sure the last vestiges of the cockroach's shadow had boiled away that he poured out the water and boiled a fresh potful for his noodles.

A funk wafted out of the fridge the instant he opened it. All it contained was a few red chili peppers, which, by the looks of them, had been in there for at least a month. No meat, no eggs—nothing.

Fuck! Did Li Baoguo buy the exact right amount of dumpling mince, down to the last dumpling? Not even an ounce left over?

He stared blankly at the pot of water for a moment, then turned the gas off.

After a tragic mental tussle between going out to eat, ordering takeout, and buying groceries to cook noodles with, he firmly decided to buy groceries. He was powerless to change his environment, so the only thing he could do was adapt. Which was easy enough to say—actually doing it was as hard as growing wings and flying.

Jiang Cheng picked up his wallet and phone, then went out to shop. Going to the local market was the sensible choice, but...after all this time and all his daily walks around the area, he still hadn't seen any kind of market nearby. He wanted to ask a passerby, but he'd gone all the way down the block without running into a single person. At this time of night, everyone would be cooking at home.

He frowned and glanced at the other street.

Gu Fei's not-supermarket would surely have some grocery items. Even if they didn't have green vegetables, there would definitely be sausage or canned fish or something... Maybe he'd been living too hard lately, but the mere thought made him salivate. He was hungry.

Look at the state of yourself, Jiang Cheng!

After admonishing himself, he still turned and walked in the store's direction.

Pushing apart Gu Fei's storefront curtains almost gave him war flashbacks now; he'd felt awkward every time he was here. The fact that he was coming here to buy things when they'd barely spoken three sentences to each other since the fight made it worse.

When he opened the curtains, he felt a dense cluster of eyes staring at him. Instead of awkwardness, Jiang Cheng startled in fright. There were seven people, for a total of fourteen eyes: Gu Fei, Gu Miao, the Fresh Out of Jail quartet, and Li Yan.

A little surprised himself, Gu Fei held his chopsticks in the air as he turned around, staring wordlessly at Jiang Cheng. And because he didn't speak, neither did Fresh Out of Jail or Li Yan. Gu Miao was the only one who stood and waved at him.

Jiang Cheng smiled at Gu Miao and walked in. "I'm here to buy some stuff."

"Go ahead," Gu Fei said.

Jiang Cheng looked around. Gu Fei's store was rather large; there were several rows of shelves. "Um... Where do you stock your sausages and that kind of thing?"

"Next to the window, at the end of the aisle," Li Yan said.

"Thanks." Jiang Cheng glanced at him, then walked over.

They had a good selection, from ham sausages and small cocktail wieners to European-style sliced salami. He took one of each, then grabbed a can of pork belly and some tinned fish.

Jiang Cheng walked two steps toward the counter, paused, then spun around to stock up on condiments too, like oil, salt, soy sauce, and vinegar. Li Baoguo's kitchen was terrifying; he was fearful of using anything stocked in it.

"Quite a pantry you got there." Li Yan stood behind the counter and totaled the bill, saying, "Are you cooking?"

"Mm-hm." Jiang Cheng hesitated. "Do you have...pots and pans?"

"Pots and pans?" Li Yan was taken aback. He glanced over at Gu Fei. "Do you?"

Gu Fei was surprised, too. He rose to his feet. "What kind?"

"Just...for stir-frying vegetables, or making soup."

"Yeah," said Gu Fei. "But you'd get better quality at the mall."

"It's fine, I'll take them," Jiang Cheng said.

Gu Fei eyed him briefly, then turned and walked into the innermost corner. From a heap of buckets and basins, he pulled out a wok for frying and a pot for soup. He waved them at Jiang Cheng.

"This size okay?"

"Sure." Jiang Cheng nodded and walked over to take them.

"Why don't you eat with us?" Li Yan braced his hands against the counter. "It's just another pair of chopsticks."

Jiang Cheng pulled out his wallet. Li Yan's words were friendly, but when he looked over and met his eyes, they were coldly taunting. Unexplained hostility annoyed Jiang Cheng the most. He dug out the bills and tossed them down, then placed a hand onto the counter and stared right back.

"Careful, your eyeballs will fall out," Gu Fei said to Li Yan as he walked over and sat back on the stool. "Cash him out."

Li Yan held his gaze a moment longer before looking down to take the money, then stared at him some more before giving him the change.

Jiang Cheng saw that Li Yan wasn't going to give him a bag, so he glanced around the counter, yanked two bags from the hanging stack, and dumped all his things in them before turning to leave.

Liu Fan looked at Li Yan. "What the hell's wrong with you?"

"Nothing." Li Yan sat. He picked up his cup and took a sip of alcohol. "I don't know why, I just don't like the look of that guy."

"You don't?" Liu Fan said. "It looked more like you fell in love at first sight. You were staring so hard I thought you were going to lick him."

"Is that any way to talk?" Li Yan glowered at him.

"Yan-ge's in a funk today," Luo Yu laughed as he bowed his head and gnawed on a bone.

"Mind your own business." Li Yan glared at him sidelong. "I made this meal. If you're not going to behave, go to the backyard and cook your own noodles."

"Honestly, Li Yan, you bought some really good cuts today," Liu Fan said. "They're so fresh."

"I got my mom to buy them," Li Yan said. "I just crave meat whenever it gets cold, it calls out to me... Er-Miao, wipe the grease off your mouth. A pretty girl like you should watch her manners."

Gu Miao took a tissue and wiped her mouth before burying her face in her food again.

"By the way, that guy didn't come back, did he?" Liu Fan asked.

"Nope." Gu Fei put some vegetables into Gu Miao's bowl. Gu Miao picked them up swiftly and tried to drop them in Li Yan's bowl instead, but Gu Fei held her chopsticks with his own. "Your face is flaking from the dryness."

Gu Miao was forced to withdraw and stuff the vegetables into her mouth.

"That must be because she isn't using skincare." Li Yan leaned in to study Gu Miao's complexion. "Er-Miao, did you use the face lotion I bought you last time?"

Gu Miao didn't speak.

"She thinks it's too much of a hassle," Gu Fei said.

Li Yan tutted. "Dunno where you get that coarse streak from. Both your mother and your brother—"

He stopped midway, stuck. In the end, he simply picked up a yam noodle and stuffed it into his mouth.

"It's fine." Gu Fei sipped his soup.

Li Yan had bought the groceries and cooked this meal. The nice thing about having unemployed slobs for friends was that they would at least come over and help out when his mother was next to useless.

When Gu Fei didn't skip class, his mother was meant to mind the store, but she usually failed to stay for even half the day at least two days out of the week. Li Yan would come over on those days to watch the place and even cook. His cooking wasn't great—just a bunch of ingredients thrown together and boiled in one pot, so it all tasted the same—but he'd always buy food in such generous quantities that the pot could barely hold it all; they had to call up help to eat the entire thing.

After they'd eaten, Liu Fan and the others left. Li Yan leaned back in his chair, tilting his head back and rubbing his belly.

"I'll get the dishes later, Er-Miao. Yan-ge needs to do some digesting—I ate too much."

Gu Miao picked up her skateboard and looked at Gu Fei.

"...Go ahead," Gu Fei said, resigned.

Gu Miao's love for skateboarding bordered on obsession. She all but hugged the skateboard to sleep.

After Gu Miao left, Li Yan opened his eyes and looked at Gu Fei. "Da-Fei, let's go somewhere fun when it gets warmer."

"Where?" Gu Fei asked.

"Dunno. Why don't we ask Xin-jie?" Li Yan said. "We can go traveling with her band."

"Forget it." Gu Fei lit a cigarette and put it between his lips. "I'm not going anywhere for a while. I still have a major-offense demerit I haven't gotten rid of."

"You care about that kind of thing?" Li Yan laughed.

"I'll at least need a high school diploma," said Gu Fei.

Li Yan held his gaze. "If you get any closer to that overachiever, you might even get into a good university."

Gu Fei gave him a look. "Do you have shit for brains?"

"Honestly..." Li Yan paused, staring at the ceiling. "If that kid weren't so unbelievably cocky...he'd be pretty fun."

Gu Fei didn't respond.

"I'm kinda into that type," Li Yan added.

"That type would beat you to a pulp," Gu Fei said. "Dumbass."

"Your hair's getting long, huh. The design's blurring." Li Yan glanced at his head. "Need a trim?"

"Are you restless from all that time on your hands?" Gu Fei exhaled a cloud of smoke.

Li Yan nodded. "Yep."

Gu Fei turned his chair so that his back faced him as Li Yan took out a toolbox from under the counter.

"How long are you planning to keep that design? Do you want a new one?"

"No." Gu Fei leaned his head sideways on the headrest.

"Ding Zhuxin's your goddess, after all." Li Yan picked up his tools and carefully trimmed the music rest symbol on the left side of his head.

"My goddess is Gu Miao," Gu Fei replied. "Stop mentioning me and Xin-jie together all the time, especially to her face."

"I know." Li Yan nodded. "You're not her little devotee anymore, and you don't look up to her like you used to. You don't even like women."

Gu Fei was amused. "Are you on her payroll now?"

"No, I just think she's pretty silly, knowing that you...and still liking the bastard that you are." Li Yan sighed. "She even changed her name. Who knows what she was thinking?"

Gu Fei didn't reply.

Ding Zhuxin's name used to be Zhuyin, which meant "sound of bamboo"; she'd later changed it to Zhuxin. Zhuxin—"heart of bamboo." Except bamboo was hollow. It had no heart.

Yeah. What was she thinking?

When he was little, he worshipped Ding Zhuxin—she was so cool, so self-assured, and in his most lost and helpless years, she was much more supportive than his own mother. Now, he still admired her; he just hadn't thought so many things would change. Change was always so gradual. It was only when you woke up to it that you realized everything was different.

Jiang Cheng spent an hour fiddling with his phone's GPS navigator before he finally found his way to the warehouse.

When the warehouse worker pushed his delivery out on a flatbed trolley, he flinched in alarm. Several large boxes were stacked into a small hill.

"Here, double check. They're all numbered." The worker handed him an inventory list.

After signing, Jiang Cheng rushed out to hire a small truck to haul the boxes back. The driver refused to help him load the boxes, even for money. Jiang Cheng had to use his own hands—all one and a half of them—to drag and shove the boxes into the cargo hold. He felt unbearably sore all over. Getting into a fight was as bad as running ten miles.

Once he loaded the boxes, the driver asked him to sit in front, but he thought it over and declined, climbing in with the cargo instead. He couldn't wait to see what his mom had sent. What kind of things would she send him after he left that home? He had a feeling that once he saw, he would better understand what she was thinking.

The boxes were all well-sealed. He grabbed a knife and cut open the heaviest one: It was a box of books.

The novels and comic books he'd bought, as well as magazines he subscribed to, were neatly and tightly packed into the box. Jiang Cheng frowned. He took a few from the top and looked under them. There, he saw the study material he'd used for his high school entrance exam.

Jiang Cheng shut the cardboard box. She had probably sent him every single book on his shelf. The box underneath was filled with books too. He wasn't an avid reader, so there wasn't much, but along with all the study material, it was enough to make the two boxes as heavy as lead—matching his mood.

He hesitated before opening a smaller box beside it. Inside this one, he found all his little odds and ends—trinkets he'd left on his desk and in his drawer, fun little toys, handicrafts, an alarm clock, a pen holder, a small eyeglass frame, even an old empty lighter.

He shut his eyes and scrubbed his face forcefully, then placed his hand on his forehead, not wanting to move anymore. By the looks of it, his mom hadn't kept any of his belongings. She must've sent everything over indiscriminately, except for the piano.

All this time, he'd been miserable, despondent, and unable to understand or accept his situation. He was even angry and resentful. It was only now, laying eyes on these cast-away things, that he felt *hurt*.

His silent fights with his family, the lectures and rebukes from his parents, being sent back to where he was born...none of that had hurt him. It was only now that he saw the things his mother had mailed over like it was a task to be checked off her list—unsorted, wholly untouched, with no thought spared for whether he actually needed these things or not—that he felt a deep pang of hurt in his chest.

This pain in his heart was more intense and harder to ignore than anything he'd felt in the past weeks. When the vehicle stopped, he almost couldn't get up.

Jiang Cheng unloaded the heaps of boxes, big and small. After the driver left, he nudged them with his foot and sighed. He leaned against the boxes and spaced out as he stared at the dirty, trampled snow by the road.

A scrap collector came up to him on a cycle rickshaw. He straightened up.

"These two boxes of books." Jiang Cheng pointed at the boxes.

The man looked at them. "We buy books at the same price as scrap paper now."

"Fine. Take them," Jiang Cheng said.

After the man weighed his books, Jiang Cheng opened the box of knick-knacks and took out the only thing he wanted to keep: a large black slingshot.

"What about these?" he asked.

"Let me see." The man rifled roughly through the box, taking the things out and peering at them. "They're all pretty useless, and there's not much we can do with their parts, either... Thirty yuan."

"Take it," Jiang Cheng said.

"The one you're holding is worth something," the man said. "Twenty?"

"It's not for sale." Jiang Cheng put the slingshot in his pocket. This guy sure was a crook, he thought, offering twenty yuan for something that had cost two hundred.

The other two boxes were full of clothes, and the man was interested in taking them, too. "And the clothing?"

"What do you think?" Jiang Cheng retorted.

The man chuckled. He took the money from his pocket and handed it to Jiang Cheng, along with a business card. "Anything else you want to sell, just call me. I live close by, and I can get here quickly."

"Okay." Jiang Cheng stuffed the money and the card into his pocket.

As he dragged the boxes of clothes into his room, he felt as if they were made of solid iron. He didn't know if they were actually that heavy, or if he was just drained. The two boxes of clothes fit in his room, at least. He sat on the edge of the bed and looked at them. All those things that he'd wasted so much money and energy moving back here, just to sell to the scrap collector. He couldn't help laughing out loud.

What a great brain you have, you overachiever.

He pulled the dirty notes out of his pocket. It was all small bills, so together, it looked like a lot of money.

Such big, heavy boxes, now turned into a few little pieces of paper.

17

GU FEI SAT BEHIND THE TILL, playing with his phone as he kept an eye on Li Baoguo, who was making his third lap around the shelves. Li Baoguo walked back and forth seemingly without purpose, occasionally glancing toward Gu Fei.

Li Baoguo had stolen from them more than once, so Gu Fei watched him openly every time he came in. But now that he'd met Jiang Cheng, he felt a bit torn between watching and not watching the man.

Li Baoguo wasn't a thief, per se. Sometimes, when he needed something but had gambled all his money away, he would buy it on credit. Their primary clientele consisted of ordinary, poor folk from the bottom of the barrel, so buying things on credit was common. But Li Baoguo always tried to sneak a bit more...

"Hey, Da-Fei..." Li Baoguo's hand slipped into his thick cotton jacket for a moment before he pulled it out again. He went to the freezer and chose a pack of fish balls, then came to place it on the counter. "Here, can I pay you in a few days? With the stuff from before, too?"

"Mm-hm, sure." Gu Fei took a notebook from the drawer. He flipped to Li Baoguo's account and noted as he spoke. "One pack of fish balls, one large bottle of Niulanshan..."

"What? I'm not buying any alcohol," Li Baoguo said awkwardly.

"The one in your pocket." Gu Fei gave him a look. "Li-shu,[15] try to ease up on the booze. You're getting forgetful."

"Oh, right." Li Baoguo forced a laugh as he patted his pocket. "Right, I got a bottle of erguotou... Give me a pack of Changbaishan too."

Gu Fei reached behind to grab a ten-stick pack of Changbaishan cigarettes for him, then noted that down as well.

"You have such nice handwriting." Li Baoguo leaned over and watched. "Hey, do you know my son?"

"Of course I know Li Hui."

"Not Li Hui. My youngest, Chengcheng." Li Baoguo propped his elbow on the counter. "I just got him back. Had to give him up for adoption when he was little, couldn't afford to raise him back then... He goes to Fourth High, too. You know him, right?"

Gu Fei nodded. "Yeah, I think so."

Li Baoguo chortled smugly. "He's real good at studying, not like Xiao-Hui—a straight-A student, you know about that? You bums are all F students, aren't you? But my youngest is a good student."

Gu Fei laughed. "Yup."

"Got them all down yet? I'll ask Chengcheng to come by in a few days with the money to pay you." Li Baoguo glanced over the notebook again and pointed. "I bet his handwriting is better than yours."

"...Sure." Gu Fei kept on nodding.

After Li Baoguo went on his merry way, Gu Fei looked down at his words on the page.

He couldn't vouch for anything else, but Jiang Cheng's handwriting...*hah*. It was so ugly that he could answer everything correctly and the teacher would still dock points out of disgust.

---

15   *Shu or shushu is a term of address for an older man roughly a generation above the speaker.*

Sometime around noon, his mother came over with a thermal food container. "I made some red braised pork belly."

"Not going out today?" Gu Fei stood and unfolded a small table. "Did you eat?"

"Where would I go?! Where can I possibly go?!" Her face filled with displeasure. "If I go out with anyone, you'll leave them half-dead! I'm not eating!"

"Can't you find a guy who doesn't beg for a beating?" Gu Fei said.

"Is there anyone you *wouldn't* want to beat up? When have you ever seen the good in anyone?!" his mother spat. "You don't like the looks of any of them. The only thing you like is your mother staying single for the rest of her life!"

"If you want me to see the good in someone, they need to have some in the first place." Gu Fei opened the lid of the container, then took out a smaller bowl and dumped half of the pork belly into it.

"Where's Er-Miao?" his mom asked.

"Out playing. I'll keep a little for her. She'll come back and eat when she's hungry."

His mother sighed. "Running wild like that all the time, and with a personality like hers... Just looking at her gives me a headache. What's going to become of her?"

"Don't look, then." Gu Fei sat and began to eat.

She stared at him for a while. "You should go down there today," she suddenly said.

"Where?" Gu Fei asked as he ate another chunk of meat, even though he knew what she was talking about.

"Don't you remember what day it is?" His mother slammed a hand against the table. "Your father's only been dead for how long, and you've already forgotten?"

"It's been pretty long," Gu Fei said.

His mother glared at him wordlessly. After some time, she pulled out a tissue and wiped her tears.

Gu Fei could never understand how she felt toward her late husband. When he was alive, they fought every day; after they fought, he would beat her; after he beat her, she would beg the heavens to hurry up and take this man to his next life. But ever since he died, she would cry at the mere mention of him. Sometimes her crying even seemed sincere, as if she really was broken up inside.

"I went to the cemetery two days ago," Gu Fei said as he ate.

"It's no use! I told you, the cemetery's no use!" His mother looked at him. "You have to go to the place where he died, or he won't be at peace! How many times do I have to say it?! If you won't go, I will!"

Gu Fei sighed. "I'll go in the afternoon."

"Burn him some offerings." His mother dabbed at her tears. "That dumbass is so good at losing money, I bet he has to beg for food on the other side."

"Stay in the store this afternoon," Gu Fei said. "And don't touch the money. If you do, I'll tell the king of hell that I'm burning fake bills for him."

His mother glared at him. "...Crazy bastard!"

The lake where his father died was a considerable distance away. It was an abandoned spot that had been roped off to build a small park, apparently, though nobody ever touched it. Since there were no residential areas nearby, very few people ever visited. The water had all but dried up in recent years, so even fewer people went; in winter, not a single person could be seen.

If the lake had been as dry then as it was now, or if the water had frozen more solidly that winter's day...his dad wouldn't have died.

But...

When he had described Li Baoguo to Jiang Cheng, his mind wandered—he was distracted. It felt like he was telling someone about his own father.

Sometimes, Gu Fei was too scared to let himself think. He was afraid of facing the truth that, in his heart of hearts, he'd once wished so ardently for the man's death—and to this day, given a second chance, he'd still want him dead.

His heart and this lake...he didn't want to approach either of them. If his mother didn't insist on him coming here to burn paper offerings every year, he'd never go anywhere near it.

After he walked out the front door, it was a left turn around the little factory and straight onward. There were no turns or forks in the road. Once you reached the dead end, you were there.

It was already deserted when he went around the factory. There was nothing but ruin and desolation as far as the eye could see; it was so bleak, it felt like another dimension.

Gu Fei pulled his cap low and hid his face behind his mask, then put on his earmuffs. Maybe it was the lack of buildings and flatness of the area, or perhaps it was just his unease, but he felt cold. No matter where the wind came from, the chill seemed to seep into his bones and spread from the inside out, layer by layer.

There wasn't much snow this year, but since there was nobody to clear it away, it still blanketed the ground. The faint crunch with each step was enough to make his heart pound hard in his chest.

He walked for a while before looking down and noticing an-other set of footprints. Surprised, he turned around to look in the direction he came. There were indeed two sets of footprints, heading in but not out.

Someone else had come to the lake at this time of year.

He frowned.

He didn't want to be seen burning offerings at the lake. He didn't want anyone to think he harbored any kind of remorse. He felt no remorse—only fear.

It wasn't a large lake, but the wind was much more aggressive near the banks. It clawed at his face so harshly that it hurt his eyes. Gu Fei walked through the sparse woods, stepping through the wild brush as he reached the lakeside. The pair of footprints from earlier disappeared in the shards of ice. He looked left and right but saw no one. After a moment's hesitation, he peered into the lake, though the lakebed was exposed in many places. No one was in there, either. Of course, even if someone stepped through the ice and fell in now... this lake could no longer drown anyone, only make them freeze to death.

Gu Fei found a tree and crouched next to its trunk. Chucking down the bag he held, he pulled out a cigarette and lit it. He didn't want to walk further inward along the lake. He was going to wait this out. Anyone who came in or out would have to pass this place; he decided to wait until whoever it was went by before burning his offerings.

But after almost twenty minutes, when he feared he might freeze if he didn't at least twitch or make a sound, he still didn't see anyone come out.

"Fuck."

He hesitated, then put out his cigarette and picked up the bag. His only option was to walk further in: partially to see who was there, and partially to find a more secluded spot.

After a few hundred yards, Gu Fei heard a crisp *crack* echo from the center of the lake. It didn't sound like a natural crack in the ice, but one caused by someone's footstep or some other kind of impact. He quickly turned to look at the center of the lake, but he saw no one and nothing.

All was quiet.

A chill went down his spine. He whipped around to check behind himself. There was nobody there, nor anything...suspicious.

Before he could right himself, another crack came from the surface of the lake. He turned again—his head could fall off from all the twisting. Again, he saw nothing. But this time, the sound was more muffled.

He slowly backed away and leaned against a tree. It was a bit childish, but putting his back against something tangible and solid gave him some sense of security.

He kept his eye trained on the surface of the lake. A few seconds later, he saw a tiny, rock-like thing fly out from the cluster of dead brush by the lake, about a hundred yards away.

It hit the ice. This time, the sound it made wasn't a crisp *crack*, but a dull *thunk*.

Was someone throwing stones? Were they *that* bored? Judging by the speed of the projectile, though, it didn't seem like it had been thrown by hand.

Gu Fei tugged his jacket close and slowly ambled in that direction. He'd gone about twenty yards when he spotted a figure moving around in a cove formed by the lake's edge. Though the tall, withered grass almost hid them, he could tell that it was a person.

Not a ghost.

He felt ridiculous for being so scared of some bored stranger throwing stones at the lakeside. Absurd. He still let out a sigh of relief, though. Instead of going any further, he backed up into the woods. He intended to wait for them to leave—and he wanted to see what they were doing.

The person didn't notice him walking over. They bent down, appeared to pick something up, then stretched one arm forward while the other pulled back.

A dark object flew out with a *swoosh* and hit the ice.

Thunk.

Gu Fei realized at once that they were using a slingshot. The person's clothes seemed a bit...familiar. He peered through the grass more carefully, then stiffened.

Jiang Cheng?

That was the coat he'd worn when they fought the other day—the ugly-as-fuck one with two stripes of gray and white across the chest about a hand's-breadth wide.

Gu Fei looked around. There was nobody else here. Jiang Cheng had found this place all on his own? And then started slingshot target practice on the ice? For a top student, he was quite the romantic, spending his free time out here playing with his slingshot rather than studying at home.

Gu Fei lit another cigarette and put it in his mouth as he watched Jiang Cheng.

He appeared to be using pebbles, but since the lakeside was frosted over, they weren't easy to find. Every time he bent down, he spent ages digging around. Sometimes he had to kick at the ground to find one.

After watching for some time, Gu Fei reckoned Jiang Cheng was in a sour mood again. He kept kicking as if he was raring for a fight—he could almost see the flames rolling off him.

Four or five shots in, Gu Fei was astonished. He felt for his glasses in his inner pocket and put them on so he could see properly. Jiang

Cheng was aiming at the same spot each time! His target was about thirty yards from the bank, but he managed to hit it squarely every time, enough to bore a hole in the ice.

Pretty impressive.

Lots of people played with slingshots. Out of the ones Gu Fei knew, many bragged about how accurate they were, how skilled— several claimed they could hit a chicken from seventy yards away. But this was his first time seeing it with his own eyes: someone actually shooting stones into the same spot a dozen times in a row.

After a while, Jiang Cheng stopped. He bent down, gouging and kicking at the ground for a long time without getting up—out of stones, probably. He paced in the same place several times, then walked in Gu Fei's direction. Gu Fei quickly drew back and crouched behind a tree.

"Fuck!" Jiang Cheng shouted angrily; he still couldn't find a good stone. His voice was loud, and having been carried over by the wind, Gu Fei heard him distinctly. He was out of stones, so it was probably time for him to leave.

But Jiang Cheng didn't leave. He stared down at the ground and struck it with his foot, kicking away a layer of snow to discover another patch of pebbles.

Gu Fei sighed.

Jiang Cheng picked up a few and stuffed them into his coat pocket. He glanced at the lakeside, then turned away. After steadying himself for a few seconds, he turned and lifted his arms, shooting out a stone.

Clang. It struck a thin steel rod in the distance, sticking out of the ground.

Damn.

Gu Fei was astounded. If he hadn't been wearing glasses, he wouldn't have even seen that steel rod.

Jiang Cheng turned and took a few steps to the side, then spun around again and pelted the steel rod with yet another stone. It hit its target and cracked into pieces.

"Oh, yeah!" Jiang Cheng clapped, then raised the slingshot in his hand and waved all around, bowing in a circle. "Thank you, thank you."

Managing to keep his laughter in check, Gu Fei slowly retreated even further. If Jiang Cheng noticed him now, the ensuing fight would probably flatten all the trees in the vicinity.

"Contestant Jiang Cheng has decided to up the difficulty! He's decided to rise to the challenge once again! Woooohooo!" Jiang Cheng narrated fervently as he drew another two stones from his pocket. This time, he didn't turn away from the steel rod. He aimed directly at it and pulled.

Gu Fei heard two sounds almost simultaneously:

Clang! Thump!

He'd shot two stones at the same time. One hit the target; the other missed and struck the ground.

"Ah, what a shame." Jiang Cheng took another stone from his pocket as he spoke. "Coach Why, do you think it was a one-off miscalculation, or is this just beyond his skill level?"

Coach Why? It took a long moment for Gu Fei to realize he meant *Coach Y.*

"I think he still has room for improvement." Jiang Cheng pulled the sling back again. "He seems to be going for a different challenge this time... Will he lower the difficulty, or continue...?"

He released his arm and the stone went flying. Before Gu Fei could make it out, Jiang Cheng followed with another pull—a second stone shot out, too, then a third.

Clang, clang, clang!

All three hit their target.

Gu Fei watched Jiang Cheng's back. Were the situation different, he really would've wanted to clap for Jiang Cheng. It wasn't just the accuracy; it was the graceful flourish of his movements. If Li Yan watched this on mute, he wouldn't say another word about not liking the look of him.

But at the end of such an impressive display, Jiang Cheng didn't applaud himself, nor wave and bow. He stood in place without a single word. After a moment, he lowered his head and sank slowly into a squat, cradling his head with both arms.

Gu Fei was baffled. Was he method acting or something? But he soon realized Jiang Cheng's shoulders were gently shaking.

He was crying.

Gu Fei smoked his final two puffs and stubbed out the cigarette by his foot. Then he got up to leave, walking further inward along the lake. He wasn't interested in watching this. Watching for a laugh was fine, but spying on someone else's pain, seeing a firecracker of a guy break down and cry—there was no fun in that.

It wasn't possible to walk in a full circle around the lake. It had a boundary: Up ahead was a hill shaped like a rotten yam. That was the farthest Gu Fei could go. He found a small clearing and spent ten minutes starting a fire. Then, he retrieved the bundles of joss paper from his bag and tossed them into the flames.

Some were golden, some yellow, and some patterned; their face value went from nil to hundreds of billions, enough to suit a spirit's every need.

Gu Fei watched the leaping flames. He stretched his hands over the fire to toast them.

He was meant to say something at a time like this. Others would say things like *Come collect the money, we're all fine here, don't worry, tell us if you need more and we'll make sure it's enough...* But if he had to speak, he wouldn't know what to say.

In silence, he watched the flames flicker and shift colors as they rose through the thick smog, swaying in the wind like a waving hand before gradually thinning out. At last, all that was left was a bluish-black wisp of smoke.

Gu Fei picked up a fallen branch and dragged it through the fire. Charred scraps of joss paper sparked and floated into the air, then all was calm again.

He stood and kicked some loose snow to cover the sooty embers before turning to go.

✦ ✦ ✦

Every year, once this day was over, Gu Fei would feel himself lighten. Now the days returned to familiar dullness: minding the store, watching over Gu Miao as she hopped all over the street like a rabbit, attending school and sitting through boring lessons, playing his stupid *Aixiaochu*, and observing Lao-Xu's valiant efforts to rescue him from the so-called darkness.

Jiang Cheng didn't cry by the lake for very long that day. By the time Gu Fei returned after burning his offerings, he was gone. When Gu Fei saw him at school, Jiang Cheng seemed no different. He was still cocksure and covered in prickly thorns, listening to lessons slumped over his desk—occasionally with his eyes shut or half-open as he wrote down his notes.

They didn't disturb each other in class. They didn't really have much to say. However, whenever Gu Fei thought of Jiang Cheng's performance by the lake, he worried he might actually laugh out loud.

"Da-Fei." Zhou Jing leaned against their desk. "Da-Fei? Da—"

Jiang Cheng picked up a book and thwacked Zhou Jing in the head with it, impatience written all over his face. He lowered his voice and said, "Just say whatever the fuck you have to say! Hasn't anyone ever beat you up for that before?!"

"Fuck!" Zhou Jing held his head and scowled at him, then looked at Gu Fei. "Da-Fei, I heard something when I went to Xu-zong's office today. He said the school's starting the spring basketball tournament next month."

"Dunno anything about that," Gu Fei said.

"Are you in? You're our class's only hope. If you don't join, we'll lose for sure."

Gu Fei pointed at him. "Leave me alone."

Zhou Jing turned back and slouched over his own desk.

Jiang Cheng grew distracted. A spring basketball tournament? Next month? Did March count as spring?

At the thought of basketball tournaments, he grew wistful. When he recalled his basketball days in his old school, the memories came with other, less happy thoughts. Yet he couldn't resist thinking about those times he ran freely across the court. Against the present, those were memories that glowed.

18

JIANG CHENG CROUCHED on the floor of his room, putting a small bookshelf together. He'd managed to work up a sweat, but it still wasn't done. This was probably the most value-for-money item he'd bought since he first started lining Jack Ma's pockets with his cash.

The small, five-hundred-yuan bookshelf was dead heavy. Just by weighing each component in his hand, he could tell it was in a different class. On top of that, there was an unusually large number of parts, and since it had an odd shape, each damned part was unique.

Jiang Cheng stared at the instruction booklet for a long time before he joined the legs to the base. Then he had to insert the screws, but the holes were too small and he couldn't twist them in, so he had to get a hammer and knock them in...

Li Baoguo pushed the door open and bellowed, "You bought that thing online?"

All his life, nobody had ever just opened Jiang Cheng's bedroom door and walked in when it was closed. Li Baoguo's roaring voice almost sent his heart flying out of his mouth to smack against the wall. *Thunk!* The hammer in Jiang Cheng's hand hit his left thumb. He clenched his jaw as a burst of pain spread through his fingertip.

"That a bookshelf?" Li Baoguo asked.

"Yeah," Jiang Cheng hissed through gritted teeth.

"How much was it?" Li Baoguo walked over and bent down to look at the planks on the floor. "You have to put this thing together yourself?"

"Yeah." Jiang Cheng sucked in a breath, finally recovering a little. He looked at Li Baoguo. "Next time, could you knock before coming in?"

"Knock?" Li Baoguo was taken aback. He burst into laughter, as if Jiang Cheng had said something hilarious. Still laughing, he slapped Jiang Cheng on the shoulder and said, "Why would I knock?! It's my son's bedroom! Why would I need to knock before coming into my own son's room? I'm the one who jizzed you out of my dick!"

Jiang Cheng was astounded. "Wh...what?"

"I'm kidding!" Li Baoguo continued to guffaw, pointing at him. "Shocked by a thing like that? You're a silly kid."

"No." Jiang Cheng stared at the boards. He was in no mood to keep building the shelf. He barely even wanted to lift his eyelids now.

"There's not that many rules in our family, you know. We're rough people, we don't put on airs like rich folks," Li Baoguo said. "Look at you, you can't even put a shelf together... But that's all right, you're a good student. Kids like you can't work with your hands—you're all brains."

Jiang Cheng listened to this logically bankrupt monologue in silence, hoping Li Baoguo would take a hint and leave once he was done talking. But Li Baoguo didn't give up. He crouched next to Jiang Cheng.

"Lemme see."

Jiang Cheng didn't move. Li Baoguo grabbed a panel and looked at it, then glanced at the finished product on the instructions. "All right. Stand aside, I'll do it."

"Huh?" Jiang Cheng turned to look at him.

"It's easy." Li Baoguo looked through the heap of wooden slats and chose two, then took a twisted wooden block and began to fix them together. "I'm telling you, this thing was a waste of money. I could've picked these bits of wood from the construction site and made you one in two hours."

Jiang Cheng watched his practiced movements without a word. Li Baoguo looked far more tolerable right now than he normally did staring at his tiles at the mahjong table.

Not half an hour later, Li Baoguo finished putting the bookshelf together without even looking at the instructions.

"Done." He dusted his hands off and looked at the shelf. "What an ugly thing. How much did this piece of...thing cost you?"

"...Three hundred yuan." Jiang Cheng wanted to say four, but he deducted further after a moment's pause.

"Three *hundred*?!" Li Baoguo hollered, appalled. "Three hundred for a wooden shelf like this?! You brat, what a waste of money!"

Jiang Cheng said nothing. He wondered whether Li Baoguo would have screamed like that if he'd said two hundred or one hundred instead. True, the shelf wasn't cheap, but it was good quality, and he really liked the design. In a place that did not belong to him before he came and would not give him a sense of belonging now that he was here, he needed something that was *his*. Something that made him feel grounded. But these were things Li Baoguo wouldn't understand, and Jiang Cheng couldn't make him.

"My son spends like a sailor," Li Baoguo sighed. "Meanwhile, his dad has to buy things on credit."

Jiang Cheng stiffened. "What do you owe this time?"

"Didn't I buy a bag of fish balls the other day, the ones you said were really tasty?" Li Baoguo said. "And that bottle of...*hmph*, that kid has really sharp eyes, or I would have gotten that baijiu without having to pay... I already owed other things before that, though, so it doesn't make much of a difference."

Jiang Cheng stared at him so hard he thought his eyes might fall out—he had a mind to put his hands under them to catch, just in case.

"How's about..." Li Baoguo seemed like he had a hard time bringing it up. "Hey, son, do you...have any money on you?"

Jiang Cheng really wished he could say no. But he couldn't deny it: As Li Baoguo spent the last half hour putting his bookshelf together, he'd been a little stunned, even vaguely touched. Though now he guessed that Li Baoguo probably only helped so it'd be easier to ask him for money...

Jiang Cheng nodded despite himself. "Yeah, I do."

"There's my reliable son!" Li Baoguo slapped his arm.

"Who do you owe?" Jiang Cheng asked. "How much in total? I'll go pay it now."

"That little supermarket on the next street... You probably know him, Gu Fei," Li Baoguo said. "It's his family's store—"

"What did you say? Gu Fei?" Jiang Cheng cut him off before he could finish speaking, his voice almost breaking.

"Yeah, he seems to know you too," Li Baoguo said. "Tell him I sent you... Hey, he's from Fourth High as well. You know him, right?"

Jiang Cheng fell silent. Shock, confusion, and an indescribable sense of shame enveloped him; he grabbed his jacket and stormed out.

It was too! Fucking! Humiliating! His own father, owing money to the store owned by his deskmate—the one he just *fought*! Being in debt wasn't a big deal—that was just the way Li Baoguo lived—but by the sound of it, he even tried to *steal*! And Gu Fei caught him!

Fuck me! Fucking fuck me! Fucking fuck me over and over...

Why do I have to go pay? Can't I just give the money to Li Baoguo and make him *pay?*

Right... Why do I have to go and disgrace myself in person?

Jiang Cheng turned and walked back. Just as he reached the end of the hallway, he heard Li Baoguo's voice. He seemed to be chatting with the upstairs neighbor. "My youngest son is so mature! The moment he heard I owe money to the supermarket, he immediately went to pay it!"

"Huh," the neighbor said. "You're lucky, then, getting a son like that for free."

"What do you mean, for free?! He's my seed, isn't he?!" Li Baoguo boomed cheerfully. "That kid's much better than Li Hui. He didn't even let me do the legwork!"

"Look how happy you are. Better get yourself together. If you keep drinking all the time, someday that new son of yours won't give you the time of day, either!"

"Bullshit!" Li Baoguo yelled, spitting for good measure. "You're the worst at making conversation in this whole building—you'd rather keel over and die than say a single nice word!"

"Why are you bragging to me, then?" she yelled back. "You'd keel over and die either way, whether you brag or not!"

Jiang Cheng couldn't bear to listen any further. Now he understood how his neighbors kept starting fights with each other—the way they squabbled, he wouldn't be surprised if they started throwing fists any second. He leaned miserably against the outside of the building, then pulled off his hat and restlessly ran his fingers through his hair.

After five minutes of inner turmoil, he finally gritted his teeth and went to Gu Fei's street. It was too damned cold—by the time he got over his internal conflict, his face was frozen stiff.

It wasn't a big deal, anyway. He was going there to pay, not to add to the debt, and definitely not to steal... He could even pay interest if he felt like it!

Past the intersection, the next street led almost straight to Gu Fei's storefront. Jiang Cheng saw Gu Fei standing in the doorway, a cigarette in his mouth as he played with his phone. The moment he caught sight of him, Jiang Cheng's great "I'll even pay interest" pride disappeared as if fleeing from disaster, probably because he'd never done something so humiliating before. And when Gu Fei looked up at him, he could feel his walk turn funny.

It was too embarrassing. How could Li Baoguo be so pathetic?

Gu Fei gazed at him expressionlessly. It was only after Jiang Cheng crossed the street and continued to walk toward him that Gu Fei took the cigarette out of his mouth and asked, "Come to buy another pot?"

Jiang Cheng saw a shop assistant walk out of the small pharmacy nearby. "...Let's talk inside."

Gu Fei turned and walked into his store. Jiang Cheng followed.

Gu Fei turned back and looked at him. "Hm?"

"Did Li Baoguo buy things on credit here?" he asked.

"Mm." Gu Fei nodded, leaning against the counter. "Not much, though. We don't sell anything expensive."

"How much does he owe?" Jiang Cheng took his wallet out. "I'll pay you."

Gu Fei gave him a look. His hand reached back to stub out his cigarette in the ashtray before opening the drawer and taking out a notebook. "With your own money?" he asked as he flipped through it.

"Yeah, no shit," said Jiang Cheng. "If he had money, he wouldn't be buying things on credit."

"If he didn't gamble, he wouldn't need to buy things on credit." Gu Fei handed him the book. "Two hundred and sixty-eight yuan. You can double check."

"It's fine."

Jiang Cheng didn't take the notebook; he fished out three hundred yuan and gave the bills to Gu Fei. He didn't want to see it at all. It blew his mind that someone could live Li Baoguo's life—could live like Li Baoguo and his mahjong buddies—and not feel the need to change his ways.

"He buys on credit every month." Gu Fei gave him the change and propped a hand on the countertop, studying him. "Are you gonna pay for him next month, too?"

Jiang Cheng looked at him. Irritated, he shoved the bills haphazardly into his wallet. "How's it any of your business?"

"What I mean is, let him pay for it himself," Gu Fei said. "He can usually afford it."

Jiang Cheng stared. He could afford it? Li Baoguo made it sound like he couldn't.

"But if someone else is here to pay for him, then naturally, he won't bother." Gu Fei sat on his chair. "Can't you see that?"

"...No, my eyes aren't good enough." Jiang Cheng sighed. "I don't wear glasses, unlike some posers around here."

Gu Fei fixed him with a look. "They're prescription glasses for nearsightedness."

"From playing *Aixiaochu*?"

"No," Gu Fei snorted. "What city did you live in before you came here? Are the people there all really patient?"

Jiang Cheng looked at him silently.

"With an attitude like yours, if you weren't my deskmate—no, if Er-Miao wasn't weirdly fond of you," Gu Fei said, pointing, "I'd beat you up so bad, not even Xiao-Ming's grandpa would recognize you."

"You?" Jiang Cheng sneered. "How, by pressing into my palm?"

"Sure, I'm not as good as you." Gu Fei pushed his sleeve up and showed Jiang Cheng his wrist. Jiang Cheng took a look and saw pink teeth marks.

"Fuck me." He was astounded. "I bit you days ago. It's still there?"

"You've got a decent set of teeth. If I knew you could bite a zipper off, I would've been more careful," Gu Fei said. "You left me a row of bleeding craters. The scabs only just came off."

Jiang Cheng fell quiet. He really didn't expect a bite to be that serious. But if Gu Fei hadn't pressed his wound open...

He was abruptly overcome with the urge to laugh—he couldn't believe he'd fought such a stupid tussle with Gu Fei. Suppressing his amusement, Jiang Cheng glanced at Gu Fei. It was obvious from Gu Fei's expression that he was holding back, too; the corners of his mouth were curving upward beyond his control.

"Shit," Jiang Cheng swore.

He and Gu Fei simultaneously burst into hysterics.

Laughter was a stupid, infectious disease. The more you tried to fight it, the harder you'd end up laughing, and the harder it would be to stop.

There was a time when the homeroom teacher had chewed out Pan Zhi in class, but despite his self-proclaimed terror, he just couldn't stop laughing. When he was eventually banished to the walkway, he'd marched out with his head thrown back in endless peals of raucous laughter.

Jiang Cheng didn't want to laugh right now, either. He was still miserable, and he didn't feel like laughing with Gu Fei—but he just couldn't stop.

Gu Fei leaned back in his chair and Jiang Cheng leaned against the shelf; they laughed together for almost a full minute. In the end, Jiang Cheng was so annoyed about the laughing that he pushed the curtain aside and walked out.

In the cold wind, he finally stopped. "Fuck!"

Jiang Cheng didn't go back inside. He stuffed his hands in his pockets and strode down the street. It was kind of depressing—one bout of hysterics only lasted for so long. The moment he stopped laughing, he was rudely dropped back into reality.

Jiang Cheng was struck by something: If he kept bottling up his emotions like this, would it develop into some kind of serious illness?

Zhou Jing's intel about the spring basketball tournament turned out to be accurate. Lao-Xu called Jiang Cheng to his office. The instant he saw the basketball on Lao-Xu's desk, he knew why he was there.

"I don't play basketball," he said.

"Look, kid." Lao-Xu brought a stool over. "Sit. Let's talk."

Jiang Cheng sat. He actually did want to play basketball, but only for fun, with a few random people—he didn't want Lao-Xu putting such an official burden on his shoulders.

"You were on the basketball team at your old school, weren't you?" Lao-Xu asked.

"Let's skip the theatrics, Xu-zong," Jiang Cheng sighed. "I think you've already mapped out the lives of my ancestors eight generations back at this point."

"It's not often we get an all-around overachiever. Of course I need to learn more about you." Lao-Xu laughed. "I thought you might say no even before I asked you here, but it was worth a shot."

"Oh."

"Our school holds a basketball tournament every year—more than one, in fact. The principal loves basketball. I've always been in charge of our homeroom class, but we've never won a match in any competition..."

Jiang Cheng was rather surprised. He'd seen Gu Fei play basketball. Even if there wasn't anyone in their class to match his skills, surely they wouldn't have lost *every* match.

"Doesn't Gu Fei play pretty well?" he couldn't help asking.

"That kid..." Lao-Xu sighed. "You can't count on him at all. He never takes part in any class activities. We're just grateful he doesn't play for another class."

"Why are you coming to me, then? I can hardly win a match on my own."

"Be the team captain," Lao-Xu said. "I think you have what it takes—"

"And where did you get that idea?" Jiang Cheng was at a loss for words.

"From your heart," Lao-Xu said.

"Oh, wow." Jiang Cheng couldn't resist putting a hand to his chest.

"If you say yes," Lao-Xu grinned, "I'll go talk to Gu Fei. The two of you, plus Wang Xu, Guo Xu, and Lu Xiaobin... That's five people already. If we find some time to train every day, I think we might have a chance."

Jiang Cheng said nothing. He didn't even know who Guo Xu and Lu Xiaobin were. But Lao-Xu kept speaking to him in that earnest voice, patiently trying to persuade him, and Jiang Cheng couldn't find a reason to say anything to the contrary.

"I just have one request," Jiang Cheng said. "I'm not gonna be your team captain. You must've misunderstood my heart, Xu-zong. Pick someone else. Then I'll play along."

Having been given the green light by Jiang Cheng, Lao-Xu was energized; he immediately went looking for Gu Fei in self-study period.

Lao-Xu rapped his desk. "Gu Fei. Come to my office."

"I haven't been late or skipped class recently," Gu Fei said, resting his forehead against the edge of the desk as he played his capital-S Stupid *Aixiaochu.*

"Not that." Lao-Xu rapped the desk again.

"I'm not playing basketball," Gu Fei said.

"Not that, either," Lao-Xu said. "Come on."

Lao-Xu turned and left. Gu Fei continued playing until he finished the level, then reluctantly rose from his seat and ambled out of the classroom.

"Hey, Jiang Cheng, Jiang—" Zhou Jing called out, then cut himself off when he thought better of it. "Is Lao-Xu talking to you two about the tournament?"

Jiang Cheng didn't answer.

"You know, you look like you can play basketball. Am I right? You play basketball, no?"

"Your class hasn't won a game—ever?" Jiang Cheng asked.

"Yeah," Zhou Jing said. "We're in the humanities stream, after all. It's to be expected."

Jiang Cheng glanced at him. "Bullshit."

Ten minutes later, Gu Fei came back to the classroom. He sat down and took his phone out to continue playing his game. Jiang Cheng thought he'd say something, but he didn't. Lao-Xu must have failed.

He glanced at Wang Xu. If Gu Fei wasn't joining and he ended up having to play with that idiot... It was a miserable thought.

"Who knew a nice old man like Lao-Xu would start lying, too?" Gu Fei murmured.

"Huh?" Jiang Cheng turned. "What did he lie to you about?"

"He wanted to talk about basketball, duh," Gu Fei said as he played. "He said you're in. Are you?"

"...Yeah," Jiang Cheng answered. "He sounded really pitiful."

"You pity everyone," Gu Fei said.

Jiang Cheng glanced askance at him. "Mm-hm. You seem rather pitiful to me, too."

"Pitiful for playing *Aixiaochu*?" Gu Fei asked.

"For being stuck on the same level for four entire days."

Gu Fei put his phone down and turned to look at him. "You've sure got a mouth on you."

Jiang Cheng plastered a large, fake smile on his face. "You can keep yours shut if it can't keep up. There's no point in arguing, anyway."

Gu Fei turned back to his game. "What position did you use to play?"

"Guard," Jiang Cheng answered reflexively.

"Let's give it a try, then," Gu Fei said. "I didn't give Lao-Xu a definitive answer either way."

"Wait," Jiang Cheng said, bewildered. "What's the big fuss? He's asking you to play basketball, not martyr yourself."

"It's annoying," Gu Fei said. "Think about it. People like Jiuri are going to be on the court."

"What's wrong with him playing?" Jiang Cheng glanced at their dear classmate Wang Jiuri, who was resting his eyes with his arms folded across his chest, looking every bit the gang boss of their class.

"There's one of him in every class… Shit!" Gu Fei chucked his phone into his desk drawer—he'd probably failed the level again. "They're fine on the court, but off it, who knows what they'll do? That's what makes it annoying."

"So are you going to play or not?" Jiang Cheng asked. "Now *I'm* getting annoyed. Try, my ass—if you're gonna play, *play*. If not, just fucking forget it."

"All right then," Gu Fei said. "If you're in, so am I."

Run Wild
SAYE

19

AFTER GU FEI TOLD Lao-Xu he'd enter the basketball tournament, Lao-Xu's excitement was so palpable that Jiang Cheng felt it was as if Gu Fei had made it into Peking University. The moment classes ended that afternoon, he called all five of the players he'd picked to his office.

Jiang Cheng glanced at everyone, finally putting faces to Guo Xu and Lu Xiaobin's names.

"No reserves?" Wang Xu asked. "Just the five of us playing the whole game?"

"You can see if any of your classmates would be good on the bench," Lao-Xu said. "As for team captain..."

Lao-Xu glanced at Gu Fei as he spoke. Gu Fei lifted a finger and pointed it at Wang Xu. "Him."

Wang Xu immediately tilted his face up, putting on a reluctant expression. "Nah, I can't. I don't want to be team captain; it's such a pain."

Just the look of him made Jiang Cheng want to laugh—what a bad actor.

"Wang Xu, then. You can all start practicing tomorrow." Lao-Xu gave the basketball on his table to Wang Xu. "This is a good ball. I checked the equipment in our gym—none of the balls there are any good, so I went out and bought this one for you. They'll use a new, good ball for the tournament, so we might as well get used to it during practice."

Guo Xu took the ball from Wang Xu's hand and bounced it a couple of times. "Thanks, Xu-zong."

Jiang Cheng watched his movements; Guo Xu seemed decent. Maybe not overly impressive, but he could dribble, at least. Wang Xu seemed quite proud, so he was probably a decent player, too. He might even think he was good at it. And though Lu Xiaobin never spoke, he was the tallest—about six foot two—and pretty buff. He was built like a brick shithouse. That was good.

It was easy enough to find benchwarmers. Though their class was in the humanities stream, there were still a lot of boys. Since it meant they could play basketball during self-study period, quite a few people wanted in. Team Captain Wang Jiuri called out everyone from the back row measuring six feet or taller, and that was that.

Lao-Xu already booked a court for them. Just watching his proactive positivity made Jiang Cheng feel exhausted on his behalf. As the head of a shitty class in a shitty school, where their grades were even shittier and they didn't even have athletic prowess to fall back on, Lao-Xu somehow remained spirited and driven.

Holding the ball, Wang Xu stood in the center of the court with the air of a team captain. "Let's see you guys' skill levels first."

"We've played together a bunch of times before," one of the guys said. "What else do you need to see?"

"We all need to get familiar with each other!" Wang Xu put on a serious face, then looked toward Jiang Cheng, who was crouching by the court. "How about you start, Jiang Cheng? Since you just transferred here, I don't know how well you play."

"Okay." Jiang Cheng rose and took off his jacket. "How do we do this?"

Wang Xu passed him the ball and moved into an intercepting stance. "Bring the ball past me."

"Sure." Jiang Cheng caught it. He dribbled a few times to get a feel for the ball's bounce, then charged toward Wang Xu.

Wang Xu stood in place. By the time he reached out to stop Jiang Cheng, Jiang Cheng had already woven past on his left, stepping into a layup and sinking the ball into the basket.

"Nice!" Guo Xu cheered.

"Wait." Wang Xu looked a little embarrassed. "I didn't say 'start'— you caught me off guard."

"Ah." Jiang Cheng caught the rebound and walked back, standing in front of him.

Once again, Wang Xu took his time to get into position. He finally lifted his chin and said, "Bring it!"

Jiang Cheng barely moved before Wang Xu launched himself forward, waving his arms in an attempt to block his way and to steal the ball at the same time. Jiang Cheng paused for a moment, then simply jumped and shot for the hoop. It went in.

"That's a three-pointer," Gu Fei called out from the courtside bench.

"Damn! We've got a chance this time!" someone hooted in excitement.

Wang Xu didn't look too pleased. Just as he was about to say something, Gu Fei cut him off. "Hurry up. It's cold."

The heating in the gym was garbage, and everyone had already taken off their jackets at this point, so they were all wearing single layers. Grudgingly, Wang Xu nodded.

"How about this: We'll split into two groups and try playing half a game to start."

Everyone agreed.

Lao-Xu had been watching them the whole time, and now he came over and said, "Let's split up Gu Fei and Jiang Cheng. We'll have one on each side."

"Why?" Wang Xu asked. "They're both good. Let them work in tandem."

"Easy for them to partner up, but if the two of them are on the same side, we might as well not play," Lu Xiaobin said. "Split them into two teams and everyone can get some practice."

"All right, then."

This time Wang Xu didn't put on any team captain airs as he finished splitting everyone into teams. Gu Fei's team was Lu Xiaobin, Guo Xu, and two other guys Jiang Cheng wasn't familiar with; Wang Xu himself was on Jiang Cheng's team, along with three people he didn't know. Jiang Cheng now had a deeper appreciation of how dire his emotional state had been recently: After all the time he'd spent here, he still couldn't recognize everyone in his class. Of the ten people on the court, he only knew five. He had to differentiate them based on their clothes; two of them he'd only just managed to tell apart today...

Lao-Xu grabbed a whistle and stood by the court. "I'll referee."

"It's only half a game, what's there to ref?" Gu Fei said.

"Play by regular rules anyway." Lao-Xu put one hand on his hip and held the whistle with the other. "We'll start with a jump and play as usual, just with a shorter time limit."

"All right." Wang Xu called the rest of his team over. "Each of you guard someone. Pin Da-Fei down and pass the ball to Jiang Cheng every chance you get—don't bring it to the basket yourselves. As soon as Da-Fei gets close, pass to someone else. That bastard's killer at stealing the ball."

"All right." The team nodded.

"We're counting on you for points." Wang Xu raised a hand, but just before it landed on Jiang Cheng's shoulder, he took it back. "Oh, I forgot—you're fussy, you don't like to be touched."

Jiang Cheng sighed.

To nobody's surprise, Jiang Cheng and Gu Fei were the jumpers for the opening tip. Lao-Xu stretched out his hand, holding the ball between them.

"Focus, now! I'm about to throw."

"What kind of referee says that?" said Gu Fei.

"Focus!" Lao-Xu stared daggers at him.

Glancing behind at Wang Xu, Jiang Cheng wondered how quick his reflexes were. Jiang Cheng had always played point guard—he'd never jumped for the tip in an official match before. He figured Gu Fei's side would probably get this one.

With a lift of his hand, Lao-Xu tossed the ball up. Jiang Cheng trained his eyes on the ball, calculating the trajectory of its fall. Then, he jumped.

In the moment, he thought he timed his jump perfectly, but as he stretched out his hand, about to touch the ball, Gu Fei's hand was already there.

As he expected.

Jiang Cheng landed and turned around. The ball was in Guo Xu's hands now. He ran it to the basket with Wang Xu on his tail. Jiang Cheng took one look and was struck speechless. They'd all agreed to guard their marks before the match started. It was bad enough that Wang Xu was running after the ball, but two others on their side were chasing after it, too. Only one guy in a blue shirt was guarding Gu Fei.

Meanwhile, Lu Xiaobin guarded Jiang Cheng tightly.

Guo Xu was decent; he carried the ball well. He just wasn't fast enough. When Jiang Cheng caught up with him, he'd only just entered the key and was about to make a pass. The other team's strategy was probably the mirror of Wang Xu's—get the ball, pass to Gu Fei.

Jiang Cheng eyed Gu Fei's position, then made a hard swerve to the right. As Lu Xiaobin followed his feint, he forced his way between Lu Xiaobin and another player, charging forward.

His timing was good. By the time Guo Xu caught sight of Jiang Cheng, the ball had already left his grasp. Jiang Cheng intercepted him with one hand.

"Head back, head back!" Wang Xu reacted swiftly, turning immediately to run.

Jiang Cheng turned to bring the ball up, but Lu Xiaobin got in his way. The guy was massive—when he rushed up, his towering stature filled Jiang Cheng's entire field of vision. He took two more steps before seizing a chance to pass the ball to Wang Xu. But that numbskull was so preoccupied with sprinting ahead, he didn't see the ball coming his way at all.

"Wang Xu!" Jiang Cheng was forced to shout.

Only then did Wang Xu turn and dash back, grabbing the ball moments before it flew out of bounds.

While Lu Xiaobin was distracted by the ball, Jiang Cheng turned and broke free, dashing toward the basket. No one was guarding Wang Xu now. If he brought the ball over, Jiang Cheng could snag the chance to score.

But not even two steps later, just as Gu Fei ran up to guard him, Wang Xu decided to pass the ball back with a loud "Jiang Cheng!"

The hell are you shouting for? Are you trying to pass to Gu Fei?!

Jiang Cheng was flabbergasted. The moment he caught the ball, he saw Gu Fei's hand reach out at the same time with astounding speed. He immediately dribbled it between his legs, shifting it between his hands as he lowered his center of gravity, planning to break free from the side.

Gu Fei didn't give him the chance. He moved almost in tandem with Jiang Cheng. Not even Jiang Cheng's jumping feints could deceive him; the bastard didn't budge an inch.

Fuck!

Fortunately, Jiang Cheng wasn't the only one with deadweight teammates—Gu Fei was just as lucky in that regard. Nobody was guarding Blue Shirt, who'd managed to slip behind Gu Fei easily. Jiang Cheng passed the ball to him between Gu Fei's legs.

"God damn it."

Lost for words, Gu Fei turned to find Blue Shirt already under the basket with the ball. But now that he had possession, Blue Shirt hesitated. Jiang Cheng could tell he wanted to pass the ball, even though he was right at the basket.

"Just shoot!" Jiang Cheng hollered.

Blue Shirt finally jumped and threw the ball.

It didn't go in. Jiang Cheng knew it wouldn't. With a stance like that, they were lucky the shot didn't fly out of bounds. The ball bounced off the backboard, miles away from the rim.

Everyone waiting under the basket jumped to grab the rebound, some faster than others; several hands tangled in the air as they fought a grudge match for the ball, fighting even between teammates. Jiang Cheng reached in through the crowd and retrieved the ball, bringing it to the sidelines.

All at once, three opponents surrounded him in a semicircle. He needed to pass it off to a teammate.

"I'm open," said someone to his right.

Jiang Cheng swiftly passed the ball over, just barely within bounds. As it sailed through the air, he suddenly realized: *That was Gu Fei's fucking voice!*

Sure enough, when he turned to look, he found the ball solidly in Gu Fei's grasp. Jiang Cheng couldn't stop himself from cursing. "Fuck!"

That sneaky son of a bitch!

Gu Fei quirked his lips into a smile.

"Jiang Cheng, what the hell?!" Wang Xu roared.

"Guard him!" Jiang Cheng snapped. "He's running all over the place by himself! Keep up!"

But it was too late to guard him now; Gu Fei was fast when he had the ball. Two others on the opposing team held Jiang Cheng back, and by the time his deadweight teammates reached Gu Fei, he was already at the foul line. Jiang Cheng could only watch helplessly as Gu Fei leaped in the air, sending the ball gently into the basket with a flick of his wrist.

Jiang Cheng had handed the ball to Gu Fei himself! He wished he could go over and shake Gu Fei by the collar. *How could you be so treacherous?!*

"Hey, make sure you know who you're passing to, Jiang Cheng," Yellow Running Shoes said. "Can't you tell us apart yet?"

"Nah," Jiang Cheng said. "Sorry about that."

"Pass to your teammates," Captain Wang said with a glare, "not your deskmate!"

"You need to stand somewhere I can pass to." Jiang Cheng glared back at him. "Their guys were the only ones in my vicinity. It was either pass to him or throw it out of bounds."

Wang Xu's brow arched right up to his hairline, plainly displeased now. Just as he was about to say something, the ball came flying over from one side.

"Don't waste time," Gu Fei said.

Jiang Cheng caught the ball and handed it to Wang Xu. "You throw in, I'll bring it up to the basket. Block them and don't let Gu Fei get close to me. Stick to him like a potsticker. Pull his arms, step on his feet—foul if you have to! Just don't leave him any openings."

Wang Xu glowered at him. "Got it."

Lu Xiaobin was probably the most dutiful of all the players. He stuck by Jiang Cheng as Wang Xu was about to throw in, and as a result, Wang Xu was stuck there for ages still holding the ball. Eventually, Jiang Cheng was forced to rush over and run past Wang Xu, who finally seized his chance to pass the ball to him.

Wang Xu wasn't a bad player, though. When Jiang Cheng advanced, he escorted him down the court, vying for space with Lu Xiaobin and squeezing against him so tightly that they might've had to resolve it with fists if it'd gone on any longer. Gu Fei didn't come to stop Jiang Cheng this time—Blue Shirt and Yellow Shoes cut him off, one in front and one behind, all but holding him in an embrace. But by the time Jiang Cheng reached center court, Gu Fei had managed to escape them both.

There was no time for a slow layup. Fueled by his fury at Gu Fei's dirty trick, Jiang Cheng charged straight to the three-point line. He didn't stop and adjust; before Gu Fei could block him, he took his shot.

The ball went high, curving in a massive arc through the air before falling through the hoop.

"Holy shit, nice shot!" Wang Xu shouted.

Jiang Cheng exhaled in relief. He glanced at Gu Fei.

"Beautiful," Gu Fei said.

There wasn't much enjoyment to be had in a half-match, especially one like this with absolutely no coordination, where the only strategy on either side was to run all over the court. They were playing as hard as they could, but points were few and far between.

Lao-Xu blew the ending whistle and clapped. "Not bad!"

What part of that wasn't *bad?* Jiang Cheng wanted to say.

"The good news is we're a team with two strong players, now," Lao-Xu said. "But why didn't any of you break a single rule the whole time? You can't play like that! Be brave! Be foul! You need to be bolder on the court. What do you think about the match, Gu Fei?"

"It was a total mess," Gu Fei said.

Unsatisfied with his answer, Lao-Xu turned to look at Jiang Cheng. "Jiang Cheng, what about you?"

"Ditto," Jiang Cheng said.

"It's only the first day of practice." Lao-Xu soldiered on by himself. "There's plenty of room for improvement! You need to believe in yourselves! Do you think you can do it?"

Nobody uttered a word.

"Do you?!" Lao-Xu waved his arms. "Answer me at the top of your lungs!"

Again, he was met with silence.

Jiang Cheng could already tell from the half-match they played that apart from himself and Gu Fei, no one here played basketball on a regular basis. Even those who knew how to play were all average at best.

"Do y—" Lao-Xu continued his rousing speech.

"Yes," Jiang Cheng answered—he couldn't bear to watch Lao-Xu's great efforts met with no response.

"Yes," Wang Xu chimed in.

The whole group of them murmured "yes" with zero enthusiasm.

"That's it! That's right!" Lao-Xu beamed. "Our goal is to make it to the semifinals! Now, do you think you can do it?"

Everyone replied with a half-dead "yes." Lao-Xu nodded, apparently satisfied.

"There's still a couple of weeks until the tournament. We have plenty of time. Outside of gym class, you can practice during the afternoon self-study period."

This special privilege was nothing to be sniffed at. Instantly invigorated, the group of them promised to practice properly.

For the rest of the practice, Captain Wang didn't continue with the match, but switched to three-on-three games—the first group to score would win and the losers would be swapped out for another team.

Gu Fei didn't play again. He sat on the bench by the court and watched.

None of them were particularly good, but Jiang Cheng hadn't relaxed like this in ages, so it still hit the spot once they got into it.

"Could you stop blocking me?!" Guo Xu said helplessly, holding the ball. "Jiang Cheng, why don't you take a break?"

"Jiang Cheng, take five," Wang Xu said. "With you here, no one else will get a chance to play."

"All righty." Jiang Cheng chuckled and let Lu Xiaobin replace him. He sat next to Lao-Xu and watched.

"So, what do you think?" Lao-Xu asked.

"Of what?" Jiang Cheng looked at him.

"The team," Lao-Xu said.

Jiang Cheng said nothing. He could feel the intensity of Lao-Xu's hope.

"Why don't you two try playing on the same side tomorrow and see how it goes?" Lao-Xu asked.

Jiang Cheng nodded. "Sure."

"Getting to the semis might be hard. Don't get your hopes up," Gu Fei chimed in. "It depends which teams we meet in the knock-out rounds. If it's Class Two, we might as well just go home."

"Don't be such a downer. Cheer up!" Lao-Xu said.

"Okay." Gu Fei looked at Lao-Xu. "Ha. Ha."

As the final bell rang, people started to pour into the gym.

"Let's go," Wang Xu said. "They're all here to practice. We can't let them know our secret."

"What secret?" Jiang Cheng asked

"Our real ability. We need to still look like a shit team in front of the other classes," Wang Xu said with a completely straight face. "We can't let anyone know that Da-Fei is playing, or that Jiang Cheng's a damned good player."

Everyone nodded in unison, expressions of excitement mixed with self-sacrifice across their faces.

"Yeah!"

"We've got two trump cards now!"

"Everyone coming in now can already see that I'm here," Gu Fei pointed out.

"No worries," said Wang Xu. "Let's put on a show."

Gu Fei sighed. He stood, put on his jacket, and turned to walk out the door.

"For fuck's sake!" Wang Xu yelled at the top of his lungs, startling Jiang Cheng. Glaring at Gu Fei's back, he said, "Can't you be a fucking team player for once?!"

Gu Fei simply flipped the bird behind himself without turning.

"Wang Xu," one of the students who just came in said with a laugh as he took his jacket off. "That's an improvement! At least Da-Fei actually came this time."

"C'mon." Wang Xu rose and led them out of the gym.

Jiang Cheng wanted to applaud Wang Xu for putting on an excellent performance; his acting skills had improved exponentially since he pretended to turn down the team captain role.

Jiang Cheng didn't see Gu Miao and her skateboard at the school gate. "Gu Miao isn't waiting for you today?"

"She doesn't necessarily come every day. Sometimes she goes off to play by herself," Gu Fei said. "Are you still going back on foot?"

"Yeah."

"Want a ride?"

Jiang Cheng hesitated. "Okay."

As Gu Fei grabbed his bike, Jiang Cheng remembered the "I'm open" line from earlier and felt vexed all over again. "Hey. I notice you play dirty."

"I was just messing around." Gu Fei clambered onto his bicycle and pushed off. "I didn't think you'd actually pass me the ball."

"Why would you say it for no reason?!" Jiang Cheng climbed onto the back of the bike. "Lunatic."

"It's useful on the court. Who knows, some idiot from the other team might actually pass it to me."

"You fucker!" Jiang Cheng cursed.

"I'll call up some guys to practice with us tomorrow," Gu Fei said. "It's no fun playing like this."

"Who?" Jiang Cheng remembered that Gu Fei had brought "Out" and "Jail" with him the last time he played basketball. "Fresh Out of Jail?"

"What?" Gu Fei asked, confused.

"...Nothing." Jiang Cheng quickly corrected himself. "I mean, the guys you were playing with the last time?"

"Who's Fresh Out of Jail supposed to be?" Gu Fei laughed. "Am I included in there?"

Jiang Cheng fell silent.

"Yep, them." Gu Fei didn't press him on it. "Fresh Out of Jail."

Jiang Cheng sighed.

They didn't speak again for the rest of the way. Jiang Cheng stared at the snow piled by the side of the road, his thoughts drifting. He was getting absent-minded lately. Every time there was silence, he would grow distracted, overthinking. He hadn't always been like this—when his mind wandered in the past, it would get so thoroughly lost he wouldn't even know where it went off to.

He wondered when he would finally escape this Mariana Trench of emotional lows.

Gu Fei cycled fast. It wasn't too long before they reached the corner of Jiang Cheng's street and he squeezed the handbrakes, slowing down.

"Thanks," Jiang Cheng said as he leaped off.

Gu Fei didn't reply. He was looking down the block.

It was then that Jiang Cheng noticed the swearing and screaming from down the street, near Li Baoguo's building. He turned in time to see several people gathered around someone who'd fallen to the ground, kicking and stomping.

"The fuck." Jiang Cheng frowned. *This street and its never-ending hubbub.* "What is it now...?"

Gu Fei got down from his bike and locked it against a tree by the road, then turned to him. "The guy on the ground is Li Baoguo."

20

G U FEI USUALLY HATED trouble. He didn't like to get involved in other people's business. But here, in this handful of city blocks where he grew up, all kinds of trouble happened every day. The kind of melodramatics you'd see in TV dramas were daily occurrences here—in fact, the TV soaps fell short of reality.

When he was bored, Gu Fei would take in these scenes as if watching a show. For a long time, these things were his inspiration for the song lyrics he wrote for Ding Zhuxin: the desperate yet un-self-aware struggles of the people living at the bottom of society. They looked hopeless, but they lived lives full of color; they would mock you for being too sensitive.

Gu Fei would come across someone getting pummeled like this every now and again. Sometimes the main character was the same, sometimes not, but whatever the case, it was hardly a rare sight. On any other day, he would have just stayed back and watched from the comfort of his bike.

But today, he couldn't. Once Jiang Cheng recognized Li Baoguo, his face contorted into an unreadable expression, like he found the situation both absurd and confusing. If Gu Fei had known Jiang Cheng just a little better—as well as he knew Wang Jiuri, maybe— he would have stopped Jiang Cheng from approaching.

People usually weren't beaten to death in these situations. Besides, nobody involved was a decent person, so no one was being wronged; a bit of blood or some broken bones would just be another lesson— sometimes even a solution.

Jiang Cheng said nothing. When he turned to walk toward them, Gu Fei felt something he couldn't quite describe. It wasn't sympathy; there were far too many people deserving of sympathy in this world, so it didn't matter if he felt bad for somebody or not.

Maybe it was helplessness.

Gu Fei hadn't known that Li Baoguo had a younger son. He didn't know if it really was as Li Baoguo had said—that he gave up his son because he couldn't afford to raise him. Knowing Li Baoguo, Gu Fei wouldn't be surprised if he'd simply sold his child for the money.

There was no way for Gu Fei to understand how Jiang Cheng felt right now. The air about him was so fundamentally different from the people who grew up here. Gu Fei couldn't begin to imagine how such a person would feel in an environment like this, with a..."father" like that.

In any case, Jiang Cheng just walked over quietly. Perhaps because of his unusual relationship with Li Baoguo, he didn't look anxious or panicked, much less angry.

Gu Fei stretched. From several yards away, he ambled over as well, fishing his glasses out and putting them on as he went.

Jiang Cheng didn't go to stop the fight. He didn't even speak. He tossed his bag to the side and drove his elbow into the back of the person kicking Li Baoguo's head. Jiang Cheng was good at using his elbow; there was a lot of power behind the strike. Gu Fei had been on the receiving end of it before.

With one smash, the man howled and turned his head. Gu Fei recognized him: He was someone from the side of town by the steelworks who went by the nickname Big Dick, though Gu Fei had no way of knowing if the nickname was true to life. He was part of a group that often came around here to play mahjong. They were okay with cheating, normally, but only if they were the ones doing it.

Before Big Dick could react, Jiang Cheng slammed his head against his face, hitting the bridge of his nose. Gu Fei felt his own nose twinge in sympathy. Then, Jiang Cheng seized Big Dick's collar and shoved him backward viciously. The man staggered and collided with the two people behind him.

The rest of the group who'd been preoccupied with beating Li Baoguo immediately noticed the sneak attack. After a brief smattering of cursing and confusion, they swiftly turned their attention to Jiang Cheng.

"Fucker! What do you think you're doing?!" someone shouted, sending a fist straight toward Jiang Cheng.

Gu Fei was surprised to see Jiang Cheng step straight toward the guy's fist instead of dodging it. As it brushed past the corner of his eye, Jiang Cheng's own punch landed solidly on the left eye of his opponent. This enraged the other, still-confused members of the group; all at once, they abandoned Li Baoguo as he curled up on the ground and swung their fists at Jiang Cheng instead.

Gu Fei frowned. He looked around, but the ground was unexpectedly clean. He didn't even have a brick at his disposal to help Jiang Cheng if he ended up too badly beaten.

"Stop!" Li Baoguo hollered, still curled up on the ground and covering his head. "Stop it!"

None of the people converging on Jiang Cheng paid him any mind. Though they had no weapons in their hands, all of them were large men—their fists were enough.

One, two, three, four... Gu Fei counted them. Four people circled Jiang Cheng, with one more bouncing on the balls of his feet at the fringes, having failed to squeeze his way in. Before the guy could bounce a third time, one of the four was launched out of the circle and tumbled to the ground; Jiang Cheng had kicked him out.

Jiang Cheng swiftly rushed out of the circle as well, stomping his foot hard into the stomach of the man on the ground.

"Fuck me!" Big Dick bellowed, his nose bloody. He leaped up and kicked Jiang Cheng in the back. Ungraceful as it was, the kick carried a lot of force. Jiang Cheng stumbled several steps forward before steadying himself. He lifted a hand and wiped the corner of his mouth.

Turning, he saw Big Dick run up to give him a second kick. Jiang Cheng stood still, waiting until Big Dick jumped—then he ducked down, rushed forward, and launched an elbow at Big Dick's... big dick.

Big Dick didn't even make a sound. He fell to the ground, gasping; his mouth gaped wide open as his face contorted in agony.

Gu Fei pushed his glasses up. If his eyes hadn't deceived him, Jiang Cheng didn't actually elbow him in the balls, or Big Dick would've passed out from the pain by now. Did Jiang Cheng miss, or was he still able to control his emotions even under these conditions?

Nevertheless, Big Dick's collapse looked so gruesome that his companions—Dick Two, Dick Three, Dick Four, and Dick Five— all hesitated briefly.

That was what these people were like. Each one was as unafraid as a gang leader when they beat up someone like Li Baoguo, but they'd shrink back the moment they met someone tough. They didn't dare to take him on alone—even as a group, they all waited for someone else to start the fight.

In their moment of hesitation, Jiang Cheng rushed toward them again, slamming into the man closest to him. Top students were always fast learners: His body-slam was supplemented by a jumping start in imitation of Big Dick, but with far more grace. He leaped shoulder-first and bashed it into the man's chin.

The man's head was knocked backward from the impact; he jumped on the spot and then fell. The blow must have split his lip or made him bite his tongue; the man on the ground covered his mouth, then drew his hand away to reveal blood.

With two down now, the remaining three seemed to feel the threat. Since they were still at an advantage numerically, they all charged at Jiang Cheng at once.

Jiang Cheng must have been hurt earlier when he was surrounded. This time, he couldn't avoid being mobbed. He took several punches in the gut and back, and those were only the ones Gu Fei actually saw. Gu Fei sighed and started crossing the street.

Just as he stepped onto the road, he saw Jiang Cheng knock someone down and launch a torrent of blows to his face, two of which hit his neck. The man struggled, coughing and yelping. The other two couldn't pull Jiang Cheng off their companion, so they began to kick him from behind. After taking a few hits, Jiang Cheng reached behind himself, grabbed a leg, and yanked, then turned around and pressed that leg back.

His victim clearly wasn't flexible, and the forced split made him howl in agony. He tried to kick Jiang Cheng but couldn't muster up the strength; he frantically flung both arms at him instead, but both were weak.

It was then that the last guy standing lifted his leg. Gu Fei could tell he was aiming for the back of Jiang Cheng's head.

"Hey!" Gu Fei shouted.

He grabbed a dictionary from his bag. When the man looked up at him, Gu Fei hurled the dictionary at his face.

It was an English-Chinese dictionary. Lao-Lu would explode at anyone who showed up to his class without it. The dictionary wasn't expensive, but it was a sturdy, hardcover book. Gu Fei had never opened it, so it was just as solid as when he first bought it—it didn't even flip open in mid-air, and its impact against the man's face was almost like that of a brick.

After the dictionary hit him, the others all stopped and looked at Gu Fei as a group.

Without a word, Gu Fei walked over to pick up the dictionary, dusted it off on his pants, and put it back into his bag.

Jiang Cheng let go of the leg he was holding and got up.

The one hit by the dictionary glared at Jiang Cheng. "You fucking—"

Jiang Cheng cut him off before he could finish his sentence. "Is there anything else?"

Sitting or standing, everyone froze. Nobody said a word.

"If there's nothing else, I'll be leaving." Jiang Cheng turned to get his bag. He picked it up and walked off down the block.

"You know him?" someone asked Gu Fei.

Gu Fei eyed him. "You should get going."

Ow.

Every damned part of Jiang Cheng's body hurt. He didn't even know where the pain was coming from anymore. He clenched his jaw and kept walking; each step he took was taxing, but at the same time, it was satisfying. It felt like he'd just run a full marathon:

He was sore and aching and weak, but every breath he gasped in poured into his whole body, the air cooling him down to his gut.

Why were they beating Li Baoguo up? He'd been planning to ask at first, but now that it was over, he no longer wanted to find out. All he knew was that this was how the man lived—squirming and crawling on the ground like a worm. He couldn't change that, and neither could Li Baoguo.

The fight had been satisfying, but also deeply depressing. This was the source of Jiang Cheng's frustration and bitterness.

He wasn't any kind of great or noble person. He didn't want to save anyone or change anyone's life. He just thought that since this guy was indisputably his birth father, he would have to do his best to adapt to this fact. But though he could strive to accommodate Li Baoguo's vulgarity, his messiness, his chauvinism, his gambling addiction, and his drinking problem...he was coming to realize that this wasn't a complete list of Li Baoguo's issues. There were many other things he couldn't adapt to or accept, revealing themselves gradually before his eyes: Li Baoguo's stealing habits; Li Baoguo getting beaten up on the street until he had to crawl on the ground.

What else was there? How much more was beneath the surface?

Behind him, someone whistled. He didn't have to turn to know it was Gu Fei, so he didn't. Turning made his neck ache.

"You should go to the hospital," Gu Fei said.

"No need," Jiang Cheng mumbled.

Gu Fei didn't catch up with him; instead, he followed at a distance. "Let's make a bet."

"What?"

"I bet your rib is broken," Gu Fei said. "Get it checked. If it's broken, do my homework for a week and let me copy your exam answers. If it's not, I'll buy you dinner."

Jiang Cheng stopped. Gu Fei walked over and stood beside him. "Is it broken?"

"Dunno, I haven't broken a rib before." Jiang Cheng swept a look at him. "You sound experienced. Do you break your ribs all the time?"

Gu Fei laughed. "I should've let that guy break your neck."

"Thanks for earlier," Jiang Cheng said.

His rib probably *was* broken. Jiang Cheng would sometimes get hit in the stomach when he fought, but it had never hurt this badly and for this long.

"Where's the nearest hospital?" he asked.

"There's one by the coal mines," said Gu Fei. "Five minutes by taxi."

"Okay." Jiang Cheng took a few steps forward, then grit his teeth and turned to add, "Thanks."

"You're so polite I feel like bowing and saying 'you're very welcome,'" Gu Fei said.

Jiang Cheng didn't speak again, just walked ahead and turned the corner. He was lucky enough to flag down a taxi after waiting less than two minutes.

"I'm finishing up my shift, go get the next one," the driver said.

"I'm going to the hospital. I'll die on the street if I wait." Jiang Cheng looked at him. "It's probably acute gastroenteritis."

The driver studied him. "Get in. I'll clock out after I drop you off."

"Thanks."

Jiang Cheng hopped in. When he sat down in the back seat, he almost cried out from the pain; adjusting his posture hurt his right rib so much it felt like someone had punched him again.

"Got into a fight, huh?" The driver glanced at him in the rearview mirror while driving. "Acute gastroenteritis doesn't do that to your face."

"Is my face messed up?" Jiang Cheng asked. He knew there was a cut inside his mouth—he kept tasting blood.

The driver chuckled. "Yes, but it doesn't look too bad. It won't affect your looks."

"Oh."

"You shouldn't be so reckless, young man. If anything happens to you, your family will worry about you, even if you don't care. You know?"

"...Uh-huh." Jiang Cheng forced a smile. The corner of his mouth seemed to be hurt as well—the slight stretch of his lips sent shocks of pain to the roots of his ear.

Your family will worry about you.

You know?

Would they, though? Who actually was his "family"?

His old family would never know how he was doing. Even back when he was living with them, he wouldn't let them know about the fights he got into. And now... His dear father had been right next to him earlier, holding his head in his hands and not saying a word the entire time.

When Jiang Cheng left, Li Baoguo didn't even look at him.

So who would worry?

What a joke.

When he reached the hospital, he went to the emergency room. There weren't that many people around.

After he told the doctor he might have broken a rib, the doctor palpated his chest and back. "Does it hurt anywhere?"

Jiang Cheng focused hard on the sensations. "...No."

"No?" said the doctor. "Let me see."

Jiang Cheng unzipped his jacket. Just as he was about to roll up his clothes, he saw bloodstains on his sweater. He froze. "The heck?"

The doctor pulled his sweater up. "Looks like a cut. It sure doesn't look like broken bones... I'll check for any grinding noises."

"...Okay."

Jiang Cheng was baffled by the seemingly paranormal way he'd been wounded to the point of heavy bleeding when his clothes weren't even torn. The doctor checked him all over before pressing the area around his wound again.

"Any bone pain?"

"Just muscle pain," Jiang Cheng answered.

"No broken bones, then," said the doctor. "We can take an X-ray if you're still worried."

Jiang Cheng breathed out a sigh of relief. "No, it's okay."

The wound on his side wasn't too serious, either. It was fine once the doctor cleaned it up and put some gauze over it. Jiang Cheng sat in the hospital chair and let his mind wander for a very long time. A lot of his physical pain was gradually fading, and the initially explosive aches had already subsided. He pressed and prodded at each of his ribs over his shirt. No pain at all.

Fuck! That nutjob Gu Fei! He'd said it with such certainty, like someone who had loads of experience with broken bones. He'd scared Jiang Cheng into coming to the hospital when he didn't even want to in the first place!

Surprisingly, Jiang Cheng's first thought when he found out his rib wasn't broken was: *Great, it won't affect the basketball tournament.* He was astounded by his strong sense of team spirit. Maybe Lao-Xu's great and noble love had quietly influenced him after all.

His phone rang in his bag. He pulled it out and stiffened when he saw the number on the screen: His mom was calling him. Though he'd deleted the whole family from his contact list, he couldn't forget her number that quickly.

He picked up. "Hello."

"Xiao-Cheng?" His mother's voice came down the line. "I know I haven't been in touch lately; it's been busy here. How are things with you?"

Jiang Cheng fell silent for a long time. He didn't know what to say—he didn't know what he *could* say. His mind was as chaotic as the brawl he just had, practically buzzing.

"Did you get the things I sent you?" she asked.

"Yeah." Jiang Cheng shut his eyes and took a breath in.

"How are you getting on with your...dad?"

"Pretty well." Jiang Cheng bit his lip. The pain from the corner of his mouth was so intense that he frowned. "He's my real dad, after all."

She laughed. "That's good. I was a bit worried. He seems rather rough around the edges. I was afraid you—"

"I'm doing *great*," Jiang Cheng said.

His mom fell silent, as if she was trying to find something else to say.

"I really am." Jiang Cheng looked down, staring at a bit of mud caked on his shoe. *When did that get there?* "Don't worry about me."

"Xiao-Cheng..." His mom sighed.

"I'm getting along great. I'm adjusting well. I have to go," Jiang Cheng said. "Bye for now."

He hung up before she could reply. After staring at his darkened phone screen for a while, he stood and left the hospital.

✦ ✦ ✦

"I wasn't planning on visiting," Yi Jing said as she stood at the cash register, hugging her school bag, "but I was in the neighborhood...

Xu-zong said you guys are playing in the basketball tournament soon. I'm guessing you won't have time to study before midterms, right?"

"I don't study whether I have the time or not." Gu Fei poured her a glass of hot water and added a slice of lemon. "You worry more than Lao-Xu does."

"Not really." Yi Jing smiled, a little embarrassed. "I just don't have much else to do."

Gu Fei smiled too. "All right, then. Why don't you let me copy today's homework? I—"

"No copying." Yi Jing immediately shot him down. "If you don't know how to do it, I can teach you."

Gu Fei was tempted to reply, *In that case, I'll just copy Jiang Cheng's.* Still, he took a textbook from his bag. "Okay. Teach me English, then. I'm only planning to do the English homework today."

"All right." Yi Jing sighed. "English is probably the only homework you wouldn't dare *not* to do."

"Mhm." Gu Fei rose and unfolded the little table next to them. "Nobody skips Lao-Lu's homework."

Yi Jing grabbed a stool and sat down. She took his worksheet and began to explain the questions to him. Gu Fei was a bit distracted. Whenever it came to studying, he could never focus—even if Lao-Lu himself was sitting in front of him, Gu Fei's thoughts would still be a world away.

Yi Jing was Lao-Xu's able assistant. Like Lao-Xu, she was full of enthusiasm for their class. Even after Wang Xu had twice angered her to tears during self-study periods at the start of last semester—and only one week into her role as class president, at that—she was still as passionate as ever.

"So this is..." Yi Jing wrote on a piece of scrap paper. "You see..."

Someone pushed open the curtain at the door. Gu Fei turned and saw Jiang Cheng rooted to the spot in the doorway, his hand still holding the curtains apart.

Yi Jing turned around and stared at him in surprise. "Jiang Cheng?"

"Ah," Jiang Cheng said awkwardly. He pointed outside. "I think I'll..."

"No, don't. You're looking for Gu Fei?" Yi Jing said hurriedly and got to her feet, just as awkward. "I was just explaining some homework to him... But if you need him, I can go... Or maybe you could explain it to him instead?"

"Huh?" Jiang Cheng froze.

"Mr. Lu says your English grades are stellar." Yi Jing smiled and packed her things. "I'll be leaving, then."

"Hey, you—"

But before Jiang Cheng could finish his sentence, Yi Jing squeezed past him and left in a fit of embarrassment.

"You went to the hospital?" Gu Fei asked.

"Yeah." Jiang Cheng walked inside and stood by the shelves, hesitating. "Now you have to buy me dinner."

"Nothing broken?" Gu Fei was a little taken aback.

"Why do you look so disappointed?" Jiang Cheng said. "Come break my rib, then."

"What do you want to eat?" Gu Fei asked.

"Dunno. Anything's fine." Jiang Cheng furrowed his brow. "I'm starving. And annoyed."

"Okay then." Gu Fei stood and paused to think for a moment. "I'll take you to eat my favorite food."

Run Wild
SAYE

21

JIANG CHENG DIDN'T KNOW what Gu Fei's favorite food was or where he was taking him, but he didn't ask. He didn't have an appetite at all in his current mood, so it would probably all taste the same no matter what.

He only came looking for Gu Fei because he didn't want to be alone. He didn't want to go back home and see Li Baoguo; he didn't want to find out how badly he'd been beaten or why he was getting his ass kicked by those people in the first place. No, he wanted no part of it. This whole heap of do-not-wants had his emptied head and heart stuffed so full he couldn't breathe.

Apart from school and Li Baoguo's house, the only place he could go in this shitty city was Gu Fei's store. It was kind of sad when he thought about it, but he didn't have a choice.

Gu Fei tidied the store and locked it up. "Wait here for me. I'll go get our ride."

"Okay." Jiang Cheng wanted to ask whether it was the bicycle or the motorcycle. He really didn't want to ride a motorcycle in such cold weather—he'd rather walk. But Gu Fei headed off into an alley next to the store before he could speak.

Whatever. How cold could it get? The spring basketball tournament was about to begin, so technically, it was already spring. *Crazy.*

A motor purred from the little alleyway, but the sound was weak and brittle. It didn't match Gu Fei's 250cc bike. Just as questions were starting to bubble up in his mind, a tiny yellow car in the shape of a steamed bun—a small steamed bun, at that—crawled out of the alley.

Jiang Cheng stared, astounded as the little cornmeal bun wobbled over and stopped before him, then opened its itty-bitty door.

Gu Fei looked out at him from inside the contraption. "Get in."

"What is this...thing?" Jiang Cheng scrutinized the vehicle. Unless he was mistaken, it was a small, enclosed mobility scooter.

"A car," Gu Fei said. "Keeps you out of the wind and rain. Burns fuel. Runs better than the electric kind."

"...Oh!" Jiang Cheng walked over and stood by the door. He studied it for a long while. "And how the fuck am I supposed to get in it?"

Gu Fei looked behind himself, then got out. "You can...climb in the back first." When Jiang Cheng hesitated, he added, "Even if this was a Beetle, you'd have to climb in to reach the back, right?"

"If this was a Beetle, I'd be in the front passenger seat!" Jiang Cheng replied.

"Hurry up." Gu Fei glanced at the time on his phone. "They close at nine."

Jiang Cheng had no choice but to squeeze in through the one-foot gap between the door and the driver's seat. Battered and sore, he almost wept as he clambered into the back. He remembered seeing an old man bringing his old lady out to town in a vehicle like this one. Just how did that old lady get in the damn thing?

Once seated, Gu Fei reached out and pushed down the back of the driver's seat. "Wouldn't it have been easier if you put the seat down first?"

Eyeing the suddenly widened space, Jiang Cheng felt an urge to climb out and fight Gu Fei again. He pointed at him. "You shut your mouth."

Gu Fei put the seat back up, closed the door, started the engine, and drove off down the street.

The car had very limited space. Sitting in the back didn't feel that different from sitting on the back of Gu Fei's bike, but it *did* shield them from the wind and rain. Looking out of the window, he felt strangely like a vagrant done with a day of begging, now riding in a little cornmeal steamed bun car searching for a bowl of noodles or something from a cheap stall on the side of the road.

"This is your family's car?" Jiang Cheng asked, knocking on the plastic shell of the vehicle.

"Yep," Gu Fei responded. "My mom bought it. We use it to haul goods sometimes. It's pretty convenient."

"...Oh." Jiang Cheng studied his own seat. "What can you even fit in a tiny space like this?"

"There's not much to haul for a store like ours," Gu Fei said. "Most of our stock is delivered to us. We only transport some of it by ourselves."

Jiang Cheng didn't say anything else as he watched Gu Fei drive across the bridge he'd passed the other day. He figured anything good to eat around here must be on the other side. What could it be?

When he had dumplings the other day, he saw a number of shops, from hot pot and barbecued skewers to sit-down Chinese food and Western cuisine. He hoped Gu Fei wasn't buying him anything too expensive. Then he'd have to buy him a meal in return, which would be a pain.

The little dumpling car drove past restaurants big and small on both sides without stopping. It kept straight on, then turned down a small lane.

Sensing that they'd left the street with the restaurants, Jiang Cheng couldn't help but ask, "We're not there yet?"

"Almost there. It's just up ahead." As soon as he spoke, Gu Fei turned down yet another street.

Jiang Cheng looked out. This neighborhood was a run-down part of the old city, just like where Li Baoguo lived. It was wholly and completely filled with life and deprivation.

The car slowed and stopped in front of a few small restaurants. Jiang Cheng peered at them. One sold buns, one sold noodles, and another...

"Get out." Gu Fei opened the car door and hopped out.

"Wait." As he squeezed his way out, Jiang Cheng grew increasingly confused. "Why do these look like breakfast places?"

"They sell breakfast too." Gu Fei shut the door and pressed the remote control.

"Shit." Jiang Cheng was shocked. "This little dumpling car has remote locking?"

"It burns fuel! Even electric scooters have remote keys, why not this guy?" Gu Fei walked toward one of the shops. "We're here."

Jiang Cheng looked at the shop. Though the lights were on and it was clearly in business, everything from the storefront to the lighting to the decor screamed "money laundering front." When he saw the four brush-stroked characters written in a hand almost as hideous as his own, he blinked.

"Wang Er's Meat Pies?" He pointed at the sign. "You're taking me out for meat pies for *dinner*?"

"They're delicious." Gu Fei lifted the curtain. "Just smell it."

Jiang Cheng wasn't in the mood to smell anything. It was his first time going out to eat meat pies with someone for dinner, and he hadn't yet recovered from the shock. But the tables were mostly full—business was booming. And when he followed Gu Fei and caught sight of the waiter carrying a large vat of soup to a customer, his eyes almost popped out of his head.

"Oh, Da-Fei, you're here!" Wang Xu plunked the soup down on the table. When he turned and noticed Jiang Cheng, he froze. "Whoa, Jiang Cheng? Your fussy ass came too?"

"Uh-huh," Jiang Cheng responded, watching Wang Xu spill the equivalent of a small bowl of soup onto the table.

"Oi! What the hell, you spilled half of it!" said the highly displeased customer.

"I'll get you another small pot of it later." Wang Xu wiped the table haphazardly with a rag and called it a day. He walked over to Gu Fei and Jiang Cheng. "Go inside to the private room, it's empty."

"*Private room*?" Jiang Cheng felt one shock after another. A meat pie shop with a *private room*?

It was indeed a private dining room, with wooden boards sectioning it off on all four sides. It even had its own air conditioner.

"What happened to your face, Jiang Cheng?" Wang Xu stared at Jiang Cheng's face after he turned on the air conditioner. "You got into a fight? Was it Mon—"

"No," Jiang Cheng cut him off. The slightest gust of wind made Wang Xu think of Monkey—Jiang Cheng felt he owed it to Wang Xu to actually go fight Monkey one more time.

"Beef, pork belly, lamb, donkey meat. A few of each." Gu Fei glanced at Wang Xu. "And mutton soup. Have you had dinner? Come join us if you haven't."

"Give me a minute, I'll get them for you," Wang Xu said. "I found two good bottles of booze my dad's been hiding. We can have a little drink."

After he left, Jiang Cheng looked at Gu Fei. "This is Wang Xu's family's shop?"

"Yep." Gu Fei nodded. "Wang Er is his dad. He's pretty famous in town. People drive all the way from the new development area just to eat here."

"Oh!" For a moment, Jiang Cheng couldn't really find anything else to say.

"I'll get the soup. We'll have a bit of that first." Gu Fei rose and walked out, too.

After two minutes, he returned holding a tray laden with three medium-sized pots of mutton soup. Jiang Cheng's wits must have finally returned: When he smelled the aroma, he felt like he could eat the bowls it was served in, too.

It wasn't too long before Wang Xu brought in a plain basket containing seven or eight meat pies. "Fresh out of the pan. Eat them while they're hot, I'll get more later."

Jiang Cheng took a bite out of one. It struck him in his chest so viscerally he could've cried; he barely chewed before swallowing.

"This one's donkey meat." Wang Xu glanced at him. "How is it?"

"*So...*" Jiang Cheng took another bite, "*good.*"

Wang Xu grinned smugly. "Of course it is. You *have* to order the donkey! Everyone who comes here gets two, at least. Da-Fei can eat ten."

Jiang Cheng thought he could eat more than that. The meat pies here weren't big, only about half the size of his palm. They had thin crusts and an enormous amount of filling. Thick and soft, one bite filled his mouth with the aroma of meat; it was rich, but not greasy...

Wang Xu snuck a bottle from his father's private liquor stash. They couldn't even tell what it was—the bottle looked dirty and had no labels.

"A little drink?" Wang Xu poured a glass and put it in front of Jiang Cheng.

Jiang Cheng shook his head. He didn't usually drink baijiu. His family never drank, and when he went out with Pan Zhi, they stuck with beer.

"Boring." Wang Xu poured two glasses for himself and Gu Fei. "Good students and their rules."

Jiang Cheng couldn't be bothered to argue. After all, it was Wang Xu's meat pies he was eating—and they were fantastic.

It was an amazingly satisfying meal, with all kinds of meat pies served along with flavorful mutton soup; it filled him to the core with warmth and contentment. Even his various physical pains with their unknown sources seemed to feel much better, subsiding from explosive points of pain into dull aches buried in his flesh.

Of the three of them, Wang Xu was the only one who talked. Jiang Cheng didn't open his mouth often. Wang Xu talked about people in their class, and since Jiang Cheng could barely tell their classmates apart, he couldn't get a word in even if he wanted to. Gu Fei didn't say much either, only grunting in reply now and then between bites. None of this affected Wang Xu's enthusiasm.

"I heard that Class Two is getting some external support this time," Wang Xu said, moving on to the basketball tournament. "Should we do that too? How else will we win?"

"You want me, Jiang Cheng, and three outsiders to play together?" Gu Fei said. "What's the point of winning, then?"

Wang Xu frowned in thought and agreed. "You're right. If we did that, I wouldn't even get to play, would I?"

"With your skills? If we got outside help, we'd have no need for you," Gu Fei said.

This irked Wang Xu. "Fuck off!"

"I'll ask some friends to come practice with us tomorrow," said Gu Fei. "We're not banking on improving our skills at this point;

we'll focus on practicing our teamwork so we're more familiar with each other."

"Right!" Wang Xu said, shooting Jiang Cheng a look. "So we don't end up passing the ball to the other team."

"I didn't pass it to 'the other team'—I passed it to my deskmate." Jiang Cheng sipped a mouthful of soup. "He's on my team."

Wang Xu made a disapproving sound. "You're splitting hairs."

"Feel free to split mine," Jiang Cheng grumbled.

They spent an hour eating meat pies at Wang Xu's shop. By the time Jiang Cheng walked out, he felt as though the injury on his abdomen was about to burst from the fullness of his stomach.

"Come by whenever you want," Wang Xu's mother said as she walked them out. "I'll give you a discount! All of Wang Xu's classmates get discounts!"

"Thanks, Auntie," Jiang Cheng said. He turned away and burped.

He'd really eaten too much. So much so that when he got back into the car, he sat half-reclined in the back seat.

"Just so you know, I'm driving drunk," Gu Fei announced as he started the engine.

"Oh, shut up," Jiang Cheng said.

Although he was happy when he was eating, when he got out of the goofy little car and looked down the street to where Li Baoguo lived, a familiar sense of fatigue washed over Jiang Cheng again. Head bowed, he shuffled helpless and slow through the wind—one step, two steps—until he finally arrived at the entrance to the building.

When he opened the door of the apartment, the lights were out. He felt at the wall for ages before he managed to find the switch and slap it on. For some reason, he still wasn't used to how the switches in Li Baoguo's home were slightly higher than the ones in his old place.

Li Baoguo wasn't in. Jiang Cheng didn't know if he was in the hospital or off gambling again. He took out his phone, but after pausing for a moment, he decided not to call.

He got washed up quickly and returned to his room. When he was done with his homework, Jiang Cheng looked at the time. It was almost eleven.

Someone upstairs was beating their kid. The child was crying and screaming; the piercing noise sent chills through Jiang Cheng's chest. It sounded like the kid might die at any second.

Jiang Cheng lay down in bed, put on his headphones, and shut his eyes.

✦ ✦ ✦

Jiang Cheng now realized just how determined Lao-Xu was to win at least one match in this tournament. This morning, Lao-Xu told them that all the students involved in the tournament could skip his Chinese class and practice basketball in the gym instead. Gu Fei was forced to call the Fresh Out of Jail guys early in the morning and ask them to come over before noon.

"None of you listen in class, anyway," Lao-Xu said.

To that, Jiang Cheng wanted to say, *If I was in class, I would be listening. I'm an overachiever, after all.*

The gym was empty in the morning. Looking at the group of guys who'd made their way over as soon as the last period ended, Jiang Cheng felt a little touched. He was under no illusion that they could actually win this competition based on skill. Whether they could win depended entirely on how bad the other classes were.

"Our special training squad will be here to practice with us soon," Wang Xu said as he squatted by the court. "First, let's have the starting line-up we decided on come up to play as warm-up."

"If anyone asks about this, say that Gu Fei brought friends to practice with us," Wang Xu said. After some thought, he added, "Remember to say it like you're really angry, so it sounds like we begged him for ages before he said yes. Like he doesn't have any team spirit at all."

Everyone nodded fervently, their faces a mask of bitter contempt. Gu Fei sighed.

The Fresh Out of Jail quartet came right on time, just as the bell rang for the start of the next class—they managed to avoid the break between periods when the school was most crowded. The fact that these guys with "Here to Make Trouble" all but flashing above their heads managed to waltz in through the front gates challenged Jiang Cheng's faith in Fourth High's administration. Even latecomers had to climb the metal gate to get in...

"Let's start," Gu Fei said. "Hurry up."

Jiang Cheng glanced at the squad. Fresh Out of Jail and Li Yan... Was Li Yan playing, too?

"Liu Fan, Luo Yu, Zhao Yihui, Chen Jie, and Li Yan. Everyone, get to know each other." Gu Fei pointed at the guys and introduced them in a single breath. "Don't worry if you can't—they're gonna be your opponents anyway."

Everyone took their jackets off and stepped onto the court. Two of the reserve players grabbed whistles and acted as referees; another one even pushed out a scoreboard. Seeing this setup, then looking at the opposing team, Jiang Cheng suddenly felt an excitement he hadn't experienced in a long time.

"I'll jump," Gu Fei said under his breath. "Remember to guard Liu Fan."

"Liu Fan?" Jiang Cheng asked.

"The one wearing the big iron chain," Gu Fei said.

"Okay." Jiang Cheng glanced over to their opponents; Liu Fan was "Out," one of the two who were playing the last time he saw them.

"That chain's made of iron?" Guo Xu asked.

"How should I know? If it's not iron, it's silver or stainless steel. Or brass, maybe." Gu Fei glanced at him. "You wanna go ask?"

Jiang Cheng turned away, holding back laughter.

"No thanks. I think it's stainless steel," Guo Xu said.

Gu Fei sighed. "Guard the guy with the big stainless steel chain."

Liu Fan was the one jumping for the ball with Gu Fei. He was slightly taller than Gu Fei, but a bit of height didn't matter much—it all came down to reaction time and jumping ability.

Jiang Cheng kept his eyes on the ball as it was tossed. Just as it reached what seemed like its highest point, Gu Fei and Liu Fan both leaped at once. Gu Fei got to it first, which mystified Jiang Cheng. Even when they jumped at the same time, Gu Fei was always able to touch the ball first.

But even though Gu Fei reached it first and hit it toward Lu Xiaobin, Li Yan ended up with possession; he charged over the instant it reached Lu Xiaobin's hand and hooked the ball away.

Jiang Cheng was aghast. He remembered the last time he watched them play, Gu Fei considered Li Yan one of the "sick, weak, injured, and elderly" ones who stayed off the court. How did a "sick, weak, injured, and elderly" guy manage to snatch the ball so easily?!

Lu Xiaobin was clearly taken aback as well; he immediately gave chase. He was so frantic and furious, he looked like the only thing stopping him from picking Li Yan up and flinging him was the rules.

Jiang Cheng, however, was in no hurry to chase the ball. Li Yan wasn't going fast; it didn't look like he intended to bring the ball up. When Li Yan tilted his head ever so slightly to the right, Jiang

Cheng saw Liu Fan the Stainless Steel Chain Guy reaching out with his hand as he ran toward the right boundary.

Jiang Cheng raced forward. Just as the ball flew out of Li Yan's hand toward Liu Fan, he accelerated and intercepted it. He didn't manage to seize the ball, but it bounced toward an arm-waving Lu Xiaobin.

Lu Xiaobin reacted well this time, grabbing the ball instantly.

"To me," Jiang Cheng said.

Before Li Yan could steal it again, Lu Xiaobin threw the ball straight at Jiang Cheng. As he caught it, Jiang Cheng thanked the gods for keeping the shotput-like throw from hitting him in the face.

Li Yan tried to cut him off, but Guo Xu held him back. Now, their team's stupid tendency to rush after whoever had the ball proved an advantage. Li Yan was a pretty skinny guy. Caught between Guo Xu and Lu Xiaobin, he all but disappeared.

When Jiang Cheng brought the ball below the basket, he looked at Gu Fei, who had just broken free from their opponents and was running toward the basket as well. Gu Fei looked back at him.

Jiang Cheng didn't hesitate. Estimating Gu Fei's trajectory, he passed the ball over; it bounced once by Liu Fan's foot before arriving securely in Gu Fei's hands.

But Fresh Out of Jail was on a different level than their class's reserve players yesterday. When Gu Fei took the ball, someone— either Luo Yu or Zhao Yihui—had already turned to cut off Gu Fei's path.

As Gu Fei brought the ball back behind him, Jiang Cheng sped between the other players. He didn't know if Gu Fei put too much trust in his teammates or just didn't have the time to think about it, but Gu Fei simply passed the ball behind himself without even looking.

Jiang Cheng caught it.

The Fresh Out of Jail squad had probably honed their teamwork well over time; their offense and defense were perfectly coordinated, and it was impossible to get near the basket. After he got the ball, Jiang Cheng was forced back beyond the three-point line.

The fast break failed; Fresh Out of Jail were all under the basket now. With just himself and Gu Fei, there was no way they could get in there.

As he held the ball, counting the seconds and looking for an opening, Gu Fei suddenly raised a hand. Jiang Cheng saw him extend three fingers.

Fuck.

Fine then. A three-pointer it was!

He bolted forward with the ball, and Liu Fan shot forward to meet him. Nearing the three-point line, Jiang Cheng put all his forward momentum into his leap; Liu Fan followed like a fucking shadow, jumping to block. Jiang Cheng had to pull back at the last second for a double-pump feint before making the shot from Liu Fan's left side with one hand.

As he twisted his torso in the air, the wound on his abdomen tore. Jiang Cheng couldn't help but let out a snarl of pain, inadvertently contributing to the hot-blooded atmosphere of competition.

"Fuck!" Liu Fan turned as soon as he touched the ground. When the ball sunk into the basket, he glanced at Jiang Cheng. "Damn."

"Nice shot." Gu Fei clapped his hands above his head. When his eyes met Jiang Cheng's, he gave him a thumbs-up.

22

EVEN THOUGH JIANG CHENG sent a very skillful and smooth shot into the basket, and let out an impressive yell... Fresh Out of Jail and Li Yan's practiced teamwork far exceeded his and Gu Fei's, not to mention their skills were much better than the other three guys on their class's team. In the first half, Jiang Cheng's team only netted fifteen points.

Jiang Cheng scored two three-pointers, while Gu Fei scored most of the rest, except for one single-point penalty shot from Wang Xu. Jiang Cheng was amazed that Wang Xu's weird, butt-sticking-out, schoolboy penalty shot even managed to go in the hoop.

During the half-time break, he glanced at the scoreboard: twenty-eight to fifteen.

The score was kind of painful to look at. With this big a difference, and their skills and teamwork being what they were, there was no way they could catch up. If this were a real match, their strategy in the second half would be based on a respectable desire to keep the gap from getting any wider.

"Let's make two swaps," Li Yan said as he sat on the court floor. "Luo Yu and Zhao Yihui will take a break—let two of your bench players take their place so they can all get some practice."

"Sounds good." Captain Wang Xu nodded. "Otherwise, the game might as well be over. Class Two doesn't play this well, anyway. Our training opponents are too good—it's killing our confidence."

Jiang Cheng sat silently in his corner. Earlier, he'd only felt the pain in his wound as he took his shot—the feeling was mostly gone when he landed. But now, after a couple of minutes of rest, the pain was searing through him again like a crackling fire.

He looked at his high-spirited teammates beside him and made no mention of swapping out. If Jiang Cheng swapped out and they depended entirely on Gu Fei, they wouldn't even be able to train their teamwork; there wouldn't be any point in practicing.

In any case, he didn't want Wang Xu to know he was injured. Wang Xu was preternaturally fixated on whether he'd fought with Monkey again—he really couldn't handle any more of that crap.

"Want to swap out for a rest?" Gu Fei asked quietly, standing in front of him.

"It's fine," Jiang Cheng said. He stood and stretched his arms. "We'll see after the match."

"Okay." Gu Fei gave him a look, then called their teammates over. "We've played half a game, so you should have some idea of how it goes now. For the next half, I'll be taking it from the sidelines to the basket. You guys continue guarding your marks. Pass the ball more—don't keep possession all the time. They're all good at stealing. Pass to Jiang Cheng, and I'll get the points."

Having missed the chance to delegate the tasks, Captain Wang Xu insisted on having the last word: "Right, what Da-Fei said."

In the first half, Jiang Cheng had the feeling Gu Fei was holding back, as if he was testing the skills of Wang Xu and the team. But starting in the second half, he played differently from before, like a wild animal let loose in an open field.

Only now did Jiang Cheng realize how frighteningly fast Gu Fei could move. Liu Fan and his group were very familiar with him, yet they couldn't mark him at all.

His strategy was straightforward: go from the sidelines straight to the basket, then receive the pass and shoot. If anyone stopped him, he would pass the ball to Jiang Cheng or some other teammate, then get the ball back from Jiang Cheng again.

Gu Fei was clearly having a good time, but Jiang Cheng found it tiring. He had to keep track of everyone's position on the court at all times while also watching out for passes from Gu Fei, who made them without even looking.

They closed the gap by five or six points, but Jiang Cheng couldn't resist saying, "Could you look and see where I am before you pass?"

"I did," Gu Fei said.

"I was ten whole paces away when you made that damn pass," Jiang Cheng gritted out in a low voice.

"You got there, didn't you? It's not like we lost the ball."

Jiang Cheng was lost for words. "...And if we did?"

"Then it's on me," Gu Fei replied calmly.

"That's bullshit! What, we don't lose points just because you say it's your fault?"

"Cheng-ge," Gu Fei laughed, looking at him, "you were captain of the basketball team in your old school, weren't you?"

"That's none of your business." Jiang Cheng looked right back. "I'm just telling you, keep an eye out."

"Got it."

After that, there was a slight change in the way Gu Fei moved: He would sweep a glance at Jiang Cheng's position out of the corner of his eye. But even after that look, he still passed the ball the same way, as if to say, "You asked me to look, so I looked, but I'll still pass it the way I want."

Jiang Cheng didn't bother commenting on it again. Gu Fei and Fresh Out of Jail played like they were on the streets, anyway. They were loose with the rules and expected their teammates to be one hundred percent in sync with them. They were like animals on the court, which even influenced the reserve players—they played like they were on steroids, making three fouls in less than ten minutes.

"Watch yourselves," Jiang Cheng said, exasperated. "We only have so many players. Who'll play if you're all sent off? Lao-Xu?"

Guo Xu waved his arms as he ran past. "It's fun!"

The game was still on. Jiang Cheng didn't have time to dwell on it; he followed them.

Wang Xu stole the ball from one of the reserves and howled like a god descending from the heavens: "Aaaahhh—!"

Jiang Cheng watched as Wang Xu was carried away by his own excitement. He had no apparent intention of either passing or advancing. Jiang Cheng had to clap and call out, "Pass the damn ball!"

Wang Xu recovered and immediately passed it with a swing of his arm. Jiang Cheng felt his heart seize. He'd just escaped Chen Jie's guard, catching a brief opening when nobody was blocking him, so any normal person would pass the ball to him. Who would have thought that Wang Xu would fling the ball to Gu Fei when Liu Fan was guarding him so closely that they were practically dancing the tango?!

Jiang Cheng could only watch it happen, speechless.

Gu Fei didn't seem to expect Wang Xu to pass the ball to him, either, but despite the circumstances he reacted surprisingly quickly, stretching his hand out and hitting the ball away before Liu Fan could touch it.

The volleyball-esque whack changed the ball's trajectory, launching it at Jiang Cheng's face.

"Fuck!" Jiang Cheng cried out in shock, feeling his heart about to leap out through the wound on his rib. Luckily, he raised his hand on reflex, stopping the ball right on time.

"Are you all fucking blind?!" he swore. Now that he had the ball, he left the rest of them behind as he charged furiously toward the basket like a tank.

Time was almost up anyway; he couldn't readjust. Now he was in the paint, he realized there was no opening for him to shoot. Liu Fan was incredibly adept at marking his opponent; he'd followed him the whole way, and one turn of his torso covered him completely.

Jiang Cheng didn't see Gu Fei in his peripheral vision, only the well-guarded Wang Xu and Lu Xiaobin. He couldn't afford to turn now, not with Liu Fan's hands waving in front of him—all it would take was a moment's distraction and he would lose the ball.

"There's no time—" someone yelled off the court.

If he didn't act now, their two points were gone. Jiang Cheng had no choice. He counted on Gu Fei being close enough to assist; if he wasn't at the basket, then he had to be behind him. So Jiang Cheng hooked one hand back and sent the ball backward. Then, blocking Liu Fan, he turned his head.

Gu Fei strode over and caught the ball securely. Without missing a beat, he jumped and made a three-point shot. The ball curved a long arc through the air.

"It's in! Holy shit!" Wang Xu screeched. "Three points!"

Jiang Cheng gave him a thumbs-up. Though the shot made no difference to the game overall, it *was* beautiful.

The whistle sounded, signaling the end of the match.

"Not bad, not bad! I think that was pretty good, even though the scores..." Wang Xu wiped the sweat from his forehead as he looked at the scoreboard. "Shit, eleven points apart? Oh, but it was still really good!"

Everyone agreed as they wiped their sweat away.

"Our teamwork's not up to par." Jiang Cheng tugged his shirt. His wound was really stinging; it must have been the sweat. "We need to break our habit of keeping our eyes on the ball instead of our teammates or opponents."

"Yeah, that's right." Wang Xu nodded, then echoed in his own words, "We need to look at our own team and the opposing side, not just the ball."

Fresh Out of Jail left now that they'd performed their duty, while the rest of them were absolutely engrossed in conversation until Lao-Xu came over.

"Quick, clean up and get changed," Lao-Xu said. "I asked for ten minutes from your Political Science teacher. Don't distract your classmates when you go back to class."

Everyone funneled into the gym bathroom to wash their faces or take a piss. Jiang Cheng waited until everyone had left to go in. After he washed his face, he lifted his shirt and looked in the mirror.

"Motherfucker," he muttered as he saw blood seeping through the gauze covering his wound. "Fucking...fuck."

He had nothing to clean the wound with right now, and he didn't want to go to the infirmary. The school nurse would take one look and report it. If Lao-Xu found out, who knew what other acts of fatherly love he would be inspired to perform...

Someone whistled behind him. Jiang Cheng quickly put his shirt back down and glanced in the mirror—it was Gu Fei.

Jiang Cheng sighed in relief. "Got any band-aids?"

"For a gash like that?" Gu Fei was skeptical. "I'll...get you some gauze from the infirmary."

"Is that a good idea?" Jiang Cheng frowned. "What if the nurse asks questions?"

"No one will ask any questions if it's me." Gu Fei examined his wound again. "This is really bad. Why didn't you say anything yesterday?"

"What's there to say?"

"Wait here for me." With that, Gu Fei left.

Bracing himself against the sink, Jiang Cheng sighed. He'd been so focused during the game that he hadn't even noticed it. Now that he was more relaxed, he felt a burning sensation radiating from the wound, along with a sharp and piercing pain, as if he'd been stabbed.

He carefully peeled the gauze off to take a look. The area underneath the gauze was red, with some blood seeping out of the wound, but it didn't look too bad otherwise.

It had been a long time since he'd sustained an injury that drew blood. He'd been in a few fights since he started high school, but most of them only left him with bruises at worst. He felt a little sullen at the sudden sight of blood on himself.

Was it for Li Baoguo's sake? Nah. He couldn't even be bothered to ask how Li Baoguo was doing. More importantly, Li Baoguo hadn't contacted him since yesterday. He had no idea if the man had gone gambling again or if his attackers had finally caught up to him. The more Jiang Cheng thought about it, the more it unnerved him. What kind of trouble had Li Baoguo gotten himself into? Was it resolved now? Would there be other altercations like that in the future? This time, he'd been beaten up on the street; would they track him down at his house next time? Would they trash the place, or would they bash his head in?

The thought made him shudder.

Gu Fei quickly returned to the bathroom with a small bag containing disinfectant, bandages, and other supplies.

"Want a hand?" he asked.

"I'll...do it myself." Jiang Cheng picked up a cotton ball and poured rubbing alcohol on it.

Ever since Jiang Cheng had realized he was more into men than women, he'd been reluctant to have physical contact with other people. Apart from Pan Zhi, anyone else's touch made him feel uncomfortable. Especially someone like Gu Fei, with his handsome face and pretty hands. He worried his thoughts would stray into inappropriate territory.

However, it was hard to maneuver with one hand lifting his shirt and the other cleaning his wound with the cotton ball. When he let go to get a fresh piece of cotton, his shirt fell and brushed against his wound again.

"Wang Xu called you fussy," Gu Fei said, watching.

"Yeah," said Jiang Cheng. "What, you want to back him up on that?"

"I do. You really are difficult. Are you trying to show how strong and independent you are?"

Jiang Cheng sighed. With the bottle of rubbing alcohol in his hand, he looked at Gu Fei. "I'm afraid you won't know how to hold back—that's how you play basketball."

"I've been cleaning my own wounds since I was four." Gu Fei took the bottle from his hand and poured alcohol onto the cotton. "I'm an old hand."

Jiang Cheng said nothing. *Four?* Bullshit. He couldn't even remember anything from when he was four.

Gu Fei's hands were adept enough, though. The cotton pressed quick and gentle against his wound; it was over before he could feel any pain. Jiang Cheng shifted his eyes to the faucet in the corner.

"This wound of yours won't heal before the tournament." Gu Fei covered the wound in gauze. "Hold this."

"It won't make a difference." Jiang Cheng pressed the gauze to the wound and quickly stole a glance at Gu Fei's fingers. They were long, especially his pinky finger. Very suited to playing piano... He turned his gaze back to the faucet.

Gu Fei swiftly used medical tape to secure the gauze. "Done. You can hold onto this stuff and change it yourself later."

They returned to the classroom to hear their Political Science teacher raging at the podium, but the buzzing students were undaunted by her ire; having just returned from practice, the basketball players were at the height of their excitement.

"Your Xu-zong has got his priorities backward!" She slapped the podium. "Forget about your midterms, you can take a basketball exam instead! I can't believe you were off playing with balls during class hours! It's not that I have low expectations for your class, but the way you behave..."

Jiang Cheng bowed his head as he hurried back to his seat. As a "good student," he normally showed teachers some respect; he would usually act repentant when they got angry and yelled.

Gu Fei was less cooperative. He ambled slowly back to his seat during her impassioned admonishment, going so far as to straighten out his jacket on the back of his chair before sitting down.

"Hey, Da-Fei," Zhou Jing turned and whispered. "Hey. Da—"

Before he could finish his sentence, the teacher slammed her palm onto the podium. "Zhou Jing! Get out!"

"Wha—?" Zhou Jing froze.

"Get out!" she roared, pointing at him.

Zhou Jing hesitated, then stood, put on his jacket, and walked out the back door into the corridor.

"And the two behind him! Get out of here!" the teacher exclaimed, pointing at Jiang Cheng and Gu Fei. "Everyone else came back before you two did! You don't even want to be in class, do you?! Go stand outside!"

Jiang Cheng stared at the teacher. While he never looked like he was paying attention in class—sometimes he skipped altogether—it was his first time getting called out directly and told to leave. But Gu Fei was fully compliant, much more so than when teachers told him to pay attention. As soon as she finished speaking, he stood, took his jacket, and went to lean against the railing of the walkway outside with Zhou Jing.

The teacher continued to point at Jiang Cheng. "You!"

Resigned to the situation, Jiang Cheng sighed. He got to his feet and walked out too. He didn't have to grab his jacket; he hadn't even gotten a chance to remove it.

Zhou Jing wasn't upset about being kicked out of class at all. Leaning over the railing, he continued his line of questioning. "Wang Xu says you guys are the shit now?"

"Not *the* shit," Jiang Cheng said, "just shit."

Captain Wang Jiuri had asked everyone to act like bitter, despairing players with no hope of winning, but apparently he couldn't resist bragging.

"Is Da-Fei playing?" Zhou Jing asked. "Wang Xu said you wouldn't agree to it even when Lao-Xu begged you."

Jiang Cheng almost burst out laughing. Wang Xu still kept loyal to his claim of Gu Fei's absence, but his random embellishments made Jiang Cheng want to interview him to see what went on inside his head.

"Yeah." Gu Fei turned. "I have no sense of class pride."

Gu Fei stood to Jiang Cheng's right; when he turned and spoke, his breath skimmed Jiang Cheng's face. Jiang Cheng quickly drew away, bounced in place twice, then calmly walked to the other side of Zhou Jing. He leaned on the railing and looked out below.

"Really?" Not entirely convinced, Zhou Jing glanced at Jiang Cheng. "You're not pulling my leg?"

Jiang Cheng stared at him. Zhou Jing wasn't a bad guy, but anyone could see that his mouth was a megaphone; if you told him anything it'd get out before you even had the time to turn around.

"Mm." Jiang Cheng nodded.

"But Wang Xu said you guys are really good now... How? It's not like I've never seen them play before." Zhou Jing frowned. After a moment's thought, his eyes lit up. "Holy shit, is this one of your strategies? Telling people that you're good?"

Jiang Cheng really wanted to ask him what the point of bragging about their team's prowess as a threat to their opponents would be, but he nodded anyway.

"Oh—" Zhou Jing wanted to continue, but Gu Fei's phone rang and cut him off.

It was Gu Fei's mother. He picked up. "Hello?"

"Are you done with school yet?!" her panicked voice blared. "I don't know what's wrong with Er-Miao—"

His heart clenched as he heard Gu Miao screaming in the background. "I'm coming home right now."

He hung up and sprinted down the stairs.

There were many reasons why Gu Miao might scream. In the past two years, it was usually water. But she only occasionally reacted that way, and his mom knew about that particular fear of hers, so she usually took extra care. This was probably unrelated to water. So what was it?

He raced out the school gate; the guard didn't even have a chance to stop him and ask where he was going.

As he dashed home on his bicycle, Gu Fei felt very tired. This exhaustion would always sneak up on him without warning; the moment it struck, he always felt as if he could shut his eyes and sleep until the end of time. It wasn't physical exhaustion—he didn't feel that part of it very much anymore, but the mental exhaustion was impossible to escape. He could ignore his mom, or shout at her sometimes to vent, but he couldn't ignore Gu Miao.

He was careful: On one hand, he taught Gu Miao to handle certain possible dangers on her own; on the other hand, he had to stay on guard for her constantly, defending her against accidental threats that could appear out of nowhere.

Sprinting up the stairs, he could hear Gu Miao's screams even through the shut door.

The old lady in the unit across the landing from them opened her door and looked at him with concern. "Is Er-Miao..."

"She'll be fine," Gu Fei said. He opened the door and went in.

His mom was sitting on the sofa, holding Gu Miao. Gu Miao buried her face in their mother's breast, wailing incessantly.

"Er-Miao. Er-Miao, quiet now. Look, your brother's home." Their mom patted Gu Miao's back. "Gu Fei's home..."

Gu Fei went over and took Gu Miao from his mother's arms. One hand stroking her back and the other gently squeezing the back of her neck, he said, "It's okay, Er-Miao. It's okay now."

Gu Miao wrapped her arms around his neck and continued screaming. She was trembling. Gu Fei frowned at this—Gu Miao wasn't scared. She was *angry*.

"What is it?" Gu Fei asked softly. "Tell me. What made you angry?"

His mom looked at him, uncomprehending. "Angry?"

He pointed at Gu Miao's backpack and had his mother bring it over to him. He took out Gu Miao's books and notebooks. As he flipped through them, he asked, "Is it your books? Did someone rip them up?"

Gu Miao's screams grew softer, though she was still shouting. He could make out one muffled word through it all: "Drawing."

Gu Fei opened her vocabulary notebook. Two pages in, he saw a page that had been scribbled all over with messy sketches of a small figure tripping; he could make out a skateboard next to it, with a caption on both sides: "*Pig. Mute. Idiot.*"

"Er-Miao, stop." Gu Fei put the notebook down and held her by the shoulders. "Look at me. Look at me."

Gu Miao finally stopped screaming. She raised her head to look at him, her eyes wide open.

"Do you know who did this?" Gu Fei asked.

Gu Miao nodded.

Looking into her eyes, Gu Fei said, "Let me take care of this for you, okay? I'll go talk to your classmate."

For a while, Gu Miao fixed her large eyes on him unblinkingly. Then, she shook her head.

"No?" Gu Fei asked.

Gu Miao shook her head again.

"What are you thinking, then?" Gu Fei asked. "Tell me."

After a very long pause, Gu Miao quietly said, "Myself."

Gu Fei didn't know how she wanted to take care of it, but Gu Miao wouldn't speak again no matter how he asked, nor would she give him any other response—she turned, went into her room, and shut the door.

On the sofa, their mom covered her face and sobbed quietly. "Why is my life like this? I married a bastard, and I barely know how to raise my own kids... Did I do something terrible in my last life to deserve this? Even when I want to find someone to keep me company—"

"Mom, just go back to your room," Gu Fei said.

"And my son's so cruel to me..." Covering her face, she sobbed as she retreated to her bedroom.

Gu Fei pinched his brow. The apartment was quiet now, without a single sound.

He peeked at Gu Miao through a gap in the door. Gu Miao lay in bed, hugging her blanket; she looked like she was sleeping. There was no sound from his mom's room, either.

He returned to the sofa and closed his eyes.

After resting like that for about half an hour, he opened his eyes and called Ding Zhuxin. "Xin-jie, are you free to come out tonight?"

23

After Gu Fei vanished from school in the middle of Political Science class without even taking his bag, their teacher was so furious that she rushed to the office and berated Lao-Xu. At the end of the morning periods, Lao-Xu came to their classroom and stopped Jiang Cheng just as he was about to leave.

"Jiang Cheng," he began.

"I don't know," said Jiang Cheng. He knew Lao-Xu wanted to ask what happened to Gu Fei, but he really had no idea.

"There has to be a reason he ran off, right?" Lao-Xu said.

Jiang Cheng only knew that Gu Fei had picked up a call and said he was going home immediately. He didn't hear anything else. But he didn't want to tell Lao-Xu about that, either. Who knew what was up with Gu Fei, and who knew if he wanted Lao-Xu to know? He didn't want to say too much.

Clearly, Zhou Jing didn't think about it as deeply as he did. As soon as Lao-Xu grabbed him and asked, he squealed. "He picked up a call and said he was going home, then he ran off. Maybe something happened at home?"

"Really, now." Lao-Xu frowned. After Zhou Jing left, he seized Jiang Cheng again. "Even Zhou Jing knows, and you don't?"

"Does it matter whether or not I know? Either way, you know now, don't you?" Bag over his shoulder, Jiang Cheng walked out.

"Will you bring Gu Fei his bag?" Lao-Xu asked behind him.

"No." Jiang Cheng turned. "Xu-zong, if ever I run out halfway through a school day and leave my bag behind, please don't ask anyone to bring it back for me."

"Why?" asked Lao-Xu.

"Because it's annoying," Jiang Cheng said. "Not everyone likes it when other people touch their stuff, let alone take it to their house. I mean it. If he wants it, he can come back for it. Even a group of thugs can walk into the school, so why would you worry about a student getting in?"

Lao-Xu stared, seemingly thrown by this. Jiang Cheng didn't say anything else. He turned and left.

Lao-Xu was an old nag. He cared too much about too many things. At their age, the last thing they needed was someone hovering over them like a mother hen. Especially Gu Fei—you could tell from a glance that he preferred being alone.

Jiang Cheng was certain Lao-Xu would call Gu Fei in a moment, and just as certain that Gu Fei would ignore the call. Theirs was a relationship that couldn't be salvaged without a major improvement to Lao-Xu's emotional intelligence.

At a time like this, Jiang Cheng suddenly missed his old home-room teacher. The instant this reminiscence began, he swiftly lifted his head and gasped in a cold breath, cutting off the wave of nostalgia before it could take root.

He wanted to eat at Wang Jiuri's meat pie place again for lunch, but he thought about how he would have nothing to say if he ran into Captain Jiuri there. He didn't want the captain to drag him around the whole time yapping about strategy. He decided to have a bowl of noodles at a little shop on the corner instead.

When he returned to Li Baoguo's place, he was surprised to find that Li Baoguo was home, sitting on the couch and smoking. He was looking at a piece of paper in the dim light. Li Baoguo's home was in a dip between two buildings, so the light was dreadful. Outside, the sunlight dazzled; indoors, it was already dusk. Every time Jiang Cheng entered, he felt the weight of it pressing down on him. He reached out and turned the living room light on.

"Oh." Li Baoguo looked up, startled. "You're back, Chengcheng?"

"Mm-hm." Jiang Cheng took one look at his father: His face was splotched with patches of green and purple, and the corner of his mouth was swollen. It looked like yesterday's beating was a bad one; if he hadn't gone over to stop it, Li Baoguo might have been in the hospital now. "Are your...wounds okay?"

"Oh, don't worry, it's fine." Li Baoguo touched his own face. "It's just a scratch. Back when I worked in the plant, I wouldn't even need one hand to take on kids like that—"

"I ate already," Jiang Cheng cut him off before going to his room. "You should eat something."

Just as he took his jacket off to lie down in bed, the door opened.

"Chengcheng." Li Baoguo stuck his upper body through the door. "You were okay yesterday, right?"

Jiang Cheng was exasperated. He didn't have a habit of locking the door; after all, for most of his life, he'd only need to shut his door and no one would open it at will. Now it looked like he had to remember to lock.

"I'm fine," Jiang Cheng said. "I just want to take a nap."

"Your dad's useless," Li Baoguo said, showing no intention of leaving. "Your dad was beaten up on the street and you had to come save him. Are you ashamed of me?"

Jiang Cheng didn't speak. It had taken him a moment to realize that when Li Baoguo said "your dad," he meant himself.

"But don't worry," Li Baoguo went on. "If anything happens to me, I won't drag you down with me!"

"Got it." Jiang Cheng tried to be patient. "I'm going to take a nap. I'm a little tired."

Li Baoguo nodded and left, leaving the door open. Jiang Cheng was forced to walk over and close it. After a moment's hesitation, he decided against locking it. Li Baoguo was outside—he would hear the lock turn. Jiang Cheng didn't want to make things too awkward.

When he lay back in bed, he felt utterly drained. He didn't know whether it was because he played basketball with an injury, or because he hadn't slept well last night.

Li Baoguo didn't go out to play mahjong during lunchtime, which was unlike him. Jiang Cheng could hear him coughing in the living room the whole time. More than once he thought about getting up and telling him to get it checked out at the hospital. Li Baoguo had had that cough since winter break; now it was almost time for midterms, and it'd continued without any improvement.

He couldn't take a midday nap listening to that racket. Upstairs, someone was beating their kid again—not the one from yesterday, but a different family. There were many families with children on this block, taking turns to beat their kids. Today it was yours, tomorrow it'd be mine; some were ahead of schedule and ended up beating them together.

Every kid screamed heartrendingly. In between the screams, neighbors who couldn't bear it anymore would come out and try to make peace, which got them an upbraiding as well. And if they couldn't stand being yelled at, it would evolve into a big verbal spat.

Basically, the old buildings around here were always noisy—full of a kind of vigorous life Jiang Cheng had never encountered before.

He heard the sound of the living room door shutting, and Li Baoguo's coughing finally disappeared. Jiang Cheng grabbed his phone and looked at the time. He was due to get up for school.

Gu Fei wasn't at school that afternoon, either.

Since school started, Gu Fei had regularly either been late for class or skipped altogether. It seemed normal enough. His classmates weren't curious, and his teachers never really asked about it. Only Lao-Xu kept on questioning it.

At the end of the school day, Jiang Cheng was accosted by Lao-Xu again. "Are you against communicating with your teacher, Jiang Cheng?"

Lao-Xu smelled of alcohol; Jiang Cheng had noticed it in the past couple weeks. Lao-Xu didn't get drunk, but the scent often lingered on him. Zhou Jing said he always took a gulp or two with his breakfast. He'd even been named and shamed by the principal in front of their whole school before, but that didn't stop him.

"On that point, at least, he's kind of badass," Zhou Jing had said.

Jiang Cheng wondered whether this was why Lao-Xu liked the poet Li Bai so much that he was always bringing him up in class during his long tangents. Whatever the lesson was about, he'd find a way to link it back to Li Bai somehow. "Speaking of so-and-so, I'd like to talk about Li Bai," was how he usually started. "Li Bai, that old geezer..."

"Have you been drinking?" Jiang Cheng asked.

"I had a bit at lunch." Lao-Xu let out a sheepish chuckle. "Jiang Cheng, I notice you and Gu Fei coordinate well in basketball. You must be quite close off the court too, right?"

"...It's just basketball. Anyone who can play knows how to coordinate."

"I called Gu Fei a few times this afternoon, but he didn't pick up," Lao-Xu said. "I should've looked out for him more—"

Jiang Cheng cut him off exasperatedly. "Okay, I get it. I'll go to his store and check up on him after school, but there's nothing else I can do apart from that. I don't know him that well, and I don't know where he lives."

"All right, great." Lao-Xu nodded cheerfully. "Tell him to come to school tomorrow... I wanted to ask Wang Xu to go, but he doesn't live as close, and you can't trust that brat..."

Jiang Cheng nodded. "I get it."

It was no big deal to go to Gu Fei's store for a look, but if Lao-Xu hadn't badgered him, there was no way he would have gone. Who wanted his teachers and classmates to keep tabs on him all the time to the point of home visits?

Jiang Cheng strolled out of the school and looked at the route map next to the bus stop outside. His wound had torn once today. If practice continued like this for the next few days, it wouldn't heal before the tournament. He wanted to get some sort of wound adhesive from the hospital when he went to change his dressing so it would heal faster.

There was a bus that went straight to the hospital, and he only had to wait a few minutes before it arrived. He squeezed onto the bus through a sea of Fourth High students; the empty bus filled up halfway at this stop alone. The next stop was some vocational school, and after that, nobody else was able to get on.

The bus was full of students happily chatting away. Jiang Cheng was stuck by the metal pole at the back door. Whenever anyone moved at the back, he would be jostled against the pole. Two stops in, he was so annoyed that he wanted to crush the people next to him to the floor.

They passed another school. Jiang Cheng looked out and saw it was an elementary school, fortunately. Their parents would pick them up, so nobody would board the bus. And it'd been ages now since elementary school let out.

He braced his forehead against the pole. His headphones were in his bag, so he couldn't take them out now even if he wanted to. All he could do was close his eyes and rest while he listened to the students around him boasting and gossiping.

Halfway between stops, he heard a commotion in the bus and opened his eyes.

"Whoa! Elementary school kids are so fierce these days!" someone said.

"Oof. Looks like they're gonna crack someone's head open with that," someone else said with a laugh.

Jiang Cheng glanced out the window and froze.

Three little boys were screeching and cursing as they ran. Behind them…a little girl with a skateboard was giving chase. Jiang Cheng didn't have to look too closely to tell it was Gu Miao.

Gu Miao chased them for several steps. The boys ran too fast for her to catch up, so she put the skateboard on the ground, stepped on it, and shot forward. As she passed the bus, Jiang Cheng saw the expression on her face. He couldn't tell if it was apathy or anger, but he'd never seen her make that expression before. His chest tightened.

The bus was slow, but it was a short journey to the next stop. They were three stops away from the hospital, but Jiang Cheng rushed off at this one, pushing through the crowd.

Gu Miao and the little boys were gone without a trace. He ran in the direction they'd disappeared in, stopping at an intersection.

Straight ahead was the main road; the right turn would lead him down an old, shabby little street.

As he was pondering where to go, he heard shouting to his right.

The moment he turned, he saw the remaining two boys running out of an alley. The other had fallen to the ground. Gu Miao was straddling him, smashing his head with her skateboard.

"Fuck!" Jiang Cheng's knees nearly buckled from fright. He sprinted wildly at them.

The people from the nearby shops all rushed out, first shouting in alarm, then trying to pull Gu Miao off. But whenever anyone approached, Gu Miao would hit them with her skateboard. Two people in a row tried and failed to get close.

The boy on the ground stopped trying to break free. He simply held his head, wailing and screaming. Gu Miao seized the chance to whack his head with the skateboard again. This time, a man grabbed Gu Miao from behind and picked her up. Gu Miao began a frenzied struggle, letting out piercing shrieks.

When Jiang Cheng reached them, the man who picked her up was at a loss, unsure whether to hold on or drop her.

"Gu Miao!" Jiang Cheng yelled as he rushed toward them.

Gu Miao's eyes were shut and she kept screaming, seeming to hear nothing. In her hands, she gripped the corner of her skateboard tightly.

"Er-Miao!" Jiang Cheng roared. "It's Jiang Cheng-gege! It's Cheng-ge!"

"You know her?" someone asked. "What's wrong with this kid? Has she lost her mind?!"

Jiang Cheng took one look at the boy, whom someone had picked up off the ground. He was howling tearfully, and Jiang Cheng could see blood on his head.

"Here," Jiang Cheng said to the man holding Gu Miao. "Give her to me."

"You can't leave! Are you her family?!" the man said. "Look how badly she hurt the other kid! We have to go to the police. Call your—"

"I said *give her to me*!" Jiang Cheng bellowed, glaring at him.

He'd never seen Gu Miao struggle and scream so desperately; she looked so frantic, and it made his heart clench. Jiang Cheng knew Gu Miao had issues, but seeing her like this made him suddenly lose his composure.

His outburst stunned the other man. Jiang Cheng went over and hugged Gu Miao, pulling her into his arms.

"You can't leave!" There were more onlookers now. They formed a circle around Gu Miao and him, trapping them inside.

"Go ahead and call the police." Jiang Cheng hugged Gu Miao. Her screams had quieted somewhat, but she wouldn't stop trembling.

The wound on the boy's head wasn't serious. There was a small cut on the back of his head, which an older lady rinsed with some alcohol. They didn't know whether there were any other injuries, though. At some point during all the commotion, someone called the police.

Jiang Cheng hugged Gu Miao tightly, rubbing her back firmly to comfort her as he pulled his phone out and called Gu Fei's number.

The ringing broke off midway. That motherfucker put his phone on Do Not Disturb!

He had to send Gu Fei a message instead.

– Gu Miao's in trouble. Call me.

Next, he called Wang Xu.

Wang Xu picked up quickly. "Oh, hey! Jiang Cheng? You're calling *me*, you uptight bastard?"

"Go find Gu Fei right now," Jiang Cheng urged in a hushed tone. "Right now! His sister's in trouble! He's not picking up!"

"Huh?" Wang Xu was taken aback, but Jiang Cheng could hear him running already. "Wait, hold on, I just got home—I'm going back out now! I'll go look for him! Where are you guys?"

"I don't know, I'm near an elementary school right now... The police will be coming soon, I don't know where we'll be after that."

Jiang Cheng looked around at the shocked and furious onlookers. If he hadn't been here with Gu Miao right now, he had the feeling they would've been beating her up.

"Got it!" Wang Xu yelled, and hung up.

The police came soon after. The instant they arrived, they were mobbed by the crowd, who all tried to explain the situation.

"Take the kid to the hospital first," said an older officer, adding after a look at Jiang Cheng, "Are you this girl's family?"

"No," Jiang Cheng said. "I go to school with her brother."

"Notify her family," the officer said. "You need to follow us to the hospital first, then we'll go to the station."

"Okay."

Holding Gu Miao, Jiang Cheng picked up the skateboard and walked toward the police car. Gu Miao was silent now, only clinging tightly to his neck. Her fingers gripped his nape hard; he felt her nails digging into his skin.

"Gu Miao. Gu Miao?" Jiang Cheng murmured softly to her. "You're digging holes in my neck. Everything's fine now. Don't be scared. Your brother's coming soon."

Gu Miao didn't react. She didn't loosen her grip at all, her body still shaking. The state she was in deeply worried Jiang Cheng. He didn't know what was wrong with her or why she'd beaten up that other child so ruthlessly, and because he wasn't her family, he didn't know if he was doing the right thing... If he made the wrong call, would Gu Fei hunt him down to seek revenge...?

Jiang Cheng covered the medical bill with his own money first. The treatment and exams didn't cost much; the biggest hurdle was the boy's parents. As soon as they arrived at the hospital, they charged madly at Gu Miao and Jiang Cheng, fists swinging; they almost hit the police officers who came over to stop them.

"Don't hold me back!" the man roared. "Pay up! Pay up! She did this to my son! I'll do the same to her, the lunatic! You know what, I know this psycho girl, she's in my son's class! Freakin' nutcase! I knew something bad would happen when I saw her in that class! You better keep her inside, or I'll beat her down the moment I see her!"

"Let the police settle this." Jiang Cheng knew that Gu Miao was at fault, but the man's words infuriated him. He suppressed the flames of his rage and added calmly, "If you touch her, I'll hurt you too, and this'll never be over."

"What the fuck?!" the woman screeched. "Mr. Police Officer, did you hear him?!"

Gu Fei finally called him back. "Where are you? I'm coming now."

"The hospital," Jiang Cheng said. "Hurry."

The moment the other family heard that Gu Miao's family was coming, they grew agitated once again. When Gu Fei arrived, the police were about to bring them all to the station.

"What's this now?!" the man shouted at the sight of Gu Fei. "Did you come to fight?!"

Behind Gu Fei were Li Yan and Liu Fan, along with Wang Xu and Ding Zhuxin.

"Gu Miao, your brother's here," Jiang Cheng whispered to Gu Miao.

"Er-Miao?" Gu Fei jogged over.

Hearing his voice, Gu Miao finally let go of Jiang Cheng's neck. She turned to look at Gu Fei, then threw herself into his arms, hugging him tight.

"She hit that kid," Jiang Cheng quietly explained. "Skateboard to the head."

"I'm sorry." Gu Fei turned to the couple. "My sister—"

"Sorry, my ass! What good is a 'sorry'?!" the woman exclaimed, pointing at him. "I won't let this go until I get my hands on her!"

Gu Fei looked at her in silence. After several seconds, he said, "Go on, then."

This seemed to shock the woman. She staggered back a few steps. "My god! What kind of attitude is this! Are you all seeing this?!"

"Let's go to the police station first." Ding Zhuxin walked over. "We'll listen to what the police have to say on how this should be resolved. If there needs to be treatment and compensation, we'll oblige, within reason."

"You—" the woman tried to continue, but Ding Zhuxin cut her off.

"Ma'am." Ding Zhuxin looked at her. "You're making such a fuss that the officers can't even get a word in. If you don't want to do this the legal way, we're happy to oblige... But it might not turn out so well for you."

"Watch your words," the police officer reminded Ding Zhuxin.

"Pardon me." Ding Zhuxin smiled at the officer apologetically. "We're all anxious when something happens to our children. We'll cooperate, of course. But cooperation can't be one-sided, right?"

As they all got ready to go to the station, Gu Fei asked, "Does my friend have to come along, too?"

The officer eyed Jiang Cheng. "Yes."

"Okay," Jiang Cheng agreed. He looked at Gu Miao as she leaned on Gu Fei's shoulder. She seemed much calmer now, no longer seized by that crazed, cold fury from before.

"Thank you," Gu Fei said.

"Forget that for now. Is Gu Miao...okay? Earlier, she looked..."

"She's fine." Gu Fei paused. "I'll tell you about it some other time."

"All right," Jiang Cheng replied. He followed the police out.

After a few steps, Gu Fei called out from behind him, "Jiang Cheng. Your..." Gu Fei pointed at the back of his neck, then reached out to tug at his collar. "You've got a cut here."

Probably from Gu Miao. That munchkin had a strong grip. But Jiang Cheng was too distracted to think about that; when Gu Fei pulled at his collar, he reflexively slapped his hand away.

"...It's fine," he said awkwardly.

24

AFTER ALMOST TWO HOURS at the police station, the matter was finally resolved.

The boy didn't admit to provoking Gu Miao. He said that Gu Miao chased after him and assaulted him for no reason. Gu Miao didn't speak the whole time—she lay on Gu Fei's shoulder with her eyes closed, so there was no way to refute him.

Jiang Cheng didn't believe the boy. The way Gu Miao was, she'd be bullied at any school. But *why* Gu Miao hit him wasn't important; even if the little boy had bullied her, the police couldn't do anything about that. The point was that Gu Miao had split his head open, and he'd needed two stitches.

Luckily, there weren't any other major injuries. His parents' predatory demands for compensation were forced back by Ding Zhuxin's thinly veiled threats, leading the police to warn her several times to watch her mouth.

Gu Fei didn't speak much. All his attention was on Gu Miao.

Li Yan and the guys were simply there to fold their arms and look like they could make good on Ding Zhuxin's threats, giving off an "if you make trouble, so will we—we don't look like decent people anyway" vibe. When they finally came to an agreement and the police sent them away, Jiang Cheng let out a long sigh of relief.

Only now did his stomach wake up, whining with hunger, except he didn't really feel like eating.

They walked out of the police station and into the cold, biting wind.

"You guys should get back. Thanks for this." Gu Fei glanced at Jiang Cheng. "Let's get a taxi with Wang Xu."

Jiang Cheng nodded. "Okay."

After they split from the group and got into the car, nobody spoke. Jiang Cheng felt rather morose, and he figured Gu Fei didn't feel much better. Even Wang Xu the chatterbox didn't say much—he cursed and sighed, but he went silent after Gu Fei shot him a look.

"Neither of you ate, right?" Gu Fei asked as they approached the neighborhood.

"Don't mind us," Wang Xu said. "Go home. I don't need the taxi to take me all the way home, either; I can get off here, I'm just around the next block... Jiang Cheng, wanna come over for meat pies?"

"No, thanks. I don't want to eat anything right now."

When they arrived at the corner, Gu Fei carried Gu Miao out of the car as Jiang Cheng followed them, holding her skateboard. After a few steps, Gu Fei turned. "Thanks for today."

"Don't mention it." Jiang Cheng looked at Gu Miao. "You should keep her out of school for a few days. I saw three boys today, the other two who weren't beaten might..."

"Even if she doesn't take time off, she may not be able to go back to school." Gu Fei sighed. "Can you tell Lao-Xu I need to be excused from class tomorrow morning? I have to go to Er-Miao's school."

"Sure." Jiang Cheng nodded. "What excuse do you want me to use?"

"I have a fever." Gu Fei touched his forehead. "A fever that rages from tonight until tomorrow at noon. It's burning my hand."

"...Okay," Jiang Cheng chuckled.

Watching Gu Fei's back as he walked off, carrying Gu Miao in one arm and her skateboard in the other, Jiang Cheng felt a mix of emotions. He used to think Gu Fei lived an unbothered life: unbothered as he let his sister run amok on that skateboard, unbothered as he skipped class and came in late, unbothered as he played basketball as he pleased—just following his heart's desires, living without a care in the world.

It seemed that wasn't the case at all. Gu Fei seemed to be the only one handling all of his family's affairs. How could someone like that truly do whatever he wanted?

Nobody could do whatever they wanted. Not Gu Fei, and not himself. The same way he didn't want to stay in Li Baoguo's house, or this unfamiliar, run-down city; the way he didn't want the life set out before him, but had no choice but to face it.

Every little change changed everything.

Even his previous habit of staying out all night was something he couldn't do lightly anymore. After all, he had nowhere to go. Not many people could actually bury their heads in the sand and not care about anything but "being themselves."

Li Baoguo didn't go out to play mahjong that evening. He spent all night coughing at home, snoring, sleep-talking, and grinding his teeth—a discordant symphony evoking the rage of mortals and gods. Jiang Cheng lay awake the whole night, staring into space in his entirely unsoundproofed room where he could hear the difference between a sandal and a sneaker shuffling around upstairs.

When he got up in the morning, he felt so sleepy that his steps seemed to float.

"Maybe you should go to the hospital?" he said to Li Baoguo, who was putting on his shoes and rushing off for a morning round of mahjong. "That cough of yours sounds serious. Is it an infection?"

"See! Now that's a *real* son!" Li Baoguo exclaimed joyfully. "It's fine, I've been coughing for years. It's an old problem, no need to go to the hospital. There's no problem at all!"

Jiang Cheng wanted to say there was a problem with that sentence, but he'd only just opened his mouth when Li Baoguo threw the door open and rushed away.

Well, shit. If he wanted to be sick, let him. Li Baoguo's attitude made him feel like he was being a delicate maiden.

On the way to school, Jiang Cheng dropped by the pharmacy and bought a box of American ginseng tablets. They helped him stay alert; he used to take them often when studying before exams. If he took one now, it would at least stop him from falling into too deep a sleep in class. He didn't want to snore in the middle of a lesson—it would be humiliating.

Just as expected, Gu Fei didn't come to school in the morning. After the morning self-study period, Jiang Cheng went to Lao-Xu's office and repeated the excuse Gu Fei gave him for taking time off from school.

"He has a fever, it's killing him. He's been burning up since yesterday afternoon, and he'll be fine by lunchtime."

As soon as he spoke, Jiang Cheng realized how severely his lack of sleep had affected his intelligence. But Lao-Xu didn't seem to notice his peculiar turn of phrase. He was too busy being delighted that Gu Fei had notified him about the absence instead of just skipping.

"See, I knew he could be redeemed," he said, overcome with emotion. "Isn't he applying for time off now? I knew it. Getting through to you kids is a matter of using the right technique..."

But Gu Fei didn't wait until the afternoon to come to school. He walked in in the middle of Chinese class, the final morning period.

Lao-Xu eyed him with great concern. "Don't you have a fever? You could come in the afternoon."

"I'm better now," Gu Fei said.

Lao-Xu nodded. He rapped the podium with one hand and said enthusiastically, "Well, let's continue where we just left off…"

Gu Fei sat down and took a look at Jiang Cheng. "Did you not sleep?"

"…Is it that obvious?" Jiang Cheng slumped over the desk, his eyelids a little too heavy to lift.

"Yeah," Gu Fei said. "It hurts just to look at you. You'd think *you* were the one with the day-old fever."

Jiang Cheng yawned. "I didn't sleep well last night."

"Sorry," Gu Fei muttered, "for keeping you for hours and making you go through all that trouble."

"It wasn't because of Gu Miao." Jiang Cheng waved a hand. "It's Li Baoguo… He didn't go out to play mahjong yesterday. He stayed in and coughed all night and the noise kept me up."

"Oh." Gu Fei dug into his pocket and pulled out a small cardboard box, setting it in front of Jiang Cheng. "Want some?"

"Wha…" Jiang Cheng opened the box to find a handful of milk candies. Speechless, he wondered what exactly Gu Fei was thinking. "Milk candy?"

"Yup. You like them, don't you?" Gu Fei took a mint candy from his pocket and stuck it in his mouth.

"I never said I liked them. I was just hungry that day," Jiang Cheng said.

"Really?" Gu Fei gave him a look of exaggerated surprise, then dropped it and took the candy away. "Give it back, then."

"Wha—" Jiang Cheng glared at him. "You're pretty interesting, you know that?"

"Do you want them or not?" Gu Fei asked.

Jiang Cheng opened his mouth just to close it again. After a pause, he said, "Give me a mint one. It'll wake me up."

Gu Fei glanced at him and searched his pockets for a long while before retrieving a handful. He rifled through it with his fingers. "I'm out of those. Why don't you take this one? It'll wake you up, I promise."

"Okay."

Jiang Cheng took the little round candy from his hand. It was tangerine-flavored, nothing especially invigorating. Jiang Cheng wrapped his tongue around the piece of candy. How the hell was tangerine supposed to wake you up? It had to at least be lemon...

Before he could finish the thought, the tip of his tongue sensed a faint sourness. Maybe the tangerine layer outside had dissolved completely, and the inside was a little sour...?

He didn't have time to react before the sourness burst forth and assaulted his taste buds. His eyes widened.

Agh! Soooooooooouuuuuuuur! Fuck, it's so sour!

The acidic taste, verging on bitter, surged right into his heart and his tear ducts. It ached so much he longed for the sweet release of death.

Gu Fei watched him sit upright and said, "Um—"

Jiang Cheng spat the candy out with a *ptooey* before Gu Fei could continue. Like a little bullet, the candy shot out and smacked into Zhou Jing's neck in front of them.

"Agh!" Zhou Jing yelped. He started and sat straight up in alarm, then turned around and touched his neck with one hand. In a hushed voice, he asked, "Shit, what was that? It went into my shirt!"

Jiang Cheng couldn't speak. Though the candy was no longer in his mouth, its traces still lingered, and the bitterly sour flavor that made him shudder uncontrollably remained.

"Face the front," Gu Fei said.

"Zhou Jing," Lao-Xu said from the podium, "please be respectful of the classroom rules."

Although the number of people who observed the rules in this class wasn't enough to form a basketball team, Zhou Jing faced the front anyway.

After two seconds, he turned again. "Shit, why is it sticky? What is this thing?"

"Candy," Gu Fei said.

"...The hell is wrong with you two?" Zhou Jing was devastated. He pulled his shirt out and shook it for ages before the candy landed in his chair.

"Sorry," Jiang Cheng said. He'd finally recovered, so he turned and stared at Gu Fei.

Gu Fei was looking down at his phone, but Jiang Cheng could see the mirth he was trying to suppress.

"Trying to get yourself killed?" Jiang Cheng said under his breath.

"You wanted something to wake you up." Gu Fei's finger slid across the phone screen. "Are you still sleepy?"

"Motherfucker!" Jiang Cheng cursed.

Gu Fei turned to look at him. "You're not sleepy now, right?"

"Want me to write you a certificate of achievement?"

"No thanks." Gu Fei turned back to his game. "Nobody can read your handwriting, anyway."

Jiang Cheng grudgingly admitted that he was now thoroughly awake. His sleepiness had been banished completely. However, his urge to whack Gu Fei with a stick had overtaken his initial desire to ask how Gu Miao's school was handling her issue.

When the bell rang for lunch, Gu Fei put his phone down. "Let me treat you to a meal, as thanks for your help yesterday."

Jiang Cheng looked at him wordlessly.

"Lunch or dinner, up to you," Gu Fei added. "Got time?"

"...You don't have to, it's fine," Jiang Cheng said.

"It's not just to be polite. If it wasn't for you, I don't know what would've happened to Er-Miao yesterday. I get scared just thinking about it."

Jiang Cheng was quiet for a moment. "Dinner, then. I'm napping at lunch."

Gu Fei nodded. "Okay."

In the afternoon they had basketball practice during the self-study period, as usual. Lately, self-study was probably Wang Xu and the others' favorite time of day.

Jiang Cheng went to the hospital at noon to get his dressing changed. He also asked the doctor to apply some apparently imported wound adhesive. They mainly practiced their teamwork in the afternoon, instead of playing a regular match. His wound was all right; he didn't feel it much.

At the end of practice, Captain Wang Xu crouched by the court, jabbing the floor with his finger. "I think we have a chance this time. The way we are now, at least... But we have to keep it a secret so nobody considers us a threat, just like before."

"As long as you don't go bragging all over the place," Jiang Cheng said.

"It's fine," Wang Xu said airily. "As long as they don't find out about you and Gu Fei. Nobody believes me when I brag, anyway."

"...Oh." Jiang Cheng looked at him. It was the first time he'd sensed this much honesty from Wang Xu; he was rather taken aback that Wang Xu confronted that harsh reality so readily.

"Da-Fei." Wang Xu turned to face Gu Fei. "Can you ask those guys to come practice with us again when they have the time? I think that was pretty useful."

"M'kay," Gu Fei answered.

"All right, dismissed." Wang Xu waved a hand. "The other classes are coming soon. Do you all remember our chant?"

"Chant?" Lu Xiaobin stared blankly. "We have a chant?"

"Oh, didn't I mention it?" Wang Xu said. "Our chant is, 'We have a secret weapon!'"

Even after he spoke, it somehow still didn't register in Jiang Cheng's mind as their chant. He froze for a moment, then turned his face away, suppressing the violent laughter that threatened to burst out of him.

Everyone silently stared at Wang Xu.

"We have a secret weapon!" Wang Xu repeated, before waving his hand again. "Dismissed!"

As he walked out the gate after school, Jiang Cheng glanced around out of habit. There was no sign of the skateboard-wielding little mob boss Gu Miao waiting at the entrance. He looked at Gu Fei, but Gu Fei made no attempt to explain, just walked off down the road with his hands in his pockets.

Jiang Cheng noticed he wasn't going to get his bike. "You didn't bike to school today?" he asked.

"Nope." Gu Fei pulled his collar. "Crappy old bicycle tire got bent out of shape this morning on the way here."

"What?" Jiang Cheng didn't understand. "Why would a tire be bent out of shape? Is it in a bad mood or something...?"

"...That's really cute." Gu Fei gave him a look. "It's not bent out of shape like it's *upset*; it's literally not round anymore."

"Oh." Jiang Cheng was impressed by his own brain, too.

"I crashed pretty hard." Gu Fei sighed.

Jiang Cheng glanced at him, but didn't say a word. If it had been Pan Zhi, Jiang Cheng would've been clapping and cheering right now.

"What do you feel like having?" Gu Fei asked as he walked.

"Dunno. Nothing in particular. You don't have to make it anything special," Jiang Cheng said. "Just whatever you usually eat with your friends. It's not some grand appreciation ceremony."

"With my friends, huh..." Gu Fei laughed. "We eat some weird things. I don't think you could handle it."

"What, do you eat shit?" Jiang Cheng blurted out. It was something he was used to saying to Pan Zhi; the two of them had numerous meaningless and childish back-and-forths they were used to saying out of habit. Sometimes he thought, *If anyone hears this without seeing us, they'll think we're a couple of seven-year-olds.*

"No," Gu Fei said, "but if you want some, that can be arranged."

Jiang Cheng sighed. "Maybe just something mundane instead."

Sighing at the thought of Pan Zhi was certainly an interesting turn of events for him. Pan Zhi's grandfather had been hospitalized recently, so the whole family was taking turns to keep him company in the ward. The two of them hadn't been in touch lately. Sometimes, looking at his silent phone, Jiang Cheng felt very lonely.

"Let's go to the supermarket first," Gu Fei said.

"The supermarket?" Jiang Cheng was bewildered. "What for?"

"Food, of course," Gu Fei said. "Raw ingredients and stuff."

"We're cooking for ourselves?" Jiang Cheng was astounded.

"Yup." Gu Fei nodded. "My friends and I usually cook for ourselves. If you want ready-made food, we can—"

"No, it's fine." It would be better to follow Gu Fei's routine, Jiang Cheng thought. He hadn't wanted to bum a meal from Gu Fei for what happened yesterday, anyway. "I should tell you that I only know how to cook instant noodles, though."

"It's okay, this is simple. We'll have a barbecue," Gu Fei said.

Jiang Cheng was surprised all over again. *A barbecue, in this weather? Where?*

After walking around the supermarket, Gu Fei bought a whole chicken, already chopped, some beef and lamb slices, marinated and ready to be grilled, and two packs of dumplings.

Perplexed, Jiang Cheng asked, "How do you barbecue dumplings?"

"You boil dumplings," Gu Fei explained, his expression serious.

"I know you boil dumplings, I just... Never mind, I'll eat whatever you make," Jiang Cheng said.

"What do you drink? Soft drinks or hard?" Gu Fei asked.

"Neither, thank you." Jiang Cheng's mind filled with the image of them standing in the rough northerly wind, half-frozen as they watched over a dying woodfire in some abandoned wilderness. The thought of drinking anything in those conditions made him shudder.

◆ ◆ ◆

After making his purchases, Gu Fei led him homeward.

If Gu Fei asked him over to his place for the barbecue... Jiang Cheng was a bit uneasy about that. He'd been spending quite a lot of time with Gu Fei recently, but they still didn't feel close. Going to his house would make him pretty uncomfortable; he didn't even like going to Pan Zhi's place.

Gu Fei didn't stop when they reached his family's store. He simply glanced inside, then kept walking. Jiang Cheng looked in, too. Through the glass, he could see a woman at the counter. Judging from her hair, it was probably Gu Fei's mother.

Further on, the street merged with the one that led to Li Baoguo's house.

Jiang Cheng had been here before. It was quite deserted. Up ahead, past the abandoned factory, there was a road that led to an almost dried-up lake... He shuddered. If Gu Fei was planning to barbecue at the lake, he'd much rather treat Gu Fei to a restaurant meal himself.

But Gu Fei entered through a small gate and headed for the abandoned factory grounds.

"Here?" Jiang Cheng followed. "This was a factory, wasn't it?"

"Yeah, the steelworks, back in the day," Gu Fei said. "It shut down ages ago... Lots of people around here used to work in the factory. Including Li Baoguo."

"Oh." Jiang Cheng looked around.

Walking in, he realized that the factory had an enormous campus. The main factory buildings were still there; they looked sturdy, but they were surrounded by desolation. Clearly nobody cleaned this place anymore—the ground was paved with ice.

Gu Fei led him all the way in. After passing several basketball courts, they entered what looked like the old office block.

"Me and...Fresh Out of Jail," Gu Fei said as he walked up the stairs, "we hang out here when we don't want to be in the store."

"You can't even get power in here, can you?" Jiang Cheng glanced at the mess around his feet.

"We pulled in our own line," Gu Fei said. "It gets pretty lively here in the summer, actually. There's a lot of open space outside. The grandmas and grandpas like to do their street-dancing here."

"*Street-dancing*?" Jiang Cheng repeated.

"Yeah. They even have dance-offs. It's all very trendy—the absolute peak of the new wave." Gu Fei reached the third floor. He took out a key and opened a door.

Jiang Cheng glanced inside. It was an empty room, very cleanly kept. A makeshift brick stove sat in the center; next to it were several low stools and padded cushions, along with a legless couch.

A flat barbecue rack and an induction stove was on the ground next to the wall. There was even a pot, along with bottles of oil, salt, and other miscellaneous seasonings.

"Damn." Jiang Cheng was amazed. "You could live here."

"What do you think? Nice, huh?" Gu Fei said, putting the ingredients down on a table. "We installed the lock ourselves. I could give you a key, if you want. Then when you don't want to go home but you have nowhere to go, you can stay here. Li Yan and the guys normally come over on weekends—it's empty the rest of the time."

Jiang Cheng didn't speak. He leaned against the wall and gazed at Gu Fei, a little upset that Gu Fei had pointed out his dilemma of frequently having "nowhere to go" so simply.

Though he was upset, Jiang Cheng was surprised to find that he wasn't angry. The fact that even his deskmate could tell his life was a mess... It was kind of laughable.

Run Wild
SAYE

25

THIS ROOM HAD ONCE BEEN a reception room for guests to the steelworks, and it came with its own restroom. Though it was neglected, someone still owned the property, so there was still running water—that was why Li Yan had snapped it up as quickly as he did.

The factory grounds looked quite desolate, but even aside from the liveliness around the factory buildings during warmer seasons, it wasn't completely deserted here. Others also came around, looking for a place to hang out—they were just less religious about visiting.

Gu Fei didn't come often, but he wanted to treat Jiang Cheng to a meal without being too far from home, and there weren't any decent restaurants around here. When Jiang Cheng said he didn't mind where they ate, he thought of this place.

"I guess there's no heating here?" Jiang Cheng sat on the couch and stomped his feet.

"Light your own fire." Gu Fei grabbed a lighter from the table and tossed it to him. "There's charcoal in the bag next to the couch. You can find some rags and stuff outside... Do you know how to light a fire?"

"Yeah." Jiang Cheng stood and went outside. A couple of seconds later, he returned with a violent bang of the door, a rag in his hand and a stiff look on his face.

Gu Fei was holding a pack of disposable plates, about to lay out the ingredients; the sound made him jump. "What's wrong?"

"Fuck." Jiang Cheng held out the rag between two fingernails. "I picked this thing up just now... and there was a dead rat under it! Scared the shit out of me!"

Gu Fei didn't understand. "Why are you still holding it so bravely, then?"

"I thought it was probably useful, so I decided to be brave..." Jiang Cheng chucked the rag into the brick stove. "It should be enough for the fire."

"You could have walked ten steps more and found something else to light the fire with. Something without a dead rat under it." Gu Fei resumed sorting the ingredients onto their plates.

"It's too damn cold, I didn't want to move." Jiang Cheng crouched in front of the stove. "I think I'm getting used to it now. At Li Baoguo's place, there are even cockroaches in the pots."

"He doesn't normally cook. They provide meals at the mahjong place," Gu Fei said.

"I can tell." Jiang Cheng lit the rag. "If they had beds as well, he could probably sell the house."

"He can't." Gu Fei brought the pot to the restroom and washed it under the faucet, then filled it with water before bringing it back out. "All the apartments belonged to the old steelworks. Most people here are so poor, the only things they own are the shirts on their backs."

"...Oh." Jiang Cheng put two pieces of charcoal in the fire and stared at them, as if lost in thought.

Once the charcoal caught fire, Gu Fei put the pot of water on top, then crushed two pieces of ginger and tossed them in. After that, he added a small sachet of pre-sorted goji berries and red dates.

"Making soup?" Jiang Cheng asked.

"Yeah." Gu Fei held the lid of the pot. "Do you prefer the soup or the meat?"

"...What's that supposed to mean?" Jiang Cheng looked at him, baffled. "You'll make a pot of chicken soup, and I have to choose between drinking the broth and eating the meat?"

Gu Fei sighed. "No. If I add the chicken when the water's cold, the broth will be more flavorful. If I add it to boiling water, the chicken will taste better."

"Oh," Jiang Cheng said, surprised. "Why?"

Gu Fei thought that Jiang Cheng's response perfectly encapsulated the mindset of an overachieving student: lacking in common sense, but full of curiosity. He didn't want to explain, though, so he simply said, "Just tell me which you prefer."

"Soup," Jiang Cheng answered simply, then took out his phone.

"Okay." Gu Fei put the chicken into the pot and covered it. "While the chicken is cooking, we can start grilling."

"All right." Jiang Cheng stood up, still looking at his phone. "What do you need me to do?"

"Eat," Gu Fei replied.

Li Yan and company really liked to barbecue here, so they were well stocked. Gu Fei set up the grill rack, then transferred some charcoal from the stove. All the meat he'd bought was prepared and ready to use after a quick dab of seasoning—it was very simple.

"When you start the chicken in cold water, the flavor of the meat is gradually released as the temperature rises, resulting in a more flavorful broth," Jiang Cheng read off his phone as he sat by the stove, basking in the heat of the fire. "When you put the chicken in boiling water, the outer layer cooks instantly, sealing the flavor inside. As a result, the chicken itself will taste better... Is that right?"

"...Yeah." Gu Fei glanced at him. "Are you going to take notes, too?"

Jiang Cheng glanced right back. "These kinds of things don't usually need to be memorized verbatim. A basic understanding of the meaning is enough."

Gu Fei turned and began seasoning the meat. When Jiang Cheng spoke like that, he gave off strong overachiever energy, the kind you couldn't really formulate a response to.

"You guys hang out here often? You've got a lot of supplies." Jiang Cheng stood at the barbecue grill. "There's even cumin?"

"Cumin, pepper, chili powder, we have it all. I just don't know whether anything's expired—who knows when they bought them."

"...Shit." Jiang Cheng picked up a bottle. "Let me see... Shelf life, thirty-six months. Should be fine. I doubt it's been thirty-something months since you bought this."

"How long is thirty-six months?" Gu Fei grabbed the bottle without even looking up and scattered it over the meat.

"Three years," Jiang Cheng said.

"The last time was a few weeks ago, at most. You sure are particular. I usually just check for weird smells."

"Is it because you can't figure out how long the shelf life is?" said Jiang Cheng.

"Yeah." Gu Fei swept his eyes over Jiang Cheng. "I can't compare with the refined life of an overachiever."

It wasn't long before the skewers on the barbecue began to drip grease. The smoke permeating the room started to smell of fragrant meat. Barbecuing wasn't a difficult task, skill-wise, and Gu Fei seemed quite practiced at it, so Jiang Cheng didn't offer his help. He sat by the chicken soup, warming himself at the fire.

It was quiet outside. The sky had gone completely dark, and the open window looked like a sheet of black cloth. It made Jiang Cheng feel cold. But in front of him, the stove and grill rack reflected the bright flames, tethering him to the ground and giving him a sense of security. Altogether it was a funny feeling, just like the other day in the ridiculously tiny car: Outside was the cold street and the bitter wind, but inside it was warm and calm.

Now, outside the window was dark uncertainty and unease, but in front of his eyes was light and warmth.

Jiang Cheng really liked this feeling.

After all this time—since he came here with his melancholy and bitterness, his confusion and helplessness, and all the other things he wasn't used to—he finally felt his feet land on solid ground. The feeling might be temporary, or just a trick of the senses, but right now, he couldn't help but quietly savor it.

"Can you handle spice?" Gu Fei asked.

"A little, not too much," Jiang Cheng said.

Gu Fei sprinkled some chili powder over the meat, then put a few skewers on a plate and handed it to Jiang Cheng. "Try it. I prefer them a little charred. These are the less burnt ones."

"I like it a little charred, too." Jiang Cheng took a bite. "Tastes pretty good."

"I thought you overachieving students didn't eat burnt food. You even check for shelf life. Aren't you scared the char will give you cancer?" Gu Fei went back to grilling the meat skewers.

"Are you done?" Jiang Cheng retorted as he ate. "What do you have against overachievers? You won't shut up about them."

"It's my first time seeing a real live one in all the seventeen years I've lived—my heart's pounding from excitement, obviously." Gu Fei put the rest of the skewers onto the plate in one tall heap, then set the plate on an upside-down wooden crate by the stove that functioned as a table. "An overachiever with a mouth on him, too."

Gathering around a fire and eating skewers when it was cold out-side was a blissful indulgence; Jiang Cheng didn't feel like bickering with Gu Fei for the time being. He continued eating without saying a word.

"Want a drink?" Gu Fei rifled through a nearby cardboard box. "There's still some alcohol here from before, I think."

"Baijiu?" Jiang Cheng asked.

"What else? Do you drink beer when it's this cold out?" Gu Fei grabbed a bottle of baijiu and placed it on the wooden box. "Times like these call for an erguotou to warm the soul."

Jiang Cheng paused for a moment, staring at the bottle, before nodding. "Fine, let's have a little."

The way Gu Fei filled the paper cups to the brim gave Jiang Cheng a bit of a shock; he'd never had baijiu that way before. But since he and Gu Fei seemed to be able to argue about anything any time they spoke, he stayed quiet as he watched Gu Fei place the liquor before him.

"You may think I don't have to formally thank you," Gu Fei said, raising his cup, "but I'm still going to say thank you."

Jiang Cheng raised his cup as well. "You may think I don't have to say 'no worries'... But I'm going to say it anyway."

Gu Fei laughed. He bumped his cup against Jiang Cheng's, then took a swig.

Jiang Cheng looked into Gu Fei's cup. The bastard chugged baijiu like he was drinking beer. Jiang Cheng had no choice but to match him and take a similarly-sized gulp. The liquor blazed a path from the top of his throat all the way to his stomach, then sent a fire burn-ing upward, setting his neck and ears alight.

Gu Fei glanced over at him. "You don't normally drink much, do you?"

"I don't drink hard liquor the way I drink beer," said Jiang Cheng.

He lowered his head and took a bite of the meat. It was deeply satisfying to chug a drink by the fire in such cold weather.

"A sip or two should be enough for you," Gu Fei said, "with that wound of yours."

"It doesn't hurt much today." Jiang Cheng pressed against the wound. He really didn't feel anything now. He hesitated, then asked, "How are things...with Gu Miao?"

"She'll stay home for now." Gu Fei took another sip. "Those parents yesterday got the other two boys to bring their families to school to pitch a fit together."

"The fuck?!" Jiang Cheng scowled. "I bet they did something to make Gu Miao react like that. She hardly even looks at people most of the time."

"They scribbled in her book." Gu Fei lifted the lid of the pot. The soup inside was boiling now; he tasted it, then added some salt and seasoning. "Er-Miao wanted to handle it herself, so I didn't go to the school about it. I didn't think she was going to handle it like that."

Jiang Cheng could guess what the scribbles on her book looked like. That age—the age where adults would excuse them with "they're only a child"—was when children were cruelest. He thought of his own elementary school days, when a slightly slower kid in his class was shunned and bullied by everyone else. Even Jiang Cheng had taken part, afraid that standing out from the crowd would earn him the same treatment.

"So they're making Gu Miao stay home?" Jiang Cheng said. "They don't care who started it? Even if she was wrong for hitting him, surely she doesn't deserve to be suspended!"

"The school didn't want to take her in the first place. I begged the principal for ages." Gu Fei paused, falling silent for a while before glancing at him. "Er-Miao was supposed to go to a special school."

"...I see." Jiang Cheng had already guessed that Gu Miao had some sort of problem, but when he heard Gu Fei say *special school*, he was still uncertain how to reply.

"She was born a little...different." Gu Fei sprinkled cumin on a skewer of meat. "She had speech issues. She only started speaking at two or three, and even then, she'd only use a couple of sounds and she could barely get her tongue around them. She has trouble learning new things, and probably with expressing herself, too. She just screams whenever she's hungry or thirsty or in pain."

"So she..." Jiang Cheng trailed off. Gu Fei stared at the food in his hand as he spoke, looking utterly indifferent, but Jiang Cheng could sense his misery.

Jiang Cheng didn't probe, and Gu Fei ended it there. They didn't talk about what exactly was wrong with Gu Miao, or where that scar on the back of her head was from—whether it really was from Gu Fei's dad, like Li Baoguo said. They didn't discuss whether the rumors about Gu Fei were true. Jiang Cheng was curious about all of it, but he decided not to ask.

The chicken soup was delicious. Maybe it was the unique allure of hot soup in cold weather, but a single mouthful was enough to send him to heaven with its warmth.

"This chicken soup is going to my head," Jiang Cheng marveled.

"Did you buy your top student credentials?" Gu Fei took a sip of his drink before holding the cup in front of Jiang Cheng's eyes, giving it a swirl. "*This* is what's going to your head."

"...Oh." Jiang Cheng paused, then picked up his own cup and took a sip too, nodding. "You're right."

The alcohol content might have been high, and Jiang Cheng might not have been a regular baijiu drinker; nonetheless, eating and drinking like this soon reduced the paper cup's contents to nearly nothing.

Maybe that was why he suddenly felt like laughing. It was the same urge as the one that struck him in Gu Fei's shop, when they were talking about their fight—he was seized by the same desire to burst into brainless hysterics.

He turned to look at Gu Fei. "I..."

Gu Fei had just taken a mouthful of soup; meeting Jiang Cheng's eyes, he turned away and sprayed it all out.

It was enough to send them both into fits of hysterical laughter.

Jiang Cheng laughed so hard he couldn't hold his chopsticks— they clattered to the table. He tried to set them down properly, but they soon rolled onto the floor. Still giggling, he bent down to retrieve them, but instead came back up with a small wooden dowel he picked up off the ground, which he put next to his bowl.

At the sight of the dowel, Gu Fei laughed so hard that half of his soup sloshed out of the bowl he was holding.

"I can't," Jiang Cheng laughed, pressing one hand to the wound on his ribs. "I'm injured, I can't laugh like this..."

Gu Fei couldn't speak. He leaned back against the wall and continued to chortle for a while before ending it with a big sigh. "I could barely breathe..."

When they'd finished laughing, Jiang Cheng's back, chilled in the wind from the open window, was now covered in sweat.

"Ahh." Jiang Cheng searched through his pockets for tissues to wipe his mouth with, but came up empty. "I'm exhausted."

"Looking for tissues?" Gu Fei pointed at the table behind him. "There."

Jiang Cheng turned around. There were several rolls on the rickety old table behind him. He reached for one, and as he took it, a sheet of paper fell from the table to his feet. When he picked it up and was about to put it back, he paused, staring at the paper in surprise.

It was a piece of kraft paper with a five-line staff printed on it, torn from a music manuscript book. It was the kind of paper he was intimately familiar with: His favorite manuscript books were made of kraft paper like this.

A sheet of music manuscript paper wasn't a strange sight in and of itself. He figured Gu Fei was the kind of useless student who would mistakenly buy this, thinking it was a workbook for English vocabulary... What surprised him was what was written on the manuscript paper: more than half a page of a score.

"Holy shit." Jiang Cheng blinked and gripped the edge of the table, forcing his eyes to focus on the doubling image in front of him. He hummed two bars. "It sounds good. What song is this?"

Gu Fei was still leaning against the wall. He stared at Jiang Cheng for a while. "You can read music?"

"No shit." Holding the sheet, Jiang Cheng leaned back so he was against the table leg, his head bowed as he pored over the page. "We top students know everything... Who wrote this?"

Gu Fei fell silent.

Jiang Cheng looked over it again, then lifted his gaze to peer at him. He pointed a finger at Gu Fei. "You?"

"Hm?" Gu Fei took another sip. "Why me? Do I look like someone who writes music?"

"No, but..." Jiang Cheng flicked the paper. "But this key signature, this sharp symbol, it's the same as your handwriting. Longer at the bottom, like someone with one hand on his hip."

"The hell?" Gu Fei snorted.

"You wrote this? Or did you copy it for someone?" Jiang Cheng waved the paper at him, then hummed two more bars. "It sounds really nice."

"Top students sure are a different breed." Gu Fei deflected his question. "You learned music notation in middle school, didn't you? And you still remember it, even."

"Shit, you underestimate us." Jiang Cheng stood and slapped the paper against the table. He really was in high spirits now, happily sloshed as he spoke breezily, "I'm going to open your eyes."

"Are you going to sing?" Gu Fei was also excited now; he stood up and applauded as he leaned against the wall.

"Wait." Jiang Cheng got his bag from the couch. "I'm not sure if I brought it... I normally bring it with me everywhere... Ah, here it is."

Gu Fei watched Jiang Cheng dig through the contents of his school bag and pick out a translucent and slender plastic case.

A flute?

Jiang Cheng's ability to read music, especially his ability to hum a melody instantly upon reading it, was astonishing enough. Even though Lao-Xu called Jiang Cheng an overachieving top student, he didn't look the type—nobody would believe it unless they saw his actual grades. His top achievements were tongue lashings and physical lashings. His prowess at basketball was much less of a surprise than his music skills.

Like Gu Fei himself, even if he'd signed his own name on the music he wrote, anyone who didn't know him would assume he'd beaten up the real composer and robbed it from him.

Jiang Cheng was probably a little hyper from his drink. There'd been no less than four ounces of erguotou in his cup, which was now empty. When someone who rarely drank downed that much liquor in such a short stretch, this kind of behavior was to be expected.

"Is that a flute? It's so thin." Gu Fei looked at the slim metal tube in his hand. It was long and black.

"Kind of. It's a tin whistle." Jiang Cheng cleared his throat. "An Irish whistle. I really like it, but I don't play it often. I didn't play it often back at home either."

"Why not?" Gu Fei asked.

"Because it doesn't look as sophisticated as the piano." Jiang Cheng snorted. "My mom... Well, she didn't think much of it. She said it was noisy. She prefers the piano."

"You play the piano, too?" Gu Fei studied Jiang Cheng's hands. He hadn't noticed before, but now, as Jiang Cheng's fingers lined up along the length of the whistle, he could see they were long. The joints of his slender fingers were defined, but not bony.

"Yeah. You wanna bow down before me? There's a cushion on the couch, why don't you bring it over?" Jiang Cheng gestured at the floor in front of himself with the tin whistle. "You can kneel down right here."

Gu Fei burst into laughter. He found himself a cigarette and lit it.

He didn't think he'd heard a tin whistle before, but when Jiang Cheng played a bar, he suddenly remembered: There was a period of time when Ding Zhuxin had been into Celtic music and listened to it every day. It was filled with all kinds of wind instruments, from wooden flutes to bagpipes. It must have included the tin whistle.

He didn't know what Jiang Cheng was playing, but it sounded very familiar.

Just as Gu Fei was awestruck that Jiang Cheng could play the tin whistle—and play it well, at that, the way his fingers danced nimbly across the holes... Jiang Cheng abruptly stopped and cleared his throat.

"Sorry. I'll start again."

So Gu Fei had to give him another round of applause.

Jiang Cheng eyed him, then put the whistle back to his lips. He lowered his eyes and his fingers danced, the notes beginning to glide out once more.

This was Gu Fei's first time listening to someone play an instrument like this right in front of him. The feeling was indescribable. Jiang Cheng's usual scowl of displeasure and annoyance vanished with the first note. His softly fluttering eyelashes looked steady and serene. In this moment, Gu Fei suddenly and sincerely made peace with the fact that Jiang Cheng was an overachieving top student after all.

Run Wild
SAYE

26

THE NOTES FROM THE TIN WHISTLE were bright, spirited, and melodious as the harmonies echoed within the closed room. Gu Fei had no idea why anyone would consider an instrument capable of producing such beautiful sounds less impressive than a piano. From where he sat, Jiang Cheng cut a rather impressive figure, leaning against the table with the thin black whistle in his hands.

The tune was a light and cheerful one, but somehow, Gu Fei managed to glean a trace of loneliness from it. He wasn't sure whether it came from the instrument itself or its player.

At last, the final note reverberated around the dancing flames and eventually disappeared. Jiang Cheng lowered his hands amidst their mutual silence.

He looked up after a moment, the tiniest smile playing at the corner of his lips. "So?"

"Aww, *wonderful*," Gu Fei cooed as he clapped enthusiastically.

"Please speak normally." Jiang Cheng wiped the mouthpiece with a small cloth. "How do you manage to make me want to smack you with a single word?"

"Bravo," Gu Fei tried again. "It must've taken a long time to learn."

"Yeah," Jiang Cheng answered automatically, but after a moment, he shook his head. "Not that long, actually. Not as long as the time I spent learning piano."

"And you managed to play so well in such a short time," Gu Fei remarked. "It's no wonder you're such a..." He paused then, leaving the sentence unfinished.

Jiang Cheng sighed. "Yeah, yeah, I'm an overachiever, I get it. Will you ever get tired of that bit?"

Gu Fei laughed for a while, then finally said, "You really do play well."

"It's not that hard, actually. It's very easy to pick up." Jiang Cheng spun the whistle in his hand a few times before offering it to Gu Fei. "Wanna give it a try?"

"...Sure." Gu Fei walked up to him and accepted the whistle. "Can I play it just like this?"

"What's your point?" Jiang Cheng asked.

"I mean, are you a germaphobe?" Gu Fei said.

Jiang Cheng started laughing. It was as if a dam had somehow been opened in him tonight, and he couldn't stop laughing at everything. After a while, he got himself together long enough to point at the walls.

"A germaphobe would've had a breakdown as soon as he came in here."

"True. And you just grabbed a dead rat's blanket, too." Gu Fei studied the whistle in his hands, mimicking Jiang Cheng as he placed his fingers on the holes. "Like this?"

"Yep." Jiang Cheng reached out and gently tapped Gu Fei's fingers. "Press down tightly, you're letting the air out."

After adjusting his grip, Gu Fei attempted to make a sound. The whistle let out a short and shrill screech like a voice cracking. Gu Fei turned his face away with a frown. "Ah, what the heck was that? Scared me."

Holding back a laugh, Jiang Cheng said, "Relax a little more.

Don't hold your breath back; you have to let it out for it to sound good."

"All right."

Gu Fei puffed up his cheeks and tried again. This attempt was much better; the note was long and loud, but it sounded like...

"Never mind," Gu Fei said, taking his mouth off the flute. "Just because it's easy to pick up doesn't mean it'll sound good. With noises like these, you'd think there was a husky in here or something."

"You're still too tense." Jiang Cheng took the flute and wiped the mouthpiece carelessly on his pants. "Watch my face. You have to relax more." He played a scale as Gu Fei watched him intently. "Understand?"

"If I say no," Gu Fei chuckled, "will you start cursing at me?"

Jiang Cheng didn't answer, continuing to play scales and snippets of tunes.

After a moment, Gu Fei lifted a finger and poked his cheek. "When you say relax, do you—"

The music abruptly stopped as the whistle smacked sharply against the back of Gu Fei's hand.

"Agh! Fuck!" Gu Fei yanked his hand back. He shook his hand out and rubbed it vigorously. "What the hell is wrong with you?"

Jiang Cheng was suddenly overcome with a wave of embarrassment so strong that he wanted to jump out the window. It might've been the alcohol, but being in such close proximity to Gu Fei made him feel like the tension in the air was thick enough to cut with a knife.

Gu Fei's voice... The caress of his breath as he spoke... All of it made him feel light-headed.

The touch of his fingertip against his cheek was light—so light that it was barely noticeable—but Jiang Cheng still overreacted. In that instant, he couldn't quite tell if that was a reflex or a subconscious evasion. But more importantly, Gu Fei was left utterly flummoxed by his smack, and it wasn't as if he could explain himself.

Hi, my name is Jiang Cheng, and I don't really like it when people touch me.

Because I like men, I especially don't like to be touched by them.

Hello, when Wang Jiuri called me a fussy bastard, it was actually an extremely accurate assessment...

"Wang Xu said you're fussy and you don't let people pat you on the shoulder." Gu Fei took the words right out of his mouth. "I see that's true."

"Uh huh." Jiang Cheng looked at him. "Did you just realize that?"

Gu Fei stared back without a word. Unable to explain himself further, Jiang Cheng could only stand there and hold eye contact.

After about ten seconds of staring, Jiang Cheng got a bad feeling: the urge to laugh. A very *strong* urge. If he ended up laughing hysterically after smacking Gu Fei with a metal tube, Gu Fei would probably fight him.

There was a lesson to be learned here: You shouldn't drink so recklessly, lest it impair your judgment.

Through the tangle of a hundred thoughts swirling through his head, he managed to clench his jaw and keep from laughing. Meanwhile, apparently tired of staring at him, Gu Fei rubbed his hand again and grumbled, "Good thing you're not a girl, otherwise you'd probably end up alone."

This was when Jiang Cheng erupted into hysterics.

What the fuck are you fucking laughing about?! What's so fucking funny?! One tiny paper cup of erguotou was enough to turn you into a total idiot!

Are you a dumbass, Jiang Cheng?
Why yes, I am.

He admonished himself internally, while on the outside, he convulsed with laughter so violent the table he leaned on quaked from the impact.

"You want me to beat you up?" Gu Fei said.

With one hand holding the wound on his rib, Jiang Cheng continued giggling. In the end, Gu Fei was infected by his idiocy once again and started laughing along. Aside from the foolishness of it all, there were certain benefits to this bout of laughter: It dissolved the brutal awkwardness that had enveloped Jiang Cheng just before.

It only made his sides ache, that was all.

"Ay…" He heaved a big sigh as he collapsed on the sofa. "Sorry, I might've had too much to drink."

Gu Fei let out a long breath, probably still waiting for the giggles to pass. He walked over to the couch and plopped heavily down on the seat next to Jiang Cheng. "Wang Xu said you were ready to fight him because he patted your shoulder once."

The sofa might have been old and tattered, but it retained a surprising bounce. Gu Fei's cannonball-like impact on its surface sent Jiang Cheng shooting right up. In his dizziness, he felt as though he was about to take flight.

"I'm not interested in fighting that scaredy-cat," he said, then patted the sofa before rising up and letting himself fall back down.

Beside him, Gu Fei bounced.

"Are you a child?" Gu Fei said, then got up and dropped himself on the seat again.

"You started it—" Jiang Cheng landed a little off-balance this time and started rolling over toward Gu Fei.

The sofa wasn't large, only a two-seater. When Jiang Cheng fell, the two of them ended up squished together, their heads almost knocking into each other.

"Fuck," Jiang Cheng cursed quietly. He reached out to brace a hand on the sofa and right himself, but he ended up pressing against Gu Fei's hand instead.

Gu Fei's hand was warm. The sensation of his knuckles grazing against Jiang Cheng's palm was clear and visceral.

This time, Jiang Cheng didn't lash out reflexively. He didn't know why, but he froze in place, as if someone had pushed the pause button on him.

Gu Fei didn't speak or move away. As he turned to face Jiang Cheng, his breath brushed along the edge of Jiang Cheng's ear.

"You..." Jiang Cheng began, though he had no idea what he wanted to say.

"What?" Gu Fei asked.

Under the effects of alcohol and physical proximity, the simple word turned into an electric current, zapping him with sparks. Jiang Cheng felt as if all the pores on one side of his body had been blasted open at the sound of Gu Fei's voice.

He turned his face and kissed Gu Fei on the cheek.

Madness.

That was the only light still flickering in Jiang Cheng's mind. Everything else had been cleared out. Emptied. There was not a single brain cell to be found.

Gu Fei remained still and silent. In that instant, they seemed to have turned into statues frozen in a pocket dimension. He couldn't discern any reaction from Gu Fei, and because his head was swimming, Jiang Cheng couldn't read his eyes, either.

All he wanted was for a lightning strike to descend at this very moment and smite away their memories.

✦ ✦ ✦

When Jiang Cheng woke up the next morning, his phone showed that it was 10:30 A.M., and he had three missed calls from Lao-Xu.

It was his first time being late for class since the semester started. Any later, and it would count as a half-day of absence.

Pushing against the bed for support, he sat up, though his head still sagged and his eyes were half-closed.

He didn't want to go to school. Absolutely not.

Obviously, it was because of what happened last night.

The last memory he had was of his lips on Gu Fei's cheek. Anything after that was gone from his head. Even if he *could* remember, he didn't want to. He'd convinced himself to black out and persuaded himself to forget. He would've forgotten the kiss itself too, if he could—it wasn't for lack of trying.

He'd tossed and turned the whole night, troubled by dreams he no longer remembered. When he tried to recall them, all that remained were clouds of smoke in grayscale.

It exhausted him. And yet, the first thing he felt after waking up was embarrassment. Well, that, and unease. He'd only known Gu Fei for the latter half of the winter break and the first half of a semester, but one drink and he'd gone crazy, kissing the guy on the cheek... Yes, it was alcohol-induced lunacy.

It *was* alcohol-induced—a great explanation. His low tolerance didn't allow him to down a huge cup of erguotou in such a short time, so he got drunk.

He got drunk, so he ran wild.

A perfect explanation.

Jiang Cheng got out of bed and put on his clothes. After calming himself down with this reasonable explanation, he washed up and gave Lao-Xu a call back before rushing off to school.

He arrived between periods. Holding his backpack, Jiang Cheng entered the classroom through the back door. Although he had been calm and composed the whole way here, he felt unsettled again the moment he stepped into the classroom and realized that Gu Fei had actually not skipped class, but was instead sitting at his desk with his head buried in his stupid *Aixiaochu*.

He swore to the almighty lord of overachievers that he had no thoughts of that kind toward Gu Fei before that kiss. Apart from normal, superficial admiration for his good looks and nice hands and whatever—feelings anyone would have—he didn't have any ulterior motives at all.

But he didn't know whether Gu Fei minded it or not.

As reluctant as he was to admit it, in all this time he'd spent in this city, Gu Fei was the only person he wanted to hang around. He was the only person he thought of as a friend.

A fear began to creep up in him: If the connection between him and Gu Fei were to be severed, who else could he talk to? Zhou Jing? Wang Jiuri? The sudden onslaught of the unknown made his heart pound in trepidation. If he'd never met Gu Fei and had remained an outsider this whole time, he wouldn't have felt it so keenly.

Jiang Cheng kicked lightly against the leg of Gu Fei's chair. "Let me get by."

"Oho." Gu Fei looked up, just as surprised to see him. "I didn't think you'd make it today."

"I overslept." Jiang Cheng squeezed past from behind. Everything seemed normal with Gu Fei, which made him feel a lot better.

"You left this behind yesterday." Gu Fei took the tin whistle out from his desk drawer.

The mention of yesterday had Jiang Cheng's hand almost shaking as he took the flute. "Oh."

"Do you still want the key to the room?" Gu Fei asked, swiping away on his phone.

"...Yes." Jiang Cheng thought about it for a moment. "Would Fresh Out of Jail mind?"

"Why would they?" Gu Fei pulled out his own keys and took one off its ring to hand to him. "They're fresh out of jail, anyway. It doesn't matter, even if they do mind."

Jiang Cheng looked at him in silence.

"They won't mind. It's not like they don't know you," Gu Fei said.

"Thanks." Jiang Cheng took the key.

"Treat me to a meal when you get the chance." Gu Fei returned to his game. "The meat pies at Jiuri's place will be fine."

"...Why?" Jiang Cheng blinked.

"I gave you the key," Gu Fei said. "Besides, I have leverage on you."

"What?" Jiang Cheng turned his whole body to face him.

"If you don't treat me to a meal, I'll tell Jiuri you took advantage of me."

"I...what...the fuck?" Jiang Cheng was so shocked that he couldn't even stop to feel embarrassed. "I was just drunk, okay?"

"Ask around, see if anyone around here gets drunk off of less than five ounces of erguotou," Gu Fei laughed.

"Well *I* get drunk off of a few ounces." Jiang Cheng was incredulous. "What, you discriminate against lightweights here? Is your intolerance against outsiders here based on their tolerance for alcohol?"

"Makes sense. You're a southerner, after all," Gu Fei said.

"...I'm not a southerner."

"Anything south of here," Gu Fei said as he set his phone down and drew a line in the air in front of them, "is the south."

"Bullshit."

"So what if it's bullshit? I've already accepted the lightness of your weight, but you won't accept the shit from my bull?"

"I..." Jiang Cheng trailed off, looking at him.

"Don't laugh." Gu Fei pointed at him. "I'm serious. If you start laughing again, I'll really have to meet you by the back gates after school."

It would've been better if he hadn't said anything. Hearing this, Jiang Cheng felt the urge to laugh again.

Fortunately, Zhou Jing chose that moment to turn around. "Jiang Cheng—Jiang Cheng? Jiang... Hey, I wanted to ask you something."

"What is it?" Jiang Cheng sighed.

"It's almost midterms," Zhou Jing said. "Can I look at your answers during the exam?"

"What's the seating arrangement like during your exams?" Jiang Cheng asked.

He'd heard his share of requests like this in the past, but his old school split the class up for every test, no matter how minor; half of them would be sent to take the test in the lab or somewhere else. They would also be seated in random order instead of by their student numbers. Destiny was the only thing that guaranteed anyone a seat close enough for copying answers.

Come to think of it, the reason he and Pan Zhi had become so close was probably because they sat for exams in the same classroom every time, and with the same papers.

"We pull the desks apart. How else?" Zhou Jing answered.

"Oh. Does the class get two different versions of the same exam?"

"Nope," Zhou Jing said.

"...Oh."

Pan Zhi would've loved to take his tests in Fourth High, Jiang Cheng thought. It was practically free answers for all.

"Just leave your paper on your desk," Zhou Jing added. "I can look at it myself."

"Oh," Jiang Cheng said again.

Satisfied, Zhou Jing flopped back onto his own desk.

Jiang Cheng turned to Gu Fei. He knew they'd been talking before Zhou Jing interrupted, but now he couldn't remember what they were talking about.

"I don't need to copy you." Gu Fei met his gaze.

"Okay." Jiang Cheng turned away, but after a moment, glanced back at him. "Do you write all your test answers yourself?"

"Mm." Gu Fei nodded.

"And you know how to answer them?"

It seemed to Jiang Cheng that the books on Gu Fei's side of the desk had never been opened. He spent class time rotating between sleeping, watching videos, listening to music, and playing his stupid *Aixiaochu*.

"Sure I do. All I have to do is pick a good-looking answer and fill it in. What's there to it?" Gu Fei held out a handful of candy. "Want some?"

Jiang Cheng spotted the tiny round candy from yesterday. "No!"

Gu Fei picked out a milk candy and popped it in his mouth, laughing.

For the next few days after that, Gu Fei made no mention of the day they drank together. Every day passed exactly like the last: He would be late to school, play with his phone during class, and go to basketball practice with the others.

Occasionally, when he skipped class, it was still without any notice. When that happened, Jiang Cheng could sense a deep sadness emanating from Lao-Xu.

He had hung the key to the steelworks room on his own keychain, which was heavy with keys. They unlocked the main door to his old home, the old garage, his old room, and a bunch of his drawers. He'd kept all of them even once he moved here.

After adding the key to the room in the abandoned factory, he hesitated for a moment, then removed all of the old ones. Looking at the lone key on the now spacious ring, he sighed.

There was only one key to Li Baoguo's apartment. Jiang Cheng's bedroom also had a lock, but the key was nowhere to be found. None of the cabinets or drawers in the place had locks, either.

Jiang Cheng squeezed the keychain in his hand now, feeling a little melancholy. But the sense of loneliness and wandering helplessness he used to feel had faded a little. Time moved forward as always, and people changed. He didn't know if he owed it to forgetting or adapting.

Gu Miao had been out of school the whole week since the incident. Jiang Cheng knew this well because she would sneak into Fourth High every day during third period, standing on the walkway outside their classroom.

She showed up even earlier today. Jiang Cheng noticed the head of the skateboard-clutching little girl poking through the doorway a few minutes before the end of second period. Gu Fei gestured with his hand, signaling for her to wait outside. She turned and draped herself over the balcony, stepping up onto the bottom railing. The fight the other day and her subsequent suspension from school didn't seem to have had any impact on her mood; she was the same as usual.

Folded over his desk, Jiang Cheng looked out the window, but his gaze was caught midway by Gu Fei's side profile.

Gu Fei was also looking out the window. The bright sunlight streamed in, tracing a faint halo around his features.

Jiang Cheng was suddenly reminded of the other night. With this one glance, what had already become blurred memories and forgotten sensations all rushed back to him at once.

Fuck!

The way he'd rolled awkwardly away to the other end of the sofa; the way Gu Fei calmly lit a cigarette, and even handed one to him; the way they'd finished their cigarettes together, and somehow the pot of chicken soup, too... All these memories that were clearly recorded in his memory but that he convinced himself to forget now raced through his mind in his moment of weakness.

Was his brain so disobedient now?!

Gu Fei turned back. "Meat pies."

"Ah," Jiang Cheng answered, reining in his thoughts. "Huh?"

"When are you buying me meat pies? The tournament is tomorrow," Gu Fei reminded him.

"Let's go today," Jiang Cheng said. "Gu Miao can come with?"

Gu Fei nodded. "Okay."

Was the tournament really tomorrow? Jiang Cheng pulled out his phone and checked the date. It was true. Time had seemed to pass pretty quickly recently, but at the same time, it went by without much attention on his part—the large red banners promoting the school tournament had been hung up for days.

Gu Miao seemed to be in a good mood today. She made circles around them on her skateboard.

"Let me make a call first." Wang Xu pulled out his phone as they walked. "My dad will have to make the donkey meat in advance and set our portion aside... Oh yeah, why don't you guys come over again after school with the others on the team? We can hand out the jerseys Lao-Xu got us and discuss some strategy."

"Sure."

Jiang Cheng's eyes were on Gu Miao. The little munchkin's hair grew pretty fast; he could already see it poking out of the edge of her hat. The only problem now was it had no shape. He thought about Gu Fei's own fancy shave with its ornate motifs, and compared it to his sister's bald head or the messy mop of hair she had now…

"Is your wound all healed up?" Gu Fei asked quietly beside him.

"Yeah." Jiang Cheng touched his own rib. "It's pretty much fine now."

Without warning, Gu Fei suddenly reached out a hand and patted Jiang Cheng's shoulder.

"What?" Jiang Cheng looked at him.

"Are your reflexes in hibernation?" Gu Fei patted him again.

It was only then that it dawned on Jiang Cheng that Gu Fei had touched him.

He lapsed into contemplative silence.

THE STORY CONTINUES IN

Run Wild

VOLUME 2

Character Guide & Glossary

Characters

Jiang Cheng 蒋丞

"Returned" by his adoptive parents, he moves to the Steelworks in the middle of a school year to live with his birth father.

Gu Fei 顾飞

Jiang Cheng's new deskmate, infamous in the neighborhood for his ruthlessness. He lives with his mother and little sister.

FAMILY

GU MIAO 顾淼: Gu Fei's younger sister. Loves to skateboard; only speaks to Gu Fei.

GU FEI'S MOTHER: Dates a lot of younger men.

LI BAOGUO 李保国: Jiang Cheng's birth father, a noisy, alcoholic gambler.

LI HUI 李辉: Jiang Cheng's older brother.

LI QIAN 李倩: Jiang Cheng's older sister.

SHEN YIQING 沈一清: Jiang Cheng's former adoptive mother.

PAN ZHI 潘智: Jiang Cheng's best friend.

STEELWORKS

DING ZHUXIN 丁竹心: Gu Fei's friend and former neighbor.

LI YAN 李炎: Gu Fei's friend.

FRESH OUT OF JAIL 不是好鸟: Four of Gu Fei's friends—Liu Fan 刘帆, Luo Yu 罗宇, Zhao Yihui 赵一辉, and Chen Jie 陈杰. They are older than him and aren't currently in school.

MONKEY: A street thug who leads a gang in their neighborhood.

SCHOOL

LAO-XU 老徐: Xu Qicai 徐齐才— Class 8's homeroom teacher and Chinese teacher

LAO-LU 老鲁: Class 8's English teacher.

WANG XU 王旭: also known as Wang Jiuri 王九日, Jiang Cheng and Gu Fei's classmate and friend.

ZHOU JING 周敬: Jiang Cheng and Gu Fei's classmate who sits in front of them.

YI JING 易静: The class president.

Diminutives, Nicknames, and Name Tags:

-**GE/GEGE:** Used to refer to older boys or men in an informal way. Literally means "older brother".

-**JIE/JIEJIE:** Used to refer to older girls or women in an informal way. Literally means "older sister".

LAO-: Usually added as a prefix to a surname as a familiar way of referring to someone older. (e.g. Lao-Xu)

ER-: Added as a prefix to a second child's name (e.g., Er-Miao).

-**ER:** Added as a suffix to turn a name into a familiar diminutive (e.g., Cheng-er).

DA-: Added as a prefix to a name as a sign of respect, especially for someone older (e.g., Da-Fei).

-ZONG: Usually used as a suffix for CEOs or people of high rank. Students attach it to the end of a surname to refer casually to a teacher, indicative of their rapport (e.g., Xu-zong).

NAME-DOUBLING: A cute way to nickname someone, adults often use this with very young children (e.g., Chengcheng).

Glossary

MAINLAND CHINESE SCHOOL SYSTEM

SCHOOL YEARS AND EXAMS: Most Chinese students go through six years of elementary school (小学), followed by three years of middle school (初中) and three years of high school (高中). At the end of middle school, all students to proceed to regular high schools will take the standardized high school entrance exams (zhongkao, 中考); at the end of high school, they take the university entrance exams (gaokao, 高考) for admission to domestic universities. The gaokao is widely considered the single most important event in a young Chinese person's life and their best opportunity at crossing the class divide.

HIGH SCHOOL STREAMING: In most regular high schools, classes are sorted first by streams (STEM or humanities), then by academic performance. This sorting usually happens before the first or second year of high school, after which the students largely stay with the same class throughout their high school years. Each class has a homeroom teacher who is responsible for that class, in addition to their usual teaching duties, and will stay with the same class of students, progressing through the years until the students graduate.

SCHOOL SESSIONS, CLASSES, AND PERIODS: A school day typically runs from early morning until noon, with a two hour break for lunch and midday naps, then continues from afternoon to evening. In addition to lessons, there are daily periods set aside for quiet study called "self-study" periods.

NORTHEAST CHINA (DONGBEI)

INDUSTRIALIZATION: The northeast was once considered China's industrial hub. In the late 1990s and early 2000s, economic changes—namely the privatization and consolidation of state-owned enterprises—led to a collapse of the manufacturing sector all over the country, especially the three provinces in the northeast. Many cities were devastated by massive layoffs, affecting millions of workers. Run Wild takes place in a bleak, post-industrialized city, living in the aftermath of this economic transition. In its heyday, there would've been a full community centered around factories similar to the Steelworks, with dedicated housing, childcare, healthcare, and social spaces, all in service of the factories and their workers. Now, the same neighborhood is populated by impoverished families struggling to eke out a living—including people like Li Baoguo, who turn to drinking and gambling to while away their time.

GENERAL TERMS

FACE: *Mianzi* (面子), generally translated as "face," is an important concept in Chinese society. It is a metaphor for a person's reputation and can be extended to further descriptive metaphors. For example, "having face" refers to having a good reputation, and "losing face" refers to having one's reputation hurt. Meanwhile, "giving face" means deferring to someone else to help improve their reputation, while "not wanting face" implies that a person is acting so poorly or shamelessly that they clearly don't care about their reputation at all. "Thin face" refers to someone easily embarrassed or prone to offense at perceived slights. Conversely, "thick face" refers to someone not easily embarrassed and immune to insults.